ANGELS LANDING

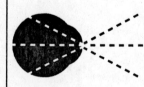

This Large Print Book carries the
Seal of Approval of N.A.V.H.

ANGELS LANDING

ROCHELLE ALERS

THORNDIKE PRESS

A part of Gale, Cengage Learning

GALE
CENGAGE Learning·

Detroit • New York • San Francisco • New Haven, Conn • Waterville, Maine • London

GALE
CENGAGE Learning®

LIBRARY OF CONGRESS CATALOGING-IN-PUBLICATION DATA

Alers, Rochelle.
  Angels Landing : a Cavanaugh Island novel / by Rochelle Alers. — Large Print edition.
    pages cm. — (A Cavanaugh Island Novel) (Thorndike Press Large Print African-American)
  ISBN 978-1-4104-5338-9 (hardcover) — ISBN 1-4104-5338-3 (hardcover)
  1. Life change events—Fiction. 2. Inheritance and succession—South Carolina—Fiction. 3. Islands—South Carolina—Fiction. 4. Large type books.
  I. Title.
PS3551.L3477A84 2012
813'.54—dc23   2012037255

Published in 2012 by arrangement with Grand Central Publishing, a division of Hachette Book Group, Inc.

Printed in Mexico
1 2 3 4 5 6 7 16 15 14 13 12

Angels Landing is dedicated to my Gullah ancestors for their pride, strength, and determination to survive.

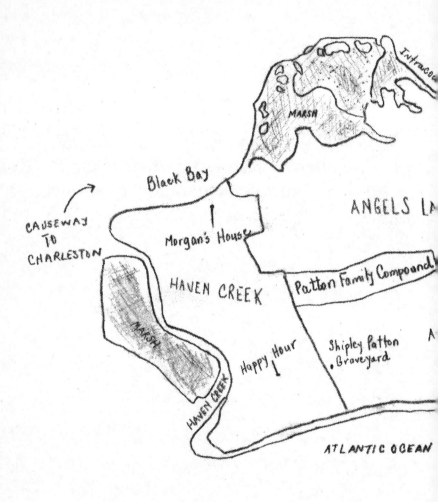

Intracoa[stal]

MARSH

Black Bay

ANGELS LA[NDING]

CAUSEWAY
TO
CHARLESTON

Morgan's House

HAVEN CREEK

Patton Family Compound

MARSH

Happy Hour

Shipley Patton
• Graveyard

HAVEN CREEK

ATLANTIC OCEAN

CAVANAUGH ISLAND

Waterway

Deborah's House

MARSH

Hamilton Residence

SANCTUARY COVE

FERRY TO CHARLESTON

LNG

Cove Inn

Muffin Corner

Jack's Fish House

The Parlor Bookstore

Landing Station

Village Square

Who is left among you that saw this house in its former glory? And how do you see it now? Does it not seem like nothing in your eyes?

— Haggai 2:3

CHAPTER ONE

"Good morning, ma'am. May I help you?"

Kara returned the receptionist's friendly smile with a bright one of her own. She'd recently celebrated her thirty-third birthday, and it was the first time she'd ever been called "ma'am"; but then she had to remind herself that she wasn't in New York but in the South. Here it was customary to greet people with "yes, ma'am" and "sir," rather than "missy" or "yo, my man."

"I'm Kara Newell, and I have a ten o'clock appointment with Mr. Sullivan," she said, introducing herself.

The receptionist's smile was still in place when she replied, "Please have a seat, Miss Newell. Mr. Sullivan will be with you shortly."

Kara sat down in a plush armchair in the law firm's waiting area. The walls were covered with a wheatlike fabric and artwork depicting fox hunting scenes. She'd planned to take a break from her social worker position at a New York City agency by visiting her family in Little Rock, Arkansas. She never anticipated having to travel to Charleston, South Carolina, instead.

The certified letter from Sullivan, Webster, Matthews and Sullivan requesting her attendance at the reading of a will had come as a complete shock. When she'd spoken to Mr. David Sullivan Jr. to inform him that she didn't know a Taylor Patton, the attorney reassured her that his client had been more than familiar with her.

Kara had called her parents to let them know she wouldn't be coming to Little Rock as scheduled because she had to take care of some business. She didn't tell her mother what that business was because it was still a mystery to her as to why she'd been summoned to the reading of a stranger's will. It was only when the attorney mentioned it had something to do with a relative she wasn't familiar with that she'd decided to make the trip.

She unbuttoned the jacket to her wool pantsuit. Although the temperatures had been below freezing when she'd boarded the flight in New York City, it was at least fifty degrees warmer in Charleston. One of the things she'd missed most about living in the South was the mild winters. By the time the jet touched down, Kara barely had time to hail a taxi, check into her downtown Charleston hotel room, shower, and grab a quick bite to eat before it was time to leave. She sat up straight when a tall, slender black man approached her.

"Miss Newell?"

Pushing off the chair, Kara smiled. "Yes."

"Good morning, Miss Newell. David Sullivan," he said in introduction, extending his hand.

His hand was soft, his grip firm, which took her by surprise. As she took in the sight of him, she realized he didn't quite fit the description she'd had. The one time she'd spoken to Mr. Sullivan, there was something in his tone that made her think he was much older than he looked. Now she realized they were about the same age. Conservatively dressed in a navy-blue pin-striped suit, white shirt, blue-and-white dotted tie, and black wing tips, he released her hand.

"It's nice meeting you, Mr. Sullivan."

David inclined his head. "Same here, Miss Newell. It's nice having a face to go along with the voice." Taking her elbow, he led her out of the waiting room and down a carpeted hallway to a set of double ornately carved oak doors at the end of the hallway.

"I'd like to caution you before we go in. I don't want you to reply or react to anything directed toward you. Taylor Patton was my client, and that means indirectly you are also my client."

A shiver of uneasiness swept over Kara like a blast of frigid air. What, she mused, was she about to walk into? For the first time since she'd read the letter, she chided herself for not revealing its contents to her mother.

"What do you mean?" Kara asked.

"I can't explain it now, Miss Newell. But I want you to trust me enough to know that I'm going to make certain to protect your interests."

When the doors opened, Kara suddenly felt as if she were about to go on trial. The room was filled with people sitting around a massive rosewood conference table. She heard a slight gasp from the man sitting nearest the door, but he recovered quickly when she stared at him. The hazel eyes glaring at her — so much like her own — were cold, angry. The resemblance between her and the man was remarkable. So much so that they could have been brother and sister. But Kara didn't have a brother — at least not one she was aware of. She was an only child.

David directed her to a chair at the opposite end of the room, seating her on his left while he took his place at the head of the table. He still hadn't revealed to Kara why he'd wanted her to attend the reading of the will of Taylor Patton, but his cautioning was enough to let her know she was involved in something that was about to change her life. The fact that she resembled several of those in the conference room led Kara to believe there was a possibility she just might be related to the deceased.

Resting her hands in her lap, Kara listened as David informed everyone that a stenographer would record the proceedings, asking those present to introduce themselves for the record. Kara glanced at the stenographer sitting in a corner, fingers poised on the keys of the stenotype machine resting on a tripod.

David touched her hand, nodding. "Kara Elise Newell," she said, beginning the introductions. One by one the eleven others gave their names.

The men were Pattons, while the women were hyphenated Pattons, with one exception. Kara glanced at Analeigh Patton's hands. Unlike the others, her fingers were bare. A hint of a smile inched up the corners of Analeigh's mouth, and a slow smile found its way to Kara's eyes.

Everyone's attention was directed toward David when he cleared his voice, slipped on a pair of black horn-rimmed glasses, and opened the folder in front of him. " 'I, Taylor Scott Patton of Palmetto Lane, Cavanaugh Island, South Carolina, do hereby make, publish, and declare this to be my Last Will and Testament, hereby expressly revoking all wills and codicils, heretofore made by me.' "

Kara felt her mind wandering when David mentioned that as the executor he would judicially pay the deceased's enforceable debts and administrative expenses of Taylor's estate as soon as possible. Taylor hadn't married; therefore, there was no spouse to whom he would have bequeathed his belongings. All of the Pattons leaned forward as if the motion had been choreographed in advance when David paused briefly. Then he continued to read.

" 'I do give and bequeath to my daughter, Kara Elise Newell, all my personal effects and all my tangible personal property, including automobiles owned by me and held for my personal use at the time of my death, cash on hand in bank accounts in my own name, securities, or other intangibles.' "

Kara went completely still, unable to utter

a sound as pandemonium followed. The room was full of screams, tears, shouts of fraud, and threats to her person. Another two minutes passed before David was able to restore a modicum of civility. "Ladies, gentlemen, please restrain yourselves. Remember, this proceeding is being recorded, so please refrain from threatening my client. By the way, there is more."

The man who'd glared at Kara stood up. "What's left? My uncle has given this *impostor* everything."

"Please sit down, Harlan. I can assure you that Miss Newell is not an impostor," David said.

Kara wanted to agree with the Pattons. Austin Newell, not Taylor Patton, was her father. She closed her eyes, her heart pounding a runaway rhythm, as David outlined the conditions of what she'd inherited: She must restore Angels Landing to its original condition; make Angels Landing her legal residence for the next five years; and allow the groundskeeper and his wife, who would receive a lump sum of fifty thousand dollars, to continue to live out their natural lives in one of the two guesthouses. In addition, she could not sell any parcel of land to a non-family member without unanimous approval of all Cavanaugh Island Pattons, and the house and its contents could only be deeded to a Patton.

She opened her eyes and let out an inaudible sigh when David enumerated names and monies set aside in trust for three grandnephews and two grandnieces for their college education. This pronouncement satisfied some, but not all. There were yet more threats and promises to contest the will.

Forty-five minutes after she'd entered the conference room, Kara found herself alone with Taylor Patton's attorney. Holding her head in her hands, she tried to grasp what had just happened. She hadn't risen with the others because she wasn't certain whether her legs would've supported her body. David had warned her not to say anything, and she hadn't, but only because she couldn't. Reaching for the glass of water that had been placed before each chair, she took a sip.

David removed his glasses and laced his fingers together. "So, Miss Newell, you are now the owner of a house listed on the National Register of Historic Places and two thousand acres of prime land on Cavanaugh Island."

Kara's eyelids fluttered as if she'd just surfaced from a trance. "I'm sorry to inform you, but Taylor Patton is not my father."

David's eyes narrowed. "Did your mother ever mention Taylor Patton's name?"

She shook her head. "No. The only father I know is Austin Newell."

"Well, I can assure you that you *are* Taylor's biological daughter. In fact, you are his only child."

Kara closed her eyes. When she opened them, they were filled with fear and confusion. "How is that possible?" The query was a whisper.

"That is something you'll have to discuss with your mother."

She would talk to her mother, but not over the phone. What she and Jeannette Newell needed to discuss had to be done face-to-face. Combing her fingers through her hair, Kara held it off her forehead. "Please tell me this is a dream."

David sat on the edge of the table, staring at Kara's bowed head, a look of compassion across his features. "Even if I did, it still wouldn't change anything." Reaching into the breast pocket of his suit jacket, he took out a small kraft envelope, spilling its contents on the table in front of her. "These are keys to the house in Angels Landing, Taylor's car, and his safe-deposit box in a bank in Sanctuary Cove."

Kara released her hair, the chin-length, chemically straightened strands falling into place. "Where's Sanctuary Cove?"

"It's on Cavanaugh Island, southeast of Angels Landing. You only have ten days to transfer the accounts from Taylor's to your name. By the way, do you have a rental?"

"No. I took a taxi from the airport to the hotel."

"Good."

"Good?" Kara repeated.

David smiled. "Yes. It means I don't have to get someone to drop it off for you. I'm going to have our driver take you back to the hotel so you can pick up your luggage, and then he'll take you to Angels Landing."

"I'm sorry, but I'm planning to leave for Little Rock tomorrow."

"Can you hold off leaving for a few days?"

"David. May I call you David?" He nodded. "When you wrote and asked me to come here, I never could've imagined that the man I've believed was my father all these years is not my father. Not to mention that I now have a bunch of cousins who can't wait to put out a hit on me so they can inherit my unforeseen assets, assets I don't need or want."

"Are you saying you're going to walk away from your birthright?"

20

"A birthright I knew nothing about."

David leaned in closer. "A birthright you need to protect, Kara. If you walk away from this, then you'll be playing right into the hands of the developers who've preyed on the folks who've lived on the Sea Island and who'll turn their inhabitants' birthright into a playground for millionaires."

Kara felt as if her emotions were under attack. "But . . . but the will states I can only sell the land to a Patton."

"Pattons who want to sell more than half of Angels Landing."

"Why would they want to do that?" A pregnant silence filled the room as she and David stared at each other.

"Greed, Kara. If they can get you to go along with their way of thinking and you sell your two thousand acres, the monies they'll receive for the sale will be divided among them evenly."

An expression of confusion crossed her face. "How many acres do they hold collectively?"

"Probably about four hundred," David said.

"Hypothetically, if I decide to hand over my shares and we sell twenty-four hundred acres at let's say a thousand dollars per acre. Are you telling me two-point-four million will be divided among twelve of us?"

He didn't respond. Instead, she did the calculations in her head. Instead of $2 million she would get $200,000. "The split seems a little inequitable, especially if I hold the majority shares."

David's dark eyebrows lifted a fraction. "They see you as an outsider, someone who will take the money and run. Please don't prove them right."

"What do you expect me to do?"

"I'd like you to give yourself a week to think about it. Stay at the house, tour the island. If you decide you prefer the Big Apple to the Lowcountry, then you walk away and . . ."

"I walk away and what?" Kara asked when David didn't finish his statement.

"The surviving heirs will contest the will, it will go into probate, and after the state of South Carolina gets its share, the family will get what's left."

She gave the dapper attorney a long, penetrating stare. He was asking for a week while her supposed biological father had asked her for five years. Right now Kara had three weeks of vacation time: one she could spend in Angels Landing and the other two in Arkansas before returning to New York. She hadn't told her parents when to expect her, so Kara decided to change her travel plans yet again.

"Okay. I'll try it for a week."

David blew out an audible breath. "Thank you." He stood, walked over to the wall phone, and pushed the speaker feature. "Please tell Linc I need him to drive a client to her hotel. He's to wait for her to check out, and then I want him to take her to Taylor Patton's house." He ended the call and came over to cup Kara's elbow when she stood up. "I'm going to call my cousin, Jeffrey Hamilton, who's the island's sheriff and have him stop in to check on you. I'll be in court for the next two days, but as soon as there is a recess, I'll come out to see you. Meanwhile, Jeff or one of his deputies will help you if you need anything."

Kara nodded her head in agreement, trying to keep her emotions in check. Taylor Patton was her biological father?

Jeffrey Hamilton leaned back in his chair, booted feet propped up on the corner of the scarred desk. He'd submitted his department's budget to the mayor and town council at the January meeting, yet it was mid-March and he was still awaiting delivery of new office furniture. Ever since he'd been appointed sheriff of Cavanaugh Island,

Jeff had attempted to refurbish his office and expand the force from three deputies to four. Sadly, things seemed to be taking a lot longer than he'd first thought.

The cell phone on his desk rang. Glancing at the display, Jeff answered it on the second ring. "What's up, David?"

"Is there anyone in your jail that needs legal counsel?"

He laughed softly. "Sorry, Cuz, but I haven't locked up anyone in more than three weeks. Are you calling to let me know that you're ready to pop the question to that gorgeous oral surgeon you've been seeing?"

"We're not even close to that. I'd like you to go out to Angels Landing and check on the new owner. Her name is Kara Newell."

"Is there anything I should know about her?" Jeff asked.

"I may as well tell you now because gossip about her is going to spread across the island faster than a cat can lick its whiskers. She's Taylor Patton's daughter."

"I was under the impression that Taylor didn't have any children."

"Most of us thought the same thing."

Jeff shifted, and his chair groaned like someone in pain. "How are the others taking the news?"

"Let's just say they're not too happy that

she exists. That's why I'm calling you."

"Don't worry, David. I'll keep an eye on her." He knew his cousin couldn't divulge how he'd come by the proof because he was still bound by attorney-client privilege, even in death.

"Thanks, Jeff. By the way, how is Aunt Corrine?"

"Grandmomma's good. Have you made plans for Easter?"

"Yep. Petra and I are going down to St. Thomas for a few days. You're welcome to join us."

Jeff stared at his spit-shined boots. After spending twenty years in the Marine Corps, he still enjoyed the age-old tradition of shining his shoes and boots. "I'd love to, but I gave my deputies time off to spend with their families."

"Speaking of families, Jeff, when are you going to settle down and have a couple of kids?"

He sat up and lowered his feet. "After you get married and have one."

David's chuckle came through the earpiece. "You've got a few years on me, Cuz, so you're first. I have to hang up because I have a meeting with a new client. Call me if Kara is having trouble with her new family."

"No problem," Jeff promised.

He ended the call, then slipped the cell phone into the case attached to his gun belt. He was walking out of his office when his clerk, Winnie Powell, entered the police station through the back door.

Winnie smiled, her bright blue eyes sparkling like blue topaz. She fluffed up her short, curly hair. "It looks like rain."

He returned her smile. "We could use a little of that." The winter had been unusually dry. "I'm going over to Angels Landing."

Winnie nodded as Jeff headed out of the station. Once in the parking lot that served the town hall, courthouse, and police station, the humidity wrapped around him like a wet blanket. He got into the Jeep and started the engine. The vehicle had been emblazoned with a sheriff logo on the passenger-side doors and refitted with a partition separating the front seats from the rear ones. Within minutes of driving, the rain had begun as Winnie predicted, the sound of the wipers breaking the silence.

Slowing to ten miles an hour, Jeff drove through downtown Sanctuary Cove, passing Jack's Fish House, the town square with its fountain and marble statue of patriot militia General Francis Marion atop a stallion, and the Cove Inn, the town's boarding-house. Once he'd taken over as sheriff, he'd convinced the town council to lower the town's speed limit to fifteen miles an hour because there were no traffic lights in the Cove and to discourage teenagers from drag racing. Amazingly, there hadn't been posted speed limits for years.

Maneuvering onto an unpaved road, he shifted into four-wheel drive. A marker pointing the way to Angels Landing came into view, and Jeff turned onto Palmetto Lane and headed to the house that had given this section of Cavanaugh Island its name. The few times he'd come to Angels Landing, Jeff felt as if he'd stepped back in time. The antebellum mansion at the end of a live oak allée was breathtaking with its columned, wraparound porch. The rose-colored limestone Greek Revival home, with its pale pink marble columns and black-shuttered tall windows, had been one of the finest homes on the island.

Jeff parked next to the vintage Mercedes-Benz sedan that had belonged to Taylor Patton. Reaching for his cap on the passenger seat, he pulled it on. The rain was now a steady drizzle as he sprinted to the front door, which opened as he wiped his boots on the thick rush mat.

27

"Why, if it isn't Corrine Hamilton's grandbaby boy. What brings you out this way?"

Jeff took off his cap and curbed the urge to roll his eyes upward. The petite woman and her groundskeeper husband had worked for the Pattons for longer than he could remember. He also wanted to remind Mrs. Todd that at forty he had left boyhood behind many years before.

"Good afternoon, Miss Iris. I'm here to see Ms. Kara Newell. Is she in?"

Mrs. Todd's dark eyes narrowed suspiciously behind her rimless glasses. "Did she do something, son?"

Jeff tightened his grip on his cap. It was apparent that the housekeeper had transferred her loyalty from Taylor to his daughter within weeks of his death. Those who lived on Cavanaugh Island joked that it was easier to gain access to the Oval Office than to cross the threshold to this historic house.

"No, she didn't, Miss Iris. David Sullivan asked me to look in on her."

Mrs. Todd opened the door wider. "Why didn't you say that in the first place?" She smiled. "Follow me. She's in the garden room."

Jeff shook his head in amazement as he followed the elderly woman, who was dressed in a crisp gray uniform that matched the coronet of braids atop her head. It had been years since he'd stepped foot into the house, but like the exterior, nothing had changed. It had the same vases, lamps, tables, and chairs. Mrs. Todd directed him down a narrow carpeted hallway to a doorway on the south side of the property.

He stopped at the entrance to a room filled with potted plants, trees, and flowers. The sound of soft music flowed from somewhere in the indoor oasis. His gaze shifted to the housekeeper when she approached the woman reclining in a cushioned chaise and spoke quietly to her.

Jeff felt his heart stop when Kara Newell swung her long, slender, bare legs over the chaise and stood up to face him.

She was absolutely stunning. Anyone familiar with the Pattons would recognize the startling resemblance between Kara and her paternal grandmother Theodora — or Teddy as she had been affectionately called by her husband. His gaze went from her tousled hair, pulled up in a short ponytail, to the tawny face with large hazel eyes, cute button nose, and lushly curved full lips, then lower to a white tank top and olive-green shorts. Each time she took a breath, the swell of her breasts were visible above the top's neckline. Scolding himself, he focused his attention on her face rather than staring at her chest. She was slim but had curves in all the right places.

He inclined his head. "Ms. Newell."

Kara smiled and offered her hand. "Please call me Kara."

Taking three long strides, Jeff grasped her hand, holding it gently within his much larger one. "Jeff Hamilton."

"David told me you would stop by. Would you like to sit down?"

"Thank you." He waited until Kara sat on a pull-up chair at a small round table covered with a floral tablecloth before sitting on the matching one.

A pair of eyes with glints of gold and green met his. "May I offer you something to eat or drink?" Kara asked Jeff.

"No, thank you." He crossed one jean-covered knee over the other. "Have you settled in?"

Kara assumed a similar pose, staring at the polish on her bare toes. "There's not going to be much settling in. I'll only be here a week."

Leaning forward, Jeff lowered his leg, planting both feet on the worn rug. "Are you telling me that you don't plan to live here?"

"No, I'm not telling you that."

"Then what is it you're *not* saying?"

"Why do I get the impression that you're interrogating me, Sheriff Hamilton?"

Jeff's impassive expression did not change with her accusation. "If I were interrogating you, Kara, you wouldn't have to ask. All I want is a yes or no as to whether you plan to live on Cavanaugh Island."

"I can't give you a yes or no, Sheriff Hamilton."

"It's Jeff."

"Okay, Jeff. As I said, I can't answer that question right now. I promised David I would spend a week on the island before making a decision. Only two hours ago I was told the man I believed to be my father isn't." She looked away from him, trying to hold back the tears forming in her eyes. "When I walked into that conference room earlier this morning and saw people staring at me who look like me . . . to say it was a shock is putting it mildly. Then I was told that I've inherited a house, two thousand acres of land that my so-called relatives want me to sell to a group of greedy developers, and I must live here for five years. If I do so, it means I have to resign from my job, give up my Manhattan apartment, which has an incredible view of the East

31

River, and lose contact with a group of friends I've become extremely close to."

"Yes, I can understand how difficult that may be. Not only will you have to uproot your entire life, but you'll also have to deal with the family issue." Jeff lifted his broad shoulders under a long-sleeved chambray shirt. "The upside is you can always get another job and make new friends. And instead of views of the river, you'll have views of the ocean."

Kara folded her arms across her chest. "You make it sound so easy."

A hint of a smile tilted the corners of Jeff's mouth. "Because it is. I gave up a military career to come back here to take care of my grandmother."

"That's different."

"You think so, Kara?"

"Of course it is. There is no discussion when it comes to family. You do what you have to do," Kara said.

"Like you have to accept your birthright and honor your father's last wishes."

"What's with this birthright thing?" she asked.

Jeff stood up. "I'll tell you sometime soon. Right now, I have to get back."

Kara also rose to her feet. "When will I see you again?"

"Tomorrow. I'm off, and if you don't have anything planned, I'll come by and take you to Jack's for lunch and give you a crash course in Lowcountry culture."

"I'd like you to answer one question for me, Jeff."

"What's that?"

"Do you have something against the Pattons?"

"Nothing personal. I just don't like it when people threaten others."

Her eyes grew wider. "Did David tell you what happened?"

"He didn't have to. You can say I read between the lines. As sheriff of Cavanaugh, I have zero tolerance for those who break the law. And to me threats are a serious offense. I'll pick you up at twelve."

Jeff didn't give Kara a chance to accept or reject his offer when he turned on his heels and walked out of the room. He'd been back for almost a year, and it was the first time that a woman had captured his attention for more than a few minutes.

There was something about Kara, other than her natural beauty, that had him enthralled. He didn't know whether it was her big-city attitude, but whatever it was, he intended to discover it before the week ended and Kara was out of his life for good.

CHAPTER TWO

Kara sat motionless, her gaze fixed on a potted palm. It had been more than two hours since David had informed her that Austin Newell was not her biological father; instead, her father was a dead man who knew about her when she hadn't known he existed. The news had stunned her, the hostility exhibited by the Pattons frightened her, and Sheriff Hamilton coming to see her made their threats even more terrifying.

Any normal person would've been overjoyed to inherit a house listed on the National Register of Historic Places and two thousand acres of land and four automobiles — three of which were classics — cash on hand, securities, and other tangibles in Taylor Patton's name. And if the house, its contents, the cars, and the land was an indication, then there was no doubt she'd become a very wealthy woman.

Kara knew she had to call her mother

because only Jeannette Newell could give her the answers she needed as to her true paternity. What she didn't want to think about was her mother's duplicity. How could she hide the true identity of the man who'd fathered her for more than three decades, while Austin, the only father she'd ever known, had become a coconspirator?

She also knew she couldn't avoid the inevitable but decided to wait — wait until her mother was at home before calling her. Normally Kara would've called Jeannette at the senior residence where she headed the nursing unit, but she couldn't find the nerve to talk to her mother just yet. She also wanted to tell her mother that her travel plans had changed and not to expect her the following day.

David has asked if she would stay on the island for a week, and she'd said she would. A week was more than enough time to uncover what David and Jeff Hamilton had warned her about giving up: her birthright.

Kara bit her lower lip. Whenever she heard the word *birthright,* she thought of her Sunday school lesson about twin brothers Esau and Jacob. Firstborn Esau cared little for his birthright, so he sold it under oath to Jacob for bread and lentil soup because he was hungry. She also recalled that Jacob had not only taken Esau's birthright, but also his dying father's blessing.

Was that what she was going to do? Walk away and give her birthright to relatives who in turn would sell it to developers? Or would they sell her two thousand acres and keep the money — a sale that would drastically affect the lives of the residents of Angels Landing and Cavanaugh Island forever?

She could take the proceeds and buy a co-op or condo in an upscale Manhattan neighborhood, maybe a house in the suburbs where she could park her own car in her driveway instead of hailing taxis or renting cars to take her whenever she wanted to go. She could also plant a rose garden and even get a little dog that would have a backyard to run in.

Kara could do a lot with her newfound wealth, but in reality it really wasn't her money, even though Taylor had believed she was entitled to all his worldly possessions. She didn't want to think that he had included her in his will out of a perverted sense of guilt. Had Jeannette come to him with the news that she was carrying his child, and he'd turned his back on her?

The questions assaulted Kara like barbs, and she was unable to parry them. Combing her fingers through her hair, Kara dug her nails into her scalp, welcoming the pain. She knew she had to pull herself together or lose it completely.

"Miss Kara?"

Her hands came down, and she turned to find Mrs. Todd standing only a few feet away. Kara hadn't heard her come into the room. She stood up. "Please call me Kara, Mrs. Todd."

The older woman inclined her head. "Miss . . . I mean, Kara. I made lunch. Would you like to have it in the breakfast room or on the back porch?"

Kara smiled. "In the breakfast room."

She hadn't believed how quickly her life had changed. She now had someone to cook and clean up after her — something that made her uncomfortable. Iris Todd had introduced herself and then informed Kara that Angels Landing had been her only home for the past fifty-five years; she'd worked for Taylor Patton's mother, Theodora, then stayed on after her death to assume total responsibility of running the household for Mr. Taylor.

She followed the tiny, doll-like woman with a sable-brown complexion and snow-white hair. "Mrs. Todd, I'd like you to tell me about my . . . Taylor Patton." Kara had caught herself before calling him "father."

Mrs. Todd shook her head. "Cain't do that. Not up to me to talk his business. God bless the dead."

"I'm not asking you to divulge his secrets."

Mrs. Todd stopped midstep, turned, and faced Kara. "There are no secrets because around here, there is no such thing as a secret. This town is so small, everybody knows everyone's business."

"What did he do?"

A network of faint lines fanned out around the housekeeper's eyes when she smiled. "David didn't tell you?"

A look of confusion crossed Kara's face. "Tell me what?"

"Mr. Taylor was an investment banker. He handled rich folks' money jest like it was his own. Made tons of money for them even though they didn't need no more."

Kara sucked in her breath, held it, and then let it out slowly. If Taylor Patton had made his rich clients even richer, then there was no doubt he had done the same for himself. "Is there a safe in this house?"

"No. Why you asking?"

"I thought perhaps Mr. Patton kept his important papers there."

Mrs. Todd squinted behind her glasses. "Why do you keep calling him Mr. Patton instead of your daddy?"

"Because I'm not certain if he *is* my daddy."

"Oh, he your father all right. You look jest like Miss Theodora. Or Teddy as the fancy folks around here used to call her. Yes, Kara. You the spitting image of your grand-momma."

So that's why the Pattons had looked at her as if she were an apparition, Kara recalled. It was obvious they'd known something she hadn't when she'd walked into the law firm's conference room, even before the reading of the will. They knew just by looking at her that she was a Patton. So why had they tried to deny her?

Kara still couldn't bring herself to think of Taylor Patton as her father and certainly not daddy.

Mrs. Todd angled her head, appearing deep in thought. "I don't know if Mr. Taylor had a safe. He took his papers to the bank in Sanctuary Cove."

Again she was reminded of the envelope David had given her with keys to the house, cars, and safe-deposit box. The first thing on her agenda the following day was to go to the bank and go through the contents of the box.

Mrs. Todd took a step, resting a hand on

Kara's arm. "Don't you worry yourself none, honey. Everything will work out in its own time. All you need is a little faith."

That's what I'm hoping for, Kara thought. She wanted to tell Mrs. Todd she needed an abundance of faith. She also wanted everything to work out so she could visit with her family in Little Rock; return to New York; and pick up her life as if she'd never heard of David Sullivan, Taylor Patton, or the Angels Landing Pattons.

"How did he die?" Kara asked.

"Mr. Taylor had problems with his heart. He went to bed one night and never woke up. My husband tried reviving him, but when the doctor from the Cove came and covered him with a sheet, we knew it was too late. It's a shame because he was only fifty-six."

Taylor Patton was fifty-six, the same age as her mother. Kara followed Mrs. Todd down a narrow hallway, into the kitchen, and to an alcove that overlooked the rear of the house. Upon close inspection she saw the shabbiness of the worn carpets and fading wallpaper. The antebellum mansion was antiquated; whoever did the interior decorating must have been arrested in a past time period. Yet despite all that needed to be done, Kara knew it could be elegant and beautiful again if restored to its original condition. Unfortunately, she knew she wouldn't have the time needed to make the repairs. She'd promised David and Jeff she would stay on Cavanaugh Island a week, and she would. But there was no way she could supervise restoring the property in that short amount of time.

After a lunch of lobster bisque, shrimp salad, and sweet tea, Kara returned to the bedroom Mrs. Todd had chosen for her. She picked up her cell phone that she'd left on a side table. She'd missed one call. Tapping the voice mail icon, she listened to her roommate's message, then tapped the key for Dawn Ramsey's number.

"Hey, Miss Dee," Kara said in her usual greeting. Walking over to an armchair, she sat down.

"Hey yourself, Miss Kay. I'd called to find out if you'd made it home safely."

Kara exhaled an audible sigh. "Yes, I did. But . . ."

"But what, Kara?" Dawn asked when she didn't finish the sentence.

"I'm not in Arkansas."

"If you're not in Little Rock, then where the hell are you?"

"I'm in Angels Landing. It's on Cavanaugh Island."

There was silence on the other end of the line. "I know I didn't do well in geography, but could you please tell me where Cavanaugh Island is? Is that even in the United States?"

"Yes. It's a Sea Island off the coast of Charleston, South Carolina."

"South Carolina! Why are you in South Carolina? Have you been holding out on me, girl? Do you have a man there you don't want me to know about?"

If the situation into which she'd found herself wasn't so serious, Kara would've laughed. But it wasn't funny. Far from it. "No, I don't have a man here. You, better than anyone, should know that I don't want to deal with any man after that last loser. Too bad I didn't have the good sense to walk away before it even started."

Dawn sucked her teeth. "You dated him for all of four months, and that was more than two years ago, Kara."

Kara stared at the threadbare rug and the fading drapes of the floor-to-ceiling windows. "I wish it'd been four seconds and two hundred years ago."

The sound of Dawn sucking her teeth again came through the earpiece. "You weren't alive two hundred years ago."

Shaking her head, Kara held her forehead. There were times when she didn't know if Dawn actually worked at being obtuse or if she was that gullible. When she'd mentioned this to her roommate, the dance teacher claimed men liked her best whenever she pretended to be an airhead. There had to be an awful lot of men who liked Dawn because Kara had lost count of the number of them who'd crossed the threshold of their East Harlem apartment.

There were times when she'd come home to a living room filled with people. She'd go directly into her bedroom, close and lock the door, and wait for the revelry to end. It did end, but not until the early-morning hours when she had to get up and go to work, while Dawn slept well into the afternoon when it was time for her to get up and go into the dance studio where she taught ballet, jazz, and tap.

"I'm here because I need to work out a few things that have to do with someone's estate."

"What are you talking about, Kara?"

She told Dawn everything, beginning with the letter from David up to and including her meeting with the sheriff. What she left out was her relationship to Taylor Patton. She wasn't ready to approach that can of worms when she could barely wrap her own head around things. "Right now, I've committed to staying here a week to sort out a few details."

"Have you lost your mind?" Dawn asked. "You just found some long-lost relatives are ready to take you out, and you talk about hanging around and giving them the opportunity for a drive-by?"

The laughter began, shaking Kara until she found it almost impossible to talk. She could always count on Dawn to make her laugh. And lately there hadn't been that much for her to laugh about. Her position as a social worker for at-risk children had her close to being burned out, and the steady stream of people coming and going at the apartment she shared with Dawn had also begun to take its toll, leaving her sleep deprived. If she could afford to move, she would have, but with exorbitant and prohibitive Manhattan rents, Kara felt trapped.

She loved Dawn like a sister, but her roommate allowing unemployed actors and dancers to occasionally crash at their apartment went beyond being a good friend. And as much as she tried to explain to Dawn that they were *her* friends, not their friends, nothing changed until Dawn asked a few of them to leave and not return because several valuables had disappeared from the apartment.

"It's not that easy to execute a drive-by down here. First of all it's an island, and there are only two ways on and off it, the ferry and the causeway, so how would they get away? And then there's the sheriff. He's definitely no-nonsense."

"Is he a good old boy?"

Kara scrunched up her nose when she recalled Jeff Hamilton. If she hadn't been so agitated, she knew she would've noticed that he probably wasn't much older than she was and that he was tall and well-spoken. He'd denied interrogating her when that was exactly what he'd done. Also like his cousin David, he had tried to convince her to remain in Angels Landing and claim her birthright.

"Not quite," Kara responded.

"What does the house look like?"

"It's a twenty-room antebellum mansion. It's rather run-down but not falling apart."

"Damn, Kara," Dawn drawled. "We could party for days in a place that big."

"That's where you're wrong. I'm not going to be here long enough to throw anything."

"Good for you. You come on back home where you belong. It's taken me awhile to turn you into a Big Apple diva, so I can't imagine you turning into a Scarlett O'Hara Southern belle, rocking on the front porch with a tall glass of sweet tea, while servants fan your moist face."

"Stop it, Dawn!" Kara said, laughing.

"Is there someone who takes care of the house?"

"Yes."

"Then you have a servant."

"She's a housekeeper."

"We won't argue about terminology, but on a more serious note, I'm worried about you, Kara. You can't dismiss the threats because you don't know how far these folks will go to get what they feel is legally theirs."

"It's not legally theirs," Kara argued softly.

There came a beat; then Dawn asked, "Are you certain?"

"Very certain."

"What aren't you telling me?"

"It's something I can't talk about right now."

"Hold up, Kara. You know you can tell me anything. We're more than friends, we're sisters. Let me be there for you . . . help you with this."

"No lie, Dawn, because if I didn't think of you as my sister, I would've moved out a long time ago." Kara chuckled uneasily.

"I know you're not talking about my friends hanging out at *our* place."

"They don't hang out, Dawn. They move in."

There came another pregnant pause from Dawn. "Why didn't you tell me you felt like this?"

Kara rolled her eyes upward even though Dawn couldn't see her. "I've told you I didn't mind them staying over for a night or two, but they'd come and never leave." Having lived with Dawn for so long, Kara knew how hard it was for an actor, singer, or dancer to wait for his or her big break. Kara was the social worker, but Dawn had become their Mother Teresa.

"I can understand. Honestly . . . I used to think you were jealous of them, particularly my guy friends."

This time Kara was at a loss for words. "Jealous, Dawn? No way! I don't have a boyfriend because I'm too stressed out from dealing with women who let their husbands or boyfriends abuse their children, then lie because they don't want to lose the man. I put myself at risk every time I report a case of abuse or neglect. And I never know when the parents are going to turn on me.

"Then there are the times when I'm on call. Do you think any man is going to

47

understand me getting up in the middle of the night to remove a child from his or her home? And every time I have to go to the hospital to see a battered child with tubes attached to their little bruised body, I lose a little bit of myself." Tears filled Kara's eyes, and she clasped a hand over her mouth to stifle the sobs. "I have to go. I'll call you in a few days."

"Kara?"

"Bye, Dawn."

She broke the connection. Wiping the tears with the back of her hand, Kara attempted to bring herself under control. She knew feeling emotionally exhausted had something to do with her current situation. Although she'd been a social worker for ten years, she was still shocked and amazed by the amount of adults abusing helpless and vulnerable children and prayed she would never get so jaded that she'd accept it as commonplace rather than the exception.

She lost track of time as she sat in the chair, staring into nothingness. Kara had always prided herself on being strong, yet this was one of those times when she didn't know what to do.

Her situation wasn't unique. There were thousands who'd uncovered they were adopted or that one parent wasn't their biological parent. The use of DNA had become quite popular to determine paternity. Maury Povich's "You *are* or you're *not* the father!" had become the show's catchphrase. Despite her startling resemblance to the Pattons, Kara knew some of them would demand she submit to a DNA test to validate Taylor's claim that she was his child and sole heir.

Pushing off the chair, Kara plugged the cell into the charger. She stood in the middle of the bedroom, her eyes shifting from one object to another. The room reminded her of those she'd seen in museums, and she was uncertain whether the massive mahogany four-poster bed was an antique or a reproduction. The posts were elaborately carved with pineapples, leaves, and vines. The design was repeated on the legs of the highboy, writing table, the drawers on the bedside tables, and on the front of an armoire. Age and countless footsteps had worn away the color and woven threads of area rugs, and the design on the wallpaper had faded.

Mrs. Todd had offered her a choice of the six bedrooms, and she'd chosen this one because the casement windows opened out onto a veranda that overlooked the rear of the property while offering panoramic views of the water. What had kept the mansion from appearing decrepit was its cleanliness. There wasn't a speck of dust anywhere.

Kara didn't know why, but suddenly she felt as if she were smothering and had to get out of the house if only for a few minutes. She exchanged her tank top and shorts for a blouse and black cropped pants. Slipping her feet into a pair of sandals, she picked up her cross-body bag and walked out of the bedroom, nearly colliding with Mrs. Todd; she'd just come out of a room carrying a plastic bucket with cleaning supplies.

"Now that it's stopped raining, I'm going out for a while."

"Are you going to walk or drive?"

Kara paused. "I think I'll drive. Where do you suggest I go?"

Mrs. Todd switched the handle of the pail from one hand to the other. "I think you should start with Haven Creek."

"Where's Haven Creek?"

"It's west of here. It's the first town off the causeway." The older woman squinted. "You do know east and west don't you?"

Kara smiled, nodding. "Yes, I do." She'd noticed Mrs. Todd squinting and wondered if she needed to have her eyes examined, then reminded herself Mrs. Todd wasn't her client and she wasn't in Angels Landing to evaluate her.

Mrs. Todd nodded. "Will you be back in time for dinner?"

She glanced at her watch. It was after 3:20. "Yes. I'm only going to be gone for about an hour."

"Until you learn the island you shouldn't be out after dark."

"Now you're scaring me, Mrs. Todd."

"I don't mean to scare you, but some of the roads don't have lights. Don't drive too fast or you'll get a ticket. The second time you're caught speeding the sheriff will impound your car for thirty days."

"Isn't that a little harsh?" Kara asked. "What if you need your car to go to work?"

"That's the law. The sheriff doesn't make exceptions."

"I'm not going to be out too late. And I'm definitely not going to speed."

The older woman nodded before Kara headed out of the door.

Minutes later, Kara drove slowly, staring out the window of the car that made her feel as if she were riding on air. The sedan was at least twenty-five years old, and kept in mint condition. There wasn't a hint of rust on the black, shiny exterior and the saddle-tan leather interior was as supple as soft butter.

As she lowered the driver's side window, the scent of salt water wafted into the car. Decelerating to ten miles an hour, Kara became a tourist and sightseer. One- and two-story homes, palmetto and Spanish moss–draped trees dotted the landscape. She spied a marker indicating the number of miles to Haven Creek.

A cyclist coming in the opposite direction waved to her as he passed, and she returned the wave. How different, she mused, Cavanaugh Island was from Manhattan where cyclists and bike messengers whizzed in and out of traffic while coming dangerously close to the many taxis playing chicken with pedestrians. Here the street and road names were flora: Magnolia, Palmetto, Honeysuckle, Oak, Gardenia, Peach, Carnation, and Cherry. In Manhattan there were street numbers running east and west and avenues running north and south.

The most profound difference was the absence of noise — no sirens or honking horns. The apartment she shared with Dawn was on the eighteenth floor, and once she closed the door all street noises ceased to exist. Kara had spent hours sitting on the balcony outside her bedroom, reading or taking in the sight of pleasure boats and barges gliding along the East River. Winter was her favorite time of the year with the falling snow making it almost impossible for her to see the lights on the many bridges connecting Manhattan with the other boroughs.

And if she hadn't had to come home and step over people in sleeping bags in the living and dining rooms, her home life would have been close to perfect. She also resented not being able to watch television in the living room because of strangers sprawled over the sofa and chairs drinking beer and eating chips. Kara loved Dawn but hated that her dogged need to take care of a bunch of freeloaders allowed her to constantly be used as a doormat.

She'd also found it hard to accept twenty- and thirty-something educated people traveling around with all of their worldly goods in a bedroll or backpack. Perhaps if she hadn't had such a stressful job, then she probably would've been more tolerant. The deliberation whether or not to leave or remove a child from his or her home was never an easy decision for Kara. Even after she'd made the decision, there were doubts. Those were the occasions when she wanted to come home to peace and familiarity.

Kara knew she could find the peace she

craved at Angels Landing. She would be the only one living in a six-bedroom, eight-bathroom house with a small and grand ballroom, two kitchens, a formal dining room, a solarium, and front and back porches. Mrs. Todd told her Taylor had lived alone, rarely had visitors, and conducted business using the telephone or Internet. She could understand his need for solidarity.

A wry smile twisted her mouth. She couldn't believe Taylor had known so much about her, yet she knew very little about him. However, in the week that she remained on the island, she would find out as much as she could about the man who supposedly had fathered her.

The landscape changed again, becoming more wooded with trees lining both sides of the two-lane road. The houses in this section of Angels Landing were smaller replicas of the house she'd inherited.

"Pattons." The name had slipped unbidden from her lips. They couldn't live in the big house, so they'd built their own Angels Landing mini-mansions.

Kara slowed and turned off the road at the marker pointing the way to Haven Creek's business district. Waning afternoon shadows slanted over a street that could've been in any small town in America. There was a sign prohibiting vehicles on the street, and she maneuvered into an area set aside for parking. She walked the short distance from the parking lot to Oak Street. Cobblestone streets, bricked sidewalks in a herringbone design, and black-and-white striped awnings shading storefronts gave the main thoroughfare a picture postcard appearance.

Peering through a window, Kara stared at a group of women sitting in a circle quilting. She'd always wanted to learn how to hand quilt. The shelves in the next shop were filled with sweet-grass baskets.

Moving along the street, Kara soon realized the area was an artists' colony. Haven Creek was a Lowcountry Taos with businesses offering photographs and paintings depicting the scenes of the Sea Islands; another shop displayed an ironworker's creations reminiscent of the late Philip Simmons's, the most celebrated of Charleston ironworkers; she passed a jewelry store featuring gold and silver pieces, another of a furniture maker, and an architectural firm. She stopped abruptly when she came face-to-face with Jeff.

He touched the worn brim of his Atlanta Braves baseball cap. "Good afternoon, Kara.

I thought I wouldn't see you again until tomorrow."

Kara felt her breath catch in her throat when she met the dark, deep-set eyes of the man who'd promised to protect her. Why, she thought, hadn't she noticed the perfection of his masculine face? He wasn't just a good old boy, but tall, dark, and very handsome.

She inclined her head. "Good afternoon. I thought I'd get out and do a little sight-seeing."

"I told you I'd take you around."

Kara focused on his face rather than the automatic handgun holstered at his waist. "I suppose I felt a little restless. I'm not used to sitting around doing nothing."

Jeff nodded to a shopkeeper and stepped to his left to allow him to pass. "What is it you do, Kara?" he asked.

Her gaze moved to the badge and name tag pinned on the chambray shirt over his heart. "I'm a social worker for a child protective agency."

Crossing his arms over his chest, Jeff whistled softly. "That can't be easy, especially in a big city."

"It isn't."

"Overworked and underpaid?"

"How did you know?"

56

Jeff smiled, drawing her eyes to the slight cleft in his strong chin. "I've met a few social workers in my travels, and they all complained about carrying too many clients on their caseloads and are paid a pittance for performing miracles."

Kara laughed for the second time that afternoon. "I've never heard it put quite that way."

"It's not much different for law enforcement when the bad guys outnumber the good guys."

She sobered quickly. "Are you saying there's a lot of crime on Cavanaugh Island?"

"Quite the contrary. There's little or no crime, especially with an islandwide policy of zero tolerance. You break the law, you pay the price."

"Like speeding?" Kara asked.

"Especially speeding because there're no stop signs or traffic lights on the island."

"I noticed there are no posted speed limits."

Jeff's right eyebrow lifted a fraction. "Do you see that as a problem?"

"It smacks of entrapment, Jeff."

He leaned closer. "How's that?"

"Just say I'm stopped for going thirty miles an hour, and you tell me the speed limit is twenty when nowhere on the island is it posted that the limit is twenty. You hit me up for a hundred dollar —"

"Two hundred," he said, interrupting her.

Kara's jaw dropped. "Two hundred dollars? That's excessive."

"So is speeding," Jeff countered. "We don't have drag racing or hit-and-runs."

"What about DWI and DUI?"

"Those fall under Charleston PD's jurisdiction." The small walkie-talkie clipped to his shirt collar crackled. "Please excuse me," he said, then took a backward step, his gaze meeting and fusing with Kara's before he turned his back.

Kara stared at the width of Jeff's broad shoulders, his trim waist and hips. He'd admitted to having been military, and his ramrod posture validated his claim. She didn't know whether he was married or involved with someone, but there was something about Jeffrey Hamilton that reminded her of what she'd been missing: male companionship.

She'd told Dawn that she was too busy, tired, or stressed out to deal with a man, when in reality she hadn't met one who could hold her interest. She'd accused her roommate of being Mother Teresa, wanting to house and feed the homeless, when she could've become a spokesperson for Save

58

the Children. Her supervisor had cautioned that she was too involved with some of her clients, but Kara's mantra was "No child will fall between the cracks on my watch."

Glancing at the time on her cell phone, Kara knew if she didn't cross the street to see the other shops, it would be dark before she returned to Angels Landing. She'd just stepped off the sidewalk when a large hand around her upper arm stopped her.

"Where are you going?"

She glanced over her shoulder to find Jeff's gaze riveted on her face. "I'm going to check out the shops across the street. I plan to head back to Angels Landing before it gets dark."

His fingers tightened, then fell away. "You probably won't have much time to look around. You can follow me back to Angels Landing, and I'll bring you back tomorrow and introduce you around."

Kara wanted to tell Jeff she didn't want to meet anyone; she wanted answers about Taylor Patton. And if anyone knew everything about anyone on the island, then it would be the sheriff.

For a long moment, she returned his stare. There was something in his entrancement that ignited a tingling in the pit of her stomach. "Okay."

Reaching for her hand, Jeff led her to the parking lot, waiting until she was seated and belted in. "I'll head out first."

Kara wagged her finger at him. "No speeding."

He flashed a white-toothed smile. "Just try and keep up."

Her eyes grew wider when she registered his veiled challenge. "Please close my door."

He bowed from the waist. "Yes, ma'am."

Starting up her car, Kara waited for the Jeep to maneuver out of the parking lot, she following close behind. When he'd said for her to try and keep up, she knew he would exceed the unofficial island speed limit. The Mercedes's speedometer hovered close to forty miles an hour as she stared at the taillights on the vehicle in front of hers.

Palmetto Lane came up so quickly Kara hit the brakes to keep from passing it. Jeff tapped his horn, she tapping hers in response. He sped off while she drove on the sandy road under a canopy of live oaks, draped with Spanish moss. Angels Landing came into view at the end of the allée, her breath catching in her throat. Waning sunlight reflected off the columns in shimmering shades of rose-gold.

In that instant Kara wondered how different her life would have been if she'd grown up in this house? Would she have viewed things differently if Taylor Patton had raised her instead of Austin Newell?

She parked the car, got out, and walked around to the door that led directly into the kitchen. She made it to her bedroom without encountering Mrs. Todd or her husband Willie. Picking up her cell phone, Kara stood at the window as she tapped speed dial. Her mother's sultry drawl came through the earpiece.

"Hi, baby. What time should your daddy pick you up at the airport tomorrow?"

Kara closed her eyes for several seconds. "I'm not coming in tomorrow."

"What's going on, Kara?"

She knew she had to choose her words carefully. "Mama, I need you to answer one question for me." Kara had decided not to wait for a face-to-face encounter with her mother to ask her about Taylor because she knew it would nag at her for the week.

A beat passed. "What is it?"

"Why didn't you tell me Taylor Patton was my father?"

Jeannette gasped. "Who told you?"

"Mama, please. Was he my father?"

"I can't talk now."

"When can you talk?" Kara asked.

"Not over the phone, Kara."

Kara knew by her mother's evasiveness that she'd validated David's claim that she *was* Taylor's daughter. "Is Daddy there with you?"

"Yes."

It was obvious her mother didn't want to talk about Taylor in front of Austin. "I'm not coming to Little Rock." She told Jeannette that she'd committed to staying on Cavanaugh Island for at least a week. "Can you get off and come here?"

"Right now I'm short staffed. Two nurses called in today with the flu. They're going to be out at least a week."

"Can you come here next week?"

"I'll try, baby."

Kara pulled her lower lip between her teeth. "You don't have to explain anything until you get here. But I need to know now. Yes or no?"

The seconds made a full revolution before her mother said, "Yes."

Walking on shaky legs, Kara sat on the padded bench at the foot of the bed. "Thank you, Mama."

"It's not what you think, Kara."

"I'm not judging you, Mama. I just needed to know the truth."

"I love you, baby."

"And I love you, too. Let me know when

you're coming, and I'll meet you at the airport."

"You take care of yourself."

"You, too, Mama."

Kara ended the call filled with a powerful relief that she knew the truth. She would now be able to face whatever challenges came her way with new objectivity. And knowing she was Taylor's daughter gave her the ammunition she needed to handle her newfound relatives' threats and intimidation.

CHAPTER THREE

Jeff had always been a light sleeper, so when he heard the distinctive ringtone he woke, reaching for the cell phone on the bedside table. Glancing at the clock, he moaned softly. It was 3:48 in the morning. Turning on the lamp, he punched a button.

"Hamilton."

"I'm sorry to bother you, Jeff, but I have a situation down here at the station."

Groaning under his breath, he ran a hand over his face. "Is it a situation or an emergency, Kenny?" Jeff had hired Kenneth Collins to replace a part-time deputy who'd remarried his wife, then relocated to Orlando to be close to their grandchildren.

"It's a situation that will soon be an emergency. Patty Calhoun called because her ex showed up drunk and threatening to kick down the door if she didn't let him in. I arrested him because of the restraining order."

"Where is he?"

"I locked him up."

"Did you call Charleston PD and tell them to pick him up?"

"Yes."

"Then what's the situation?" Jeff asked.

"Patty's here pitching a fit because she doesn't want her man to get locked up. And Jimmy's threatening to kill himself if I don't let him out."

Throwing an arm over his face, Jeff cursed softly. "She should've thought of that before she took out a restraining order. Make certain there isn't anything in the cell he can use to hurt himself."

"What about Patty?"

"Tell her to go home or you're going to lock her up, too. Is that her screaming?" Jeff asked when he heard a screeching sound.

"Yeah."

Lowering his arm, he sat up. "Put her on the phone, Kenny. . . . Patty, this is Sheriff Hamilton." Normally he would've introduced himself as Jeff, but right now he and Patricia McFarland weren't former classmates. She was a resident of Sanctuary Cove and he sheriff of the island.

"Yesss," came her tearful reply.

"Where are your kids?"

"They . . . they're at home."

"Are they home alone?"

"Yes . . . but —"

"But nothing, Patty!" Jeff practically shouted. "You left your kids home alone to follow a man who beats you on a regular basis. Either you get home and take care of your kids or when the Charleston police come for Jimmy I'll have them pick up your kids, too. Both you and Jimmy will have to stand before a judge. You for abandoning your children and he for ignoring the order to stay away from you. It's your choice. Let me know now what you plan to do?"

There came a pause. "I'm going home."

"Don't play games with me, Patty."

"I'm going home, Jeff. I swear."

Jeff hated playing the bad guy, especially with someone he'd grown up with. Life hadn't been kind to Patty. She'd grown up with an abusive alcoholic father and had found herself in the same situation when she married a man like her father.

"I'm going to give you five minutes to get home; then I'm going to call your house. If one of your kids answers the phone, then I'm coming to arrest you, but not before I call child protective services to have them remove the children from your home."

"Please don't, Jeff. I'm going home now."

"Put Kenny back on the phone."

He heard muffled voices before his deputy returned. "She just left, Jeff."

"Give her ten minutes to get home, then call the house," he ordered. "Call me right away if she doesn't pick up."

"What are you going to do if she doesn't pick up?"

"I'll call CPS and have them put her children in foster care. Between Patty and Jimmy, those poor kids are going to be messed up."

"I hear you, boss," Kenny intoned.

"How's Jimmy?"

"He's quieted down, but I know he's going to start up again when they come to get him."

"It won't matter because he'll no longer be our responsibility."

"You're right, Jeff. I'm sorry to disturb you, but you have a better relationship with the people on the island than I do."

Sliding back to the mound of pillows supporting his shoulders, Jeff smiled. "That's because I grew up here and you didn't." His smile faded as quickly as it appeared. He was scheduled to be off for the next two days, hoping his deputies would be able to handle whatever came up until his return. "Good night, Kenny. Or should I say good morning?"

"Good morning, Jeff. I'll try not to call you again."

"You do that."

He ended the call, turned off the lamp, and readjusted the pillows. Threatening to remove Patty's children from their home reminded him of Kara. As a social worker she'd been entrusted to protect children from situations that threatened their safety.

Jeff had consciously tried not to think about Kara, but the image of her face and body lingered around the fringes of his mind when he least expected it. When his cousin had called to ask him to check on Taylor Patton's daughter, to say he was shocked was putting it mildly because he along with others who'd spent their lives on Cavanaugh Island believed Taylor didn't have any children.

Although Jeff had spent twenty years in the corps, returning home whenever he had leave, he knew if Taylor had fathered a child, he definitely would've heard about it only because there were very few secrets on Cavanaugh Island. And he knew not to ask David how he'd learned that Taylor had a daughter because his cousin would've claimed attorney-client privilege.

Resting his head on folded arms, he closed his eyes and attempted to go back to sleep, but it proved elusive. Reaching for the television remote, he turned on the flat screen and began channel surfing, passing numerous infomercials until he found a sports channel. The Super Bowl was over, baseball's spring training had begun, and the NBA and NHL seasons were in full swing. Jeff would be the first to admit he was a rabid sports fan, becoming an armchair spectator only because South Carolina did not have a professional sports team. He always took his dinner hour at Jack's Fish House just to watch the televised games on the many flat screens installed at the island's popular restaurant.

He muted the sound, turned on the closed caption feature, staring at the images until he felt his eyes closing. When he woke hours later, the television was watching him, and Jeff felt more tired than he had when he'd gone to bed and turned off the TV.

Bright sunshine filtered through the blinds at the windows, threading its way over the hardwood floor. Sitting up and swinging his legs over the side of the bed, he walked on bare feet out of the bedroom and across the hall to the bathroom. The first thing he'd done once he returned to Sanctuary Cove was to have an architect draw up plans to expand the house by adding a first-floor bedroom, bath en suite, and sunroom for his grandmother after her cardiologist cautioned her about climbing stairs. Corrine had pouted whenever he carried her up and down the staircase until the renovations were completed; then her attitude changed once he suggested they go into Charleston to shop for furnishings to decorate her new living quarters.

It had become role reversal when he looked after his seventy-nine-year-old maternal grandmother much like she'd cared for him after his mother died in childbirth. Corrine had become mother, father, and grandmother, and after his grandfather passed away, she'd also stepped into that role. She'd been forthcoming when it came time for her to tell him about sex. She was emphatic about his using protection whenever he slept with a woman and cautioned him about using women just to relieve his own sexual urges. What had surprised Jeff was he was more embarrassed about the discussion than his grandmother. Always taller than the boys his age, he hung out with older boys, most of whom were sexually active and proud of their exploits and conquests. However, his respect for the woman who'd raised him outweighed that of his peers, and he was discriminating and very discreet whenever he'd become involved with any woman.

Jeff did what he'd always done on his days off: yard work. He mowed the lawn, raked leaves, and bagged everything for the weekly trash pickup. His grandmother had voiced her concern whenever he opted to stay home with her instead of going out with a woman, fearing he would go through life alone. At forty he wasn't as concerned about marriage or fathering children as he was about taking care of the woman who'd sacrificed so much for him.

He'd been back a year, and his love life was nonexistent. There were single women on the island, but none had interested him. He'd found them shallow, immature, and gauche, unlike the women with whom he'd been involved when he was stationed in the States or abroad. Jeff had had two serious relationships — one that had prompted him to propose marriage — yet at forty he was still a bachelor. There was a time when he'd looked forward to marriage and becoming a father, but lately he'd reconciled to the possibility of that not happening in his immediate future. This didn't mean he wasn't looking for a woman with whom he could have a comfortable ongoing relationship. He just wasn't sure if he'd found her yet.

Twenty minutes later, dressed in sweats, Jeff walked into the kitchen and kissed his grandmother's cheek. "Don't you know how to sleep late?"

Corrine patted his stubble. "It's your day off. Don't *you* know how to sleep late?"

He smiled tenderly at the tall, thin woman with smooth skin the color of café au lait, tugging gently at the silver curls hugging her scalp. There were a few lines around her eyes whenever she smiled. "Remember, I have to clean up the yard."

"The yard can wait until next week, Jeffrey."

"No it can't, Gram. Then I would have twice as much to do." He only called her Gram whenever they were together and usually referred to her as Grandmomma when speaking of her to others.

Corrine filled a mug with freshly brewed coffee from the blue enameled pot on the stove, handing it to him. "What else do you have to do on your days off? You get up the same time as when you'd go to the station, you work in the yard, and then you come back inside and watch every game imaginable on that darn idiotic box."

Jeff cut his eyes at her. "Would you prefer I go to a bar, pick up women, guzzle beer, and chomp on peanuts all day?"

"No. I'd like you to find a nice young woman to marry and give me a few great-grandchildren before I die."

"Please, Gram, don't start on that again."

Corrine pushed her hands into the pockets of the bibbed apron covering a floral shirtwaist dress. "You gave up something you loved for me, son."

"And you gave up your life for me, Grand-momma!" Jeff shouted. "I'm sorry about raising my voice," he apologized when her jaw dropped. "You had the chance to marry again after Grandpapa died, but you didn't because you didn't want to put a man ahead of me." He held up a hand when she opened her mouth. "I overheard you when you were talking to Miss Dean about Mr. Hawkins wanting to marry you, and you said I came first in your life."

"You were eavesdropping on grown folks' business?" Corrine asked accusingly.

Opening the door to the stainless steel refrigerator-freezer, Jeff removed a container of cream, poured a dollop into his mug, then replaced it and closed the door. His grandmother had also balked when he updated the kitchen with top-of-the-line appliances, complaining that she liked her old stove. He'd also bought a single-cup coffee-maker that she refused to use, declaring her enamel pot made better coffee. How, he mused, would she know that when she hadn't drunk coffee for more than a year?

"No. I was bringing something to your classroom when I heard you talking with Miss Dean. That's all I heard before I waited at the end of the hall for her to leave."

"You couldn't have been more than six."

"I was seven, Gram."

Corrine removed her hands from her apron, clasping them in front of her. "And you waited all this time to tell me this, Jeffrey?"

Jeff took a sip of the warm brew, staring at his grandmother over the rim of the mug. Corrine Jefferson Hamilton's life was measured in numbers. She'd graduated high school at fifteen, married her high school sweetheart at eighteen, graduated college at nineteen, gave birth to her only child at twenty, became a grandmother at thirty-eight, and was widowed at forty. A former teacher and elementary school principal, she was the only one on Cavanaugh Island who called him Jeffrey. To everyone else he was Jeff, Sheriff Hamilton, or Corrine Hamilton's grandbaby boy.

"I didn't say anything because at that time I'd felt as if I was in the way and also a burden on you."

"What do you mean by 'in the way'?"

"There was talk, Gram. Folks used to say it was a shame that you'd raised a child and then you had to turn around and raise your grandchild when you had the chance to remarry after Grandpapa died. Some said I was standing in the way of your happiness, while others — most of them — praised you for your selflessness. It wasn't until I was older when I realized that if you'd wanted to remarry, then you would have."

Corrine walked to the table in the corner of the eat-in kitchen and sat down. She traced the design of the hand-stitched embroidery with her fingertips. "I did what I had to do, Jeffrey. Your mother died giving birth to you, and there was no way I was going to let you go to some foster home or let some strangers adopt you. Not when I still had breath in my body. I didn't marry Mr. Hawkins because I found out later that he was as mean as a junkyard dog whenever he drank. Your gramps never raised his hand or his voice to me, and I wasn't about to involve you in a situation where that may happen. Even if I would've put up with it, I know you never would once you got older."

Jeff sat opposite Corrine. Placing his hand over hers, he gave her fingers a gentle squeeze. "No one will ever hurt you, Gram. Not while I have breath in *my* body."

Eyelids fluttering, Corrine blinked back tears. "Drink your coffee, and take care of the lawn. I'll have breakfast ready for you when you're finished."

Leaning over, he kissed her cheek. "I'm going to pass on breakfast this morning because I'm meeting somebody for lunch."

"Who is she? It is a she, isn't it?"

He smiled. "Of course, it's a she."

"Who, Jeffrey? Do I know her?"

"No, you don't know her, but there's no doubt you'll hear about her before the sun goes down."

Reversing their hands, it was Corrine's turn to squeeze her grandson's fingers. "I guess I can wait for the rumor mill to start working overtime."

Kara had just come out of the bathroom when she heard soft knocking on the bedroom door. "Good morning, Mr. Todd."

The groundskeeper stood in the hallway outside her bedroom. He was the complete opposite of his wife in looks and personality. Tall, light-skinned with a face covered with freckles, and his once reddish hair now liberally sprinkled with gray, he spent most of his day landscaping the many acres that made up Angels Landing, sitting on the riding mower and pruning trees.

Mr. Todd crushed a battered straw hat between his large hands. "The sheriff is here to see you, Miss Kara."

She nodded. "Thank you. Please call me Kara," she reminded him. The man was old enough to be her grandfather, yet he'd insisted on calling her Miss Kara.

Mr. Todd's solemn expression didn't change. "As I said, the sheriff is downstairs."

"Thank you, Mr. Todd."

A hint of a smile tilted the corners of his full lips. "And you can call me Willie."

Kara plucked the navy-blue pashmina shawl off the back of the armchair, looping it around her neck, then picked up her handbag. "I can't do that, *Mr. Willie.*" If Mr. Todd had spent his life in the South, then he knew children were taught to address older people by miss or mister, regardless of first or surnames.

He stepped aside. "You should leave now. The sheriff isn't a very patient man."

Kara glanced at the clock on the fireplace mantel. It was 11:45, fifteen minutes earlier than when Jeff had promised to pick her up. "Please let him know I'm coming down." She waited until Mr. Todd left, then followed him, he taking the back staircase and

77

she taking the one that led to the front of the house.

Her pace slowed as she stepped off the last stair. Jeff stood in the middle of the living room, staring at the paintings of former owners of the house that had given the town its name. He looked a little sinister dressed in black: slacks, sweater, and jacket. Facets of light from the massive chandelier shimmered on his smooth jaw and dark brown skin. There was something about Jeff that was so masculine, virile that she found swallowing and breathing difficult.

"Good morning." Jeff turned at the sound of her voice. He stared at her as if she were an apparition. "Is there something wrong?" Kara asked.

Jeff blinked, his gaze moving slowly from her face to her feet. Kara appeared quite the chic, urban sophisticate. "No, Kara. Everything is fine." He closed the distance between them while extending his hands. Kara placed her hands on his outstretched palms, he leaning down to kiss her cheek. "You look beautiful."

Kara glanced down at the navy-blue wool gabardine pantsuit and matching patent leather pumps with a sturdy four-inch heel. "Thank you." Her head popped up. "I hope

I'm not too overdressed for lunch at Jack's."

Tucking her hand in the crook of his arm, Jeff gave her a reassuring smile. "No. If anything, you'll bring a little class to the joint."

She pulled back, but he tightened his grip on her much smaller hand. "I'll go up and change into something less businesslike."

"Please don't. Our lunch will be a combination of business and pleasure."

Jeff didn't want to tell Kara she was like a breath of fresh air. The ponytail was missing, and in its place was a sleek hairdo, parted off center to frame her face, the blunt-cut ends falling inches above her shoulders. A light cover of makeup accentuated her best features: her eyes and lips. His gaze lingered on the curve of her mouth outlined in a soft orange-brown shade.

"Pleasure?"

"The food at Jack's is pleasure personified. You don't believe me, do you?" he asked when she gave him a skeptical look. "I know you have good restaurants in New York, but they can't compare to Jack's."

"We'll see."

"Okay, Big Apple skeptic, let's go find out." Jeff led Kara out of the house and to his parked car. He released her hand, seating her in the low-slung, silver two seater.

"Nice, sexy little car," she crooned.

He hadn't thought of the Miata as sexy but practical for his lifestyle. In essence, it was a bachelor's car. His grandmother had accused him of being selfish when he'd first purchased the two seater, but after he'd taken her into Charleston for a test-drive, she changed her mind. The only thing Corrine complained about was that it was too low to the ground and she much preferred her four-door Camry. Jeff wasn't certain how much longer she would continue to drive, leaving that decision up to her doctors. What he wanted was for his grandmother to remain independent for as long as possible.

"Thank you," Jeff said to Kara as he slid in behind the wheel.

"It smells new."

The engine of the Mazda MX-5 Miata roared to life when he pushed the Start Engine button. "It is. I picked it up from the dealer a couple of months ago. My last car was eighteen years old, and I used to work on it whenever I came home on leave, but then after a while, I was unable to replace the parts, so I sold it for scrap."

"Did you give it a proper farewell?"

Throwing back his head, Jeff laughed, the rich sound bouncing off the roof inside the small vehicle. "To be honest, I couldn't look when the tow truck driver hooked it up and drove away."

There was a comfortable silence as he continued in an easterly direction toward the Cove, Jeff more than aware of the woman sitting less than a foot away. Everything about her screamed big-city sophisticate: coiffed hair, pantsuit, shoes, and the pearl studs in her ears. He'd told a little lie when he said she wasn't overdressed because it'd been awhile since he'd gone out with a woman like Kara. It wasn't that the women on the island didn't dress up, but those who were stay-at-home mothers or shopkeepers tended to be more casual.

"How large is Cavanaugh Island?" Kara asked, breaking into his musings.

"The entire island is about eight square miles."

"If it's that small, then why is it divided into towns?"

Jeff met her eyes for a second. Sunlight coming through the windshield had turned them into large pools of green and gold. "There were rumors that Thomas Cavanaugh, whom many suspected was a pirate, used the island as his home base. He and his band of men would lay in wait in the marshes and fire on merchant ships moored off the coast. Although British authorities could never prove he was responsible for the dastardly acts, they forced him to give up his claim to the island when he was impressed into their navy. Others came seeking their fortune in what had been the American colonies, and they were awarded land grants for their service to the king."

"Why is the house called Angels Landing when the town is also called Angels Landing?"

Jeff shifted into a lower gear as he approached the newly built road connecting Angels Landing with Sanctuary Cove. "Now that's a long story."

"Remember, Jeff, I'm not leaving tomorrow."

He laughed again. "It definitely won't take a week to tell, but I want to warn you that it has everything to do with your people."

She went completely still. "When you say my people, are you talking about the Pattons?"

"Yes."

"Is it something I don't need to know?"

A beat passed. "There's an old Gullah saying that 'you can't know where you're going if you don't know where you've come from.' "

"Are you saying I'm Gullah?"

"If you're Taylor Patton's daughter, then yes, you *are* Gullah."

Kara closed her eyes. "I still don't want to believe the man I thought to be my father for all these years isn't."

"That happens to a lot of us."

She opened her eyes. "Us?"

"I never knew my father," Jeff stated in a strained tone. "I wouldn't know him if I met him on the street. But it's different with you because you don't have to share DNA with a man for him to assume the role as dad."

"The man I call Daddy is awesome."

"That's all that counts, Kara."

He maneuvered into the parking lot at Jack's Fish House, pulling into the last space. The lot was filled with pickup trucks belonging to the fishermen who came to the restaurant for the luncheon specials. There were also out-of-state license plates belonging to snowbirds that came down to spend the winter on the island.

"Is the lot always this crowded?" Kara asked.

Jeff realized Kara had asked a lot of questions because she was trying to sort things out for herself. Some he could answer, and others she would have to uncover on her own. He'd grown up not knowing his mother or father, yet he'd never felt disconnected. He didn't remember his grandfather, but the stories Corrine told him about her beloved husband and photographs she'd saved of him made Malachi Hamilton come alive in Jeff's imagination.

"Most of the time. By twelve thirty nearly all of the fishermen on the island come for lunch, then around five or six it's the dinner crowd."

Kara gave Jeff a tender smile. "Well, Gullah man, you promised me a wonderful lunch, so let's go."

Jeff opened his door, planting one spit-shined, booted foot on the ground, then turned and smiled at Kara over his shoulder. "It appears as if I'm not the only Gullah here."

She ran an imaginary line down the middle of her body. "Only half."

His smile grew wider. "One drop of Gullah blood makes you Gullah."

Waiting until he came around to assist her, Kara tilted her chin. Jeff's eyes sparkled in amusement. "Do you speak Gullah?"

He shook his head. "But I do understand it."

"I was hoping you'd give me a crash course. Sometimes Mrs. Todd will lapse into dialect, and it takes a while before I realize what she's saying."

"My grandmother could teach you, but a week isn't long enough for you to pick up even the simplest phrases."

Kara wrapped her arms around her body to ward off a gust of cold wind coming off the ocean. "I'm staying more than a week."

Jeff stared wordlessly as if he couldn't believe what she'd said. He replayed her statement over and over in his head. "You're staying longer than a week?" She nodded. At that instant he didn't know whether to shout like a crazy man or kiss Kara. Twenty-four hours ago he hadn't known she existed. But now it was different. David had told him she wasn't married, yet that still didn't mean she wasn't committed to someone back in New York.

He didn't know what it was that drew him to Kara other than she was different than any of the women on the island. She was a transplanted Southern girl who wasn't reticent when she'd accused him of interrogating her, yet underneath the feigned tough-girl exterior, she was a vulnerable woman whose very existence had proven to be a lie.

Their eyes met, and he smiled. "I'll introduce you to my grandmother. She was a teacher for forty-five years, and I know she'd like nothing else better than having you as her student."

Kara's expression changed. It stilled, becoming serious. "I can't impose on her like that."

Wrapping an arm around her waist, Jeff led her out of the parking lot toward the restaurant. "I wouldn't have mentioned it if I thought it was an imposition. If it will make you feel more comfortable, you can ask her yourself."

Opening the door, he held it for Kara, watching her reaction as she walked inside the restaurant where the cuisine had become legendary throughout the Lowcountry. Tantalizing and mouthwatering aromas filled the air as the waitstaff pushed their way into and out of the kitchen's swinging door, trays laden with dishes piled high with lunch orders.

Kara's eyes were as large as silver dollars. "Oh my . . ." Her words trailed off when a waitress placed platters of fried chicken, catfish, biscuits, red rice and sausage, collards and chitlins on the table of six diners who'd tucked napkins under their chins.

"Did I not tell you?" Jeff whispered in her ear when she leaned back against his chest.

"If that's lunch, then what are they going to eat for dinner?" she asked softly under her breath.

"I don't know."

The waitress beckoned to them. "Jeff, there's a table for two near the side door. If you don't want to sit there, then you can wait for an empty one."

Jeff lowered his head, pressing his mouth to Kara's ear. "Do you want to wait?"

"No!"

Her reply was so emphatic that he was hard-pressed not to laugh. Resting a hand at the small of her back, Jeff directed her to the table. As if on cue, the entire restaurant fell silent, all eyes directed at them. He knew most of the locals were either curious or shocked to see him bringing a woman into Jack's. In fact, they hadn't seen him with a woman since he'd returned to the Cove to live. Whenever he ate at the restaurant, it was usually alone, with his deputies, or his grandmother.

"Damn, Jeff! She's hotter than a bushel of peppers!" boomed a male voice.

Jeff never broke stride. "Watch your mouth, Bossier. And you will respect the lady, or I'll lock you up for disturbing the peace!"

A few guffaws and titters followed his warning. Those who didn't laugh knew he never issued idle threats. Jeff seated Kara, then came around the scarred oak table hewn from massive tree trunks. "What's the matter?" he asked when she looked at him, a strange expression on her face.

"Does this usually happen whenever you bring a woman here?"

Leaning back in his chair, he gave her a long, penetrating stare. "No, it's happening because I don't bring women here. The exception is my grandmother."

"What about your wife?"

His eyebrows flickered slightly. "I don't have a wife."

It was Kara's turn to lift her eyebrows. "What about a girlfriend?"

"I don't have a girlfriend."

She angled her head. "I know this is a little personal, but do you like women?"

Jeff smiled, flashing his teeth. "I happen to love women."

"But you don't date local women," Kara said perceptively. Her question was a statement.

He nodded. "Not from the Cove, Landing, or the Creek."

"What's wrong with them, Jeff?"

"Nothing."

"Nothing?" Kara repeated. "There has to be a reason why they don't appeal to you."

Propping an elbow on the table, he rested his chin on his fist. "Do you want me to set

88

up a session where you can analyze me?" He knew he'd embarrassed Kara when a rush of color darkened her face. "I'm sorry," he apologized quickly. "That was uncalled for. Will you forgive me?"

Kara stared at something over his shoulder. Her eyes were now a deep green. "I'll think about it."

Reaching across the table, Jeff grasped her hand, tightening his grip on her fingers when she tried pulling away. "I'm really sorry, Kara, for not answering your question." He thought for a moment. "I don't know why, but I've never been attracted to the girls on the island."

Her gaze swung back to meet his. "Is it because you resent being Gullah?"

"No! Why would you think that?" he asked, letting go of her hand.

"I don't know, Jeff. It just seems odd that you don't find any woman on an eight-square-mile island attractive."

Jeff lowered his arm. "That's where you're wrong. I find you attractive."

Kara blushed again. "I don't count."

"And why not?"

"Because I don't live on Cavanaugh Island."

A pregnant silence ensued as they stared at each other. "What if you do decide to stay?" Jeff asked, "would you be opposed to going out with me?"

There, he'd said it. Depending on Kara's answer he would know whether she was or wasn't involved with someone either in New York or Little Rock. And he hoped it was the latter.

A hint of a smile softened Kara's mouth. "I'm having lunch with you, aren't I?"

Crossing his arms over his chest, he nodded slowly. "Yes, you are. But it's not really a date."

"Then what is it, Jeff?"

"It's keeping a promise to my cousin that I would look after you. And that includes showing you around and making sure that certain people like that jerk who disrespected you won't do it again."

"So I'm safe as long as I'm with you?"

Lines fanned out around his eyes when he smiled. "As safe as you'd be if you were locked in a bank's vault."

"You just reminded me of something."

"What's that?"

"I have to go to the bank. I have power of attorney to open Taylor's safe-deposit box."

"Do you have the key?"

"Yes. David gave me an envelope yesterday with the key and some other papers that I never took out of my bag."

"After lunch I'll take you to the bank."

Kara let out an audible sigh. "How can I thank you?"

"Go to the movies with me," he said quickly. "I'm off duty tomorrow."

"Is there a movie theater here on the island?"

"There's one on the Cove, but most of the films are at least two to three months behind the ones they show in Charleston. There's also a small theater in the Creek. They only feature foreign films and black-and-white movies from the thirties and forties. The Creek is our artist community. Most of the people who live there are artisans and farmers. All of the chickens sold on the island come from the Creek. There's still a dairy farm and a couple of hog farms. Every Wednesday the farmers set up an outdoor market where you can buy fruits, veggies, and home-baked goods.

"Angels Landing is different because it is solely residential. The Cove offers both. It has a bank, post office, pharmacy, bakery, boardinghouse, supermarket, liquor store, ice cream parlor, and bookstore. It also has a unisex salon. Last year the island got its first resident doctor in more than a decade. Dr. Monroe has an office off Main Street and Moss Alley, and he makes house calls."

"So folks really don't have to leave the island if they don't want to."

Jeff shook his head. "No, they don't. Every town has a school with grades one through eight. Once they graduate they go into Charleston for high school."

"Do the kids from Charleston ever come to the island?"

"Many of them do once they form friendships with the kids who live here. It's like culture shock for many of them because life here is very laid-back. Everyone knows one another, and there is zero tolerance for crime. Old folks say kids can cut the fool on the mainland, but we don't tolerate that here."

"What about churches?"

"Each town has its own church."

A waitress with neatly braided hair covered with a hairnet came over to their table. Her dark skin glistened with good health as she nodded to Jeff, then Kara. "Would you like to see a menu?"

"Yes," Jeff said, answering for himself and Kara.

Within seconds, menus were placed on the table along with a pitcher of sweet tea, two tall glasses, and a plate of biscuits. "We are a little backed up in the kitchen, so it may take awhile before you get your food.

92

But I could start you off with a bowl of gumbo."

"Would you like to try the gumbo?" Jeff asked Kara.

"Yes, please."

Chapter Four

Kara was tempted to undo the button on her slacks. She couldn't remember the last time she'd eaten so much. The gumbo could've been a meal because it wasn't just celery, okra, tomato, onion, corn, and peppers; the chef had added pieces of smoked meat, spicy sausage, crabmeat, oysters, and shrimp.

When she couldn't decide what to order she'd insisted that Jeff order for her, and much to her delight he'd selected red rice and sausage, shrimp, crab and salmon cakes, and mustard greens with cornmeal dumplings.

Kara placed her napkin beside her plate. "I can't eat like this every day."

"You hardly ate anything. Are you sure you don't want dessert?"

She groaned. "Quite sure. Lunch for me is usually a tuna salad or a half a bagel left over from breakfast."

94

Jeff dabbed the corners of his mouth with the napkin. "I hope you're not one of those women who monitors everything they put into their mouths because they don't want to gain two pounds."

"No way. It's just that I don't have time to eat. Between seeing clients and field visits I'm lucky if I eat two meals a day."

"Do you ever take a vacation and just chill out?"

"That's what I'm doing now," Kara explained. "I've accrued so much vacation leave that if I hadn't taken at least three weeks I would've lost it."

"Oh, so you can stay three weeks."

Kara bit back a smile when she saw the look of expectation on Jeff's handsome face. There was something about the man sitting across from her that was intriguing. He still had the drawl verifying that he'd grown up in the American South; however, there was a worldliness about him that probably had come from his time in the military.

"I can stay a maximum of three weeks, then it's back to New York and the grind." She saw Jeff angle his head and stare at her as if he were committing her face to memory. "What's the matter?"

"Why do you work at something you refer to as a grind, Kara?"

"I only say that because it's the same routine day in and day out. I'm certain it was the same with you when you were in the military."

"Not when you're in a war zone."

A slight gasp escaped Kara. "You were in Iraq?" Jeff's expression changed, the warmth in his eyes was replaced by something she could only interpret as pain.

"Afghanistan. Two tours."

She slumped back in her chair. "I'm sorry if what I said sounded so glib."

"It's all right. You didn't know."

"Were you in the army?"

"Hell no."

"Ouch!" Kara held up her hand, palm facing Jeff. "You must have been a jarhead."

"You've got it," Jeff admitted proudly.

"Once a marine, always a marine?" she teased.

"You better believe it." He shrugged out of his jacket, pushed up the sleeve to his sweater, and showed her the insignia and motto of the corps on his left forearm.

She stared at the tattoo of an eagle, globe, anchor, and *Semper fidelis* on his muscular arm. "How long have you had your tattoo?"

"Almost twenty years. I got it after successfully completing OCS and the NROTC program."

Kara tucked a thick lock of hair behind her right ear. "So, you were an officer."

"I'd attained the rank of captain in the military police before I put in my discharge papers."

Shock after shock slapped at Kara with this disclosure. "My dad was also in the corps as military police. He retired last year after thirty years as a sergeant major."

"Hot damn! My man!"

She brought her hand up to stifle a giggle. "It can't be all that, Jeff."

"Baby, you just don't know what it means to be a marine."

"I do know," Kara countered. "My mother lived on base with Dad for the first eight years of my life. She didn't like it, and I didn't like moving from base to base and leaving my friends. We moved back to Little Rock, and I lived there until I left to go to college."

She felt as if she'd known Jeff for years when she told him about moving to New York to attend college, earning an undergraduate degree and MSW, and sharing an apartment with a professional dancer.

"Do you like New York?" he asked.

"There was a period of adjustment, but I've grown used to the noise, grittiness, and the pulsing excitement that's so contagious.

The first time I went to Times Square during the summer I couldn't believe I had to jostle for space on the sidewalk at three in the morning."

"Well, it is touted as the city that never sleeps," Jeff reminded her.

"And it doesn't. What made you decide on a military career?" Kara asked, deftly steering the focus of conversation from her to Jeff.

"A recruiter approached me within days of my enrolling in college, and his pitch sounded so good I signed up."

"Do you miss it, Jeff?" Her voice was soft, almost a whisper.

He pulled down his sleeve and stared at the initials carved into the table. "Yes and no. I miss the brotherhood, seeing the drills, the dress parades, and the silent drill platoon. I still get together with some of the officers whenever they come to Charleston."

"Your mother must be very proud of you." Without warning Jeff sobered, and instinctually she knew she'd mentioned something that should've been left unsaid. She also recalled he'd talked about his grandmother, but not his mother. "I'll understand if you don't want to talk about her."

"There's not much to talk about. My mother died giving birth to me."

98

Kara's eyelids fluttered as she attempted to bring her emotions under control. She'd been trained as a therapist to remain detached, not get emotionally involved with her clients, but Jeff wasn't a client. He was the man whom she'd found herself drawn to; a man who made her feel things and react to him when she didn't want to.

He'd openly admitted he was attracted to her, while she didn't and couldn't tell him ɜhe felt the same. There was no way she would permit herself to get involved with Jeff when she knew she would be leaving Cavanaugh Island in three weeks or maybe even less. It had taken only one devastating relationship for Kara to learn never to let her heart rule her head. If she had planned to relocate to Angels Landing, she would seriously consider dating Jeff. He was intelligent, a wonderful conversationalist, and very easy on the eyes.

"I'm sorry, Jeff." She exhaled a breath. "Why is it we keep apologizing to each other?" He angled his head in a gesture she found endearing and had come to look for.

"I don't know, Kara. Actually there isn't anything to apologize for. I —" Whatever he was going to say was preempted when the waitress approached their table.

"Is there anything else I can get you,

Sheriff Hamilton?"

"Just the check, Bessie."

Reaching into the pocket of her apron, Bessie placed the check facedown on the table. She stared openly at Kara. "You have to be a Patton because you look just like those folks in the Landing. Which one are —"

"Thank you, Bessie, and keep the change," Jeff said, handing her several twenties and cutting her off. He pushed to his feet, came around the table, and pulled back Kara's chair. "Please let Otis and Miss Vina know that everything was delicious."

"That wasn't very nice," Kara chastised once they were out in the parking lot.

"It wasn't very nice that she tried to get in your business like that," he countered.

"I am a Patton, Jeff, and that means I don't have any business — at least not on Cavanugh Island. Right now, I feel as if my life is a puzzle with several missing pieces. Meanwhile, I have to wait until my mother gets here before she can give me the piece about her relationship with Taylor. Then there's the financial component and the mandate to restore Angels Landing. It's not only a lot to take in, but a great deal to handle in just a couple of weeks. The only constant is that I'm still Kara Newell and

Austin Newell is and will always be my father."

Jeff glanced at his watch. "Speaking of finances, I'd better get you over to the bank before it closes."

Three minutes later, Jeff sat in his car in the business district parking lot behind the bank waiting for Kara. He'd revealed things about himself that he never would have said to another woman during their first encounter. He'd thought of it as an encounter and not a date. David had asked him to keep an eye on her, yet keeping an eye on Kara did not translate into asking her to go to the movies with him. She hadn't said yes or no to his offer, so as an optimist he'd hoped she would go with him.

Jeff reclined the seat, crossed his arms over his chest, and closed his eyes. He didn't know what prompted him to tell Kara about his mother, because whenever anyone asked about Juanita Hamilton his reply was she was dead. His mother had died in child-birth, but the details of the events leading up to her death were imprinted on his brain like a permanent tattoo.

Whenever kids asked about his father, he'd either refuse to talk about him or say he'd died a hero. It was easier to lie and tell them his father had died in Vietnam than say he didn't know who his father was.

The drawback to growing up on Cavanaugh Island was no one had to ask who your folks were because everyone knew everyone. Although he rarely interacted with the Pattons, Jeff knew them all. Even when he'd been away for years and returned on leave, his grandmother would catch him up on what had been going on not only in the Cove, but also in Haven Creek and Angels Landing. She'd given him an update on who'd died, gotten married, divorced, moved back and the names and sex of newborns, some who'd been delivered by a midwife and some who were born in hospitals on the mainland.

It wasn't until the year he'd celebrated his tenth birthday that his grandmother felt he was ready to deal with the circumstances behind his birth. Juanita left the island to go to college and had found herself involved with an older student. Corrine had believed she was living on campus when in reality Juanita had moved in with her boyfriend. Juanita hadn't realized she was pregnant until she went into labor late one night. It was only when she'd begun hemorrhaging that her baby's father drove her to the hospital; he'd panicked, leaving her in the hospital's parking lot and drove away. Her body was found the following morning, barely conscious. Juanita was lucid enough to give the ER doctor her contact information and how she'd gotten to the hospital. What she did not reveal was who'd left her there. She delivered a three-pound baby boy but did not survive the ordeal because she'd lost too much blood.

When Corrine and Malachi came to claim her body, they were unable to bring home their grandson until he was able to breathe on his own. Jeff was four months old when his grandparents finally brought him to the Cove. When asked, Corrine told everyone the baby was their grandchild and their daughter had died giving birth to him.

There was gossip that if Corrine hadn't kept her daughter on such a tight leash, Juanita wouldn't have gone buck wild when it came time to leave home for college because Corrine had established a reputation as a strict teacher and an even stricter no-nonsense principal.

Jeff never got to see that side of his grandmother; he'd never had her as a teacher and had only known her as a soft-spoken and somewhat overindulgent grandparent. He didn't know whether her spoiling him was because she'd wanted to make up for him not knowing either of his parents, but that aside he realized he'd had a wonderful childhood. He knew how much his grandmother valued education and Jeff studied longer and harder than necessary, eventually becoming an overachiever.

Once he'd become sexually active there was never a time when he hadn't assumed the responsibility of using protection. Even when a woman claimed she was using an oral contraceptive, he still wore a condom.

A light tapping on the window garnered his attention, and Jeff sat up. Kara had returned. He got out of the car. The wind had picked up, blowing her hair around her face. The temperature had dropped twenty degrees from the day before, topping out at forty instead of the average sixty. He tucked several strands behind her ear. "Did you finish what you had to do?"

Kara shook her head, her windblown hair moving with the motion. "No. I left a message with the manager's secretary that I'd like to see him tomorrow morning. I decided on a morning meeting because I didn't know when you wanted to go to the movies."

Jeff was hard-pressed not to pump his fist. Kara had given him her answer. She would go out with him. However, he had to be careful, very, very careful not to become too emotionally involved only because she was going to leave, just like the other women in his life. He'd lost his mother, past girl-friends, fiancée, and it was inevitable he would eventually lose his grandmother.

"Would you like to take in a matinee, then eat afterward, or see a later show?"

"I'll leave that up to you," Kara said.

"Are you all right?" he asked when he saw her chewing her lip.

Kara flashed a quick, too bright smile, then looked away. "Of course."

Cradling her face in his hands, Jeff forced her to look at him. "What's the matter, Kara?" He lowered his head, their mouths inches apart. "Whatever it is, I want you to remember that I'm here to help you."

Kara anchored her arms under Jeff's shoulders, feeding on his warmth and the strength in his muscular upper body. How could a man she'd known twenty-four hours make her feel so safe, protected? There were men she'd dated for months, a few for years, and she'd continued to see them because it was better than sitting home alone. They took up the empty hours when she wanted and needed to get out of the apartment. However, none of them made her feel quite like she did with Jeff. He'd parried the outburst from the man in the restaurant with a warning about disrespecting her, while she'd lost count of the number of ribald comments and lecherous gazes directed at her whenever she walked down a street or entered a traditional male bastion with another man who'd kept walking as if he were deaf *and* mute.

Going on tiptoe, she pressed her mouth to his ear. "Taylor has been hiding cash in a deposit box," she whispered. "Lots of money."

Jeff froze. "How much are you talking about?"

"I don't know. I stopped counting at fifty thousand."

He buried his face in her hair. "Call David and ask him what you should do."

Kara patted his back when she wanted to kiss him. "Thanks for reminding me. I'll call him later."

Turning his head, Jeff kissed her hair. "I want you to forget about what you found inside the bank and come with me. I'm going to give you an up close and personal guided tour of the island." He glanced down at her feet. "Are you comfortable walking in those shoes?"

"I'm good."

She'd been truthful. Given their height, the shoes were very comfortable. She could wear them all day, walk up and down stairs, and then go out dancing in them. However, she couldn't remember the last time she'd danced. Dancing around the apartment whenever one of her favorite songs came on the radio didn't count. Dawn had accused her of not knowing how to have fun. What the dancer failed to understand was that she would've been more animated if their living arrangements hadn't impacted her very essence.

Kara wanted to be able to walk around in a state of half-dress, hang out in the kitchen on weekends and cook enough food to last her and Dawn for several meals, because her friend and roommate's cooking skills were wholly deficient.

Suddenly she realized spending time on Cavanaugh Island was a respite from the fast pace and noise of her adopted city; the revolving door of people coming and going in the apartment; and not having to deal with clients, updating case records, and listening to her supervisor's critical assessment of the work she did every two weeks. Jeff took her hand, holding it protectively. She hadn't realized how tall and powerfully built he was until they stood side by side.

She giggled like a little girl when he bowed gracefully.

"We'll begin the tour with the bank. They are now open on Saturdays in keeping with the banks on the mainland. Next we have the pharmacy, which also houses the post office."

"Does each town have a post office?" Kara asked, shading her eyes with her free hand when she peered through the plate glass window.

"No. It's always been here on the Cove. Before the state built the causeway, mail was delivered by ferry, and the ferry only docks at this end of the island."

She strolled with Jeff, stopping when he entered each store and introduced her to the owners. There was no mistaking their shock when Jeff introduced her as Newell and not Patton.

They'd just walked out of Rose Dukes-Walker's sweet-grass basket shop, A Tisket A Basket, when Jeff waved to a slender blonde woman pushing a stroller with a flaxen-haired little boy. "That's Alice Parker. Her husband is US Representative Jason Parker. His folks were originally from Haven Creek, and they moved from Charleston to the Cove last year. It turned out to be a good thing for the Cove and

Landing because it was Jason who made certain we got enough money from the Department of Transportation to build the road between the two towns."

"Where to next?" she asked.

"We won't stop at De Fountain because it's impossible to go there and not buy something. All of the ice cream, sorbet, and gelato are made on the premises. During the summer months there is always a line out the door. Folks come from Charleston just to buy ice cream."

Kara gave him a sidelong glance. "It's *that* good?"

He nodded, smiling. "It's that good."

"The next time I come to the Cove I'll be certain to pick some up."

They strolled past a wine and liquor store, a florist, and a supermarket with a deli and gourmet food sections. "This is Dr. Monroe's office, and his wife's bookstore is on the corner."

Tugging on Jeff's hand, her eyes dancing in excitement, Kara said, "I need to go to the bookstore."

He gave a smile parents usually reserved for their children. "Slow down, baby. If someone sees you running, they'll think I'm chasing you."

"People don't run on Cavanaugh Island?"

"Only on the beach."

"Let go of my hand, Jeff."

"Jeff Hamilton, when did you start dating a Patton?"

Kara heard Jeff when he mumbled an expletive. He smiled, but the gesture did not reach his eyes. "Good afternoon, Miss Hannah."

Bright green eyes darted between Jeff and Kara. The frames on the oversized glasses perched on the end of her nose matched the vermilion color on her mouth, while clashing with a head of teased champagne-pink hair.

"Good afternoon, Jeff. Aren't you going to introduce me to your *girlfriend?*"

Kara opened her mouth to tell the garish-looking woman that Jeff wasn't her boy-friend, but the slight pressure on her hand when he tightened his grip on her fingers stopped her.

"Kara, this is Mrs. Hannah Forsyth. She's the Cove's librarian and the island's histo-rian. Miss Hannah, Kara Newell."

Hannah blinked, reminding Kara of a heavily lidded owl. "You're not Kara Pat-ton?"

"No, ma'am."

"You have to be related to them because you look just like Theodora Patton when

110

she was your age."

"We're sorry to rush off, Miss Hannah, but we have to get to the bookstore."

The librarian patted her cotton candy wisps. "I just came from there to welcome Deborah back from her maternity leave. Deborah opening the bookstore, and she marrying Dr. Monroe is just wonderful for the Cove."

"I agree," Jeff said at the same time he moved past the librarian. "Have a good evening, Miss Hannah."

"You, too," she said to his departing back.

"What was that all about?" Kara asked when they were out of earshot.

"I should've introduced her as the island gossip instead of the historian. She's a walking tabloid."

Kara couldn't fathom how Jeff knew everyone on the island whereas she didn't know all of the people who lived in the six apartments on her floor of the twenty-two-story high-rise. She'd recognized a few whenever they rode the elevator together but didn't know their names. Most New Yorkers were too busy and self-absorbed with making it in a city that offered something for everyone. They didn't have time to dawdle because they were always going or coming from somewhere.

She didn't know why, but Kara hadn't expected to find a bookstore on the island. So many bookstore chains in large cities had gone out of business or were closing with the advent of the super bookstores that offered coffee shops and reading rooms.

Jeff opened the door to the Parlor Bookstore, and the inviting warmth of a parlor enveloped Kara. The concert piano, comfortable leather grouping, area rugs, Tiffany style floor lamps and hanging fixtures, low tables, flat screen, and wall-to-wall, floor-to-ceiling shelves packed tightly with books beckoned her to come and stay awhile. It was the perfect place to relax and read.

A tall, slender woman with a profusion of curly hair framing her bare face greeted Jeff with a hug and kiss. She appeared casually chic in a pair of fitted jeans, ballet type flats, and man-tailored white shirt. He lifted her effortlessly off her feet with one arm.

"Welcome back. How's the family, Debs?"

She rested a hand on Jeff's cheek. "Everyone's well. Georgia told me you stopped by every day when you're out on foot patrol to check on the store."

He nodded. "How's the baby?"

Deborah smiled. "He's getting so big."

Curving an arm around Deborah's waist, he led her to where Kara stood watching the interaction. "Kara, this is Deborah Robinson-Monroe, owner of the Parlor. Debs, Kara Newell."

Kara and Deborah shared a handshake and smile. "It's nice meeting you, Mrs. Monroe."

Deborah waved a hand. "It's Deborah. You're welcome to look around, and as a first-time customer you'll be entitled to a fifteen percent discount — that is, if you decide to buy something."

There was something about Deborah that Kara liked immediately. She had an infectious smile that lit up her entire face. "Thank you."

"There's tea and sweet breads on the table," Deborah offered.

"Oh, no thank you. Jeff and I just came from Jack's."

"Was it your first time there?"

"Yes. And it definitely won't be my last. Do you have any books on gardening?" Kara asked Deborah.

"Yes. They're at the end of this row on the right."

Kara found the section and was surprised to find quite a few books on the subject. Although she hadn't planned on living in Angels Landing, she'd thought about putting in a rose garden.

After a quarter of an hour she decided on a coffee-table book on designing gardens. Deborah processed her credit card, taking off 15 percent and placing the book in a recyclable bag with the bookstore's logo.

"I hope you'll come again."

Kara and Jeff exchanged a glance. "I'm certain I will."

Deborah hugged Jeff again. "I want you and your grandmother to come by the house during Easter week. Whitney will be home from college, and it will be the first time we'll all be together since Christmas."

"I'll make certain to bring her by."

"I like Deborah," Kara told Jeff once they left the bookstore to return to where he'd parked his car.

He took the shopping bag from her. "Debs and I go way back. Her grandmother was the first black teacher to integrate the Cove's white school."

"Don't you think it's strange that she's the only one who didn't mention my resemblance to the Pattons?"

"Maybe that has something to do with Debs not growing up on the island. She doesn't have the same sensibilities as the rest of us."

"Where did she grow up?"

"Charleston. She used to spend her summers here with her grandparents."

Kara smiled. "I bet spending summers here was better than going to a sleepaway camp."

"It was wonderful for kids. After we did our chores we used to hang out on the beach. Once we were teenagers we were allowed to hang out on the beach at night. We'd light a fire and roast marshmallows and make s'mores. The trick was eating them without ingesting sand. The only thing we couldn't do was swim at night. Years before a couple of kids had gone swimming at night and one drowned. It was weeks before his body washed up off Saint Helena Sound."

"The island is like living in a huge gated community."

Jeff angled his head. "I never thought of it in that way. But you're right. Everyone looks out for one another. The kids who live here are careful not to do anything they're not supposed to do because they never know who's watching them. It's not like kids on the mainland when parents take the keys to the car because of an infraction. Here they're truly on lockdown. Once the news gets out that Jamal or Keisha are grounded, it spreads through the island like a lighted fuse. Some of them call me and ask that I stop by the house to check and see if their kids are there."

"That's invasive, Jeff."

"No, it's not. It's about concerned parents, Kara. How many stories have you heard about kids sneaking out and getting into trouble, or they were at the wrong place at the wrong time?"

"Unfortunately too many," she confirmed. "There's no fast-food restaurant or Starbucks on the island, so where do the kids hang out?" Kara asked Jeff.

"There's always the beach, and the Cove and Creek have town squares. Many of them gather there on weekends and in the summer. Most of them entertain their friends in their backyards. A few who have cars drive to Charleston, and those who don't take the ferry. However, the ferry doesn't run all night, so that acts like an unofficial curfew."

"What happens if they miss the ferry?"

"Then they'll have to come out of their pocket for a taxi. The mayor of the towns negotiated with the taxi companies on the mainland to charge a flat fee; otherwise it would be prohibitive to pay what's on the meter."

"Why isn't Cavanaugh Island listed as one of the best places in the country to live and raise children?"

"We want that to be our little secret. That's one of the reasons why we don't want developers buying land here. They'll put up condos, golf courses, and country clubs, and the folks who live here will become second-class citizens in their own towns. Taxes will probably triple and quadruple, and when someone on a fixed income whose family has owned a plot of land for more than a hundred and fifty years can't pay the taxes, they'll lose everything."

Kara thought about her dilemma. Developers wanted Angels Landing and the two thousand acres it sat on. If she did sell it, then it would only impact two people: Willie and Iris Todd. Taylor Patton's will stated that the groundskeeper and his wife would continue to live out their natural lives in one of the two guesthouses. That might prove problematic if the developer who purchased the land sought to displace them. She couldn't do that to the friendly couple.

"You can't do what?" Jeff asked.

Giving him a confused look, Kara then realized she'd spoken her thoughts aloud. "I can't sell Angels Landing."

His eyebrows lifted. "You were thinking of selling it?"

"Not consciously. But what am I going to

do with a house with twenty rooms?"

"The same as Taylor did once his mother passed away. Live in it. Angels Landing is on the National Register of Historic Places; its contents and the land are worth millions and much too important to give away to a bunch of greedy developers."

Kara slipped into the car when Jeff held the door for her. She'd complained to him about living alone in a house with double-digit rooms yet complained to Dawn about the number of people crowding their two-bedroom apartment, aware that she couldn't have it both ways. Either she return to New York and accept Dawn's need to take care of the less fortunate or accept her birthright and restore the house as stated in Taylor Patton's will. Settling back against the leather seat, she stared out the side window. She had time in which to make a decision to stay or leave.

Jeff drove slowly enough for her to see the town hall, the courthouse, and the library. She noticed signs pointing to the school, ferry, and the Cove Inn, the town's boardinghouse.

"Where are we going?" she asked when he turned off Main Street and onto a road that didn't lead to Angels Landing.

"I want you to meet my grandmother."

"I'm not ready to meet your grand-mother."

Jeff gave her a quick glance. "When will you be ready?"

"I don't know."

"Are you always this indecisive?"

"No. And I'm not indecisive."

"You're not ready to meet my grand-mother, you don't know whether you'll sell Angels Landing, and you haven't decided whether you're going to stay or leave. In my book, that adds up to indecisiveness."

Kara pushed out her lower lip as she'd done as a child when she was angry or bothered. "You're reading the wrong book."

"I don't think so, Kara. If you want to know about Taylor, then you have to ask Corrine Hamilton, because Gram and Theodora Haynes Patton were once what kids refer to nowadays as BFFs."

CHAPTER FIVE

Corrine Hamilton stared at the young woman standing next to her grandson, feeling as if she'd stepped back in time, a time when she and Theodora Haynes were as close as sisters.

An uncertain smile flitted across her features. "Please come and rest yourself."

Jeff placed a hand at the small of Kara's back. "Gram, this is Kara Newell. Kara, my grandmother, Corrine Hamilton."

Kara inclined her head. "It's a pleasure to meet you, Miss Corrine. Jeff speaks very highly of you."

Corrine waved a hand. "That's because Jeffrey is quite biased when it comes to me, and I must admit I'm a bit partisan with him, too." She nodded to the object of her admiration. "Jeffrey, please take Kara into the sunroom. I'll be in directly."

What she didn't tell him was that she had to spend a few moments alone just to compose herself. Jeff had introduced the young woman as Kara Newell when he should've said Kara Patton. She looked enough like her childhood friend to have been her clone.

Walking into the kitchen, Corrine sat down because she didn't think her shaking knees would support her body. She was still sitting when Jeff entered the kitchen. "I'm coming as soon as I get some sweet tea from the refrigerator."

Jeff hunkered down in front of her. "Are you all right, Gram?"

She nodded. "I'm fine, Jeffrey. It's just seeing that girl gave me quite a shock because it's like seeing Teddy come back to life."

Jeff held her hands. "Don't worry about the tea, Gram. I'll bring it in for you."

Corrine stared into a pair of eyes so much like her own. "She's Taylor's daughter." The statement was also a query.

"Yes," he confirmed. "She just found out yesterday when David read the will."

"That poor child must have been shocked."

"She's that and more." Jeff told her about the Pattons' reaction when they were told that Kara had inherited everything. "David asked me to keep an eye on her."

Placing a hand over her mouth, Corrine

tried to process what she'd just heard. "You know they want to sell that land," she said after lowering her hand.

"They've been quite vocal about that. And it's not about improvement or growth progress, but greed."

"How does Kara feel about this?"

"She's mentioned that she doesn't want to sell, but . . ."

"But what, Jeffrey?"

He didn't meet Corrine's eyes. "The will states she has to make Angels Landing her legal residence for five years and restore it or the house and the land will revert to her money-grubbing relatives who don't give a damn about anything or anyone but themselves. And you know they'll sell the land quicker than a cat can flick its tail."

Corrine closed her eyes and shook her head. "I've seen what happened to folks on the other islands in the Low-country when developers buy their land, but I thought it would never happen here." She opened her eyes, the dark orbs flashing fire. "Kara can't sell it, and she can't leave."

"I've tried to be subtle when I kind of said that. But subtlety has never been my strong suit," Jeff admitted.

"You're about as subtle as a runaway loco-motive."

Leaning forward, Jeff kissed her cheek. "Thanks, Gram."

The seconds ticked by as grandmother and grandson stared at each other, Corrine seeing something in his eyes that she hadn't seen in a while. "I know David asked you to look after her, but what is it about this girl that makes you take a more than passing interest in her?"

There came another pause. "I like her, Gram."

"Like her how?"

He smiled. "Enough to ask her to go to the movies with me tomorrow."

Corrine leaned back in the chair, her gaze narrowing. "You asked her out after knowing her for one day?" There was no mistaking the slight trace of wonder in her voice.

"I had to, Gram, because she was only going to be here a week." Corrine's jaw dropped. "But that's before she told me she would extend her stay to three weeks." He paused. "It's not what you think."

"Now, how do you know what I'm thinking?" Corrine asked.

"Because you have the same look on your face that you had when I told you I'd proposed to Pamela. It's nothing like that," Jeff added.

Corrine gave him a skeptical look, deciding to drop the subject. "Let me get up and entertain that girl before she thinks we've forgotten our manners." Extending her hands, Corrine allowed Jeff to ease her up off the chair, thinking of how their roles had changed.

From the time she and Malachi had brought their grandson back to Cavanaugh Island, there had never been a time when she'd made a decision without taking into consideration how it would affect Jeff. Most of the time she was left to raise the boy on her own whenever her merchant seaman husband went to sea for months at a time. He'd return with souvenirs from the countries he'd visited, while always bringing her exquisite bolts of fabric from which she fashioned the latest styles she saw in magazines or pattern books.

Her Malachi had died much too young, leaving her to raise Jeffrey on her own. Her period of mourning was brief because she had to focus all of her energies on a toddler that relied solely on her for his very existence. Although she'd had several opportunities to see men and/or remarry, Corrine knew that wasn't going to be possible as long as she had to take care of her grandchild. Her mantra was that she would never put a man before him.

She entered the sunroom to find Kara studying the framed artwork of renowned Southern painter Jonathan Green mounted on a wall of the room that had become her sanctuary. Kara must have sensed she wasn't alone because she turned slowly, eyebrows lifted questionably.

"Yes," Corrine confirmed with a smile, "they are originals. *Majestic Sheets, Richard's Piano,* and *Red Lips* are three of his newer paintings."

Kara turned back to the artwork. "They don't look like oil or watercolor."

"They're acrylic on paper. That's why I could afford to purchase all three." She approached Kara, pointing to a larger painting. He painted *Grays Hill Blankets* in oh eight, and it was the only oil on canvas I was willing to pay five figures for."

Kara's eyes shimmered with excitement. "You have a very valuable art collection."

Corrine smiled. "It would be a lot more valuable if I bought the one I really want, but I can't see myself putting out a hundred fifty thousand for *Young Bride.* How did you come to know about Jonathan Green's work?"

"There are a lot of street vendors in New York, and one in particular carries reproductions of his artwork."

"Please sit down, Kara." She gestured to a love seat covered with a sunny-yellow fabric with bright green leaves. Waiting until her guest sat, Corrine took her seat in a matching armchair opposite her and rested her feet on a like-patterned footstool. Her sharp gaze took in everything about the young woman who unknowingly had enthralled her grandson, even if he wasn't willing to admit it. She'd noticed the proprietary way Jeffrey had placed his hand at the small of her back and the softening of his gaze whenever he looked at Kara. He was in denial with a capital *D* and unaware that she knew him as well as she knew her own mind.

Corrine knew Jeffrey had been less than lucky in the romance department and that he'd sworn off forming lasting relationships with women, but that was when he was in the military. What he still hadn't accepted was that the life of a civilian was vastly different from that of a career soldier. Her fervent prayer was he'd realize that before she passed on.

Crossing her feet at the ankles, she met Kara's steady gaze. "Does it bother you when folks say you look exactly like Taylor's mother?"

"Do I?" Kara asked softly.

Corrine was preempted from answering when Jeff entered the room with a pitcher of tea. He placed it on a glass-covered table. "Aren't you going to join us?" she asked him when she saw he'd brought only two iced tea glasses.

"Not right now. I just got a call from Dr. Monroe that some kid came into his office with a superficial gunshot wound. The boy claims his older brother was cleaning his handgun and hadn't realized there was still a bullet in the chamber. Apparently he pulled the trigger and the gun went off, the bullet grazing the fleshy part of his upper arm."

"But you're off duty, Jeffrey."

Leaning down, Jeff kissed her hair. "I'm never off duty. I'll be back as soon as I check out their story and file a report." He gave Kara a long, penetrating stare, then turned on his heel and walked out.

Kara pushed off the love seat. "Do you mind if I pour the tea?"

Corrine smiled. "Not at all. Thank you," she said when Kara handed her a glass. Waiting until Kara had filled her glass, she took a sip, then set it on a coaster. "Is it sweet enough for you, Kara?"

"It's perfect."

"Good. Now, back to your question about

you looking like Theodora Patton. The answer is yes. Teddy was one of my best friends even though kids from the Cove didn't mix too freely with those from the Landing or the Creek."

"Why was that?"

Corrine ran a hand over her short, silver curls. "I don't know. It'd been that way for years and continues to this day."

"How did you meet her?"

"At that time all of the black children on the island took the ferry to a segregated mainland school. We socialized in school, but once the ferry dropped us off, we went our separate ways. However, it was different for Teddy and me. I'd beg my mother to let me have playdates with her, and it continued until they finally integrated the schools on the island. She made new friends, and I bonded with the kids here."

"Did you continue to keep in touch?" Kara asked.

Corrine toyed with the tiny gold hoop in her left ear. "Yes. We'd call each other, and once we left for college, we'd write. Teddy shocked everyone when she announced her engagement to Cornelius Patton because no one knew they were seeing each other. The Haynes were working-class folks who brainwashed Teddy into believing that she had to marry up, and landing a Patton was like having the cake with the icing and the cherry. They had a big, lavish wedding at the mansion, and I knew then we'd moved in different directions because I wasn't invited to the wedding."

Kara gasped. "That's horrible."

"I'd thought so, too. I later learned her mother said she didn't want me in the wedding party because I'd lowered my standards to take up with a man without a college education. She was a fine one to talk because she hadn't finished high school. My late husband worked for the post office before he signed up as a cook on a merchant ship. It was hard at first because he was out to sea nine months out of the year, but whenever he came home, it was Christmas and New Year's all rolled into one. My parents took care of our daughter while I taught, and when she was old enough to go to school, I took her with me.

"Every time Teddy had a baby she threw a lavish party with everyone bearing gifts as if the new baby was royalty. She had two sons and three daughters before she had Taylor. He was a beautiful baby with a wonderful disposition. Everyone doted on him: his parents, grandparents, and his sisters. Once he became a teenager and showed an inter-

est in girls, Teddy sabotaged every relationship he had."

Unconsciously Kara's brow furrowed.
"But why, Miss Corrine?"

"There were rumors that she wanted him
for herself."

"Oh no," Kara drawled at the same time
she scrunched up her nose.

"As I said, there were rumors. By this time
Cornelius was a deputy solicitor general,
and when the Supreme Court was in session, he divided his time between South
Carolina and Washington, DC. The girls
went off to college and married and had a
bunch of babies. When it came time for Taylor to go to college, Teddy wouldn't allow
him to attend an out-of-state school."

"But he had to go to an out-of-state college if he'd met my mother."

Corrine paused to take a sip of tea. "She
relented when Cornelius resigned his position and came back to South Carolina and
opened a practice in Charleston. That's
when Taylor left to enroll in Morehouse."

Kara bent her head and studied her
clasped hands. "My mother went to
Spelman." Her head came up slowly as she
awkwardly cleared her throat. "I suppose
that's where they met." Spelman and More-
house were brother and sister colleges. Her

eyes filled with tears, and she blinked them back.

"Are you all right, baby?"

"I'm fine, Miss Corrine."

"I can stop now if you want."

"No, please don't. I need . . . want to hear as much about . . . Taylor before I talk to my mother."

Kara's expectant stare bore into Corrine. The poor child didn't know who she was because someone had lied to her about her paternity. She didn't blame the girl's mother as much as she did Taylor Patton. He knew he was her father, yet he'd withheld that information, revealing it only in death. As far as Corrine was concerned, it was the coward's way of settling an old score.

"Taylor came home changed."

"Changed how, Miss Corinne?"

"It was like he'd grown up overnight. He'd left South Carolina a boy and had returned a man. Many said it was because he'd gotten out from under Teddy's thumb. After he graduated he went to work in a bank in Columbia. His daddy died, and Teddy was like a lost soul. Then his oldest sister was diagnosed with an inoperable brain tumor, and she died. Teddy became an emotional cripple and rarely was seen outside the house. She neglected her award-winning

131

garden, most of the flowers going to seed, and she had the plaque designating Angels Landing a National Register of Historic Places removed because she claimed it reminded her too much of Cornelius. Last year it made National Historic Landmark status.

"There was talk that Teddy had come down with insomnia. Lights burned at the house twenty-four hours a day, seven days a week. Iris was concerned because she'd stopped eating. Taylor held onto his mother for as long as he could, but toward the end she had to be confined to a nursing home."

"How long did she live there?"

"She didn't last a month. The family had a private funeral with just a graveside service. I don't know if you've had a chance to tour the property, but there is a cemetery . . . no, I take that back. There are two cemeteries at Angels Landing. One white and one black. That practice ended with Cornelius when he was buried in the white section. I always thought it so asinine that people have separate cemeteries based on race and religion when dirt is dirt, and the Lord said he would be the one doing the separating."

Kara smiled for the first time since Corrine began her discourse on the Pattons. "I agree. Was Angels Landing a working plantation?"

Corrine nodded. "It was the largest plantation producing Sea Island cotton, rice, and indigo. The east end of your property is a swamp with poisonous snakes and gators, and heaven knows what else is lurking below the surface of the water. There are also egrets, herons, and someone took a picture of an eagle's nest in a cypress tree. Cabins were built near the swamp as a deterrent for slaves attempting to run away."

"Where would they go, Miss Corrine? After all, they were on an island surrounded by water. And if they did make it to the mainland, where would they hide?"

"Not everyone in the South was pro-slavery. There was a wealthy cotton merchant, James Whitcomb, who hid runaways, then took them North with him, passing them off as his slaves. He'd managed to get away with the ruse for a year until a patroller recognized him, called the authorities, and he was sentenced to hang. The governor commuted his sentence to twenty years because James was a distant cousin. He was sent to Old Jail, the same prison where Denmark Vesey spent his last days in the tower before being hanged. It remains a mystery to this day, but James had managed to escape and stow away in a ship transporting cotton to the mills in the North. After that, increased restrictions were placed on slaves and free blacks in Charleston as a result of the Vesey insurrection, and at that time the law required that all black seamen be housed in the Old Jail while they were in port."

Leaning forward, Kara caught and held Corrine's eyes. "Were any of those escaped slaves from Angels Landing?"

"A few. But they weren't your ancestors."

"Are you saying that Taylor's ancestors were so wedded to their servitude they made no attempt to escape?"

"Why would you run away when you were already free?" Corrine had answered Kara's question with a question of her own. "Please excuse me," she said when the phone rang. She picked up the receiver, listening to the velvety soft, deep voice. "Okay. No problem." She hung up, watching Kara staring at her. She did look like Theodora, but upon closer inspection she was softer, prettier. Her face was rounder, cheekbones higher, and her mouth was lush. It was her eyes with glints of greenish-gray and gold that reminded her so much of Theodora.

"That was Jeffrey. He's tied up at the station house and won't be able to drive you back to Angels Landing. I'll take you back."

"Are you certain I won't put you out, because I could always call Mrs. Todd and ask her to pick me up?"

Corrine lowered her feet and stood up. "Of course you're not putting me out. Since I retired I have to find things to do to keep myself busy. Last year I had a health scare when I found myself in the hospital with a blocked artery. It weakened my heart, so I have to be careful not to get exhausted."

Kara rose to her feet. "I'm going to be here for at least three weeks, and if there is anything you want me to help you with, just let me know."

"Thanks for asking, baby, but I'm okay here. Jeffrey hired someone to come in twice a week to clean, so there's not much for me to do except cook. Speaking of cooking, I'd like to invite you over for Sunday dinner."

"I'd love to come, but I'm not certain when my mother is coming to town."

"Bring her with you. I'm certain she'll be tired from traveling and would enjoy sitting down to a home-cooked meal."

"Thank you, Miss Corrine. That's very kind of you."

"It has nothing to do with kindness and everything to do with Lowcountry hospitality."

■ ■ ■ ■

It wasn't until she was back at Angels Landing that Kara thought about what Jeffrey's grandmother had said about Lowcountry hospitality. Her newfound relatives hadn't shown her the warmth and welcome but blatant hostility. They viewed her as an interloper, taking what they'd considered theirs because they were legitimate Pattons.

Sitting on a rocker on the front porch, she stared out at the verdant landscape that resembled green velvet. Countless trees, draped in Spanish moss, stood like sentinels along the path leading up to the historic house. Closing her eyes, she imagined horse-drawn carriages filled with men and women in their silks and finery coming up the unpaved path to Angels Landing for a ball.

Instead of horses it was now cars that brought people to the house. She opened her eyes. Mrs. Todd told her that not much had changed over the years with the exception of indoor plumbing and electricity and updated appliances, while the antebellum mansion upon close inspection still looked run-down. The smaller kitchen hadn't changed. There was still the massive black wood-burning stove with an oven large enough to roast a small pig.

Something Corrine said about the property receiving landmark status the year before made her think of Taylor's mandate that she had to restore the house to its original condition while making Angels Landing her residence for the next five years. She wasn't certain how long it would take to complete the restoration; however, she knew the cash in the safe-deposit box was more than enough to pay an engineer to ascertain the house's structural stability and to refinish floors and replace wallpaper, drapes, and rugs. And she had to make sure that Mr. and Mrs. Todd received a lump sum of fifty thousand dollars for their dedication and loyalty.

Opening the door, she switched on the light, staring at the space where Taylor had probably spent hours working for his clients. It was quintessentially masculine from the massive carved antique mahogany desk and cordovan leather sofa and chairs. She stared at the faded rug with a narrow strip lighter than the rest, leading her to believe this was where Taylor had paced up and down its length.

Built-in bookshelves were packed tightly

with books, some with worn leather bindings. Kara walked over to an armoire and attempted to open it, but the doors didn't budge. Then she realized it was locked. She thought of the envelope David had given her with keys. There had to be one that unlocked the armoire.

She retrieved the envelope, spilling the keys out on the top of the desk. There was one skeleton-type key, and when she inserted it into the lock and turned it, Kara wondered what she would find behind its locked doors.

She couldn't control the runaway beating of her heart when opening a drawer to find bank statements with staggering balances. There were statements from five different mainland banks and the one in Sanctuary Cove. She opened another drawer, finding copies of Taylor's tax returns for the past ten years. He'd reported income from his corporation, interest and dividends from bank accounts and bonds. There were copies of checks on the taxes owing attached to the forms.

Sinking down to the floor, Kara clapped a hand over her mouth. She felt faint and had begun to hyperventilate. How could she go from a middle-income, overworked social worker who was lucky if she could save fifty dollars a month to someone with enough money to buy an apartment in Trump Tower?

It was all too much for her take in so quickly. She lay back on the rug, staring up at the ceiling. Even if she didn't work another day in her life, she would have enough money to last her for the rest of her days.

"She must restore Angels Landing to its original condition." David's words echoed in her head as if he were in the room with her. He wasn't talking about the house but the entire plantation: the house, gardens, and outbuildings.

The doorbell chimed throughout the house, and Kara scrambled to her feet. Mrs. Todd worked from eight to six, then retreated to her two-bedroom guesthouse to spend the evening with her husband.

Kara made her way down the hallway to the staircase, curbing a childish urge to slide down the banister. The marble floor in the living room and entryway felt cool under her bare feet. Going on tiptoe, she peered through the security eye, seeing the distorted image of a familiar face. She unlocked the door and opened it. Standing on the porch wearing a black T-shirt and jeans was Jeff, and seeing him caused her mouth to suddenly go dry. She had only caught a glimpse of his upper body when he'd taken off his jacket to show her his tattoo, but the cotton fabric stretched over broad shoulders, massive pectorals, and bulging biceps left little to the imagination.

"Hi." The single word was torn from the back of her throat.

"May I come in?"

"Of course." She stepped aside and he walked in, and that's when she saw what he held in his hand. "You brought my book."

Jeff felt as if he'd been punched in the stomach. He knew Kara was sexy, but seeing her in a skimpy tank top and shorts made him feel things he didn't want to feel at that time, as he thought of what he'd wanted to do with her. And because of his height advantage he could see her breasts.

He handed her the book. "I thought you'd want to read it."

"Thank you." A blush darkened her cheeks. "I'm forgetting my manners. Would you like something to eat or drink?"

Jeff had just stopped by to drop off the book but quickly changed his mind. "I'll take coffee if it's not too much trouble for you."

"Of course not." Kara gave him a sensual

smile. "I usually have a cup before I go to bed because drinking something hot helps me fall asleep."

He wanted to tell her there were other things guaranteed to help her sleep but quickly banished his traitorous musings. Perhaps his grandmother was right. He'd been without a woman much too long.

He loved how she looked from the front but didn't mind the view as she walked away. He followed her, his gaze fixed on the shape of her behind in the shorts that revealed more than they covered. If he didn't get it together, Jeff knew he was going to embarrass himself. At forty he still had a healthy libido, but he'd learned to control his urges with strenuous physical workouts. There were mornings when he would get up and run the length of the island or do a hundred push-ups. The "once a marine, always a marine" motto carried over to daily physical training and conditioning. At six four he'd managed to keep his weight at 225, and if he went five pounds above what he considered his peak weight, he substituted more fruit, vegetables, and protein for the carbs.

He'd accused Kara of having a possible eating disorder but seeing so much of her body proved him wrong. She was slender but definitely not skinny. Women he'd found himself attracted to usually were more full figured, yet that hadn't stopped him from pursuing Kara. He was definitely interested in her and had to admit that bringing her the book was just an excuse to see her again.

"My grandmother said she loved talking with you this afternoon."

Kara stared at him over her shoulder. "All I did was ask questions. She did most of the talking. Please sit down." She gestured to a chair in the dining nook. "I'm glad I did get a chance to talk to her because she helped me to make up my mind about something."

Jeff watched as Kara washed her hands and went through the motions of measuring coffee into an automatic coffeemaker. "What was that?"

"I'm going to stay."

He went still. "What do you mean stay?"

"I'm going to stay and restore the property."

"How long will that take?"

She filled the carafe with water from the sink and poured it into the well. "I don't know. I have to call an architect and have them come out and inspect the house and outbuildings. I'll also have to hire a landscape architect to see if the gardens can be revived."

"That's not going to take three weeks, Kara."

Resting a hip against the countertop, she folded her arms under her breasts. "Very funny, Jeff."

He smiled, coming to his feet and closing the distance between them. Wrapping his arms around her waist, he lifted her off her feet until their faces were level. Not giving her a chance to react, he brushed his mouth over hers in a light kiss. "I'd like to offer you a very special welcome to Cavanaugh Island."

Curving her arms around his thick neck, Kara pressed her cheek to his. "Do you welcome everyone like this?"

"Hell no! Just the pretty women."

Jeff didn't want to believe Kara felt as good as she looked and smelled. He buried his face against the column of her neck, not wanting to let go. But he knew he had to because he was becoming more aroused with each passing second.

Kara kissed his cheek. "Thank you for the very special welcome."

Slowly, deliberately, he let her down until her feet touched the floor. He cleared his throat. "You made this decision without talking with your mother?"

Her catlike eyes smiled at him. "Yes. The

pieces of the puzzle are coming together."

"I'm happy for you, Kara."

"Thank you."

His expression stilled, becoming somber. "You know this news isn't going to sit too well with your cousins."

Kara sobered. "Even if I give them what they want, they still won't be satisfied. When it comes to greed, you have to ask yourself, when is enough, enough? And the answer is it's never enough."

Cradling her face in his large hands, Jeff kissed the end of her nose when it was her mouth he wanted to kiss and smiled when he heard the soft intake of breath. It was as if he couldn't stop touching her. "I'm still going to stop by whenever I go on patrol. I'll tell my deputies to do the same."

"Don't you think you're overreacting?" she asked.

"No, I'm not. After all greed is one of the seven deadly sins."

Kara patted his shoulder. "I promise I'll be careful. Would you mind if we postpone going to the movies tomorrow?"

"No," he said when he wanted to say the opposite. "Now that you're staying we can go anytime."

"Thank you for being so understanding."

"What I understand is that you're going

to be a very busy woman. I'm not going anywhere, and neither are you."

Easing out of his embrace, Kara stared at the middle of his chest. "I think the coffee is ready."

"Aren't you going to join me?" Jeff asked when he noticed she'd only taken down one cup.

"I'll have mine later. I'm not ready to go to bed now." She set the cup on the table, then opened the refrigerator to get a small container of cream. "There's sugar on the table if you want it."

"No thanks. I usually drink my coffee without sugar."

Standing behind him, Kara rested a hand in the middle of his back. He went completely still when he felt the warmth of her palm through his T-shirt. Jeff knew they were playing a dangerous game touching each other, but he didn't want it to stop.

"What's the matter, Sheriff Hamilton? You're sweet enough?"

Reaching around his body, he pulled her to stand between his outspread legs. "Oh, sweet thing. Don't you know you're my everything?" he sang.

"Uh-ah, Chaka Khan wannabe."

"Don't knock her, baby. The girl can still blow."

"I know that," Kara admitted. "Drink your coffee before it gets cold. I'm sorry I don't have any doughnuts in the house. Maybe next time."

Jeff gave her a layered look. "Now you're trying to stereotype me. Not all cops drink coffee and eat doughnuts."

"The ones in New York do."

"Again, that's a stereotype. What if I said all social workers are bleeding heart liberals?"

"It wouldn't bother me none because I am."

Jeff gave her a long look. "Good for you."

Her eyebrows lifted a fraction. "You approve?"

"I approve." He took her hand. "Come sit with me." Jeff took longer than he normally would to drink the coffee, taking furtive sips to prolong the time spent with Kara. "Thanks for the coffee," he said after he'd drained the cup.

She stood up, took the cup, and placed it in the sink. "I'll walk you out. I don't know if your grandmother told you, but she invited me to Sunday dinner."

This disclosure shocked Jeff. When he'd returned, his grandmother hadn't mentioned this to him. "Are you coming?"

"I told her I would if my mother doesn't

come in before then."

"Bring her with you."

"That's what Miss Corrine said."

Jeff stopped at the door. "The deputy will probably come by tomorrow, but I'll definitely see you Sunday afternoon."

Going on tiptoe, Kara kissed his cheek. "Thank you for showing me around."

"Remember, we still have to see Haven Creek."

She nodded as he opened the door, then closed it behind him. Standing on the porch, Jeff waited until he heard the locks click into place. Walking to his car, he didn't know what to make of Kara. His past experience with women had always been tenuous because of his dedication to the military. Many of them had become Miss Right Now. Pamela Singleton had been the exception. He'd found himself in love with her and proposed marriage; however, she'd ended the engagement once she realized she hadn't wanted to become an officer's wife.

Jeff knew it would be different with Kara. He was now a civilian, and she'd made a commitment to live on the island. He'd thought of her as a distraction — a very welcome distraction that he couldn't help wanting to be around.

Other than reuniting with his grand-mother, Jeff was glad he'd come home.

CHAPTER SIX

Kara woke more tired than she had been when she'd crawled into bed after two in the morning. She spent hours going through Taylor's financial records. She also found a slip of paper in an envelope marked "computer password." His password was the month and day of her birth: Kara1219. Once she logged on, Kara lost track of time as she researched design companies specializing in historic restoration. She'd found two based in Charleston. There was also the architectural firm in Haven Creek she planned to contact.

Her eyes were blurry by the time she'd searched out historic places and landmarks in South Carolina and other Southern states. If she was going to restore Angels Landing, then she wanted to know what it entailed. Kara's fatigue disappeared when she happened upon the website for Middleton Place on Ashley River Road in between

North Charleston and Summerville. Her excitement escalated once she realized there were tours of the house and the landscaped gardens. Transfixed by the colorful photographs of the well-preserved, mid-eighteenth-century house, ideas were swirling around in her head as she printed out the pages. Corrine had mentioned Theodora's garden, and Kara believed it was a coincidence that she'd purchased a book devoted to designing gardens.

Jeff and Corrine had answered her questions, yet she still had more. The issue of her paternity would come from her mother, but would anyone tell her why Theodora had elected to leave the house to her bachelor son rather than her children who'd married and had children of their own? Wouldn't it have been better to hear the footsteps and laughter of her grandchildren in the twenty-room mansion than near or complete silence by a single soul?

Rising slightly on an elbow, she peered at the clock on the bedside table. It was after eight, time to get up and start the day.

Fortified with a breakfast of grits, eggs and strips of melt-in-your-mouth Smithfield ham, and a cup of coffee, Kara set off for Haven Creek. She'd left a voice mail message for David, and he'd returned her call.

When she explained what she'd found in the safe-deposit box, David revealed he was aware that Taylor had stored cash in the box the same way people either put money under their mattresses or in shoe boxes. He'd reminded her she had power of attorney and that she should close out Taylor's accounts and reopen them in her name within ten days from the reading of the will.

Her decision to contact the local architectural firm was predicated on their familiarity with the island. There was no doubt their archives would have plans and photographs of the 160-year-old house and outbuildings. Decelerating to less than ten miles an hour, Kara maneuvered into the parking lot behind the two-story building. Her appointment was for eleven and she was ten minutes early.

Walking around to the front, she opened the door and stepped into a reception area. Rattan chairs and love seats covered with plush colorful seat and back cushions, a raffia rug, and ceiling fans made her feel as if she'd stepped into a Caribbean bungalow. She gave the receptionist her name, then sat down to wait for Morgan Dane.

Kara's head popped up when a woman approached her. Tall, slender, and dressed entirely in black — turtleneck, stretch pants, and high-heeled booties — she'd pulled her braided hair into a ponytail. The large turquoise pendant suspended from a thick silver chain matched the studs in her ears. With her flawless sable-brown skin, delicate features, and thin body, she could've been a model.

"Miss Newell?"

Kara stood up. "Yes."

"I'm Morgan Dane." Her dark eyes sparkled when she smiled. "I know you were probably expecting a man, but my mama decided to name me after my granddaddy."

"Kara."

Morgan offered her hand, smiling. "Please call me Morgan. Come with me. We'll talk in the conference room because workmen are painting my office."

They sat at a small round table in a conference room with walls covered with black-and-white photographs of historic buildings and homes. Kara recognized Middleton Place and Drayton Hall.

"Are you familiar with Angels Landing?"

"The house or the plantation?" Morgan asked.

"The entire property. I've just inherited the house and —"

"So you're the one who has the Pattons going ballistic," Morgan interrupted.

Momentarily speechless, Kara thought the woman was mocking her until she saw her smirk. "You've heard?"

"Who hasn't?" Morgan's expression and tone changed when she said, "When the receptionist gave me your name, I had no idea who you were. This is not gossip, but you should know that a few of the Pattons have been less than complimentary where it concerns you. Harlan in particular."

Kara's jaw tightened. "What I'm about to propose is going to make them even more upset. I plan to restore the property, and I'd like an appraisal from your firm. I also want to be candid and let you know I intend to check out two other architectural firms before I make a final decision."

Morgan laced her fingers together in her lap. "I appreciate your candor. However, I doubt whether the other firms would be as familiar with the property as I am since I live here. Would they know that the east end of Angels Landing is a cypress swamp? That there is evidence of several winnowing barns? And that seven of the original cabins in the slave village are still intact?

"I'm certain they could," Morgan said, answering her own questions, "but it would take them a lot longer to gather all the information than I would because I've lived on Cavanaugh all my life. I left to attend the Savannah College of Art and Design, and instead of accepting a position with a very prestigious firm in California, I decided to return home because I wanted to preserve the Gullah culture, and that can only be done if Gullahs take care of what has been passed down for generations."

"You sound very passionate about what you do," Kara said, smiling.

"I'm as serious as a heart attack. I'm more than aware of developers sniffing around the Landing like bloodhounds chasing an escaped prisoner, and I don't like it. If one person sells out, then that translates into everyone selling out. All they have to do is wave some paper around, and it's all she wrote. If you sell off ten acres and the developers put up a hotel or an inn — they prefer the term *inn* because it sounds warmer and fuzzier than hotel — what do you think is going to happen to the Cove Inn?"

"It'll probably lose business."

"No, Kara. It won't lose business. It will go *out* of business. Once you build an inn, you'll have to feed your guests. A restaurant will be in direct competition with Jack's Fish House. And of course they'll have to have a souvenir shop. That would put folks here on Haven Creek in direct competition with what they're selling in their shops."

Kara stared at Morgan, complete surprise freezing her features. She'd sought out the architectural design firm to get an idea of what it would cost to restore her property, not to get a history lesson or listen to a rant defaming developers. First it was David, then Jeff, and now Morgan.

Slowly, as if pulled by a taut wire, Kara leaned forward. "I did not come here to talk about selling the property, Morgan. I'm here because I need an estimate of how much it would cost and how long it will take for your firm to restore Angels Landing Plantation to its original state circa 1854. I understand your opposition to developers coming in and literally changing the landscape and their impact on the lives of the people who live here because I'm now one of those people. I may be a couple of things, but I've never been accused of being a sellout." Morgan lowered her eyes in a gesture Kara could only interpret as embarrassment.

"I'm sorry if I offended —"

"I'm not offended," Kara said, interrupting her. "It's just that I didn't expect to be reminded about giving away my birthright yet again."

"I'm not the first person to tell you?"

Kara laughed, the sound seemingly shattering the tension. "No. I've heard it from David Sullivan and Sheriff Hamilton. There are probably a few others who feel the same way but haven't said anything to me. At least not yet."

Twin dimples kissed Morgan's cheeks when she smiled. "Folks here usually don't bite their tongues when they have something to say."

"Like you?"

Morgan nodded. "Yes, like me."

Kara stared at the photograph of Middleton Place. "When it comes to historical restoration I know we're on the same page." Her gaze swung back to the woman sitting across the table from her. "This is only my third day on the island, and I have yet to tour what you call the Angels Landing Plantation; so other than the guesthouses, I haven't seen any of the outbuildings."

"Do you want me to go with you to see them?"

Taken aback by the question, Kara hesitated. "When would you like to see it?"

"What about now? That is if you don't have anything planned for this afternoon."

Kara glanced down at her pencil skirt. When she'd gotten dressed earlier that morning, she hadn't planned on traipsing over several thousand acres in a fitted skirt, cashmere twinset, and pumps. She smiled. It was about time she looked over what Taylor had bequeathed to her and what her cousins so passionately coveted.

"No, I can't right now. What other time would you be able to meet?"

Morgan checked her watch. "Let's make it one."

Pushing back her chair, Kara stood up and extended her hand. "Great, then I'll see you at one."

Kara returned to Angels Landing, Mrs. Todd opening the door before she could turn the knob. The house remained unlocked during the day. It was only at night that Kara felt uncomfortable leaving the doors unlocked, especially since she lived there alone.

"Good afternoon, Mrs. Todd."

"Good afternoon. I was just leaving to bring my Willie his lunch." She held up a cloth-covered wicker basket. "Once that man gets on his riding mower he doesn't want to get off."

Men and their toys, Kara thought. "I know. It's like getting a brand-new car. I've known men to sleep in theirs. Someone is coming here at one, and we're going to tour the property to ascertain what needs to be done to make this place beautiful again."

Mrs. Todd nodded slowly. "Mr. Taylor knew what he was doing when he left everything to you. If some of his nieces or nephews got this property, the scavengers would've been here minutes after the will was read to start taking this place apart."

"Don't worry, Mrs. Todd. That's not going to happen. Not now or years from now. I'll make certain of that."

"You may look like your grandmomma, but you got your daddy's heart. Out of all of Miss Teddy's children, Taylor was the best. Enough jawin'. Let me get this to Willie 'fore it gets cold. I left your lunch in the warming drawer."

Bending slightly, Kara kissed her cheek. "Thank you." Knowing she'd shocked the housekeeper with the display of affection, Kara walked into the house, leaving Mrs. Todd staring at her back.

With a light step, she raced up the staircase to her bedroom to change. Fortunately she had packed a pair of rain boots. Kara entered her bedroom, stopping abruptly when she saw the bouquet of pale pink roses on the table in the sitting area. Attached to the vase was a balloon stamped with "Welcome Home."

Walking over to the table, she picked up the card. A smile curved her mouth when she read the bold script: "Thank you for staying. Hugs, Jeff."

"You're welcome," she whispered to the empty room, reminding herself to call Jeff and thank him for the thoughtful gesture.

If he was glad she'd decided to live on the island, she was equally excited she'd made the decision to stay. This is not to say it had been an easy decision because she would have to resign her job and give up a way of life she'd grown accustomed to for fifteen years. She'd come to New York to attend college and stayed. Except for her noticeably Southern drawl, she'd become a New Yorker in every sense of the word.

Kara had learned to walk quickly in order to navigate the sidewalks teeming with pedestrians, and she also learned to push her way into a crowded subway car so she wouldn't have to wait for another that would be just as crowded. She'd adopted the practice of not making eye contact with anyone on the street; not speaking to strangers; not responding to ribald catcalls from men; and not picking up her drink at a bar, a club, or party once she'd averted her gaze. And she didn't give out her address, home or cell numbers arbitrarily.

The men she'd dated were usually friends of friends. Several had progressed beyond the platonic stage, and a few ended before they'd begun. Kara could not get used to men expecting her to take off her panties on the first date. Firstly she hadn't known them well enough to take their relationship to the next level, and secondly she didn't know whether they were some crazed deviant who would rape or, even worse, kill her.

Kara knew she had to call Dawn and let her know that she'd decided to relocate. She retrieved her cell and punched in Dawn's number, activating the speaker feature as she undressed. "Hey, Miss Dee."

"Hey you," Dawn drawled.

"Did I wake you up?"

"No. I was just taking a power nap before I go into the studio. Kara?"

"What is it, Dawn?"

"You're right about the apartment becoming an SRO. Jackie stopped by yesterday with a couple of guys, and they stayed up all night drinking beer while playing poker. I didn't get more than an hour of sleep. And you know I have to be alert when working with my students. Their parents pay big bucks for me to teach the little cherubs to dance."

160

Kara slipped into a pair of jeans, buttoning the waistband. They fit a bit more snugly than they had when she'd worn them before, and she knew it had come from eating three meals a day. She made a mental note to begin walking along the beach for exercise.

"I'm not going to say I told you so."

"Tell me, girl, so I can experience a reality check."

"I told you so, Dawn Ramsey."

"Thanks. Now I can get rid of the guilt."

"Since you're newly guilt-free, what are you going to do about it?"

"I'm going to take a break from friends. Maybe your pep talk and not having you around for a few days brought me to my senses."

"You're not going to have me around for more than a few days, Dawn."

"What aren't you saying? And please don't tell me something I'm not equipped to deal with right now."

Kara knew putting off the inevitable wouldn't make it any easier for Dawn or herself. "I'm staying." The two words made her heart sink like a stone in her chest.

"You can't, Kara."

"I have to, Dawn."

Kara told her why she'd decided to relocate to Angels Landing. "I can't walk away, not when I have a chance to possibly build a relationship with a family I never knew I had."

There came a pregnant pause until Dawn said, "I understand where you're coming from because you told me you don't have a large family, but that still doesn't make me feel any better."

"I'm not going to leave you hanging, Dee. I'm going to send you a check for my share of the rent until the lease expires."

"You've got it like that?"

Kara smiled. "Yes, Dee. I've got it like that."

"Well, damn! Did you hit the mother lode?"

"Just about," she admitted. "I want you to take off and come visit me."

Dawn's distinctive Eddie Murphy laugh came through the earpiece. "I thought you'd never ask."

"Come on, sister. You know you can come hang out with me anytime. The only thing I'm going to ask is that you not bring your funky bunch with you."

Dawn laughed again. "Have you forgotten that I'm trying to rid myself of the funky bunch?"

"That should be easy, Dawn. We live in a building with a doorman, and when he calls to ask if he should let Freeloader Freddie in, just say no. Or you could call management and tell them that you're not accepting visitors. That way you can save face whenever you run into them. Better yet. Blame it on management, and tell them that your neighbors are complaining about the number of people who are hanging out at the apartment, and if it continues, then you're going to lose your lease."

"You're a genius, Kara."

"No, I'm not. I'm just a little more practical than you are. Look, Dee, I have to go. But I promise to call you in a couple of days with an update of my life in the Lowcountry."

Kara didn't know why, but she felt like crying. She'd heard the pain and indecision in her former roommate's voice when Dawn said she understood why Kara had decided to live in South Carolina but still wasn't too happy about it.

What she hadn't told Dawn was that she was frightened, more frightened than she'd ever been in her life. New York City had become her second home. Of course, she'd experienced some anxiety moving from Little Rock to New York, but that was normal for college students when they attended out-of-state schools. They were little birds ready, yet hesitant to leave the nest.

First there was the college tours, then the monumental decision of what college they would attend.

Her parents didn't want her to move so far away. After all, she was their only child, and both tried to hold onto her for as long as possible. She'd reassured them New York wasn't that far away, and in the end they relented. Kara suspected they were more concerned with her living in a big city than the actual distance, and for the first six months she called them weekly to let them know how she was doing.

After a while the calls decreased to every other week, then finally to once or twice a month. She had made new friends and had her first serious boyfriend, who'd eventually become her lover. They parted amicably during her junior year, and Kara concentrated on pulling up her grades because she'd planned to enroll in graduate school.

She dated sporadically throughout grad school and had a serious liaison with another social work intern. She wanted a commitment while he wanted an open relationship wherein they would date other people. Doubt and cynicism dogged Kara whenever she was introduced to a man, and after a while she could care less whether she dated or not.

Kara knew the decision to relocate to Angels Landing would've been a lot more difficult if she had someone with whom she was in love. She'd always told her mother she wanted what Jeannette had: a loving, loyal, and protective husband.

Opening a drawer in the triple dresser, she took out a lightweight wool sweater. Daytime temperatures were in the low forties, almost twenty degrees lower than the average high for the region. She pulled on her patterned houndstooth rain boots and pushed her cell into the back pocket of her jeans. Running a large-tooth comb through her hair, she swept it up in a ponytail and secured it with an elastic band. The doorbell chimed as she reached for a baseball cap and a pair of sunglasses.

Quickening her pace, she jogged down the hallway to the stairs. Kara was halfway across the expansive living room when the bell rang again. She opened the door, expecting to see Morgan, but the woman standing on the porch elicited a shiver of uneasiness.

"Hello, Analeigh."

The petite woman with sandy-brown twists and dark eyes smiled. Her white midi blouse, navy-blue pleated skirt, and penny loafers were better suited for a schoolgirl.

"I'm surprised you remember my name."

"I remembered because you were the only one who didn't give me a screwface." Kara estimated she and Analeigh were about the same age.

"May I come in?"

Kara opened the door wider. "I'd love to sit and chat with you, but I'm expecting someone any moment. Is there another time when you can come back?"

"Tomorrow. Same time."

"Do you want to give me an idea of what you'd like to talk about?" Kara asked.

"I'll wait until tomorrow."

"I'd rather know now if you don't mind."

Exhaling a breath, Analeigh twisted her mouth. "I thought we could be friends."

"Friends?" Kara questioned. "I thought we were cousins."

"We are, but I'd like for us to get to know each other."

Something told Kara not to trust Analeigh, but on the other hand she'd never been one to reject an offer of friendship. "Okay. Please come back tomorrow, and we'll have lunch."

Analeigh pressed her palms together. "Should I bring something?"

"Yes."

"What would you like me to bring?"

166

"Yourself."

Analeigh's face fell like someone pulling down a window shade. "Me?" The single word sounded like a squeak.

Kara would've laughed if her cousin's eyes hadn't filled with tears. She hugged her instead. "Yes, you. You're the guest of honor." She gasped when Analeigh put her arms around her neck, squeezing her tightly. "Please, Analeigh. You're choking me."

"Thank you, Kara. I told the others you were nice, but they wouldn't listen to me."

Reaching up, she pried Analeigh's arms from around her neck. "Thank you for speaking up for me."

"Are you nice, Kara?"

Kara saw movement out of the corner of her eye. A Jeep came to a stop in front of the house. The passenger-side door bore the logo of the sheriff's department. "Excuse me, Analeigh." She walked out onto the porch, watching as the stocky-built man climbed the steps. The buttons on his red flannel shirt strained across his broad chest. A round face, ruddy cheeks, and beer belly made him the perfect candidate to play Santa.

He touched the brim of his baseball cap. "Afternoon, Miss Newell. I'm Deputy Sheriff Collins. I'm just stopping to check on folks in the Landing."

"I'm well, thank you."

Analeigh stepped from behind Kara, flashing a lopsided smile. "Hi, Mr. Deputy. How you doing today?"

Deputy Collins stared at her as if she were an apparition. "What are you doing here, Analeigh?"

Wrapping her arms around her body, Analeigh angled her head and closed her eyes. "I came to see my cousin. Did you know she is my cousin?"

He glanced around. "No. How did you get here?"

Analeigh moved closer to Kenny. "I walked."

"You walked all the way from your house?"

She took another step. "Yes, sir."

Kara blinked as if coming out of a trance. She realized Analeigh's childlike behavior wasn't an act. "Deputy Collins, can you please drop Analeigh off at home?"

He touched his hat again. "Of course. I'll let Jeff know you're good here."

A nervous smile found its way across Kara's features. She wanted to tell Deputy Collins that she wasn't so good. An obviously mentally or emotionally disturbed woman had come to her home with the intent to befriend her. The uneasiness when she'd opened the door to find Analeigh standing there wasn't imagined, but real.

"Thank you, Deputy. If you speak to Jeff, please tell him to call me on the house phone."

"No problem, Miss Newell."

Crossing her arms under her breasts, Kara watched as the deputy escorted Analeigh to his truck, helped her inside, and drove away. She was still on the porch when Morgan drove up in a white late-model Cadillac Escalade. "I just have to get my sunglasses," Kara told Morgan when she got out of the vehicle.

"I'd like to do a once-over of the interior of the house first." Morgan held up a digital camera. "A picture is worth a thousand words once you look at the before and after photos."

"Do you want me to go with you?"

"No. I won't take long."

Kara nodded. "I'll wait on the porch." She folded her body down to the white wicker rocker with baby-blue cushions, recalling what Dawn said about her turning into a Southern belle while sitting on a porch drinking sweet tea. Even though she'd spent the last fifteen years of her life in New York, she was still a Southern girl at heart.

She rocked slowly, marveling at how the

dictates of a dead man were determining her future. Kara knew she didn't have to follow the mandates set down in Taylor's will, yet strangely, she felt compelled to honor his wishes.

If she had known Taylor was her biological father, would he have been willing to share her with Austin or would he have legally exercised his right to share custody with Jeannette? Or would her mother have agreed to let her spend her summers on Cavanaugh Island? The maybes nagged at Kara until Morgan returned, camera in hand.

Kara rose to her feet. "What do you think?"

"The house and the furnishings are magnificent. Of course, the wallpaper has to be replaced. You'll also have to replace the drapes, and the rugs will need to be cleaned. The rugs are Aubusson, and that alone makes them priceless. I suggest once they're restored you use them as tapestry wall hangings. Some of the floors are warped, so they'll have to be replaced. An engineer will examine the foundation to make certain it's sound and can hold up to some of the brick and plasterwork. An electrician should rewire the entire house, and I recommend heating registers installed in the floors to make them less conspicuous."

"Where would you find the people to do the restoration?" Kara asked Morgan.

"Most of them would come from Haven Creek. There are at least four master carpenters, and a few that are experts in brick and plasterwork. There is also a father and son team that put in parquet floors with herringbone or inlaid designs that will take your breath away. The advantage to using local artisans is that they're always available and take a lot of pride in their work because they have to maintain their reputations. The fabric for the chairs can be ordered from a firm on the mainland that specializes in patterns that are almost an exact match to what you have."

Kara put on her sunglasses. "We can talk while we walk." She knew there was a lot of land to cover, and she wanted to see as much as she could before nightfall. She waited until Morgan drove her SUV around to the rear of the house, then they took off walking.

Afternoon shadows had fallen, and the air was much cooler when they finally returned to the main house. Morgan gave her an overview of life in the Sea Islands when rice-producing plantations provided much of Europe with "Carolina Gold." It was African

American slave labor that had perfected irrigation techniques using tidal water and man-made dikes.

She saw the ruins of what Morgan had referred to as winnowing barns where rice grains were processed for shipment. The architectural historian compared Angels Landing to Mansfield Plantation as only two American plantations to be saved from development and reclaimed by a direct descendant of the original owner.

Kara didn't want to believe she was a direct descendant of the men in the paintings. Uncovering who her ancestors were and how Cornelius Patton had come into possession of Angels Landing was another missing piece of the puzzle. *You can't know where you are going if you don't know where you've come from.* The Gullah saying wasn't far from the truth as it referred to her.

Morgan had pointed out that the original owners had built the main house on a hill to provide them with views of the ocean and river. There were more buildings: a schoolhouse, a chapel, and a dilapidated shed filled with blacksmith tools. There were two cemeteries, one for the white family and the other for blacks. The area in the undeveloped northeast section was made up of a densely forested woodland and swamp.

Kara felt like crying when she saw the cabins that had made up the slave village. The one-room shacks were structurally unsafe to enter, but when she'd peered through the windows she saw items that had been essential to those who'd lived there: broken pottery, spoons, a chair, table, and frames for several beds. Morgan took pictures of everything: trees, several ponds, outbuildings, and what had once been gardens.

"I don't know if you realize what you have here," Morgan said to Kara.

"Yes, I do. Angels Landing is like a pretty girl covered in dirt and grime. And I know it's going to take time to clean her up where everyone sees her beauty."

"You're very lucky Angels Landing is here instead of on the mainland because it probably wouldn't have escaped the Civil War when Union soldiers either occupied or burned plantations when they came through Charleston. I took photos of the books in your father's office, and many of the titles go back more than one hundred years. They alone are worth a small fortune. I'm certain private collectors would act like rabid fans at a music concert if they saw them."

Kara stared at the avenue of live oak trees leading up to the main house. "How long do you think it would take to restore everything?"

Morgan supported her back against one of the massive pale pink marble columns. "Probably two, maybe even three years."

She closed her eyes. "That long?"

"That's not very long, Kara. As a student at SCAD, I'd worked on projects that were ongoing for more than six years. My recommendation would be to start with the house and the gardens. The outbuildings would be the last because I would have to search for authentic artifacts to re-create life as it was more than 150 years ago."

Kara opened her eyes, staring at Morgan. As they walked she'd also regaled Kara with how she'd become an historical architect. Morgan had admitted her first choice when enrolling in Howard University's College of Engineering, Architecture and Computer Sciences was engineering but quickly changed her concentration when she took an architecture course. She graduated as an architect, then returned to South Carolina to enroll in the Savannah College of Art and Design to pursue a degree in historic preservation.

"Who would supervise the project, Morgan?"

Morgan stared off into the distance.

"Most likely it would be one of the partners."

"You do all the legwork, and they get to supervise? No pun intended," she added when Morgan looked at her. "Right now my legs are screaming for mercy. I can't remember when I'd walked so much."

Morgan nodded. "It's like running a half marathon. And to answer your question as to supervision. I'm only an assistant. One of the partners or senior architects will probably oversee the project."

"How long have you been with the firm?"

"Two years."

"If you don't mind my asking, how old are you?"

"Thirty-two."

"How many years will it take before you're more than an assistant?"

Morgan lifted a shoulder. "I don't know. Probably at least another ten years, give or take a few."

Kara took a deep breath, held it, then exhaled slowly. She'd known she was going to use Morgan's firm within an hour of their surveying the property. However, she'd hoped to work directly with her, not the owners of the architectural and design firm.

"How would you like your own firm?"

Morgan stood up straight. "What are you

talking about?"

"I just came into more money than I know what to do with. Taylor . . . my father's will states I have to restore this property, and that's what I intend to do. Right now, I don't have the patience to go through what I've just gone through with you. I'll hire you if you set up your own firm."

"But I don't have my own firm," Morgan whispered.

"Open an office here on Cavanaugh Island, and I'll be your first client."

Morgan's eyelids fluttered wildly. "I don't have that kind of money. And besides, I'd never open an office in Haven Creek. I'd be in direct competition with Ellison and Murphy."

"What about Sanctuary Cove? I noticed there were a few vacant stores in their business district. I'll loan you the money you'll need to be operational."

"Why are you doing this, Kara?"

"Why wouldn't I, Morgan?" She'd answered her question with one of her own. "We're both young, single black women who have to fight to make our way in this world. I'm an overworked and underpaid social worker with a male supervisor who refuses to give me a favorable evaluation even though I go above and beyond what is called for in my job description. I've lost track of the number of times I was tempted to resign and set up a private practice. That is virtually impossible in Manhattan because I'd have to rent an office or a desk with another group of social workers and/or psychologists.

"I barely make enough money to pay rent on the apartment I share with a friend, buy food and a monthly Metro-Card for the bus and subway. Then there are movie tickets that are nearly twenty dollars, and please don't buy popcorn or a soda. If I go to a club and give the bartender a twenty for a drink, I'm lucky if I get back two dollars, which becomes his tip. It's not easy for us, Morgan, and if you don't want to accept my offer, then I'll respect your decision."

"Damn, Kara. You really know how to pile on the guilt."

"That's what my roommate says."

Morgan smiled. "What do *we* have to do to make this a reality?"

"Are you familiar with the law firm of Sullivan, Webster, Matthews and Sullivan?"

"No."

"David Sullivan Jr. was Taylor Patton's attorney and is also my attorney. I'll ask him to draw up an agreement stating that I'm an investor and silent partner in your firm."

"Aren't you afraid I'd run out with your money?" Morgan asked.

Kara chuckled. "Where are you going, Morgan? Didn't you tell me you live here? And I have to assume your family still lives here."

Morgan nodded. "They do."

"Would you embarrass your family when word got out that you're a thief? I don't think so," she added when Morgan gave her a wide-eyed stare. "I'm giving up a lifestyle I've come to like and a career I love despite all my bitchin' and moanin' to fulfill a dead man's wish. Together we can make it happen, or the new owners of Angels Landing may not look like you or me. And I don't have to tell you that developers could care less about preserving the Gullah culture once they put in their golf courses, condos, and country clubs."

"I won't say anything to my supervisor until I'm ready to leave."

"Good for you."

"I'll take time off and check out the vacant stores in the Cove. Once the news gets out that I'm renting space in the Cove, the proverbial shit will hit the fan."

"What's the worst they can do, Morgan? Fire you?"

Morgan laughed until tears ran down her

face. "By that time it'll be too late." She sobered. "I'll need office furniture and equipment."

"What about employees?"

"All I need is a receptionist who will handle the phone and paperwork. I have a good working relationship with the artisans in the Creek, so that eliminates looking for them. You know, Kara, I think this is going to work."

"Of course it is. I don't want to be rude, but I'm going inside to soak in the tub for a while. My calves are singing the hallelujah chorus right about now. You have my numbers, and I have the one to your cell. I'll call you tomorrow after I speak to David."

Morgan threw her arms around Kara's neck. "Thank you, girlfriend."

"You're welcome, girlfriend."

Kara opened the door and walked into the house that held memories and secrets of those who'd lived before her. Hiring Morgan to restore the house was another piece of the puzzle that would soon be in place.

CHAPTER SEVEN

Jeff couldn't wait to return home. He'd played phone tag with Kara even before he'd left the island to attend a crime prevention conference. With the proliferation of illegal firearms and an increase in drug-related crimes, the governor and law enforcement officials had convened with a joint task force that included police departments from as many as two hundred small towns.

By the time Kenny called to say that Kara wanted him to call her at home, it was after eleven and much too late to call. Then Spencer White woke him at dawn, apologizing because his secretary had misplaced a letter from the governor requesting his presence at the conference and he had to leave for Columbia posthaste. Jeff was tempted to refuse the mayor's directive because he suspected Spencer was so busy campaigning for his upcoming reelection that he had misplaced the letter and decided to blame the secretary.

He'd asked his closest neighbor to look in on his grandmother during his absence, although he doubted she would do anything to exert herself. The cardiologist had inserted a shunt into her heart to divert the flow of blood from one chamber to another because he'd wanted to avoid a bypass procedure.

Jeff knew Corrine didn't like curtailing her normal activities yet resigned herself to following the doctor's directives. Corrine had been very active up until the attack, and she still talked about not being able to bowl. For years she'd belonged to a bowling league that met every Sunday night at the Charleston bowling alley. She'd also been an avid swimmer and like most children on the island had learned to swim by jumping off the pier.

He wasn't certain why Kara wanted him to call her, but when he'd checked in with his deputies, they reported back that Mrs. Todd said Kara was spending a lot of time in Charleston. Sending her flowers and the balloon had been a knee-jerk reaction when he'd passed the florist. Jeff hadn't wanted to believe it had taken less than a week for Kara to change her mind and move to the island. She'd revealed that she was required to stay for five years, but five years was a great deal longer than one or even three weeks.

Jeff felt his mind drifting when thunderous applause shook him from his reverie. He still hadn't figured out what it was about Kara that he'd found so attractive. He knew it wasn't her looks because he'd dated beautiful women before and a few that were so overtly sexy they turned heads wherever they went. Unfortunately their looks weren't enough to get him to commit to something other than a physical relationship. The only one who'd gotten him to commit was a North Carolina schoolteacher he'd met when he was assigned to Marine Corps Base Camp Lejeune.

Pamela wasn't as pretty as she was charismatic. Her infectious smile, the timbre of her sultry voice, and the dedication she'd shown her students were what had won him over. He'd waited thirty-six years to find someone like Pamela, and when he'd proposed marriage, she accepted without hesitation. Then when he was transferred from Camp Lejeune to Camp Pendleton, Jeff realized their relationship was on shaky ground. Pamela had been appointed to assistant principal, and she'd postponed their wedding date because she had to think about whether she'd wanted to become a military wife. A month later she returned his ring, declaring she'd made a mistake accepting it when she knew he would never give up his military career to live a normal, more stable life.

A scraping of chairs and more than three hundred men and women representing police forces all over the state filed out of the auditorium. Gathering the many handouts they were given, Jeff shoved them into his plastic folder stamped with the conference title and made his way out to the parking lot. He'd left Cavanaugh Island Wednesday morning, and it was now Friday afternoon. The drive between Columbia and Charleston would take approximately two hours, barring traffic delays. He was anxious to see his grandmother . . . and Kara.

One hour and forty-five minutes later, Jeff smiled when he saw his grandmother sitting on the porch knitting. She hated sitting around doing nothing, so she'd picked up her needlework. If he had to recall one thing from his childhood, it was a basket filled with squares of fabric for quilting or colorful skeins of yarn Corrine used for her knitting, crocheting, or embroidery projects. She even knitted or crocheted when watching television.

He parked his car under the carport beside her Camry and came around to the front porch. Leaning over, he kissed her forehead. "How's my favorite girl?"

Corrine gazed up at him with loving eyes. "Your grandmother is just fine. You should be asking that question to that cute little girl you brought here earlier in the week."

"She's just a friend, Gram."

"She needs to be more than a friend, Jeffrey. I may not leave this house every day, but I do manage to hear the gossip."

Flopping down on a chair beside her, Jeff stretched out long legs. "What gossip now, Gram?"

"She's staying. And someone saw that pretty little architect from the Creek over at the house. That can only mean that Kara plans to fix it up. And there has been other talk . . ."

Jeff shook his head. He was away from the Cove for three days, and the gossipmongers were busy. "Spit it out, Gram."

"You had flowers delivered to Angels Landing."

Taking off his hat, Jeff placed it on his knee. "Since when is buying flowers for someone a crime?"

"It's not a crime, Jeffrey. It just sends a

message that you're interested in the young lady."

"Do you want me to say that I'm not interested in Kara?"

"Oh no! I think it's wonderful that you are. It's just that I want you to be prepared in case you start keeping company with her."

"Prepared for what, Gram?"

"For all the talk about you and Kara."

Running his hand over his face, Jeff closed his eyes. "Grandmomma, I could care less about what folks say. Spending two years in Afghanistan taught me to take one second at a time. When I saw men who'd become my brothers in every sense of the word get blown up right in front of my eyes, I promised myself that nothing or no one, could get to me. The exception is you." He pushed to his feet. "I'm going inside to shower and catch a few winks before I go over to the station house."

"Don't you want something to eat?" Corrine asked.

"No thank you. I'll grab something from Jack's before they close if I get hungry." Leaning down, he kissed her again. "It's good to be home."

Kara sat at the table in the kitchen drinking coffee and flipping through the pages of the book she'd bought from the Parlor Bookstore. Not only did she want to revive Theodora's garden, but she also wanted to plant a vegetable and herb garden.

Even though Mrs. Todd prepared most of the meals, she wanted to begin cooking for herself, even if it was only the evening meal. She'd thought she would be bored, but she'd been anything but. It had taken three trips to Charleston to complete her banking. The accounts in Taylor Patton's name were closed and reopened in her name. She'd met with an investment banker at each branch who'd recommended which accounts she should utilize to maximize the greatest yield. What she'd refused to do was put her money into accounts that weren't insured by the FDIC.

Morgan had called to say she found a small shop two doors from the Muffin Corner on Moss Alley. It was perfect because it was off Main Street. The owner of the property had waived the security fee and the first month's rent because he'd been trying to rent the space for more than a year and a half. Morgan said she would take the space, then made him swear an oath that he would not reveal who the new tenant was until it came time for her grand opening.

Kara had David draw up the papers making her a silent partner in M. Dane Architecture and Interior Design. He'd met with Morgan and convinced her to set up a corporation for which he would file the necessary paperwork.

Morgan had given her a projected budget of what she would need to start up the business, and Kara had checks drawn on her Charleston accounts to minimize someone inadvertently leaking the news that Kara had given Morgan a check for six figures. What they didn't know was the amount on the check was minuscule compared to the price of restoring the property and would be deducted from the final cost.

She studied a page featuring a pond in a meadow surrounded by ornamental grasses and irises. When walking the property, Kara had discovered several ponds and an underground stream. She jumped when she heard the doorbell chime and glanced at the clock on the microwave. It was 10:50.

Lowering her feet she'd rested on another chair, she went to answer the door. It hadn't taken her long to get used to locking the door right after Mrs. Todd left for the evening.

Peering through the security eye, she saw Jeff standing on the porch. When he hadn't returned her call, she thought either he forgot or had intended to call her. He'd done what David had asked him to do and was keeping an eye on her. His deputies continued to stop by every day to ask about her as they did with most residents and businesspeople on the island. It was something Jeff had instituted to stay connected. Morgan said the former sheriff was distant, reinforcing the stereotype that people shouldn't trust law enforcement.

She opened the door to find him grinning at her like a Cheshire cat. He was wearing his badge and gun, so she assumed he was on duty. "Good evening, Sheriff Hamilton."

He nodded and angled his head. "Good evening, Miss Newell. I heard you were asking for me."

Kara shivered slightly. Not from the cool night air but from the way Jeff was staring at her. Pulling back her shoulders, she managed a tight smile. "Yes. I wanted to thank you for the balloon and the flowers." She noticed he was staring at a spot below her neck, and when she glanced down, she saw her distended nipples were clearly visible under the cotton fabric of her pajama top.

Jeff's gaze inched up to her face. "May I come in?" Taking a step back, Kara opened the door, and he stepped into the entryway. "I would've come sooner, but I was away at a conference."

Kara closed the door but didn't turn around. "You don't have to explain yourself to me, Jeff."

He took a step, pressing his chest to her back. "What if I feel the need to explain myself?"

"Why?"

Her heart was pounding in her chest like a trip-hammer. Jeff dwarfed her as she stood there in her bare feet. His heat, the scent of his cologne, and the solid wall of his chest against her back reminded her of what she'd missed and had been missing for years. She wanted to trust him but couldn't because of the men in her life: Taylor and the other men in her past. Even Austin had deceived her when he'd elected not to tell her he wasn't her biological father. And yet despite her angst, her body betrayed her at the exact time his arm went around her waist.

"Because I missed you," he whispered in her ear.

"You haven't known me long enough to miss me," she murmured.

"I don't measure my life in days, weeks, or years but in seconds. You look at life differently once you stare death in the face every second of your life. I grew up hearing the old folk talk about tomorrow isn't promised to you. My mantra is today isn't promised, either."

Kara was certain he could feel her trembling. "What is it you want, Jeff?" His deep chuckle caressed her ear.

"You really don't want to know what I want."

She smiled in spite of her pleasurable predicament. "Yes, I do."

"Right now I want to kiss you."

"Is that all?"

He laughed again. "What else were you expecting?"

"Nothing," Kara said much too quickly to sound convincing.

"You're an incredibly beautiful liar." He pressed his mouth to her hair. "I want that too but only when you're ready.

She bit her lip and nodded. "What if I'm never ready?"

"Then we'll have a relationship without the sex. I just want to be with you."

Turning in his loose embrace, Kara met his eyes, looking for a trace of guile. His expression was closed. "You're kidding, aren't you?"

"No, I'm not. Do you believe I'm so self-centered that I think all women want to sleep with me?"

"Most of the men I've known or met

expect me to sleep with them."

His eyebrow lifted a fraction. "You've been hanging out with the wrong guys."

"It appears as if I have," she said under her breath. What she couldn't tell Jeff was that if she were given a choice she *would* sleep with him.

She hadn't told anyone (and that included Morgan) that after she restored Angels Landing, she planned to move into the vacant guesthouse and convert the main house into a museum. The revenue she derived from tours would be used for preservation. Once she had lived there for five years, she would decide what she wanted to do with the rest of her life. At thirty-eight she would still be young and wealthy enough to do whatever pleased her.

Jeff cradled her face. His head dipped as if in slow motion, and Kara breathed in his scent seconds before his mouth covered hers in a kiss that stole the breath from her lungs. Going on tiptoe, she anchored her arms under his shoulders, holding onto him as if her life depended on him and only him.

Arousal snaked through her body, scorching her from head to toe. She opened her mouth to his searching tongue, losing herself in the moment and the man. It took herculean strength but Kara managed to tear away before she begged Jeff to take her upstairs and make love to her. A soft groan escaped her parted lips when he fastened his mouth to the column of her neck.

"My grandmother wants to know if you're coming for Sunday dinner."

"Will you be there?"

"I can arrange to be there if you want me to."

"It really doesn't matter," she quipped, offering him a saucy grin.

His eyebrows lifted a fraction. "Oh, really? What do I have to do to make you change your mind?" he teased, pulling her closer and lowering his head to kiss her again.

"Leave before we start something we can't finish."

"Yes, ma'am."

Jeff's arms fell away, and Kara felt his loss even before he walked out of the door. Something about being in his embrace felt so right, so natural, as if they'd done it before in another time and place. "Good night," she said in a hushed whisper.

Amusement shimmered in his eyes. "Oh, that it will be." Turning on his heels, Jeff opened the door. "I'll pick you up on Sunday."

Kara could still see his broad shoulders, cropped hair and remembered the sparkle in his dark eyes long after she'd locked the door. She felt a warm glow of satisfaction when she realized he hadn't forgotten her. In fact, he'd admitted to missing her.

"I missed you, too." She didn't know why it was so hard for her to have admitted that to Jeff.

Kara returned to the kitchen and poured the lukewarm coffee in the sink, rinsed the cup, and put it in the dishwasher. Leaving the light on in the hallway, she walked up the back staircase to her bedroom. When she climbed into bed, she felt a pang of emptiness. She'd slept alone for so long it almost seemed natural for her. Since meeting Jeff, Kara realized she didn't want to sleep alone.

She didn't want to end up like Taylor living in a twenty-room house with no one to tell him that they loved him. He'd grown accustomed to being alone and had died alone. How sad for a man in the prime of his life and who'd amassed a great deal of wealth to have no one to share it with.

Kara shook her head as she pulled the sheet and blanket up and over her body. No. She would not go out like that. Even if she never married, she would adopt a child or children, anyone who would enjoy their grandfather's legacy.

■ ■ ■ ■

Kara felt as if she had butterflies in her stomach when she saw her mother's name and number come up on her cell as she prepared to leave the house to walk along the beach.

"Mama?"

"I got someone to cover for me, and I'm on my way to Charleston."

She closed her eyes. It was time to discover another piece of the puzzle. "What time is your plane coming in?"

"I'm driving, Kara."

"Is Daddy with you?"

"No. This is something we need to talk about without him being present."

"Where are you now?" It was about nine hundred miles between Little Rock and Charleston, and Kara hoped her mother hadn't attempted to make the drive without stopping.

"I just crossed into South Carolina. I'm going to stop in Columbia, check into a hotel for a couple of hours, then come on in."

"Mama, you'd better sleep for more than a couple of hours."

"Once I get to Charleston, I'll need directions for Cavanaugh Island."

"Call me and I'll meet you."

"Okay."

"Mama? Please get some sleep."

"Okay, baby."

Kara tapped the button, ending the call. Walking on shaky knees, she managed to make her way over to the bedroom's sitting area. Dropping into a deep armchair, she rested her feet on the footstool. The bottle-green, watered silk fabric was faded and frayed.

She couldn't wait to see her mother — not just to uncover the details of her paternity, but because Jeannette was the stabilizing factor in her life. The last time she'd seen her mother cry was when Austin was being transferred to another base, the third in four years, and Kara had become hysterical because she didn't want to leave her friends. Jeannette had risked her marriage when she told her husband she wasn't going with him, that she was returning to Little Rock to live with her mother and father until he voluntarily resigned or retired from the corps.

Kara knew the ultimatum had shocked Austin, and he'd accused Jeannette of not supporting him, but Jeannette remained resolute when she said her daughter's

emotional well-being was first and everything else secondary. It was the first time
Kara remembered her mother's reference to
her being *her* daughter and not *their* daughter. However at eight years of age she hadn't
understood any of the dynamics surrounding her parents' marriage. The only thing
that mattered was she was going to go to
the same school year after year and she
didn't have to leave her new friends.

Kara loved Austin, but even at a young
age she knew she didn't like military life
when her family moved every few years, and
there were times when she rarely got to see
him. Would it, she mused, have been that
way if Jeff was on active duty and they were
in a relationship? She knew whatever they
would've had would have failed because she
was not willing to embrace that lifestyle.

Sitting and thinking about her past was
not helping to ease her nerves about the
pending meeting with her mother. And if
she didn't get up, she wouldn't, and she
wanted to make it to the beach in time to
watch the sun rise.

When she got there, Kara discovered she
wasn't the only one on the beach. There was
an older couple walking slowly while holding hands. She passed two young women
jogging at a fast pace who nodded to her

but didn't break stride. She walked in the opposite direction, heading for the Cove and where the Black Bay connected with the southwest bank of the Ashley River. Slowing, she watched the magnificent sunrise as the cold, gray, angry surf pounded the beach.

"Awesome, isn't it?"

With wide eyes, she spun around to find Jeff standing several feet away. She forced herself not to stare at his bare chest. Beads of perspiration dotted his forehead and upper body despite the cold wind coming off the water. She could see every one of the abs on his flat belly.

"Yes it is." He was talking about the sun, and she was talking about his body. "Aren't you cold?" She'd elected to wear a cotton turtleneck under her sweats, while Jeff had opted for sweatpants.

He began jogging in place. "You don't feel the cold if you keep moving." He took her hand. "Come jog with me."

"I hadn't planned to jog."

He gave her a sidelong glance. "You don't look as if you're out of condition."

She quickened her pace to keep up with him. Jogging on sand was much more difficult than on a track. "My mother is coming in today."

"What time is her flight?"

"She's driving. I told her I would meet her in Charleston."

"She's welcome to join us tomorrow."

"I'll tell her." Kara's breathing was becoming more labored. If she'd joined a gym, the extra exertion wouldn't have tested her endurance. "You're either going to have to slow down or let go of my hand. Oh no!" she screamed when he swung her up in his arms and continued running. "Put me down, Jeff," she yelled between clenched teeth.

"Hold on, baby."

She held onto his thick neck to keep her balance. "Are you hard of hearing? I told you to put me down."

"Stop talking and enjoy the ride."

Kara couldn't believe he was carrying her as if she were a child. "You're going to pay for this."

"Ooo-wee! I'm scared." Jeff shook himself for effect.

"I'm not kidding, Jeff."

"Please stop talking, darling."

"I'm not your darling."

"You could be."

"What if I don't want to be?"

"Your mouth says one thing today, while the other night your lips said the opposite."

"Do you have to remind me of that?"

"Why not? I can't forget it."

"Stop it, Jeff. You're embarrassing me."

He slowed, then came to a complete stop. "Are you a virgin?"

Her jaw dropped, heat suffused her face, appalled that he thought her so prudish that she could've been a virgin. Was it that obvious because it had been a while since she'd been in a man's company? She had been alone for far too long.

"Do you realize how old I am?"

"That's not what I asked you. Have you ever slept with a man?"

"Of course I have. And why would that interest you?"

"There's an innocence about you I find endearing."

"Too innocent for the worldly military man?"

Jeff grinned, his teeth showing whitely against the stubble on his lean jaw. "Never." Bending slightly, he set Kara on her feet. "It's time I start back. Some of us have to work for a living."

She scrunched her nose. "Very funny. Remember, I'm on vacation."

He cradled her face and brushed a light kiss on her mouth. "I'll call you tomorrow."

Kara stood watching as Jeff turned and

raced down the beach, sand spewing under bare feet. As she turned to retrace her steps to the parking lot, she noticed two women watching her. By the looks on their faces, they'd seen the entire encounter.

CHAPTER EIGHT

Kara and her mother stood at the rail of the ferry, watching the skyline of Charleston growing smaller as the ferryman deftly steered the boat through the narrow inlet until he reached open water.

Jeannette placed a hand over her mouth, smothering a yawn. "I suppose I still didn't get enough sleep."

"That's why you're going straight to bed once we get to Angels Landing." Shifting, Kara leaned back against the rail. "Even with bags under your eyes, you still look beautiful, Mama."

The older woman yawned again. "And you always know what to say to make me feel better."

Kara studied her mother, noticing a few more strands of gray in her thick, stylishly cut, coiffed hair. Kara had inherited her mother's hair and body, but that's where their resemblance ended. Her eyes were hazel, her coloring a golden-brown, while Jeannette always joked that her eyes and skin were an exact match: henna.

"It's the truth. I'm surprised Daddy didn't insist on coming with you. You know he has a jealous streak as wide as the Mississippi."

Jeannette flashed a demure smile. "I told him we were going to have a girls' week. After all, he has his boys' week with his military buddies whenever they go camping and do Lord knows what."

Kara smoothed back the wisps of hair that had escaped her ponytail. It was the last week in March, and spring was definitely in the air. Daytime temperatures now topped out at seventy. "Did his jealousy have anything to do with Taylor?"

An audible breath came from Jeannette. "Come, let's sit down, Kara." They moved over to sit on padded benches, far enough away from the other passengers so they wouldn't be overheard. She smiled when Kara rubbed her back. "Austin and I grew up together. He was my first and only boyfriend until I met Taylor. I'd left home to go to college while Austin enlisted in the Marines. Austin and I hadn't slept together, and he made me promise to wait for him.

"My college roommate was dating a More-house brother, and I sort of paired up with his roommate. Taylor and I became real good friends. Outside of class you rarely saw me without him and vice versa. One night when he'd had too much to drink, he told me about his family, his overly protective mother in particular, and how he'd had to fight for his independence. I was close to tears once he admitted that he'd never slept with a woman. He was a handsome, brilliant man who'd been afraid to approach a woman because his mother had turned him into a social cripple. Then everything changed during our senior year. Instead of going home for spring break, we took off for Virginia Beach, checked into a hotel, and a sorry sight it was with not one but two bumbling virgins. We managed to get it right, and for one glorious week I felt as if I'd died and gone to heaven.

"My period was late, but that didn't raise any warning bells because my cycle was never regular. It wasn't until after I'd graduated and moved back to Little Rock that I realized I was carrying Taylor's baby."

"Did you tell him?"

Her mother nodded. "I'd called his home and left a message for him to return my call, but either he didn't get the message or he'd decided to move on. I wrote him a letter, and that too went unanswered. That's when

I knew I had to tell Austin that I was carrying another man's baby. I'd expected him to walk away, but he insisted we marry as quickly as possible. We went to the courthouse, got married, and moved into off-base housing. You were born a week before Christmas, and when Austin held you for the first time and called you his baby girl, I knew I'd been given a second chance. I had a wonderful supportive husband and a beautiful daughter."

"How did Taylor know my birthday?"

A slight frown furrowed Jeannette's smooth forehead. "What are you talking about?"

"His computer password is Kara twelve-nineteen, which just happens to be my birthday."

"I don't know, Kara. After I sent him that letter, I'd mentally exorcised Taylor from my mind."

"It's incredible, but he knew everything about me, Mama. My full name, birthday, my New York City address, and who knows what else. He left me everything: the house, land, antiques, classic cars, cash, bonds, et cetera, et cetera, et cetera. I'm told he never married or had any other children. No one ever saw him with a woman, and he lived and died alone. I'm certain it wasn't too difficult for him to hire an investigator to collect whatever information he needed on me." A beat passed. "You never told him you had given birth to his daughter, yet it wasn't until after he died that I was made aware that Taylor Patton, not Austin Newell, was my biological father. Why didn't you tell me, Mama? Why did I have to find out from a dead man?"

Jeannette took a deep breath, holding it until she was forced to exhale. "Austin and I never talked about it. I was your mama and he was your daddy. It'd become our tainted little secret."

A cynical laugh escaped Kara. "One thing I've learned living here is there are no secrets."

"Living? Don't you mean visiting?"

Kara made circular motions on her mother's back as if to ease the blow of what she was about to tell her. "I'm going to live here, Mama."

"What! You can't, Kara!" Her protest was pregnant with shock and fear.

"I have to," Kara countered. "If Taylor was out for revenge, then he has exacted a heavy price." She revealed the terms of his will.

"How can he ask you to live here for five years?"

"I don't know, but he did. At least the

mandate comes at a good time in my life. I'm not married, and I don't have to worry about uprooting a child."

"Are you certain this is what's best for you, Kara? You have a beautiful apartment in one of the greatest cities in the world and a wonderful career. Why would you want to give that up?"

"I own a house here that is listed as a National Register of Historic Places, and the property is a National Historic Landmark District. Don't forget that I'm a CSW, and I can always work as a school-based or hospital social worker in any city. Or I could open a private practice, an option I didn't have in New York because I didn't have the time or money."

Pushing away Kara's arm, Jeannette slid over, putting distance between them. "Don't tell me you're doing this because of money."

"Mama!"

"Don't 'Mama' me, Kara. Is it about money?"

Kara felt as if she'd been stabbed through the heart, left to bleed invisible blood. She did not want to believe that her mother thought she was that greedy, avaricious, and narcissistic. That she'd agreed to carry out a dead man's wishes because he'd made her wealthy. It wasn't just about money; it was about the future of Cavanaugh Island and its inhabitants.

"I can't believe you said that," she whispered. "If I'd wanted to make a lot of money, I never would've become a social worker. Please look at me, Mama," she pleaded. "It's not about me," she continued when Jeannette stared at her.

"What is it about?"

"It's about connecting with relatives I never knew I had. It's also about getting involved in a restoration project that will take years to complete and may even permit me to start up a new business." What she didn't tell her mother was the possibility of a relationship with an attractive man — something she hadn't had in a long time.

"I can't believe it's taken only a week for you to become this impassioned about something you knew nothing about."

"A week ago I had no idea that the man I call Daddy isn't my biological father. But that doesn't change anything because DNA aside, Austin Newell is and will always be my father . . . even though everyone says I look exactly like Theodora Patton."

"He loves you, baby."

Kara inched over and hugged her mother. "Nothing's changed because I still love him. I don't know why Taylor left me everything when he should've left it to his brother, sisters, nieces, and nephews."

Jeannette's round, sherry-colored eyes grew wider. "He disinherited them?"

"I wouldn't call it disinherit because they're not his heirs."

"That probably didn't make them too happy."

Kara didn't tell her mother about the outburst in the lawyer's office following the reading of the will. "He did set aside monies for some of the younger Pattons' college education, and he has provided for the housekeeper and her husband. The more I think about it, the more I believe my inheritance is attributed to his guilt. Taylor knew about me but was either too much of a coward or too intimidated by his mother to reach out to you."

"I don't know, Kara."

"Would you have married Taylor if he'd asked you?"

"In a heartbeat. I loved Austin, but I was in love with Taylor."

"Are you in love with Daddy now?"

"Yes. Our marriage hasn't been perfect, but we've sacrificed a lot to make it work. I know he felt cheated that I never got pregnant again, and that put a strain on our marriage once he was diagnosed with a low sperm count. My decision not to become a military wife was as difficult for me as it was for Austin. I would've followed him around the world if it'd been just me, but there was someone else to consider, you. It wasn't easy not having my husband with me for your parent-teacher conferences, when your cheerleading team went to Orlando to compete, and your high school graduation."

Kara rested her head on her mother's shoulder like she'd done as a child. "It was never easy for me to make friends, so when we had to move so much, I couldn't deal with it."

"I know." Jeannette gave her daughter a tender glance. "Have you made friends here?"

"Sort of."

"What do you mean 'sort of'?"

"The sheriff is my attorney's cousin, and he's sort of taken me under his wing. I met his grandmother, and we're invited to have dinner with them tomorrow."

"Do they know I'm coming?" Jeannette asked.

"Yes."

"Is the sheriff your only friend?"

"No. I think Morgan and I are going to get along well."

"It appears as if you have guy friends. Don't you think you need at least one girl-friend?"

Kara laughed. "Morgan is a girl."

Jeannette's mouth formed a perfect O. "I see."

The ferry slowed as it neared the dock and landing for Sanctuary Cove. Kara and Jeannette were the last cars off the boat. Kara had paid the ferryman for a bumper sticker for her mother's car. Other than official vehicles no vehicle was allowed on island roads without a permit.

"Follow me," Kara told Jeannette before she slipped in behind the wheel of the Mercedes.

She drove slowly away from the pier and through downtown Sanctuary Cove. It was Saturday morning, and people were out and about shopping. They drove past the town square. The benches were filled with retirees taking advantage of the warmer weather. Kara smiled when she saw Jack's Fish House, remembering her unofficial date with Jeff that seemed so long ago when it'd only been a week. What she couldn't forget were his kisses, kisses that fired her blood while reminding her why she'd been born female: that she was a woman with needs only a man could assuage.

Kara had no preconceived notions about having a relationship with the handsome lawman. He was a forty-year-old confirmed bachelor who lived with his grandmother on an island with a total population of less than 2,300 residents. She'd made home visits to New York City public housing projects with more than 2,300 tenants in the development. And like those on Cavanaugh Island, everybody knew everybody and their business.

She didn't believe she would be able to live on the island and have a normal relationship with a man. Mrs. Todd had revealed Jeff didn't bring the flowers to Angels Landing but had had them delivered. How long, she mused, had it taken for the news to sweep over the island that Jeffrey Hamilton had sent flowers to Kara Newell.

Kara had never been one to flaunt her affairs, and she knew she had to develop a thicker skin *if* she was going to date Jeff. Peering up into her rearview mirror, she saw her mother slowing down. It was apparent she was driving and sightseeing. Jeannette had taken a week's vacation, and that was more than enough time for Kara to show her the island and Charleston's historic district.

Signaling, she took the newly constructed

two-lane road to Angels Landing. She maneuvered off the road, signaling again, before driving slowly under a canopy of live oaks draped with Spanish moss. The sight of the pink house at the end of the allée never failed to elicit a feeling of incredulity that the massive trees had survived countless generations that had owned and inhabited the grand house.

She came to a stop, parking in front of a trio of carriage houses that had been converted to two locked garages used to house Taylor's three classic cars. Kara motioned for her mother to pull up alongside her.

"Pop the trunk, and I'll take your bag inside." When she saw the direction of her mother's gaze, she smiled and said, "Close your mouth, Mama." Using the side door, she led her mother into the main kitchen with brick walls and flooring. A massive fireplace took up half of an entire wall.

"Oh my word!" Jeannette gasped. "This reminds me of Williamsburg."

"I read that the house was built sometime around 1832. There was a fire in 1854, and the first floor was completely destroyed. The house remained unoccupied until 1858. After extensive repairs a gambler, who'd won the house on the turn of a card, moved in with his mistress. Then came the Civil

War and he joined the Confederate Army and died in the Battle of Rivers Bridge two months before the war ended."

"What happened to the mistress?"

Smiling, Kara shook her head. "I don't know yet. I'm still reading a book about the history of Cavanaugh Island. Come, let me show you to your room. After you're rested I'll give you a tour of the house and introduce you to Mrs. Todd once she returns from the dentist. She and her husband are off on the weekend."

Jeannette followed Kara down a narrow hallway to a staircase at the rear of the house. "Are you losing weight?"

Kara glanced over her shoulder. "Quite the contrary. I think I've gained now that I'm eating three meals a day. I've also started exercising."

"Where do you exercise?"

"I walk along the beach."

"Don't exercise too much because you look better with a little more weight."

"Spoken like a mother."

"That's because I am a mother, who one day would like to be a grandmother."

"That's definitely not going to happen now. This is your room. You also have a private bathroom."

Kara had chosen the bedroom at the far

end of the hall for her mother. Embroidered mosquito netting draped the four-poster bed. Kara had dubbed this the yellow room because of the coverlet, pale pine floors, yellow bed dressing, and green fabric on the settee and chairs embroidered with yellow butterflies.

"How many rooms are in this house?"

"Twenty."

Jeannette closed her eyes. "I can't imagine one person living here alone."

"I guess you get used to it."

She gave her daughter a long, penetrating stare as she placed her luggage on the bench at the foot of the bed. "Is that what you intend to do, Kara? Do you really want to ramble around this . . . this monstrosity of a house alone like Taylor did?"

Crossing her arms under her breasts, Kara met her mother's glare. "No."

"Didn't you tell me the housekeeper and her husband live in a guesthouse? And if that's true, then you are here alone."

"Can we talk about this later? Right now, I have to draft a letter of resignation because I'd like to put it in the mail on Monday. I'll either be in the kitchen or on the front porch if you need me."

"I'd like to do a little shopping and sightseeing later this afternoon."

"I'll take you to Haven Creek for shopping; then we'll go to Sanctuary Cove for dinner."

Jeannette slipped out of her lightweight wool jacket. "Why don't we eat in Angels Landing?"

"Angels Landing isn't zoned for businesses. It's the only town that's solely residential. Even folks who own large houses with the intent of turning them into boardinghouses can't because the town council won't give them a variance."

Kara had spent most of her spare time researching the history of the island and the house she would now call home. She knew her property was exempt from the town's building codes because of its landmark status; once the restoration was complete, and she made it known she was turning it into a museum, she knew there would be little or no opposition.

"Isn't there some way for them to get around that?"

She smiled. "There is always a way to circumvent the law. All they have to do is apply to the Secretary of the Interior for landmark status."

Resting her hands at her waist, Jeannette's smile matched her daughter's. "What do you plan to do with this place?"

"You can't mention a word of this to anyone, Mama. Not even Daddy."

It took a full minute before Jeannette said, "Okay."

"After the house, the gardens, and the outbuildings are restored, I'm going to turn Angels Landing into a museum. People will be able to purchase tickets for tours. I'll offer discounts to schoolchildren and senior groups. When I spoke to my attorney, he suggested setting up a foundation with a mission to sustain the highest level of preservation. I've been thinking about building an inn not far from the formal gardens to attract corporate groups who wish to hold a conference in a different kind of setting. Then there are always the destination weddings. Why go to the Caribbean when you can marry in the Lowcountry? Again, I would offer discounts on weddings on Fridays and Sundays in May and Friday, Saturday, and Sunday in June."

Staring at her only child, it was as if Jeannette was seeing Kara for the first time. "You are truly *his* child."

"What are you talking about, Mama?"

"Whenever Taylor had to come up with a business plan for any of his business courses, he would always draft two schematics. Then he would submit the least probable of the two while saving the best for himself. His rationale was why give away something he could possibly use for his future."

"I was told he made a lot of money for his clients as an investment banker." A smile played at the corners of Kara's mouth. "And based on his net worth, he also made quite a bit for himself. Aside from the appraised value on this house and the two thousand acres it sits on, Taylor left me close to five million dollars. That's only cash on hand in banks. There are still bonds and other securities that I have to get an accountant to interpret for me."

Jeannette pressed a hand to her throat. "I don't believe it!"

"I must admit, it is a little overwhelming."

"It's mind-boggling, Kara."

"I know you and Daddy refinanced your house, so I'm going to give you an early Christmas gift and pay it off."

"You can't!"

"I can and I will," Kara countered. "You and Daddy struggled to send me to a private college, then paid for grad school out of your pocket because you didn't want me to end up with student loans. I never would've been able to rent an apartment in Manhattan if I'd had loans. Taylor owes you this, and because he's not around to repay you, I will." She held up her hand when Jeannette opened her mouth. "And Mama, please don't start with me because you're only going to lose this argument."

Jeannette narrowed her eyes. "Are you finished mouthing off to your mother?"

Kara struggled not to laugh. Her mother only pulled rank when she believed she was losing an argument. "Yep. I'll see you later." Turning on her heels, she left the bedroom, closing the door behind her.

Jeannette tugged at Kara's arm. "I want to go inside and look around." They'd stopped in front of a window display of miniature jars of jellies, jams, and relishes.

Kara followed her into the Cannery, the most delicious aromas wafting to her nose. Her mother had slept for more than four hours, and when Jeannette joined her in the kitchen, it was as if they'd never discussed the awkward subject of money and her intent to pay off their mortgage . . . or her biological father.

She liked what could be interpreted as the hustle and bustle of Sanctuary Cove, but it was the laid-back attitude of the artisans in Haven Creek that really appealed to her. Morgan mentioned hiring many of them for the restoration project, and she wanted to stop by the shops to look at samples of their work.

The tiny bell over the door rang, alerting the shopkeeper that she had a customer. A woman with graying dreadlocks smiled and nodded. "I'll be with you directly. Feel free to sample the spiced apple butter."

Kara walked over to the shelf with mason jars filled with fruit and vegetables: corn, beets, cherries, zucchini, peaches, pears, and an assortment of berries — blackberries, raspberries, and gooseberries. She picked up a small jar of Asian chili/salsa and one of chowchow, placing them in a wire basket. She'd known women in Little Rock who'd canned fruits and vegetables, but she'd never learned the process and neither did her mother.

The bell rang again. Kara turned and froze when her gaze met and fused with one of the women who'd sat in the conference room during the reading of Taylor's will. Her gray eyes and sable-brown skin told Kara she was a Patton. She was casually dressed in a pair of fitted jeans, white silk man-tailored blouse, navy blazer, and black leather slip-ons. The solitaire in her wedding set was much too large for her delicate hand.

Kara was the first to end the stare-down

impasse when she smiled. "Hello."

"It's Kara, isn't it?"

"Yes."

"I'm Virginia Patton-Smith. But most folks call me Virgie."

Kara offered her hand and wasn't disappointed when Virgie took it. "This is my first time coming here. Perhaps you can recommend something."

Virgie picked up a jar of cherries, handing it to Kara. "I use the cherries as a topping for pancakes and ice cream."

She placed the jar in her basket. "What else?"

"You've got to be a Patton because we all have a weakness for chowchow."

"You don't believe I'm a Patton?" The question was out before Kara could censor herself.

"Please, don't get me wrong, Kara. I believe you're one of us because you look exactly like my grandmother. But some of my relatives still believe you're an impostor."

"I can reassure you that I'm not an impostor."

Virgie patted her shoulder. "I wouldn't worry too much if I were you. Give them time, and I'm certain they'll come around. We have a family tradition that we all get together for Sunday dinner. We rotate homes; that way it becomes more equitable. This Sunday it's my turn, and I'd love to invite you, but I don't want you to be blind-sided by some of our less than hospitable relatives."

"It's okay. I wouldn't have been able to make it even if *our* relatives were ready to welcome me with open arms. I happen to have a prior engagement."

"Good for you. I'd really like us to get together before you go back to New York."

Hazel eyes met a hoary-gray pair. "I'm not going back. I've decided to make Angels Landing my home." Kara thought Virgie was going to faint when she swayed slightly. She reached out to steady her, but Virgie took a backward step.

"You're kidding, aren't you?"

Kara almost felt sorry for Virgie when she saw her expression of confidence replaced with fear. "Not at all."

"But why?"

"Why? You heard the conditions outlined in my father's will. I've been directed to restore the property and live in the house for five years. And that's —"

"Kara, baby . . . Oh, I'm sorry I didn't realize you were talking to someone."

She gave her mother a plastic smile. "This

isn't just someone, Mama. She's Virginia Patton-Smith, and she happens to be my cousin."

Virgie recovered enough to give Kara's mother a friendly smile. "It's nice meeting you, Ms. Newell."

Jeannette nodded. "Same here."

"I'd invited Kara to share Sunday dinner with the family, but she told me she has a prior engagement. I'd love to stay and chat, but I have to keep to my schedule or I won't get back in time to pick up my daughter from her dance lessons." She wiggled her fingers. "I'll call you, Kara. I hope to see you again, Ms. Newell."

"Why do I get the impression that she didn't mean a word she said," Jeannette whispered in Kara's ear.

"It's called being fake," Kara whispered back. "Let's finish up here so we can stay on schedule."

Jeannette cut her eyes at her daughter. "You know you're bad, don't you?"

"I learned it from my mama," she intoned.

Kara and Jeannette left the Cannery with their purchases in a recyclable shopping bag. Haven Creek's town council had recommended business owners replace plastic bags with recyclable ones to offset polluting the island's environment.

Mother and daughter had become teenagers turned loose in a mall with a no-spending limit. Jeannette couldn't make up her mind which size sweet-grass basket she wanted to buy for her sister while Kara sat on a tall stool patiently waiting.

"Kara, please help me out," Jeannette pleaded.

Sliding off the stool, she walked over to the table. "I like the large tray."

"Do you think it would look nice on a coffee table?"

"Mama, stop wondering where Aunt Denise would put it. It's a beautiful piece."

Jeannette turned it over, staring at the price sticker. "I don't know if I want to spend this much for it."

Kara took the exquisitely woven tray from her mother, walked over to the counter, and gave it to the salesclerk. "I'll take this one, and I'd like you to gift wrap it," she said, handing her a credit card.

"Kara!" Jeannette hissed.

"Mama?"

"What is it?"

"You're giving me a headache."

"That's because you need to eat. The only time you get headaches is when you don't eat. What did you eat today?"

Kara rolled her eyes upward. "Can't you

stop being a mother for five minutes?"

Jeannette stood up straight and pulled back her shoulders. "No. Once you become a mother, you'll know exactly what I'm talking about."

"That's not going to happen any time soon." Jeannette moved closer, placing her ear against Kara's chest. "What are you doing?"

"I'm listening to your biological clock. It's getting louder."

"No comment."

Those were the last two words Kara exchanged with Jeannette until they sat at a table for two at Jack's Fish House. They'd had to wait twenty minutes before they were seated because it was Saturday night and the island's date night. She found herself glancing around the crowded restaurant for a glimpse of Jeff. Even if she closed her eyes, she was able to recall every feature of his face, the sound of his mellifluous voice, and his body's clean, masculine scent. What she didn't want to think about was the awesome sight of his magnificent chest or how her body had reacted when he'd kissed her on the beach.

Kara had told her mother Jeff was her friend when she wanted him to be so much more. She didn't think that was possible because on an island as small as Cavanaugh everyone would be in her business, while in New York she didn't know the name of her closest neighbor. The only way she and Jeff could hope for a measure of anonymity would be to go into Charleston.

"I can't believe this menu."

Jeannette's voice had broken into her thoughts. "What about it?"

"It has all of my favorite dishes. I'm beginning to like the Lowcountry."

Kara smiled. She, too, was beginning to like the Low-country *and* Sheriff Hamilton.

●

CHAPTER NINE

Kara was sitting on the porch with her mother when Jeff drove up the live oak alleé. He'd called the house earlier that morning to let them know he would come by at two.

"He's gorgeous," Jeannette whispered when Jeff got out of the car.

"That he is." Kara sighed, like a vapid heroine in the Regency novels she favored.

"Is he married?"

Kara didn't have time to answer when Jeff placed a booted foot on the first stair. Rising to her feet, she extended her hands. "Hello again," she crooned when he towered over her.

Dipping his head, Jeff kissed her cheek. "How are you?"

"I'm well. How are you?"

His dark eyes shimmered like polished jet. "Wonderful." His gaze shifted to Jeannette. He held out his hand, gently easing Jeannette off the cushioned rocker. "Jeff Hamilton, Mrs. Newell."

"It's Jeannette," she insisted, smiling.

Kara watched the dynamics play out between her mother and the sheriff of Cavanaugh Island. Jeannette stared up at Jeff under lowered lashes. The gesture was unequivocally seductive. Was that how she'd looked at Taylor Patton, where a man who'd never had a physical relationship with a woman had succumbed to her subtle seduction? Or was it Taylor who'd initiated making love after four years of a platonic friendship?

If David hadn't requested her presence at the reading of the will, Kara realized she never would've known the circumstances surrounding her birth. She didn't blame her mother or Austin for keeping her paternity a secret for thirty-three years. After all, Jeannette did reach out to Taylor to inform him that he was going to be a father not once, but twice, and she had no recourse but to get on with her life.

Thankfully Austin hadn't rejected the woman who'd promised to save herself for him, but married her, claiming another man's child as his own. Kara may have shared Taylor's DNA, but she doubted whether he could ever be the father Austin was.

Kara's gaze lingered on Jeff's spit-shined boots, black tailored slacks, and a crisp light blue shirt open at the neck. She smiled when she saw the engraved corps belt buckle. Her smile became a full grin when he offered Jeannette his arm and led her off the porch to his grandmother's Toyota Camry.

"Aren't you coming?" Jeannette called out as Jeff seated her in the passenger seat.

Kara locked the front door and then looped her cross-body bag over her chest and picked up a decorative shopping bag off the table. Jeff met her as she made her way off the porch. "Your mother is as pampered as she is beautiful," he said in her ear.

She smiled up at him. "Oh, you noticed."

He nodded, patting her free hand tucked into the bend of his arm. "It's no wonder Taylor couldn't resist her."

Kara had no comeback as Jeff escorted her to the sedan, holding the rear door open and waiting for her to get in. Relaxing against the leather seat, she stared at the back of her mother's head. There was no doubt Jeannette was enjoying herself. Kara thought about their meal the previous night.

Instead of entrées, they'd ordered appetizers at Jack's, allowing them to sample dishes they liked and some that were unfamiliar.

Jeannette did something Kara rarely saw her do. She ordered a beer with her meal. There had always been beer in the house whenever her father came home on leave. The first few days of his leave he would go into the equivalent of a mancave, sink in his favorite chair, grab a beer, and watch sporting events around the clock. He wouldn't even move to eat, asking his wife to bring his meals to him. By day number three, after he'd gone through twenty-four hours of military withdrawal, he emerged from the cave ready to immerse himself into civilian life.

It took only ten minutes to drive from Angels Landing to Jeff's house, door-to-door. Corrine was standing on the porch when Jeff parked alongside the updated two-story house. During her trips throughout the island, Kara had seen homes ranging from those that were one story, built high off the ground, and some with tin roofs to sprawling two-story colonials along private roads where the owners had named their plots. Jeff's house claimed white vinyl siding, dark green shutters, and a wraparound porch.

Not waiting for Jeff to assist her, Kara exited the car and climbed the porch steps. "Thank you for having us, Miss Corrine," she said, kissing the older woman's smooth, scented cheek.

"I want you to remember that you're always welcome here. And you don't have to wait for Jeffrey to invite you."

"I'll be certain to remember that, Miss Corrine." She handed her the shopping bag. "I hope there's something in here you like."

Corrine peered into the bag, smiling. "Who told you I liked onion and chow relish?"

"I haven't lived in New York that long that I've forgotten Southerners love their relishes."

"You're right. Go on in and rest yourself while I meet your mama. It's going to be at least half an hour before we sit down to eat."

Walking into the parlor, Kara inhaled a plethora of mouthwatering aromas. It smelled like Easter, Thanksgiving, and Christmas all rolled into one. There were a few times when she didn't come home for Thanksgiving and Easter, but she'd never missed spending a Christmas in Little Rock since leaving at eighteen.

She sat on a pale pink love seat with green leaves. There was a green one with pink roses facing her. The parlor was intimate, inviting one to come sit and relax. Live plants in painted bowls sat on side tables, and a trio of flowering begonias sat on a runner lining an oak credenza.

Jeff entered the room and sat down beside her. "Gram just found out that she and your mother are sorority sisters."

"That explains the pink and green," she said laughing. "Where did your grandmother go to college?"

"B-CU."

"So she's a Bethune-Cookman Wildcat."

Jeff smiled. "So you're familiar with the Wildcats?"

"B-CU was on my college tour list."

"Where did you finally end up?" Jeff asked.

"Columbia."

He whistled. "Miss Ivy League." He draped an arm over her shoulders. "How long is your mama staying?"

"She says a week."

"How does she like the Lowcountry?"

Shifting slightly, Kara turned to look directly at Jeff. "She really likes it."

"Did you tell her you're staying?"

Kara closed her eyes. When she opened them, she saw Jeff staring at her, an impassive expression freezing his features. Whenever he looked at her like that, she felt as if he'd put up a shield to keep her from getting close. Was this the way it had been with the other women in his past? Show an interest and he'd shut down emotionally?

Don't analyze the man, Kara, the silent voice reminded her. It had been that way with all of the men she met. Within minutes of their introduction, she would begin to analyze his body language and everything that came out of his mouth.

"Yes. Even though she's accepted my rationale, she still doesn't like that I'm living alone."

"Do you live alone in New York?"

"No," she said, shaking her head. "I have a roommate."

"I see her point."

"Why are you taking her side?"

Jeff rubbed several strands of her hair between his fingers. "It's not about taking sides, baby. You have to understand where she's coming from. You're her child, and she has a right to be concerned about you."

"I'm a thirty-three-year-old woman, Jeff. I've lived on my own for the past fifteen years, fifteen years in a city of eight million people. If I can survive in New York City, then I believe I can survive anywhere. There are probably more people living in my

Manhattan high-rise than in all of Angels Landing."

"And doesn't that make you feel safer in Angels Landing?"

"Yes. I'd never leave my door unlocked in New York."

"We do have crime here, but it's basically with teenagers coming from the mainland."

"What about the kids who live here?"

"They know better. Either they'll get the business from me or from their parents. Within days of installing security cameras in the Cove, the tagging of fishermen's boats stopped. Folks in the Creek and Landing don't want cameras because they feel it's an invasion of their privacy, but I know they'll change their tune once there's a rash of break-ins or vandalism."

Kara leaned into Jeff. "Are you saying I should lock my doors during the day?"

Lowering his head, he buried his face in her hair, seemingly inhaling the scent. "I want you to be careful, Kara. Kenny told me about Analeigh showing up at your house. She doesn't drive, so that meant she walked almost a mile to come to see you. Anyone who comes over on the ferry or causeway could do the same. And I'm certain you'd either open your door or talk to them because you don't know who they are. I make it my business and that of my deputies to do foot patrols. This way they get to familiarize themselves with everyone on the island."

"I'll be careful."

"Say it like you mean it, Kara."

Kara rested her hand alongside his face. "I promise I will be very careful."

Jeff kissed her forehead. "That's better."

"Jeffrey, please turn off the stove and plate the chicken."

Kara and Jeff sprang apart like teenagers who'd been caught doing something they weren't supposed to be doing. She met her mother's questioning gaze. Jeannette winked at the same time, a knowing smile softening her mouth, and Kara returned it with one of her own. There were very few things she could hide from her mother, so she'd learned never to lie to her.

She pushed off the love seat. "Show me where I can wash my hands, and I'll help you," she said, following Jeff as he headed toward the half bath off the kitchen.

"Move over," Kara ordered when they crowded into the small space. "You're hogging the sink."

Shifting, Jeff stood behind her and held his hands under the running water. "I need soap."

Kara felt his breath on the nape of her neck and his hardness pulsing against her hips. "Move back."

He fastened his mouth to the side of her neck. "First it's move over, and now it's move back."

"I can feel you, Jeff."

"Now you know what I feel whenever I'm around you."

Lowering her head, she closed her eyes. "Please don't do this to me."

"Do what?"

"You're getting me aroused."

He laughed softly. "Why should I be the only one aroused?"

"My mother and your grandmother are waiting for us."

"To be continued," Jeff whispered.

Five minutes later they sat at the table, passing serving bowls and chatting casually. "How come you didn't pledge a sorority like your mother?" Corrine asked Kara as she handed her a serving bowl.

Jeff took the bowl from her, holding it while she placed a spoonful of cabbage on her plate. "I didn't have time. I was carrying eighteen credits every semester."

Unfolding her napkin, Jeannette placed it on her lap. "You could pledge as a graduate."

Kara stared across the dining room table at her mother. "I don't have time to pledge, Mama."

"You're going to live here, so what's stopping you from finding a Charleston chapter."

"If you were to pledge, which sorority would you choose?" Jeff asked.

She gave him a sidelong glance. When Corrine set the table, she'd sat her and Jeff together while she and Jeannette sat side by side. "I don't know."

"You don't know?" Jeannette and Corrine chorused.

Kara slowly chewed and then swallowed a forkful of chicken. Corrine had prepared a delicious dinner: stewed chicken with dumplings so light and fluffy they melted on the tongue, steamed cabbage, baked sweet potatoes, and corn bread.

"I don't like the pink-and-green combination."

"It's on and poppin' now," Jeff said under his breath.

Jeannette then Corrine launched into a discourse that it wasn't about the colors but the organization. Then each went on to talk about all the notable AKAs and their service projects.

Laughing, Kara put up a hand. "Please

stop. I feel as if I'm sitting under a hot light being interrogated *and* intimidated into confessing to a crime I didn't commit."

"Easy there, baby," Jeff drawled. "Let's not start with the cop jokes."

Kara pressed her shoulder to Jeff's. "Ooooo. Aren't we touchy," she teased.

"No I'm not."

"Let it go, Jeffrey. She's not intimidated. And I think you've finally met your match."

"To be continued," he said, repeating the promise he'd made to Kara in the bathroom.

The conversation shifted to local politics, Corrine recounting what she'd heard about another developer who'd approached several of the Cove's older residents. "Now they're going after folks who don't have any children or grandchildren to look after their property once they die."

Jeff took a swallow of sweet tea. "I don't know why they continue to sniff around the Cove because they know no one is going to sell to them."

"What about Haven Creek?" Kara asked.

Corrine looked directly at her. "They're sixty-forty against the developers. It's a bit different in Angels Landing."

"The last survey put them at seventy-thirty," Jeff added. "And with the Pattons leading the charge that percentage could go higher."

Kara set down her fork. "Why would they want to sell their land? And if they did, where would they go?"

Corrine dabbed the corners of her mouth with her napkin. "I know you haven't been here long, but how much contact have you had with your relatives?"

"Very little."

"You should try and keep it that way."

"Gram!" Jeff chastised.

Corrine waved her hand. "I'm right and you know it, so don't 'Gram' me. Those folks are not right. Ever since Teddy left everything to Taylor, they've been out for revenge."

A warning voice whispered in Kara's head as she recalled the threats directed at her. "Revenge against who?"

"Whoever is the owner of the house."

Jeff placed a hand over Kara's knee under the table. "Gram, you're frightening her."

"There's no need to sugarcoat it, Jeffrey. She needs to hear the truth."

"Is my daughter in some kind of danger?" Jeannette asked.

"No," Jeff said quickly. "Nothing's going to happen to Kara."

Jeannette massaged the back of her neck.

238

"Can you guarantee that, Jeff? Because right now I don't feel very comfortable with the direction of this conversation."

"Yes. I guarantee it," he said with such conviction that everyone at the table looked at him. "Gram, I think it's time Kara hears the truth about her ancestors."

Corrine pushed back her chair, coming to her feet. "Let's go into the sunroom where it's more comfortable."

Kara stood up when Jeff pulled back her chair. "I'll help clear the table."

Corrine shook her head. "Please leave it. I'll do it later. After I tell you about your folks, we'll have dessert and coffee."

Jeff rested a hand at the small of Kara's back when they filed out of the dining room and into the expansive enclosed back porch. The space reminded her of the garden room at Angels Landing.

Corrine sat in an easy chair and rested her feet on the ottoman. She waited until everyone was seated, then said, "People have always thought of the Pattons as Low-country royalty but the griots tell a much different story. They told stories long before they were written down, passed down from one to another. It began back in 1830–something when Shipley Patton bought land

239

here to start up a rice plantation. He was already growing cotton on the mainland but decided Carolina Gold was much more profitable. He was an architect by profession and drew up plans for what would become the grandest house on the island, calling it Angels Landing. Meanwhile he had the swamps drained so he could plant his rice, Sea Island cotton, and indigo. Shipley was an anomaly in his day because all his skilled laborers were free blacks. It took two years to complete the house and furnish it. He moved his family from what is now Goose Creek, and he and his wife hosted a lavish ball, inviting people from the mainland.

"That summer he lost his wife and two daughters to swamp fever. After that he always took his two remaining sons back to the mainland during the summers. A year later he remarried, and his second wife eventually gave him two sons and four daughters. Even though dueling was outlawed, Shipley challenged another planter to a duel. The man supposedly had spread a rumor that Shipley's youngest son wasn't his and the boy's father was a mulatto slave. Unfortunately Shipley's gun jammed, and he was mortally wounded. It took him two weeks to die."

Kara was barely able to control the gasp that escaped her. "Was he the child of a mulatto?"

"The slaves said yes while his wife denied it. Fortunately for her, Oakes looked more white than black. Mrs. Patton closed up the house and moved her children to Charleston to be closer to her parents. Years later a smallpox epidemic swept through the Low-country, and all of the Pattons except Oakes and his half sister were among the many casualties. She joined a convent, and Oakes inherited everything.

"Oakes eventually married a local girl who refused to move to the island because she feared coming down with swamp fever. She hosted glittering parties while he entertained himself at Angels Landing when he made nightly visits to the slave village. He fathered a lot of black children, but when he saw a slave woman from a neighboring plantation, he knew he had to have her. Word was he paid nearly five thousand dollars for her, an unheard-of sum during that time. Once the woman with whom he'd found himself enthralled told him she was pregnant, he moved her into the main house and did something most slaveholders refused to do. He freed her children on their first birthday."

Kara closed her eyes for several seconds. "Why did he free her children when he hadn't freed the others?"

"Wasn't it obvious, Kara? He was in love with her. Their relationship was scandalous because they were living together as husband and wife. Most married men didn't bring their mistresses into their homes."

"How many children did they have?"

"It was either three or four. Everything changed when word got back to his wife, and she'd become the laughingstock of Lowcountry society. And what made it even worse to Rebecca Patton was that he'd refused to sleep with her and give her a child.

"Rebecca waited until her husband had sailed to England to meet with a cotton broker; then she paid several men to bring her to Angels Landing. Waiting until nightfall, she had them douse the house with a flammable liquid and then set it afire. Everyone inside the house died from smoke inhalation. Rebecca believed she'd wiped out her husband's mistress and his bastards, but there was one child who'd escaped the carnage. Jacob was a two-year-old boy who was prone to sleepwalking. That night he'd crawled out of his crib and out of the house. The next morning he was found sleeping under a tree. I'd heard that my great-great-great-grandmother took Jacob in, hiding him in case Rebecca would come back to kill him, too. When Oakes returned to find his home damaged by fire and his mistress and children dead, he abandoned the property and never returned to Angels Landing."

Jeannette held her throat. "What happened to Rebecca?"

A slow smile spread over Corrine's face, a smile so much like Jeff's. "What's the expression about revenge best served cold? Well, Rebecca Patton got hers served hot. Apparently she'd gotten up one night, lit a candle, and went downstairs to sit on the porch because she'd become an insomniac. She probably tripped, and the lighted candle landed on her nightdress, and she went up in flames. By the time house servants heard her screams, she'd been burned over half her body."

"Did she die?" Kara asked.

"The Lord wasn't that merciful. She recovered from the burns, but never left the house because of the scars to her hands, face, and neck. One day she took an overdose of laudanum and never woke up. Oakes started drinking, and he gambled away Angels Landing. Once word reached the island that Becky was dead, Oakes was told that his youngest child had survived the fire. He had someone retrieve the boy, and they went to live in Europe for several years. Jacob had trained to be a doctor at the University of Edinburgh, and once he and his father returned to the States after the Civil War, Jacob was fully fluent in French, Italian, and Spanish.

"Unlike his father, Jacob couldn't pass into the white race, so he lived in Charleston as a free man of color. However, he was treated with polite respect because he was a doctor. After the war, rice production became too expensive, and soon, most plantations on the Sea Islands fell into bankruptcy and were sold off to new owners. Jacob's driving ambition had been to make enough money to buy the house where he'd been born and restore it."

"Did he?" Kara had asked yet another question.

"He couldn't do it directly because antiblack sentiment was rampant throughout the South, and the Klan had begun burning the homes, schools, and churches of former slaves. He finally convinced his father to negotiate the sale for him. Oakes agreed, and once again Angels Landing belonged to a Patton. Jacob relocated his practice to the island, and the folks here had their first colored doctor. He lived in one of the outbuildings while the main house was being renovated. He married a Gullah woman from Edisto Island, and they had eight children, six that lived to adulthood. I remember the old folks talking about how the Pattons, whether dark or light, all had Oakes's gray eyes, and in each succeeding generation they had at least one or two children who'd die young. Some say Rebecca put a curse on her husband's children and his children's children."

Jeff shook his head. "Come on, Gram. That's just superstitious nonsense."

"Is it, Jeffrey?" Corrine asked. "Taylor's sister wasn't thirty when she died from that brain tumor." She turned to Kara. "It's not the men in the family, but the women they marry who turn into villainesses. Cornelius was a gentle soul, but very few people could stand Theodora. Once she became Mrs. Patton you'd think she was the queen of England. She could never keep any help because she systematically bullied them. The only ones who stayed were Willie and Iris Todd.

"She practically destroyed her children when she pitted one against the other. Taylor had become her favorite, and as a result his siblings hated him. He'd tried reaching out to them, but they turned their backs on him. The only time they did come together was when it came time for them to make a decision on whether to put Teddy in a nursing home. That's when it became unanimous because they were glad to be rid of her. Taylor was the only one to visit her, and she rewarded him when she left him everything in her will: house, land, and money.

"His brothers and sisters talked about him as if they didn't share blood, so Taylor withdrew from them completely. He'd put the word out that if any of them stepped foot on his property, he would shoot them on sight for trespassing. I don't believe they were notified of his death until after he was cremated and his ashes were scattered in the ocean. Now you know the story of your people. Their entire lives were shrouded in secrets, lies, illegitimate babies, arson, and murder — all the ingredients for a very interesting novel. I only tell you this because you're not going to know where you're going if you don't know where you've come from."

"Why don't you write the novel, Gram?"

Corrine's mouth tightened into a thin line as she glared at her grandson. "It's not my place to presume to write about someone else's people. It's the past, so let sleeping dogs lie."

Hours later Kara stood on the porch, staring out at the encroaching darkness. It was only now that she was able to react to Corrine's account of her biological father's family.

"Lives . . . shrouded in secrets, lies, illegitimate babies." It was as if Corrine was talking about her. She'd lived more than three decades believing one man was her father when he wasn't. Her mother had lied by omission because she had no intention of telling her Taylor Patton was her biological father if he hadn't written her into his will. And last but certainly not least, illegitimate babies. If Austin hadn't married Jeannette, then Kara would've become one of an endless list of babies out of wedlock. In essence her entire life had been a lie. This is not to say she didn't have a wonderful childhood, but if she couldn't trust her own mother, then who could she trust?

"Kara?"

Her eyelids fluttered. Kara had been so deep in thought that she hadn't heard her mother come up behind her. "Yes, Mama?"

"It's after midnight."

"I know."

"Don't you think it's time you go to bed?"

She shook her head. "I can't sleep."

"Is it because of what Corrine told you this afternoon?"

"Yes," she admitted. "It was and still is a lot to take in."

Jeannette took a step and put her arms around her daughter's waist. "What's bothering you, baby?"

Kara didn't know why, but she felt like crying. "Everything."

"Do you want to talk about it?"

She shook her head. "No, because what you want to talk about is something we should've discussed a long time ago. You say you love me, but it's apparent you didn't love me enough to trust me with your tainted little secret. Did you actually believe I would've loved you or Daddy any less if you'd told me about Taylor? I talk to my clients about trust issues, and right now I'm having a bit of my own."

"Why now, Kara? You didn't seem that upset this morning when I told you about Taylor."

"I guess it's taken a while to sink in."

Jeannette made a sound that came from the back of her throat. "You wouldn't be like this if Corrine hadn't filled your head with all that talk about people who have nothing to do with you."

Kara pushed her mother's arms down, turning around and looking at her. "That's where you're wrong. They have everything to do with me. You may not share blood with the Pattons, but I do. I'm not proud of some of the things they've done, but they are still my family."

"A week ago you didn't know these people existed!" Jeannette shouted, her voice carrying easily in the silent night.

"Don't shift the blame, Mama. I should've known about them as soon as I was old enough to understand that I had another family. What were you afraid of? That I would judge you for getting pregnant from one man when you were practically engaged to another?"

Jeannette ran her fingers through her hair, pushing feathered bangs off her forehead. "Now that I look back, I realize not telling you was a mistake, but I thought it was best because I didn't want to confuse you. You're angry and you have every right to be, but I did it because I wanted to protect you."

"Protect me from what, Mama? The truth?"

"No, baby. I wanted to protect you from the ugliness that's so insidious to the Pattons. Corrine said a lot of things about Taylor's family I didn't know. But there were other things I did know, and that's why I wanted to protect you from them. They're no better than a pit of vipers turning on themselves. However, you seem so hell-bent on living here among them when it's obvious they would prefer to see you gone."

"I'm not afraid of them. If they expect me to pack my bags and leave, then they don't know who I am. One thing I learned having a marine as a father is that they never ran and never will. I'm going to stay and do what I have to do."

"Do you intend to shoot them if they come on your property like Taylor threatened to do?"

Kara couldn't help but smile. Austin had taught her how to shoot the year she turned thirteen. The recoil from the automatic had nearly knocked her off her feet, but after he'd shown her the two-hand grip, she was proficient enough to hit her target.

"I would if I could find Taylor's gun. If I have any problems with the Pattons, then I'll report it to the sheriff's office."

"What about an emergency, Kara? Do you think the sheriff can get to your place in three minutes or less?"

"If Jeff can't, then one of his deputies can.

The deputies live in each town, so response time will be less than three minutes."

"The only thing I'm going to say before I go inside is be careful."

A nervous smile trembled over Kara's mouth. "I will." She moved closer and kissed Jeannette. "Good night, Mama."

Jeannette hugged her as if she feared she would disappear in front of her eyes. "Good night, baby."

Kara waited for her mother to retreat inside the house before she walked over and sat on a rocker. Back and forth, back and forth. She rocked until she felt herself relaxing. Then she rocked some more until her eyelids started to droop. Then something woke her. Sitting up straight, she squinted in the darkness as the shape of a vehicle came closer.

Pushing to her feet, she stood in a corner of the porch to make herself a smaller target. A smile parted her lips when she recognized the Jeep, then the man who stepped out.

"What are you doing here?"

Jeff placed a foot on the first stair. "I'm out on patrol. I didn't expect to see you up this late."

Kara rested a hand on the column, its coolness seeping into her palm. "I'm glad

you drove up because I was falling asleep."
He mounted two more steps until his head
was level with hers.

"Go inside, Kara, and don't forget to lock
the door."

She leaned close enough for his moist
breath to feather over her mouth. "I'd like
to reciprocate and invite you and Miss Corrine to dinner whenever you have a day off."

"Are you catering it?"

Kara pulled back. "No. I'm going to
cook."

"You can cook?" he teased.

"You can go home now."

Cradling her face, Jeff brushed a kiss over
her parted lips. "Go inside and lock the
door."

Easing back she affected a snappy salute.
"Yes, captain!"

Jeff's hand cupped her hip, holding her
captive. "You're pushing it."

Kara rested her hand over his. "Good
night, Jeff."

Tightening his hold, he cupped the back
of her head and slanted his mouth over hers,
stealing her breath away. It ended as quickly
as it'd begun. "Good night, Kara."

With her mouth burning, knees shaking,
and her heated blood racing through her
body, Kara managed to make her way to

the door before she begged Jeff to make love to her. She didn't know what it was about him that elicited a desperate need to lie with him.

She opened, closed, and locked the door like an automaton. Jeff had come at the wrong time to check on her, or she'd picked the wrong time to sit outside. Now she would go to bed aroused, remembering Jeff's confession of his own arousal.

Crossing her legs at the knees, she waited for her traitorous body to return to normal. Kara knew she and Jeff had to stop — stop the sexual teasing before they embarked on something or a situation that could prove disastrous, at least for her. She'd never been able to engage in a physical relationship and remain emotionally detached. She had never learned to love with her head and not her heart.

Maybe, she thought, it was time she learned.

CHAPTER TEN

Jeff sat opposite Spencer White, the mayor of Sanctuary Cove, acknowledging him with an imperceptible nod. He, not Spencer, would chair the session. When Spencer set up the meeting with the mayors of Angels Landing and Haven Creek, the two men expressed a reluctance to attend because they had always felt like the Cove's stepchildren. Whenever tourists came to Cavanaugh Island, it was the Cove that took in the lion's share of tourist revenue. Lacing his fingers together on the conference table, Jeff curbed the urge to fist his hands and reveal his frustration. "Don't you think your constituents would like to hear what I propose before you preclude to speak for them?" he asked Harlan Patton.

Harlan's hazel eyes narrowed as he leaned forward. "I read Spencer's memo, and I speak for my constituents."

Jeff smiled at the man who was a masculine version of Kara. "No, you don't. You speak for yourself, Harlan."

"It's Mayor Patton to you, Sheriff Hamilton."

Spencer White, an attorney with movie star looks, brought his palm down on the table. "Enough, Harlan! We're here not to attack one another, but to come together for the good of the island. Jeff didn't spend three days in Columbia with more than two hundred other law enforcement officers for you to blow him off."

Haven Creek's mayor, Douglas Rosen, nodded. "Spencer's right. I want to hear more about the governor's small-town crime prevention initiative."

Jeff nodded to the portly man with a thinning pate. Douglas, a direct descendant of Thomas Cavanaugh, the pirate that had given the island its name, was a retired FBI forensic analyst. "Thank you, Doug." He directed his attention to Harlan again. "Perhaps, it's because you're the only mayor on Cavanaugh Island lacking law enforcement experience that you're opposed to installing security cameras in Angels Landing. You've seen the cameras in the Cove's downtown area and know they're not that conspicuous. They would be even less conspicuous in the Landing because it's more densely forested. But just knowing they're there should be enough to deter burglaries."

"Where would you put the cameras?" Harlan asked.

"Along all the roads, both public and private."

"Which means you'll see everyone coming and going."

Jeff leaned back in his chair. "Do you see that as a problem, Harlan?"

"Do you think folks want Big Brother spying on them?"

"Only if they have something to hide," Jeff countered. "Not only would my deputies spend less time driving around on patrol, but we would also save on fuel."

"I'm in agreement with Jeff," Douglas said. "Fuel costs for our official vehicles this past year were outrageous."

Spencer nodded in agreement. "It's the same in the Cove."

Picking up a pencil, Jeff drew interlocking circles on a pad. "That's because the Creek and the Cove have to cover fire calls for the Landing because they still don't have a fire department. Perhaps, Harlan, it's time the residents of Angels Landing share in the cost of the other two towns responding to fires and medical emergencies."

A rush of color suffused Harlan's face. "Two years ago Spencer and Doug agreed, in a show of good faith, to have their volunteer fire departments cover the Landing because it would be cost-effective rather than erecting a building and having to buy a pumper truck."

Jeff knew it was time to proverbially cut Harlan off at the knees. "That agreement is due to expire before the end of the year, and I suggest you revise your projected budget to include a line for fire prevention, safety, and emergency services."

Harlan's gaze shifted from Jeff to Spencer and Douglas, then back to Jeff. "Are you really going to leave the residents of the Landing without access to a fire department?"

Crossing his arms over his chest, Jeff slowly shook his head. "No, Harlan. I don't have the authority to make that determination. But you can't have it both ways. Last year you saved money by not having to pay the salary and benefits of a full-time sheriff while you managed not to raise property taxes because you don't have a fire department. The security cameras and the command center won't cost us anything. Fortunately, Spencer had the wherewithal to apply for a grant to offset the expense of installing and maintaining it."

Harlan's jaw tightened. "I don't want our people spied on."

The frustration Jeff felt whenever he met with the mayor of Angels Landing escalated. "What the hell do you have to hide, Patton! You keep talking about *'our people'* when I suspect it's you. I shouldn't have to remind you there's crime on Cavanaugh Island. And statistics show there are more domestic situations, vehicle infractions, and 911 calls from Angels Landing than the Cove and Creek combined. My part-time deputies are hardly part-time when they have to work twelve-hour shifts three days a week."

Doug rested a hand on Harlan's shoulder. "Pick your battles, Patton. When your people hear that cameras are a deterrent to crime in the Cove and the Creek and that Spencer and I decided not to renew the fire department agreement, they're going to vote you out of office. And I shouldn't have to remind you that the Landing has the highest property taxes on the island because you don't want a business district."

Harlan shook off the hand. "Is that all you have? Threats and intimidation?"

Jeff blew out a breath. "You can't continue to hide behind the privacy pretext. Excuse me, gentlemen, but I'm still on duty." He rose in one fluid motion, his lethal gaze pinning Kara's cousin to his seat. "I'll see you around, Patton."

"I guess you will whenever you come sniffing around Kara. You think I don't know about your so-called night runs when you supposedly are checking up on her. How is she, Jeff? Is the little schemer a screamer or —" The words were snatched from Harlan's open mouth when Jeff reached across the table and slapped him with an open hand.

In a movement too quick for the eye to follow, Jeff grabbed the front of Harlan's shirt, pulling him half on and half off the table. "If I ever hear something like that come out of that filthy mouth again, I will hit you again. And next time, it won't be a bitch-slap." He released Harlan as if he were throwing away a soiled garment.

"You saw that!" Harlan gasped, pressing his hand to the left side of his face. "I want him arrested for assault."

Spencer stood up, Douglas rising with him. "I didn't see anything. Did you, Doug?"

The forensic analyst shook his head. "Sorry, Harlan, but you must be hallucinating." The three men burst into laughter when Harlan raced out of the office. Doug wiped the tears from his eyes. "Jeff, Spencer, I'd love to stay and talk, but I have to meet my brother who's been bitchin' and moanin' about losing his only female architect because he's too cheap to pay her what she's worth. It would serve him right if she opened her own office next door and gave him some serious competition."

"I'm not going to touch that," Jeff remarked.

Doug inclined his head. "Mayor, sheriff. It's always a pleasure." He shook hands with Spencer and Jeff, then left the room.

Walking over to the door, Spencer closed it, turning to face Jeff. "I know there's always been bad blood between you two. Just don't be surprised if Harlan goes to the Charleston PD to file an assault charge. And if I'm called as a witness, I'll have to tell the truth. I can't afford to risk jeopardizing my license to practice if I'm charged with perjury."

"Don't worry about it, Spencer. I don't think Harlan's going to risk his so-called playboy reputation when he admits I slapped him like he was a girl."

"You're probably right. Harlan's all about image. But does he know something I don't about you and Taylor's daughter?"

Jeff told the mayor about his cousin's phone call following the reading of Taylor's will. "Just say the Pattons were less than hospitable in welcoming their new cousin."

"They've always been a strange lot, Jeff. Collectively they have more money than any family on the island, but what I don't understand is their competing with one another."

"Crabs in a barrel, Spencer. That's the only way to describe them." Picking up his baseball cap, Jeff put it on. "When can I expect to see my new office furniture?"

"I'll have my secretary call the vendor, then get back to you. Now that we have the grant, you and men will be expected to wear uniforms."

Jeff wanted to remind Spencer that he'd worn a uniform for more than half his life. Getting his deputies to wear one when on duty was another matter. He left the conference room, nodding and smiling at the mayor's administrative assistant. He knew slapping Harlan went against his training, but if he'd hit the potty-mouthed man the way he truly wanted, then Harlan would've wound up with either a broken jaw or, worse, a broken neck.

He and Harlan had never gotten along. As a schoolboy Harlan had put the *b* in bully. Jeff had permitted Harlan to intimidate him because of his grandmother's warning that intelligent people used their brains instead of their fists to settle an argument. It only stopped once they'd entered high school. Jeff had joined the football team, and at six four and weighing close to two hundred pounds, he'd become a human wrecking machine, known for setting a school record by sacking opposing teams' quarterbacks — a record that still stood. Not only was he strong, but he was also very fast.

Instead of taking the tunnel connecting the town hall with the court and the station house, he walked out into the bright sunlight. He needed to get outdoors and clear his head. Reaching for his cell, he hit speed dial. "Winnie, Jeff. I just left Mayor White's office. I'm going down to the Muffin Corner. Do you want me to bring something back for you? . . . Today, Winnie," he told his clerk when she changed her mind for the third time.

"Can you stop at the supermarket deli and bring me back a tuna salad on a bed of lettuce. Please ask them if it's fresh. If not, then I'll take chicken salad on a bed of lettuce. And make certain they give you crackers and a pickle."

Jeff exhaled an audible sigh. "Aren't you going to give me a third choice, Winnie?"

"You must be feeling good today."

"Why would you say that?"

"Because you're trying to be a comedian. And I must say not a very good one."

He headed in the direction of Main Street. "I'll see you later."

Jeff knew his hitting Harlan had everything to do with Kara and not because he still harbored a grudge against a man who'd made his boyhood a living hell. Although each town had its own elementary-middle school, half the students from the Landing were bused to the Creek and the other half to the Cove when their school burned to the ground from an electrical fire. It'd taken two years for it to be rebuilt. The construction had been delayed for almost a year when the school board had to decide on whether it should be a brick or wooden structure. In the end it was stucco.

It'd been the worst two years of his life, but it taught Jeff something about himself he hadn't known he had: extraordinary self-control. At least he had until Harlan opened his mouth to mention Kara. Harlan hadn't known Jeff to retaliate with a physical attack. He could rationalize and tell himself that it was payback for past bullying, but he would be lying to himself.

It had everything to do with Kara and his growing feelings for her. It'd been so easy for him to use David's warning as an excuse to see her. But how long would he be able to continue in that vein before she saw through the ruse. The more he saw Kara, the more he wanted to be with her. She turned him on, made him want to make love to her, and he couldn't remember when he'd met a woman whose intense appeal triggered a lust he found impossible to ignore. She was easy to talk to, made him laugh because there were times when he took himself and life much too seriously. Kara understood his dedication to his job as island sheriff and the sacrifices he'd made to care for his grandmother.

Jeff was aware that resigning his commission and returning to Sanctuary Cove had changed him. In the past his grandmother had taken care of him, but now it was his turn to take care of her. At that time the military had become his extended family, the men under his command his brothers in arms, and his dedication to his country and corps unwavering.

Then there were his past relationships; they were never smooth or easy. The women complained they would've preferred competing with another woman for love and affection, not his career. He was also aware that his past relationships hadn't worked out because he feared loving and losing.

Resigning his commission and moving back to the Cove was one of the easiest decisions he'd ever made in his life. It'd become a case of no contest. His grandmother's heart attack had become a reality check that he could lose her like he'd lost his mother, and he intended to hold onto Corrine Hamilton for as long as he could.

A smile tilted the corners of his mouth when he thought of Kara. There was something about her that had slipped under his emotional radar where he felt the need to protect her, too. Harlan's outburst and his distasteful reference as to her moral character spoke volumes, and if the other Pattons felt the same as Harlan, then Kara would fare no better than her father. They'd banded together for a common cause: greed.

"Good afternoon, Jeff."

He waved to the elderly man standing in the doorway to the liquor store. "Good afternoon, Mr. Washington. How's the family?" he asked slowing his stride.

"Everybody's good. Praise the Lord. I want to tell you that those folks who want to buy us out are back. One of them offered my brother more money than he'd ever made in his life to sell his house."

Jeff stared at the man who'd served with

valor during World War II. "What did he tell them?"

"Something I can't repeat in public. But it wasn't nice. Why should he sell his house and land to a stranger when he can save it for his grandchildren? His grandbaby girl just got married, and she and her new husband are trying to buy a house, but the bank wants so much money down. Harry told them they could move in with him."

"Are they going to take him up on his offer?"

"Yup."

Jeff smiled. "Good for them. We need more young folks living here. Meanwhile, tell your brother stay strong. And you stay well, Mr. Washington."

"You, too."

Jeff hadn't realized how much he'd missed Cavanaugh Island until he'd returned — this time to stay. He still did police work but at a much slower, more laid-back pace. The crime on the island was something he could control, and if it reached the courts, then a stern warning from the judge, a fine, or a couple of nights in jail usually was a deterrent for the defendant not to repeat the offense.

Most cities in the country had surveillance cameras to protect their citizens and to make police work easier. Living on the island had led many of the residents to believe they were immune to a lot of the big-city social ills, but Jeff knew otherwise. Unlike his predecessor he'd begun the practice of foot patrols to reacquaint himself with the townspeople and gain their trust. He'd taken an oath to protect and serve, and he wanted everyone who lived on the island to know that he was there solely for that purpose.

What he or Spencer hadn't revealed to the mayors of Angels Landing and Haven Creek was an increase in the number of residents that were approached with offers for them to sell their land. Installing the security cameras would monitor the comings and goings of those who were not permanent island residents. Everyone was aware that those in Angels Landing wanted to sell out while Haven Creek was split evenly.

Sanctuary Cove had become the only holdout. Several had called to say they believed they were being threatened, while others had felt intimidated. Jeff couldn't stop the developers from coming to the island or even canvassing potential clients, but what he wouldn't tolerate was their scare tactics to force residents to sell their property.

He turned off Main Street and onto Moss Alley, waving to Deborah as she adjusted the bookstore's window blinds. Several doors down from the Parlor he saw workmen inside a vacant storefront. A year ago there had been enough vacant stores in the downtown business district to count on both hands. Now there were less than six. It was apparent the Cove was recovering from the downturn in the economy.

Jeff walked into the Muffin Corner. The smell of brewing coffee and sweet breads was intoxicating. Mabel Kelly came from behind the counter to hug him. He kissed her cheek. "Where have you been hiding yourself? When I asked Lester about you, he said you'd run off with another man."

Pulling back, Mabel gave him her trademark gap-toothed smile. Her braided hair was covered with a black-and-white pin-striped bandana. "I don't think so. There's no way I'd give up my Lester for all the oil in Saudi Arabia and the money in Dubai. I took a couple of weeks off to go up to Atlanta to help my sister with her new baby. She had a C-section and unfortunately had complications. How's life treating you, Jeff?"

"Life is good."

"How's Miss Corrine?"

"She's good."

Mabel stared up at him. "Do you think she would like a little dog?"

Jeff shook his head. "Unfortunately, no. My grandmother is not equipped to run after a dog. Right now, the doctor doesn't want her climbing stairs. What's up with the dog?"

"My sister is a dog breeder and she gave me a little Yorkshire terrier. He's adorable, Jeff, and it's a shame I have to leave him home all day. I want to give him to someone who has the time to take care of him. He's had all his shots, he's housebroken, and he responds to his name."

"What's his name?"

"Oliver."

Jeff twisted his mouth. "That sounds a little wimpy."

"He's a little dog. Do you know someone who might give him a good home?"

"Don't give him away until I ask around. I'd like a large container of my usual."

"What about something sweet, Jeff?" Mabel asked when she walked over to the commercial espresso coffee-maker.

He peered into the showcase with trays of tarts, cookies, brownies, and mini-doughnuts. "What's the special for the day?"

Mabel added a generous amount of cream to the coffee. "It was apple crumb cake, but

269

it sold out before eleven."

"What do you recommend?"

"The doughnuts are always good." She held up a hand. "It's not because you're a cop, Jeff."

"No harm done, Mabel. Give me a dozen. I'll give them to the staff."

"By the way, I'm sure you heard about the dude going around bugging folks about selling their homes. Every spring and summer the vultures come and roost. When are they going to give it up?"

"I don't know, Mabel. They'll continue to come until everyone on the island is of like mind. If we stand united, then maybe they'll get the message."

He paid for his purchases, then retraced his steps, stopping at the supermarket deli for Winnie's lunch.

When Jeff returned to the station, Winnie Powell glanced up from working on a crossword puzzle. "A tuna salad on a bed of lettuce with crackers and a pickle for the boss, and doughnuts for the staff," he teased.

Winnie blushed, her cheeks turning pink. "Are you ever going to let me live that down?"

He winked at her. "Never." Before he'd taken over as sheriff, Jeff had overheard Winnie telling someone on the phone that

270

she'd run the police station for more than twenty years, and she would continue to run it no matter who the sheriff was. "I'm going to be in the break room."

Jeff drank his coffee, then lay on the sofa to relax. He hadn't slept well the past two nights; he'd found himself tossing and turning as the sounds and images of war came back vividly, never allowing him to return to sleep. He'd gotten out of bed, went down to the front porch, and sat there until the sun came up. He was still there when his grandmother woke. She'd asked him what time he had to go on duty, and when he told her, she suggested he try and get a few hours of sleep and that she would wake him later. The nightmares didn't come as frequently as they had in the past, but they were still there.

He'd just closed his eyes when he heard Winnie calling his name. "What is it?"

"I just got a call from a Jeannette Newell. She said there's someone out at Angels Landing trying to talk her daughter into selling her house."

Jeff sprang up like a jack-in-the-box, reached for the small two-way radio and gun belt. "Call her back and let her know I'm on my way."

■ ■ ■ ■

Kara opened the door to find a conservatively dressed young black man standing on the porch. His blue blazer; buttoned-down light blue shirt; red, white, and blue striped tie; gray flannel slacks, and black slip-ons were prep school chic. The only thing missing was a pair of glasses.

Her gaze lingered on his pleasant features. "Yes?"

"I'm looking for a Ms. Kara Newell."

Nice voice, she thought. "Who's asking?"

"Porter Caldwell."

"I'm afraid I don't know a Porter Caldwell."

His eyebrows shot up. "You're Kara Newell?"

She nodded. "Yes, I am. Why are you looking for me?"

Porter gestured to the half-opened door. "Can we go inside and talk?"

"I'm sorry, but I'm not in the habit of inviting strangers into my home. It comes from living in New York," Kara added quickly. "Would you mind if we sit here on the porch?"

Porter recovered quickly. "Of course not." He moved over and pulled out a chair, waiting for her to sit before sitting across from her. He stared out at the allée of live oak trees. "What a magnificent view."

Kara noticed the direction of his gaze. She didn't think she would ever get used to seeing the century-old trees forming a natural canopy over the road leading up to the house. "It is. Mr. Caldwell, what exactly do you want to talk about?"

Crossing one leg over the opposite knee, Porter stared at the young woman. "Please call me Porter. Mr. Caldwell sounds so formal. I hope you don't mind if I call you Kara."

"Not at all." Kara thought of Porter, as he wanted to be called, as a throwback to men who epitomized the term Southern gentleman. "Before we begin, I'd like to know how you've come to know my name and where I live."

"I'm here on the island looking to purchase property, and someone told me you might be interested in selling."

A slight frown appeared between her eyes. "Who told you that?"

"I don't remember. But you do have a magnificent home. It's obvious it needs some work, and there's no doubt it will be spectacular after the repairs are completed."

Kara leaned forward. "Who do you represent, Mr. Caldwell?"

"Excuse me?"

She smiled, the gesture not reaching her eyes. "I do believe you heard me, Mr. Caldwell. I'm asking who sent you to see me."

He pulled his shoulders back. "No one sent me. I told you I'm looking to purchase property on Cavanaugh Island, and I happen to love old houses."

Kara stared at the rose-pink polish on her toes, paying him no attention, noticing a chip on the big toe of her right foot. She'd missed her regularly scheduled mani-pedi back in New York. She looked up. "Do you have any idea how much this house is worth?"

Porter gave her a direct stare. "I do."

"If I threw out a figure, would you be willing to match it?"

He nodded. "Throw it out."

"Three million. And that doesn't include the furnishings." Kara was surprised that his impassive expression did not change when she'd said the first thing that had come to her mind. "Five million with the furnishings. And that's only a conservative figure because I don't have an updated appraisal."

"That's a little steep for my wallet, but if

you exclude the furnishings, then it may be doable."

"Are you saying that you can give me a bank check like yesterday if I decided to sell you my home?"

"That's exactly what I'm saying."

"If you don't mind answering another question, I'd like to know how many people would live in this house if I sold it to you. Because right now I'm the only one living in a twenty-room slightly dilapidated mansion in South Carolina Lowcountry."

"There will be my brother, his fiancée, and myself."

"Are you aware that Angels Landing is listed as privately owned on the National Register of Historic Places and the property on which it sits is a US National Historic Landmark District?"

He whistled through his teeth. "I wasn't aware of those facts."

Kara wanted to tell the young man that she wasn't as gullible as she appeared. If living in New York had taught her anything, it was that hustlers came in all colors, sizes, and manners of dress. "Do you really think I would sell something so valuable for even ten million?"

He wouldn't meet her eyes. "Hypothetically, if you were to sell everything, what would be your asking price?"

"Five hundred million. And that includes the two thousand acres and everything on it."

"A half billion dollars! No property is worth that."

Kara smiled. "That's where you're wrong, Porter. It's worth that and more to developers who plan to turn it into a billionaire's playground. Hypothetically," she drawled, "they could build five thousand-square-foot condos and sell them for five million a pop, and poof, they've recouped most of their money. Then don't forget the golf course fees and country club memberships. That should bring in another cool half billion a year. Mr. Porter Caldwell, just because I speak a little slow that doesn't mean I'm slow up here." She tapped her forehead.

"You're wrong, Kara," Porter said quickly.

She decided to try another approach. "I hope I'm wrong. Leave me your business card, and I'll seriously think about your offer."

Opening his jacket, Porter reached inside his breast pocket, then patted his pants pockets. "I seem to have forgotten my cards. May I set up an appointment to see you again? I promise I'll have my cards."

"Can you go and pick them up now?"

"Today?" he asked.

"Yes, today."

Porter raised his arm and stared at his watch. "That may pose a problem because I have an early dinner meeting." Kara stood up, he rising with her. "Perhaps we can get together again tomorrow?"

"What makes you think I'm going to change my mind?"

He leaned closer. "I was hoping you would change your mind."

"Only if you meet my price."

"What if we meet over dinner? I know a wonderful little intimate restaurant on James Island that serves the most incredible seafood in the Lowcountry."

Kara couldn't wrap her head around the notion that a man she hadn't known fifteen minutes ago had just asked her out to dinner. Did he actually believe he could turn on the charm, and she would be so impressed that she would sign on the dotted line?

"I'm sorry, Porter. That's not possible."

"Why not?"

"Why not?" she repeated. "Isn't it obvious?"

"What is obvious is that I like you, and I'd like to see you again."

Kara didn't know whether to laugh in his

face or turn around and walk back into the house and slam the door for dramatic effect. They stared at each other, the seconds becoming a full minute. Then Kara saw movement out of the corner of her eye. Her mother was standing in the doorway watching the exchange, and she wondered how long she'd stood there and how much she'd heard. The sound of an approaching vehicle caught her attention, and Kara turned to find someone speeding up the path to the house.

"What I'd like is for you to leave now."

She walked barefoot down the steps at the same time Jeff stepped out of the Jeep. He extended his arms, and she went into his embrace. "How did you know?"

"Your mama called me. She thought you could use some help."

Kara had her answer. It was apparent her mother had eavesdropped on their conversation. "Please get him to leave," she whispered in Jeff's ear when he dipped his head.

"Did he hurt you?"

"No, but he's annoying."

Jeff kissed her forehead. "Work with me, baby."

With his muscular arm around her waist, Kara climbed the stairs to the porch. "Porter, Sheriff Hamilton. Sweetheart, this is

Porter Caldwell. He's interested in buying the house, but I told him he couldn't afford it."

"Isn't that just like a woman," Jeff drawled, shaking his head. "Why do they always presume to make decisions for us? Did she ask you if you could afford it, *son?*"

Porter's face brightened as if he'd just discovered an ally. "No, she didn't."

Jeff squinted at Kara. "Baby, didn't I tell you about that?"

She was hard-pressed not to laugh. "Yes, you did, but I figured he wasn't serious because he doesn't even have a business card."

"I . . . I forgot my cards, but I offered —" Porter stammered nervously.

"You offered what?" Jeff asked when Porter didn't finish his statement.

"I'd offered to take your girlfriend out to dinner so we could discuss it."

"He wants to take me to James Island for incredible seafood," Kara added innocently when Jeff glared at Porter as if he was ready to attack the man.

It was obvious the developers had sent a boy to do a man's job. Dawn had given her an overview of how neighborhoods, particularly those in New York City, were changed dramatically when they were gentrified.

When tenants moved out of rent-controlled or stabilized apartments, landlords allowed them to remain vacant along with a gradual decrease in services. The remaining tenants would eventually move out or the owners would employ more drastic measures by either forcing them out or setting fires. The buildings would remain abandoned, sometimes for years, until a developer would buy up the parcels and rebuild luxury apartments, the selling prices far beyond the means of those who'd lived in the neighborhoods for generations.

Kara had listened to David, Jeff, and Morgan talk about the developers as if they were a small growth, feeding on the residents of the Sea Islands until they became a malignancy, destroying the Gullah culture and their legacy for future generations.

They'd sent a clean-cut, preppy boy wearing a handmade tailored suit and imported footwear, instead of a slick, fast-talking, more experienced man, believing he would be more acceptable and approachable. Well, they were wrong. Even if Kara hadn't decided whether to stay or leave, the impromptu meeting with Porter had justified why she should stay.

Jeff, dropping his gaze, stared out into the distance. "I can't believe you asked my woman to go to James Island with you when it's known that Jack's Fish House is the best seafood restaurant in the Lowcountry. And it just happens to be a few minutes from here." His gaze swung back to Porter who looked as if he was ready to bolt off the porch if Jeff made a sudden motion. "Do you think if you took my woman to James Island, I wouldn't hear about it?" His voice was soft and dangerous.

Porter held up both hands. "Look, man, I wasn't trying to hit on your woman. I just wanted to talk to her about selling the house."

"I'm sorry to tell you," Jeff continued, "but she's not going to sell. Not for you or for me. I've tried to talk her into selling it to come live with me, but she's as stubborn as a mule."

Kara rested her hands at her waist. "I'm not living with you, Jeffrey Hamilton. My mama didn't raise me to shack up with a man, so stop asking me."

Porter lowered his hand. "I'm sorry, but I have to leave now." He nodded to Kara, then Jeff. "It's nice meeting you." Turning on the heels of his imported footwear, he practically ran to his car, jumped in, and started it up in one continuous motion.

Jeff took out his cell phone and punched

in several letters and numbers. "No speeding, son!" he called out as the gleaming black BMW swerved before it was able to regain control and drive along the allée of oaks and away from Angels Landing.

Kara began laughing and couldn't stop as tears ran down her face. Jeannette, who'd overhead everything, joined her as they collapsed on the love seat. "Did you see his face, Mama?"

Jeannette held her belly with both hands. "I heard and saw everything. You and Jeff were hilarious."

Sobering, Kara stared at her mother. "How long were you standing there?"

"Long enough to hear his spiel. The boy couldn't sell water in the desert."

Jeff came over and sat on a chair facing the love seat. "I'll find out soon enough exactly who he is and who sent him."

"What are you talking about?" Jeannette asked.

"I got his plate number. Unless that young man has a rich uncle, I doubt whether he'd be able to afford a car with a sticker price starting at six figures."

Kara met his steady gaze. "I told him I'd sell the house for three mil, and he claimed that figure was doable. Either he does have a very rich uncle or he's involved in some criminal activity and just happens to have a few million lying around."

"I'll find out soon enough. I know someone who still has connections at the bureau, and we'll find out who Porter Caldwell is and what he's all about."

Jeannette moved to the edge of the cushion. "Do you think Kara is in any danger?"

Reaching out, Jeff patted her hand. "Of course not. But I'm glad you called me. I'm certain Kara would've gotten rid of him, but if he believes there's something going on between the two of us, he won't approach her again."

Jeannette placed her hand atop Jeff's. "I'm leaving here tomorrow, and I want you to look after my baby."

"Mama!"

"Don't 'Mama' me, Kara. You're my only child, and I don't want anything to happen to you."

"Don't worry, Miss Jeannette. I'll make certain nothing happens to her."

"You promise?"

"I promise." Jeff stood, bringing Jeannette up with him. He smiled, then kissed her cheek. "What time are you leaving tomorrow?"

"Around eight in the morning. Why?"

"I thought I'd treat you to breakfast before

you leave."

"I'd like that," Jeannette said quickly.

He kissed her other cheek. "I'll meet you here at six thirty." His eyes met Kara's. "I'd like you to join us."

Smiling, Kara nodded. "Thank you."

Jeff turned to leave, then stopped. "Kara, do you like dogs?"

Her eyes lit up like a child's on Christmas morning. "I love them. Why?" He told her about the Yorkshire puppy. "Oh, please I'd love to have it."

"I'll let Mabel know. I'll call you before I bring him over."

Kara and Jeannette stood together, their arms around each other's waists, watching as Jeff drove away. "This was one time I didn't mind you being the nosy mother," she said softly.

"He's a keeper, Kara."

"What are you talking about, Mama?"

"Jeff. He's a keeper."

"He's a forty-year-old confirmed bachelor," Kara countered.

"That's only because he hasn't met the right woman."

"And you think I'm the right one?"

"I know you are." Jeannette dropped her arm. "I'm going inside to take these rollers out of my hair. Are you coming in?"

"Not yet. I'm going to look around to see where I can put in a rose garden."

"Wait for me to comb my hair, and I'll join you."

"Okay."

Kara had never known her mother to be so clingy. Even when she'd moved to New York, she'd appeared resigned that her little girl had matured enough to make her way in such a big city. She was now thirty-three, living on Cavanaugh Island with a population of 2,300 instead of on Manhattan Island with a million and a half, and Jeannette was freaking out.

And if she were to ask her mother about her inconsistent behavior, Jeannette's comeback would be *"wait until you're a mother and you'll understand."*

Well, she was about to become a mother of sorts, and she was looking forward to taking care of what would become her four-legged baby.

CHAPTER ELEVEN

Kara didn't realize how much she'd missed her mother until she got up that Sunday morning and waited for Jeannette to join her on the front porch. Both had always been early risers, and not to have her to sit with and watch the sunrise reminded Kara of how sterile her life was. If it hadn't been for her stressful job — a job from which she'd resigned — and Dawn, now her former roommate, her day-to-day existence would've been as exciting as watching paint dry.

Aside from Dawn, she didn't have any close friends. And if Dawn hadn't been her roommate, she wouldn't have had any. She'd lost touch with her childhood buddies, electing not to return to Little Rock for her tenth high school reunion because she hadn't wanted to run into a boy she'd had an intense crush on.

When she'd confided this to whom she'd

believed was her BFF at the time, Chantal couldn't wait to tell Chris Day. The next day Chris approached her in the cafeteria and told her he would consider taking her out, but only if she would do something for him. He then whispered in her ear that he wanted her to go down on him because every girl he went out with did; no girl was going to blame him for getting her pregnant and jeopardize his athletic scholarship. The shock and horror must have been evident when everyone at her lunch table burst into laughter. Unfortunately for Kara, she hadn't been privy to Chris's sexual exploits and spent the last two years of high school as a loner, finding it easier to form relationships with boys than she did girls. It had all come down to trust.

She'd trusted her mother, and even Jeannette had deceived her when she felt she was protecting Kara. In essence, she was protecting her own reputation. Jeannette wasn't the first and she definitely wouldn't be the last woman to have a child and pass it off as another man's. It was ironic that she'd become Jeannette's and Taylor's only child, and now that she knew the circumstances of her birth, Kara wondered if Austin had felt cheated that he hadn't fathered a child with his wife, that *their* daughter was a constant reminder of his wife's affair with another man. Jeannette had called her husband to let him know to expect her arrival in Little Rock late Sunday night and to say that she loved and missed him.

Overhearing that conversation reminded Kara that it'd been a long time since she'd told a man that she loved and had missed him whenever they were separated. She didn't have a husband or lover, and now she didn't have a best girlfriend or even coworkers she could hang out with whenever they got together to celebrate someone's birthday, promotion, wedding, or baby shower.

She'd become Taylor Patton, living alone in a house that had become as sought after as a cure for a communicable disease. The Pattons wanted her to sell the land to them, and in turn they would sell it to developers.

Things weren't going as smoothly as she had hoped, and Kara felt inheriting Angels Landing was more a curse than a blessing. However, she still planned to turn it into a museum.

She knew without a doubt that her decision to stay in Angels Landing had a lot to do with Jeff, but she wasn't ready to openly admit that to anyone. Despite his military experience and extensive travels, he had the small-town sensibilities she found totally charming.

It was now two weeks since she'd last seen Jeff. He'd come by, as promised, early Sunday morning to escort her mother to a Charleston twenty-four-hour diner for breakfast. After she was stuffed with shrimp and grits, a Low-country staple, Kara and Jeff waited until the taillights from Jeannette's car disappeared from view as she headed toward the interstate; then they returned to the island on the ferry instead of taking the more direct causeway.

Kara remembered standing at the rail next to Jeff not exchanging a word during the trip. He'd dropped her off at Angels Landing, saying he would see her around, and left with a hug and a kiss. She'd found his behavior puzzling but decided not to make too much of it. He didn't owe her any explanation, and as sheriff of Cavanaugh Island his responsibilities went beyond his becoming her personal bodyguard.

The news of her resignation had generated a firestorm of questions, firstly from her supervisor who wanted to know if he'd been responsible for her abrupt departure. Kara reassured him he had nothing to do with it and that she'd decided she needed a different lifestyle because she'd been close to burnout. He'd offered to cut her case-load, but Kara refused to relent and wished him the best.

Then came the phone calls from coworkers blowing up her cell. Many wanted to know if she'd found a man in Little Rock and had decided not to come back. A few were gauche enough to ask her if she was pregnant, and that's when she programmed her calls to go directly to voice mail.

She'd called Dawn asking her to box up her personal items and ship them to Angels Landing. She had also invited her to come down during the spring break because Dawn never taught classes at that time. She knew Dawn was still angry with her for leaving when she said she would think about it. What was there to think about when Kara had offered to pay for the flight? Dawn's response dampened her mood for several hours until she left the house and went to the beach. Sitting on the sand and watching the choppy waves and pounding surf wash up on the beach was soothing and hypnotic, and by the time she returned home she'd felt a gentle inner peace.

Kara was on the computer in Taylor's office when Mrs. Todd knocked softly on the door. "Corrine Hamilton's grandbaby boy is here to see you. He's waiting in the kitchen."

She smiled when hearing Jeff announced that way. When, she wondered, would he ever stop being Corrine's grandbaby boy? "Thank you. Tell him I'll be right down."

Kara hadn't realized how fast her heart was beating until she went into her bedroom to exchange a pair of too-short shorts for a pair of capris. At the last possible moment she reached for a brush and put her hair up in a ponytail. She'd put off going into the Cove to have her hair styled. Most times she washed it, let it air-dry, then pulled it into a ponytail. She knew she had to snap out of the rut of not taking care of her appearance, or she would end up like many of the mothers of her former clients who drifted from one day to the next, oblivious of the world going on around them.

It was so easy to become a recluse in the large house that held good and not-so-good memories. She rarely saw Mrs. Todd, who floated in and out of rooms like a specter, leaving only the scent of lemon and gleaming surfaces behind her.

Taking the back staircase, Kara walked into the kitchen, her heart stopping, then starting up again, when she saw Jeff. He was a visual feast in a pair of jeans; a black, waffle-weave, long-sleeved T-shirt; and shiny black leather boots. The badge pinned to his chest and the deadly-looking automatic strapped to his waist told her he was on duty. There was something poignant in seeing a man his size cradling a small puppy to his chest. She began imagining him with an infant.

"Hello, stranger."

Jeff stared numbly at Kara, unable to believe that after two weeks he still could recall everything about her. He'd deliberately stayed away from Angels Landing because of gossip, no doubt spread by Harlan, that he was sleeping with Taylor's impostor daughter. It had been his grandmother who'd warned him about ruining Kara's reputation. He reminded her that it was the twenty-first century and Kara was an independent woman, but his explanation did not sit well with her. Corrine had countered with *If you don't plan to do right by Kara, then stay away from her.* He wasn't certain what his grandmother meant, but he had no intention of hurting Kara — directly or indirectly. All he wanted to do was protect and care for her.

And he wasn't about to argue with his grandmother that there wasn't anything going on between him and Kara, but took her advice and had stayed away. Until now. He'd had his deputies stop by to check on her and had got up before the sun came up to run along the beach. It was only when he went to bed that the images of the horrors of war were replaced with her face and the sound of her voice. And when Mabel called for him to pick up the dog, Jeff knew he had to see Kara again.

"It's been a while. I was down one deputy, so I wasn't able to take off," he said truthfully, "but hopefully that's going to change with a new hire."

"Who are you considering?"

He told her about Marine Reserve Sergeant Nelson Lambert who had returned from Iraq and had come to Jeff to apply for the vacant deputy position. As soon as he received approval of Nelson's background check, he would be added to the payroll. Nelson still would have to attend classes at the Charleston police academy during his probationary period.

"With Nelson's hire we'll have deputies living in each of the towns. Kenny will still cover Angels Landing, and Nelson will move from the Cove to Haven Creek. I would love to have a third deputy, but there isn't enough money in the budget."

"Are they part-time or full-time?"

"They're part-time. I'm the only one that's full-time. There was a time when each town had a full-time sheriff, but that wasn't cost-effective. Once I was hired to replace the Cove's sheriff, the mayors decided I would police the entire island, and deputies from the Landing and the Creek would provide part-time oversight in their towns."

"Can they make ends meet on a part-time salary?"

Jeff angled his head. "Always the social worker, aren't you?"

She gave him a wide smile. "I'm not going to apologize."

"And I don't want you to. Kenny is a retired correction officer, and my former deputy was a probation officer. They take on the position to supplement their pensions." He watched Kara approach, her gaze fixed on the terrier. "Don't you want to take him?"

"Will he come to me?" she asked. There was a slight tremor in her voice.

"Hold out your arms." Jeff placed the puppy in her arms, then stepped back. The terrier had whined incessantly when Mabel had placed him in a crate but soon had settled down during the drive. He refused to come out of the crate until Jeff reached in to carry him out, the tiny canine shaking

294

uncontrollably.

Kara smiled when the dog yawned. "What's his name?"

"Oliver."

Her eyebrows lifted. "For Oliver Twist?"

"I don't know. If it were me I'd call him Killer or Bruiser."

Kara gave him an incredulous stare. "You can't be serious. This little thing probably doesn't weigh more than three pounds."

"Two and a half. I have his papers in the car with his breed and the date of vaccinations. Mabel also gave me a crate, wee-wee pads, food, and a bag of doggy-grooming supplies."

Burying her face in the soft fur, Kara pressed a kiss on the puppy's head. Oliver was gold and gray with round brown eyes and a black dot for a nose. "Why are you shaking, baby? Mama's going to take good care of you."

"I take it you've had dogs before."

Kara nodded. "I've had dogs, cats, birds, fish, rabbits, and guinea pigs."

Jeff crossed his arms over his chest. "It looks as if Oliver is going to have a good home."

"Thank you for thinking of me. This little guy and I are going to have a lot of fun together. I must admit this is the first time

I've ever had a dog this small. Most of my other dogs were hounds, and they stayed outdoors. The exception was when temperatures were close to freezing; then my mother would let them in."

"How is your mother?"

"She's good. In fact, she asked about you, and I told her I hadn't seen you in a while."

"Tell her that's going to change."

Kara gave him a blank stare. "What are you talking about?"

"I now have time to fulfill my promise to take you to the movies. And there's still the Sunday dinner you owe me."

"I'm always here, Jeff. You know where to find me."

"You *and* Oliver."

She pressed another kiss to the dog's silky hair. "Me and Oliver. By the way, did you find out anything about Porter Caldwell?"

"We're still checking."

"Will you let me know what you uncover?"

"I will, but only if it doesn't entail police business. And pouting will not get me to change my mind," he added when she pushed out her lips.

"Fine. Be like that, Jeff."

He smiled in spite of the potential seriousness of the situation. "The developers are getting bolder and more aggressive," he said, suddenly sobering. "Millicent Baily, who's a Haven Creek sweet-grass weaving instructor, called me to say someone had come to her, asking whether she was willing to sell her late father's house and farm. When she told him no, he'd asked whether she'd ever seen *The Godfather* when Don Corleone said to make him an offer he can't refuse. She interpreted it as a veiled threat and felt compelled to call and report it."

Kara whistled softly. "That's scary."

Jeff nodded. "My men are on full alert when it comes to strangers hanging around." Having Nelson policing the Creek would make it possible for the recent war combatant to closely monitor what was going on in the smallest and least populated of the three towns.

"How's Miss Corrine?"

Jeff smiled thinking of his grandmother. "She's doing quite well. She just joined a book club discussion group at the bookstore and is talking about coming to the Haven to join a quilting club."

"Good for her. Please let her know I asked about her."

"I will. Let me go and get Mr. O's things." Jeff returned to the Jeep and managed to bring in the crate and a large plastic bag with the supplies. Mabel had vacillated between wanting to keep the terrier and giving him up but in the end decided giving him up was in the canine's best interest. Oliver, bored at being left alone all day, had begun gnawing on furniture and soiling the carpet whenever she came home.

Kara examined the contents of the bag. "Did he have any chew toys?"

Jeff stared down into the eyes that made him feel as if he were drowning in pools of green and gold. "That's all Mabel gave me."

"It doesn't matter. I'll buy him some."

He took a step toward her, bringing them inches apart. "I have to get back so my clerk can go to lunch. I have your numbers. I'll call you and we'll go out."

"I'd like that," Kara said softly.

Placing an arm around her waist, he dipped his head and kissed her. It had been so long since he'd tasted her mouth that he had almost forgotten how sweet she was. "I promise I won't stay away so long again."

"Don't make promises you can't keep," she whispered against his mouth.

"I never break a promise, baby." Jeff kissed her again, wishing for the first time in his life that he didn't have to go back to work. But he'd never been one to shirk his duties or disobey an order.

Kara patted his chest. "Go before your

boss fires you for theft of services."

Jeff laughed loudly, startling Oliver who let out a yelp. "Sorry about that Mr. O. I happen to think I have a rather nice boss."

"Who's that?"

"Me."

"Aren't you appointed by the mayor?" Kara asked.

"No, baby. My position is an elected one. Only the people can vote me in or out. I served several months of my predecessor's term, then ran unopposed a month later. I'm up for reelection in thirty-three months."

"Do you plan on running again?"

"Probably. I'd thought it would be difficult adjusting to small-town life again, but so far it's been good."

A beat passed before Kara asked, "If your grandmother wasn't still living here, would you have come back?"

There came another pause as Jeff replayed Kara's question in his head. "Yes. I've traveled all over the world, and I've never felt the connection with those places that I feel here. This is home, Kara." An expression he could only interpret as indecision filled Kara's eyes. "What's the matter?"

She lowered her gaze. "I keep telling myself this is home when it really doesn't feel like it. Maybe that's because I'm only staying here temporarily."

Pressing his mouth to her forehead, Jeff said, "Don't rush it, Kara. First you were only staying a week, then it became three weeks, and now it's five years. A lot can happen in five years."

"You're right." She turned her head and kissed his cheek. "Go to work before your boss writes you up."

"Do you mind if I stop by when my boss isn't clocking me?" he teased.

"Of course. I'll even cover for you if he comes around looking for you," she said, smiling.

"You're definitely a keeper," he said.

Later that afternoon Kara had another visitor. This time it was Morgan. She put Oliver in his crate and closed the door. She'd finally calmed the puppy enough where he'd stopped shaking. She'd temporarily placed the crate near the back staircase, covered the fleece dog mat with wee-wee paper, and placed bowls of food and water in a corner.

Kara studied the renderings and photographs Morgan had spread out on the dining room table. "It's amazing."

"What's amazing?" Morgan asked.

She pointed to an early photo of one of

the guest bedroom suites. "It looks so shabby when compared to the rendering."

"It's the same room and furniture but with different wallpaper, rugs, windows, and bed dressing. The other accessories in the room will look the way it did a hundred fifty years ago."

Moving along the table, Kara stared at each photo and its accompanying rendering. "What about the fabric on the chairs?"

"I deal with two fabric houses specializing in eighteenth and nineteenth-century patterns. One is in Charleston on King Street and the other in Atlanta's Buckhead neighborhood."

"Which one do you recommend?"

Morgan smiled, dimples deepening. "The local one of course."

"Do I have to keep the same colors? Because whoever decorated appears to have been obsessed with green."

"I noticed that, too. We can always change the colors. What colors are you thinking about?" Morgan asked, opening a book with fabric samples.

Kara met Morgan's dark eyes. "Every piece of furniture in this house is either light or dark, so I'd like each of the bedrooms to have a different palette."

"How do you like these?" She pointed to

swatches of fabric that paired white with blue, rose, black, lavender, and cream. "The light-colored furniture is mid-1700s French. These pieces were probably purchased when the house was first built in 1832. The mahogany pieces came later."

"Are they antiques or reproductions?"

"They're antiques. Why? Are you thinking of auctioning off a few pieces?"

"No, actually," Kara admitted. "I was thinking of donating a few pieces to a museum. I found several chests filled with china, crystal pieces, and silver. There are duplicates of everything."

"Why don't you give them to an auction house? Of course, they'll take their fee, but you could always use the money for the upkeep of the property. Restoring Angels Landing isn't a onetime endeavor. You're going to have to hire people to maintain the gardens, make repairs and. . . . Why are you looking at me like that, Kara?"

She knew it was time to level with Morgan, inform the historical architect of her future intentions for the property. "If we're going to work together, then we must trust each other."

"You don't want me to restore the property?"

Kara rolled her eyes upward. "Morgan,

please don't get melodramatic on me," she remarked when the other woman pressed her palms to her chest as if she was going to faint. "Of course, I want you to restore the property." Morgan twisted a plait around her finger, and Kara saw that her hand was shaking. She knew the architect had taken a huge risk resigning her position to go into business for herself, even if someone had put up the money.

"Remember when you told me why you didn't want developers here?" Morgan nodded. "That they would take business away from island merchants?"

"Yes. Where are you going with this, Kara?"

She told her everything, watching as Morgan's eyes danced with excitement. "I want Angels Landing to become part of the Gullah tours. Those who take the tour would be able to buy sweet-grass baskets from artisans on the island if I decide to open a souvenir shop. In fact, everything in the shop will come from Cavanaugh Island. If it's not made here, then it won't be sold here. Think destination weddings and business meetings. We can have a restaurant on the property that can be a spinoff of Jack's Fish House. And I've heard that Lester Kelly is the island's cake man."

"And he makes the most incredibly beautiful wedding cakes," Morgan added. "You know you've just appealed to my historic gene."

"So you like my idea?"

"Don't play, Kara. You know I love it. What makes it so ingenious is it's like living off the land. You'll use what you have here, not like outsiders that will take from us. That way the plantation will take care of itself."

"I really don't like that word."

"Neither do I," Morgan agreed, "but it is what it was. It's a word that has been around since the fifteenth century, and some of the first plantations were established in Ireland. A lot of tourists come to the island in the summer, but it's the Cove that draws most of the business, then the Creek, and the Landing is last because it's totally residential."

"I went to college with a girl who was from Savannah, and she could trace her family tree back to the Revolution. She told me her house was listed on the Savannah tour of homes and gardens. It could be the same with Angels Landing if some people were willing to open their homes and gardens like they do in Savannah."

Leaning over, Morgan took her iPhone

from her bag, touching the Notes icon. "Take a look at this," she said, handing Kara the phone. Kara's smile grew wider as she read the note.

"Yes!" Kara gave Morgan a high five, then did a happy dance while still seated. "I can't believe we've come up with a similar plan."

"What do they say about great minds? Why should the developers reap all the profits? I gave you that little pep talk to get you thinking about the possibilities for Angels Landing. I also didn't want you to think I was trying to coerce you into doing something you weren't comfortable with."

"Were you testing me?" Kara asked.

Pressing against the worn fabric on the back of the dining room chair, Morgan ran her hands over her neatly braided hair. "I wasn't testing you, Kara. This is your property and your project so the final word rests with you. Angels Landing is similar to Middleton Place, Mansfield Plantation, Drayton Hall, or Borough House Plantation in that they have private governing bodies and are registered as a historic place and/or historic landmark. The difference is you're female, African American, and a direct descendant of Shipley Patton. Once the word gets out, Angels Landing will operate like the other historic homes, and I hope it will put a stop to the developers preying on Cavanaugh."

Kara felt as if a weight had been lifted off her shoulders. What she'd planned for the property wasn't an original idea, but after spending hours on the computer research-ing historic sites throughout the South, she'd felt she could do the same for Angels Landing. She felt a warm glow flow through her. The puzzle was beginning to take shape, and soon she would be able to see the whole picture.

"Let's hope it does. I don't know why, but I feel like celebrating. Is there any other place, other than Jack's, where we can go and have a little fun?"

"Hey," Morgan drawled. "I'm down if you are. There's Happy Hour in the Creek. It's the only bar on the island. And it's happy hour from the time it opens around five until it closes. They cater to an under-forty crowd and offer a wonderful buffet."

"Is it a popular place to hang out?"

"It is for the locals. We get a lot of folks from the mainland on Friday and Saturday because of the live music. There is a cover charge, but I always get around that because one of my cousins is a partner in the club."

"Is everyone on the island related?" Kara asked, laughing.

"No. And those who are make it known. We can't have cousins marrying cousins like they do in some states," Morgan joked.

"You know that's wrong. Incest is illegal."

"Tell that to some folks." Morgan checked her watch. "It's a little after five. If we get there before eight, then we should be able to get a table."

"That gives me a couple of hours to wash my hair and flat iron it."

Morgan flipped her braids. "That's why I have low maintenance hair. Wash and go."

"I had my hair braided once, and I had to take them out the next day because they were so tight I sat up all night in ppppaaaaii-iinnnn." Pain had come out in four syllables, causing Morgan to laugh and Kara to laugh with her.

Gathering up the photographs, Morgan left the renderings for Kara. "I'll come back and pick you up between 7:15 and 7:30."

"I'll be ready."

CHAPTER TWELVE

Kara felt as if every eye in the Happy Hour was fixed on her and Morgan when they wove their way through the crowd in the dimly lit club. It could've been a Friday in Manhattan instead of Friday night on Cavanaugh Island. Instead of taxis and car services dropping off passengers in front of clubs sandwiched between buildings in mostly commercial neighborhoods, these clubbers had parked their cars in a lot large enough for one square city block. Young, attractive, and casually chic, they could've come from any major city in the world. Most of the men had shed their ties and suit jackets, their dates preening in designer dresses, power suits, and stilettos.

She wore the ubiquitous New York City black — a sheath dress with an asymmetrical neckline; narrow, black patent leather belt around her waist; and four-inch black patent leather pumps — while Morgan turned heads in black stretch pants, silk blouse, and strappy stilettos. She wouldn't have had anything to wear tonight if she hadn't stopped at a boutique when she'd gone into Charleston to do her banking. She thought of the dress and shoes as an impulse buy that had served her well. And if she was going to socialize with Morgan, then that meant she had to make a few more purchases before Dawn packed up her clothes and shipped them to South Carolina.

A man with a shaved pate leaned in close to Kara, crooning, "Hello, hello, and hello!"

She laughed. "Hello to you, too." Prerecorded music pumped loudly as Kara and Morgan followed the hostess to a small table.

"I called my cousin and told him to save us a table," Morgan shouted over her shoulder as they sat down. She signaled a waiter and ordered a sex on the beach, while Kara ordered an apple martini.

The waiter stared at Kara, a slight smile playing at the corners of his mouth. "I need to see some ID."

She stared at him, tongue-tied. "Excuse me?"

"I need to see some ID," he repeated, his smile now a full grin.

Kara opened her tiny purse unable to believe she was being carded. She handed the man her driver's license. "Nice photo, Kara," he drawled, handing her back the license.

"If you wanted to know my name you could've asked." She smiled at his look of embarrassment.

"I'll be right back with your drinks."

Kara and Morgan waited until he walked away before they burst into laughter. "Do you think I hurt his feelings?"

"I told Damon that asking for a woman's ID is played out, but you can't blame him for trying."

Kara leaned over the table. "I'm certain seeing the New York State license threw him for a loop."

"Don't delude yourself into believing that. People know who you are, Kara. Damon thought asking for your license would flatter you because he wanted you to believe he thought you didn't look old enough to drink."

"It's been a while since I've been carded." What she should've said was that it had been a while since she'd gone out for drinks. Most Friday nights found her at home, in bed, and trying to catch up on lost sleep before Dawn's transients invaded the apartment.

Kara missed her roommate. She missed Dawn coming into her bedroom and flopping down on her bed to talk about what had gone on in her busy life. Kara thought of Dawn, a native New Yorker, as a Big Apple diva. She knew how to talk the talk *and* walk the walk, teaching and helping Kara navigate the frenetic lifestyle of the celebrated city.

"People know who you are."

Now that they knew who she was, what were they going to do with that information? Kara knew the Pattons weren't happy about her being on the island, and she wondered who else felt the same. Had the others thought of her as an outsider, too? Had they also shunned Taylor or had he avoided them as well?

"Should I be concerned, Morgan?"

Morgan stared at the lighted candle on the table. "I don't think so. There's going to be a lot of talk once the repairs begin on Angels Landing. Folks are going to want to drive by and check out what's going on. The supervisor of the work crew will probably put up barriers on the road leading up to the house where only workmen will be permitted to access the property. My former boss — it feels so good to say that — threw a hissy fit when I handed in my resignation, accusing me of being disloyal. Once he finds out that I'm working for you, he'll probably bad-mouth me as if I stole something."

"What's the ditty about sticks and stones?"

"Yeah, I know. Why don't you go and get something to eat before Damon brings the drinks. I'll go after you come back."

Pushing back her chair, Kara stood up and walked over to the buffet table where patrons stood two deep waiting to serve themselves. She liked the vibe in the club. It wasn't as large as some of the ones she'd gone to in Manhattan, but what it lacked in size, it more than made up in atmosphere. A U-shaped bar was the centerpiece, and mirrored walls made everything appear bigger. Tables seating two, four, and six were positioned closely together to maximize capacity. The waitstaff wore white shirts with black ties, armbands, slacks, and shoes. Everyone was patient, polite, and talking softly, but it was the number of people attempting to be heard over the ear-shattering music that increased the noise decibels.

"You can get in front of me."

Kara smiled up at a man with wavy, sandy-brown hair and soulful green eyes.

"Thanks, but I'm in no hurry."

"Did you know that you're beautiful?"

She felt heat sting her cheeks. "No."

"Well, you are. Why is it I've never seen you here before?"

Kara knew he was trying to either engage her in conversation or pick her up. She didn't mind talking to him, but she definitely was not going to be receptive if he wanted more than that. "This is my first time."

He extended his hand. "Steve Young."

She shook his moist palm. "Kara Newell."

"Are you here alone?"

Kara groaned inwardly. He wasn't being just friendly; he wanted to pick her up. Any normal woman would've been flattered to have an attractive man come on to her, but she wasn't interested. If he'd been Jeff, then she wouldn't have been so standoffish. She would've been cheesing so much, he would've been able to see her molars.

"No, I'm not."

"My loss."

Picking up a plate and flatware, Kara moved slowly along the table, spearing small portions of salad greens and toppings. There were the customary dipping sauces for wings, sushi, calamari, chicken fingers, and zucchini sticks. She chose an assortment of

313

cold antipasto and mini–crab cakes.

Morgan stood up. "Is that all you're eating?" she asked, looking at Kara's plate.

"It's only the first course."

"Good for you. I know a few women with eating disorders, and I just couldn't be around them because there's only so much lettuce one could eat without passing out."

Kara set her plate on the table. "Not me. I like food too much." She picked up a fork and cut into the crab cake. Her hand halted when she spied David sitting with a woman. She couldn't hear what they were saying, but judging from their expressions, they didn't appear to be a happy couple. Damon returned with their drink order, and Kara paid him, adding a generous tip.

"I paid for the drinks," she told Morgan when she sat down.

"The next round is on me." They touched glasses. "Here's to friendship."

"Friendship and Angels Landing."

The food was delicious, the cocktails perfect, and once the jazz quartet replaced the driving, thumping baseline beat, the music became melodious and soothing. Kara was content to come to the Happy Hour just to listen to the live music. Morgan touched her arm, garnering her attention.

"Your attorney isn't having a good night. It looks as if his girl just walked out on him. And judging from the number of glasses on the table, I think he's had more than enough to drink. I think you'd better do something, Kara."

Shifting slightly, she stared at David. The confident lawyer responsible for monitoring and protecting her legal interests was missing, and in his place was a dejected man. There were several glasses on the table, and he'd motioned the waiter over.

Kara's relationship with David was strictly business, and she didn't want to ingratiate herself into his private life. Opening her purse, she scrolled through the directory and tapped a number.

Jeff had just stepped out of the shower when his cell phone rang. Looping a towel around his waist, he answered the call when Kara's name and number came up on the display. His twelve-hour shift had ended, and he looked forward to relaxing until it was time for him to return for the eight o'clock shift.

"Hey, Kara. What's up?"

"David's here at the Happy Hour. He doesn't look so good, and I think he's had too much to drink —"

"I'll get there as soon as I can," he said,

cutting her off.

Jeff could not understand what had sent his cousin over the edge because he rarely drank. Even as teenagers, when they shouldn't have been drinking, David was always the designated driver. He'd taken a lot of ribbing from the rest of the guys in their crowd, but that didn't seem to bother him. Jeff had never known anyone to be more focused than his cousin David. Jeff dressed quickly and bounded down the stairs, stopping to look in on his grandmother.

She was in the sunroom, shades drawn, television tuned in to a cable channel, piecing squares of cotton. "I'm going out, Gram."

Corrine peered at him over a pair of half glasses. "I thought you were staying in tonight because you have to work in the morning."

"I need to meet someone. Don't wait up for me," he teased.

"I stopped that years ago. Be careful, Jeffrey."

Walking over, he kissed her cheek. "I'm always careful, Gram. Love you."

She smiled. "Love you more."

It was a game they'd played when he was a child. He would tell her he loved her, and she would always say she loved him more. They would go back and forth until they lost count of who loved the other more.

He did love his grandmother unconditionally, and Jeff's greatest fear was losing her like all of the other women in his life. Corrine was his only link with a woman who'd given up her life to give birth to him. He'd known kids who didn't know or had never met their fathers, but he had been one of the rare cases where he hadn't met either parent. His grandmother was his only link to his past, and he intended to hold onto her for as long as he could.

David was his grandmother's greatnephew. Corrine's sister had left the island to attend college and never returned. She married a lawyer, and after graduating they put down roots in Charleston where David's father set up a law firm with two of his fraternity brothers. After David graduated law school, he, too, joined the firm, becoming a junior partner. His cousin loved coming to the Cove to spend the summers. When people asked who David was to him, Jeff would say "my little brother" instead of his cousin.

Right now, his little brother was in trouble, and Jeff wondered how or what had shaken the brilliant attorney so much that he was

317

attempting to escape into a bottle of alcohol.

He got into the low-slung sports car and started it, backing out of the driveway faster than he normally would. The no-speeding rule did not apply this night when Jeff pushed the racy car past sixty as he navigated the unlit narrow road. He sped past Angels Landing, slowing only when he reached the town limit for Haven Creek. The downtown business district was dark, quiet. Jeff drove another quarter of a mile before the neon lights of the Happy Hour came into view. Maneuvering into an empty space, he was out of the car as soon as he cut the engine. He opened the door and stepped inside. Track lights appeared like stars against the black ceiling.

"What's up, Jeff?" asked the man at the door with biceps as large as a child's waist.

"Not much, Dwayne," he said, exchanging handshakes before they pounded each other's back.

"Yo, man, you still hard as a rock," Dwayne remarked. "You workin' out?"

Jeff smiled. "I just do push-ups and run along the beach whenever I can."

"Keep doin' what you're doin'. I have to say, I'm surprised to see you here. There hasn't been any trouble."

"I'm here to meet someone."

Jeff had only come to the club whenever there was a problem with a patron or when he stopped by to make certain they weren't serving alcohol to minors. The owners strictly enforced the "we card everyone under twenty-five" rule because they didn't want to risk being fined, have their liquor license suspended, or even worse, close down permanently.

"Go on in."

Waiting until his eyes adjusted to the darkness, Jeff wended his way through tables, around throngs of people waiting at the bar, until he found David standing in a corner with two women. He recognized Morgan Dane immediately, then Kara as she struggled to keep David from falling.

Moving quickly, he took over, holding David under his armpits. The smell of alcohol on his cousin's breath was revolting. "What's going on, Cuz?"

David tried to focus his eyes. "She cheated on me, Jeff."

"Who?"

"Petra. I was going to take her away and propose marriage, but she cheated on me."

Jeff managed to get David to sit without falling off the chair. His gaze swept over Kara in the body-hugging dress. It moved lower to her bare legs in a pair of sexy heels before reversing itself to her face. Seeing her dressed like that made him think that she'd come to the club to meet a man or men, and jealousy rocked him to the core.

But he knew in order to feel jealous he had to care about her . . . a lot.

"Kara, could you please order some black coffee for him."

She gave him a demure smile. "Of course."

His gaze was trained on the gentle sway of her hips as she walked away. He swallowed a groan when the flesh between his thighs stirred to life. Hunkering down in front of his cousin, he placed a hand on the attorney's shoulder. "We're going to sober you up before I take you home."

David's chin touched his chest. "I want to hate her, Jeff, but I can't. I still love her."

Jeff patted his cheek. "Love is overrated, David. What you should've done was let her love you more than you loved her." He felt someone next to him, and when Jeff glanced up, he saw Kara staring at him as if she'd seen a ghost. "What's the matter?"

"Nothing. Someone is bringing the coffee."

Morgan hunkered down next to Jeff. "How will you get him home?"

"I'm going to call someone to follow me in David's car; then I'll drive them back."

"Why don't you let him sleep it off at my house? I have two extra bedrooms," Morgan said quickly when Jeff gave her a questioning look. "After he sobers up he can drive himself to Charleston."

"Are you sure he won't put you out?" Jeff asked Morgan.

She smiled, dimples winking at him. "Come on, Jeff. The worst he can do is throw up, and if he ruins anything in my house, then I'll make him pay for it. Besides, he's probably going to sleep all night."

He thought about her suggestion, deciding it was better than calling someone in the middle of the night to help him take his inebriated cousin home. And it was better David not be left alone. Plus, Jeff could always stop by in the morning to check on him.

"You're right, Mo. As soon as I get some coffee into him, I'll drive him to your place in David's car." He turned to Kara, handing her the key fob to his car. "You'll have to drive my car to Mo's; then I'll take you back to Angels Landing."

Now I know why's he single, Kara thought as she watched Jeff force David to take furtive sips of the scalding-hot brew until he pushed the cup away. Is that how it'd been with Jeff and the women in his life? They loved him while he pretended to love them back?

Why couldn't he see that his cousin was hurting, that he'd truly loved a woman who'd deceived him by sleeping with another man? She blinked as if coming out of a trance. Maybe she'd found herself attracted to the wrong cousin. Despite his disheveled appearance, there was something about David that was refined, urbane while Jeff projected an aura of the bad boy athlete. Kara didn't know why, but she'd always found them far more exciting, yet had been reluctant to take up with one.

Jeff had made it known that he liked her, and he knew it was reciprocated when they'd shared the erotic moment in his grandmother's bathroom. She knew if they'd been alone, there was no doubt she would've asked him to make love to her. It had been a long time since a man had aroused her sexually and even longer since she'd slept with one. Could she, Kara mused, sleep with Jeff and remain emotionally detached? Knowing how he felt about falling in love was certain to make it easier for her.

Her heart turned over in compassion when David patted his shirt pocket, then those in his suit trousers. He extended a trembling hand to Jeff who shook his head. "I need my car keys."

"Not tonight, David. I'm going to drive you to Morgan's house where you're going to sleep it off. I'll stop by in the morning to see you."

David clenched his jaw. "I want to go home."

"I can't let you drive drunk. If you don't hurt yourself, then you'll probably hurt someone else."

David closed his eyes. "I'm not drunk. Now, give me my keys."

Jeff shook his head. "No."

"Give me my keys, Jeff," David insisted between clenched teeth.

Jeff caught his cousin in a savage grip under his shoulders. "Keep mouthing off and I'll charge you with drunk and disorderly conduct. And even in your inebriated state you know that's a minimum one day in lockup. What's it going to be, *counselor?*"

Closing his eyes, he nodded. "Let's go."

"Are you sure you can walk, or should I carry you?"

"Dammit! I . . . I can walk," he slurred.

Kara and Morgan shared a glance when David exhibited a display of belligerence for the first time. They left the club through a side door, David's uneven gait indicating he was no doubt under the influence.

Kara got into Jeff's car, smiling when she felt the power of the engine after she'd pushed the Start Engine button. It was definitely a pedal to the metal vehicle. The lingering scent of the masculine cologne inside the car was a blatant reminder of the man who made her feel things she'd forgotten, a man whose kisses left her mouth burning and wanting more, a man who made her throw caution to the wind when she'd admitted to him that he'd turned her on. So turned on she'd been ready to beg him to have sex with her instead of making love to her because he'd professed to finding love overrated.

Shifting into gear, she followed Jeff as he drove David's Lexus along pitch-black roads. Occasionally lights from homes in the distance punctuated the night as Kara concentrated on following the taillights of the sedan. No matter how hard she tried, she couldn't forget Jeff's off-handed comment about falling in love. The lyrics to Tina Turner's "What's Love Got to Do with It" came to mind: *It's physical, only logical. You must try to ignore that it means more than that.* Was that how it would be between her and Jeff? Whatever they would share would be purely physical?

Kara waited in the Miata as Morgan parked her SUV, got out, and opened the door to a one-story house with a front porch. She watched Jeff hoist the limp body of his cousin over his shoulder and carry him inside.

The haunting hooting of an owl came through the open window, and Kara pressed a button on the armrest, raising the window. Morgan's house had been built in a clearing surrounded by palmetto trees. Ten minutes seemed like an eternity when Jeff finally stepped out onto the porch with Morgan. He hugged her and then came over to the car.

Kara lowered the window. "Get in. I'll drive back."

He leaned into the window. "Are you sure you know how to get back?"

"Very funny, Jeff. Please get in."

She waited until he folded his long frame into the passenger seat and fastened his seat belt, then executed a perfect U-turn and drove back the way they'd come. "How is David?"

"Sleeping like a baby. I managed to get him out of his shirt and pants, but I didn't want to strip him naked. I wanted him to retain a little of his dignity when he woke up in a strange woman's bed. Thank you for calling me. I'm certain when he's lucid he'll also thank you for protecting his reputation as a straight arrow."

"Morgan's not a stranger to David." The admission had come out before Kara could censor herself.

"How does he know her?"

Kara knew she'd made a faux pas and had to think fast to cover it up. "Morgan went to Charleston with me when I had to take care of some legal business, and I introduced her to David."

"I didn't know you and Morgan were friends. Slow down, baby," Jeff warned. "There's a blind curve coming up, and you won't be able to tell if there's another car coming at you until it's too late."

She downshifted, slowing the car. "I hired Morgan to restore Angels Landing." It would become common knowledge that Morgan was the architect on the restoration project once work began; the fact that they were business partners would remain their secret, known only to her, Morgan, and David.

"So you're the one who lured Morgan away from Lenny Rosen?"

"I didn't lure her away, Jeff. She resigned because she felt stymied, and despite holding degrees in architecture and historical architecture, she probably would never advance beyond an assistant if she'd continued to work for him."

"We'll see."

"What do you mean we'll see?"

"Restoring Angels Landing will become her litmus test."

"Are you saying this because she's a woman?"

"Keep your eyes on the road," Jeff ordered when Kara turned her head to look at him.

"Why aren't there any lights?"

"It's because we don't want lighted roads. Once the sun sets you should either be home or on your way home. And to answer your question about Mo. It has nothing to do with her being a woman. The best commanding officer I ever had was a female lieutenant colonel. She truly was awesome, so please don't presume that I'm a sexist."

There was only the sound of their measured breathing and the *slip-slap* of tires on the roadway as Kara turned off on the path leading to Angels Landing. "Will you accept my apology? I didn't mean to imply you were sexist," she said after a lengthy silence.

"I'll think about it."

"Don't you know how to be gracious?"

"I'll think about it," Jeff repeated.

Kara slowed, the car coming to a complete stop, and then shifted into Park. "This stop is Angels Landing. All passengers getting off at Angels Landing please exit the vehicle," she said in a teasing tone. Light from the porch lamps reflected off the pearlescent columns.

"Turn off the car, Kara."

"Why?"

"Because I'm not going to let you go into an empty house alone."

She shut off the engine. Unbuckling her seat belt, she shifted in her seat and stared directly at him. "Have you forgotten that I stay here every night by myself?"

Stretching his left arm over her headrest, Jeff stared at her. "And I worry about you."

"Why?"

His hand touched her hair. "Do I have to wear a sign around my neck that reads, 'Jeffrey Hamilton Likes Kara Newell'?" He leaned closer. "I mean really, really likes her."

Kara stared at the strong masculine mouth. "Show her," she whispered.

Jeff slanted his mouth over Kara's at the same time a sharp sound rent the stillness of the night. He went still, then sprang into action, reaching for the small holstered automatic at his ankle. He pushed open the car door.

"Don't move."

"Jeff!"

He was there, then he wasn't when he disappeared, running around to the back of the house. Kara disobeyed him when she did move. Grabbing her purse off the console, she got out of the car, raced up the porch steps, and unlocked the front door. It was then she heard the sound of breaking glass along with Oliver's frantic barking.

She dropped her bag on the table in the entryway, kicked off her heels, and ran to see about her pet. The terrier was howling and cowering in a corner of the crate. Going to her knees, she unlatched the door and scooped him up.

"It's all right, baby. Mama's here."

"Didn't I tell you not to move!"

Kara spun around to see Jeff standing over her. "Don't you dare talk to me like that!"

He glared at her before his expression changed, softening. "I'm sorry, but you can't disobey an order, Kara."

"This is not the corps, Jeff, and I'm not one of your subordinates."

"I know that."

"Then please don't treat me like one."

Jeff took a step, resting his hands on Kara's shoulders. "I saw some kids who were throwing rocks at the house running away. It may have been a childish prank, but pranks can turn deadly. What if you'd been standing in front of the window when they threw them?"

She closed her eyes against his intense stare. "I don't want to think about that."

"Neither do I." He kissed her forehead. "Take care of Oliver while I clean up the glass."

Kara opened her eyes. "You don't have to."

"Yes, I do. And I'm going to spend the night in case they decide to come back."

Twin emotions of anticipation and confusion twisted inside her. Jeff had appointed himself her protector. Though she appreciated all that he was doing, she wasn't certain she was ready for the sexy lawman to stay under her roof. "There's no need for you to spend the night because some kids decided to pitch rocks at the house."

"I'm staying."

Judging from his expression and his voice, Kara knew anything she said wouldn't get Jeff to change his mind. "I'll prepare one of the guest bedrooms for you."

"No," he said, shaking his head. "I'm not going to let you out of my sight."

"What aren't you telling me, Jeff? Please,"

she pleaded.

"Two words were painted on the rocks."

Kara felt as if her breath had solidified in her throat. "What are they?"

"*Leave, bitch.* I wish there was something I could do, but rocks can't be dusted for prints."

Her mood shifted from uncertainty to anger. Working as a child protection advocate had given her the tools needed to face down enraged parents once she recommended removal of their children, and becoming a social worker had fortified her resolve to fight for and protect those who couldn't defend themselves. Well, it was time for her to defend her own turf.

"I'm not going to leave."

"And I don't want you to leave," Jeff said.

Oliver squirmed to get out of her arms, and Kara placed him on the floor, watching his tiny black nose sniff her bare toes. "I'm going to have a security company install closed-circuit cameras in the house and around the property. Then I'm going to go through this house and try to find Taylor's gun. If I don't find it, then I'll buy one of my own."

Jeff cradled her face. "I don't want you carrying a gun."

"I'm not going to carry it. I'm just going

to have it around in case I need it."

"You can't shoot kids for throwing rocks, Kara."

"Did I say I would shoot a child?" she asked him. "Someone put those kids up to throwing rocks at my house. Weren't you the one who said that their so-called prank could've turned deadly?" She watched Jeff's chest rise and fall as if he'd run a grueling race. "You know and I know they're going to come back. Whoever put those kids up to stoning my house will try again. And I doubt they'll send a kid to do a man's job the next time."

"Baby, baby," he crooned. "Leave the police work to me and my deputies."

Rising on tiptoe, Kara's lips brushed against his. "Think of me as police auxiliary."

"No, Kara. I will not put you in the line of fire."

"But I'm the target, not you."

"They don't want to hurt you," he argued softly. "What they want is to frighten you enough so you'll sell out and leave."

"I'm not selling."

"I don't want you to sell."

"And I'm not running," she insisted.

He smiled. "I don't want you to run, either." He kissed her again. "Take care of

Oliver while I clean up the glass and tape something over the windows. I'll be up as soon as I'm finished."

"You can stay. But just for tonight."

Jeff gave her a withering stare that she was sure had intimidated men who'd dared to try him. "I'll stay tonight, tomorrow night, and the next night until the property is secured."

Kara couldn't help but become excited at the thought of having Jeff close by.

CHAPTER THIRTEEN

Kara lay in bed, her face buried in a pillow. It wasn't until she'd stood in the bathroom, staring into the mirror while removing her makeup, that the enormity of what could've been hit her. She hadn't been able to stop the tears; however, by the time she'd finished with her shower, she was back in control.

Someone had gotten teenagers to throw rocks through her window to get her attention. Well, they had gotten it, and she heard their message loud and clear. Kara didn't want to think of what would've happened if Jeff hadn't come home with her. He said they were kids, but she'd known kids who'd killed their friends because they believed they'd disrespected them. Children so young they were tried as juveniles who'd turned on their parents, seriously injuring or killing them for an excuse as flimsy as not buying them a new pair of sneakers or a video game. And she didn't want to think someone would want to do more than throw rocks to get her to leave Angels Landing.

She managed to drift off to sleep, but then something woke her. She lay there, listening to what sounded like moaning. Sitting up, she saw Jeff slumped in the armchair.

"Jeff?"

When he didn't answer, she turned on the bedside lamp, slipped out of bed, and walking on bare feet, approached him. His eyes were closed, chest rising and falling heavily, his breathing raspy.

Kara shook him gently. "Jeff, wake up."

"No, Briggs! Don't stand up! Medic! I need a medic over here."

A cold chill raced through Kara. She was witnessing PTSD firsthand. Jeff was having a flashback. Cradling his face, she held his head firmly. "Jeffrey. Baby, please wake up." He moaned, trying to escape her hold. "It's okay, baby. That's it, wake up."

His eyelids fluttered wildly until he managed to focus. "I'm sorry for waking you. Go back to bed, sweetheart," he whispered.

She stroked his handsome face. "No." Kara was afraid if she left him in the chair the nightmare would return. "Come to bed with me."

"I can't."

"Yes, you can." Reaching for his hands, she tried pulling him off the chair, but he weighed too much. "Work with me, Jeff. Stand up." She watched his expression change, as if he was seeing her for the first time. It was then Kara realized he'd finally emerged from a place where he'd relived the horrors of war in his dreams.

Jeff stood up, towering over Kara in her bare feet. "I can't sleep in the same bed with you."

"Yes, you can."

"Are you sure?"

She smiled. "Very sure. Come on. Take off your clothes and get into bed."

Walking back to the bed, she got in and turned her back to give him a modicum of privacy. The sounds of Jeff undressing were magnified in the quiet room. She and Jeff having sex wasn't a concern to her. His flashback was.

During family therapy, Kara had led groups where either the mother or father had served in Iraq or Afghanistan. Most of them had returned with a myriad of emotional problems ranging from insomnia, depression, and paranoia to having flashbacks. Their transition back into civilian life was slow and painful for the soldiers and for their families.

She felt the mattress dip, then the warmth from Jeff's body as he lay beside her.

Jeff couldn't believe Kara had asked him to sleep in her bed. When he'd entered the bedroom after the ordeal, Kara was sleeping soundly. When he'd told her that he wasn't going to let her out of his sight, he was true to his word. The armchair in her sitting area had become his bed, he stepping into the role of her bodyguard. But as he slept the disturbing images that always plagued his mind resurfaced. This time they weren't as vivid as the others, and when Kara woke him, he wasn't in combat mode, ready to go after anything that moved. He was getting better and for that he was thankful.

"Do they come often?"

Jeff knew she was talking about his nightmares. "Not as often as they used to. There was a time when I had them every night, sometimes two or three a night." He froze when she pressed her breasts to his back. She might as well have been wearing nothing because the fabric of her nightgown was not much of a barrier between her and his boxers and T-shirt.

"Have you talked to anyone about them?"

He nodded and then realized she couldn't

see him in the darkened room. Shifting, he turned to face Kara. "Yes. I was seeing someone at the VA hospital. The psychiatrist wanted to put me on antianxiety medication, but I don't want to take anything."

"Do you feel anxious?" Kara asked.

"No. I don't think it has anything to do with anxiety. It's more like accepting that war is a game of odds and chances. When it's your time to die, nothing or no one can change that. But when it isn't, then you're coming home whole or maimed. I managed to come home whole, while others weren't so fortunate." He paused for a moment. "I'd lost count of the number of men who returned without arms, legs, or horribly scarred from IEDs."

"You can't feel guilty that you came home unscathed, Jeff. Have you thought that maybe you weren't injured because you had to take care of your grandmother and not the other way around?"

He smiled. "No. Thanks for reminding me."

"How often do you get to see your buddies?"

Jeff stared at Kara. "Are you going to bill me for this session?"

Kara looped her leg over Jeff's. "I didn't know you were a comedian."

He went completely still when her smooth leg touched his. He didn't want to believe she could be so trusting. They were in bed together, and only a cotton nightgown and his underwear kept them from being completely naked. And Kara was now well aware of how easily he'd become aroused whenever they were together.

"Well, you do ask a lot of questions."

"It comes with the profession. Speaking of professions. I repeat, how often do you see your buddies from the corps?"

Jeff rose on an elbow and rested his cheek on his fist. "Not as often as I would like to."

"My daddy has what he calls boys' week when he goes camping, fishing, or hunting with his friends from the corps. He had mild PTSD when he returned from the Gulf War, and adjusting to civilian life wasn't easy for him, so reconnecting with his buddies four or five times a year keeps him sane. Why don't you do something similar?"

"We usually meet in Charleston."

"And do what? Go to a bar and reminisce over drinks?"

"What's wrong with that?"

"Jeffrey, you can do that at the Happy Hour. What about inviting them to come here for a couple of days? Then hire a pleasure boat and go fishing. Sail down to

Hilton Head or Savannah and spend some time soaking up the atmosphere before coming back."

"It sounds like a wonderful plan, but I wouldn't feel comfortable leaving my grandmother alone for that length of time. A night or two is okay but not a week."

"She doesn't have to be alone, Jeff. You could hire a certified home health aide to stay with her."

"Grams would never allow a stranger to stay in her home."

"Would she allow me to stay with her?"

Pushing into a sitting position, Jeff supported his back against the headboard, then turned on the lamp. Kara also sat up, and a shaft of golden light illuminated her face. Resting his hand on her cheek, he kissed her forehead. The warmth and sweet smell that he associated with Kara seeped into him. Never had he wanted to make love to a woman so badly. And he meant making love, not having sex. Sex was something he could have with any woman.

"I think she would love to have you stay with her."

Reaching for the sheet, Kara pulled it up to her chin. "How do you feel about it?" she asked him. "Are you comfortable with me staying in your home while you're not there?"

"Of course. Why wouldn't I be?"

"You're very protective of your grand-mother."

He glanced away. "I have to be. She's all I have, and I'm all she has." Jeff's gaze shifted back to the woman whose very presence made him feel things he hadn't felt in a while. It wasn't her natural beauty or intel-ligence that drew him to her, but her empa-thy and compassion. "I never could've imagined sharing a bed with you for the first time without making love to you. I wanted it to be different."

Kara smiled up at him. "You wanted to date me first."

"How did you know?"

"You've been talking about taking me out ever since we met. But sometimes life works backward. I read a story in a magazine where this couple met, slept together on their first date, and then decided to get mar-ried because of their strict religious upbring-ing. They weren't in love when they mar-ried but learned to love each other."

Jeff covered her hand with his. "Are they still married?"

"They were celebrating their fortieth an-niversary with their four children and twelve grandchildren when the article was written."

"Is that how you see us, Kara? Making love, getting married, and settling down with children and then grandchildren?" She tried pulling her hand away, but Jeff tightened his hold on her slender fingers.

"No, Jeff. That's not how I see it at all. I'm not looking for a husband or children — at least not at this time in my life."

"What are you looking for?"

"If you would've asked me that question three weeks ago, I would've told you that I wanted my roommate to stop turning our apartment into a halfway house for the indigent. And instead of spending three weeks' vacation in Little Rock, I would've preferred spending at least two of those weeks in Paris. Everyone says springtime in Paris is magical."

"What's wrong with springtime on Cavanaugh Island?"

Kara rested her head on his shoulder. "There's nothing wrong with it. In fact, it's beautiful here. If it weren't for electricity and indoor plumbing, I would've thought that I'd stepped back in time. The swamps and marshes are primordial, the island's lifestyle is laid-back, and most people I've met are warm and friendly, but . . ."

"But what?" he asked when her words trailed off.

"I can't make plans for my future when I only plan to stay five years."

"If that's the case, then why stay at all?"

"Because of Taylor's will."

"Are you staying to spite your relatives?"

"No! The Pattons have nothing to do with my decision."

"You stay five years and go where, Kara? Are you going back to New York and pick up where you left off? Or is there a man in New York who promised to wait for you?"

She shook her head. "There's no man. And there hasn't been one in two years."

"You're kidding, aren't you?"

"No, I'm not."

He stared at the woman who'd tugged at his heart within minutes of meeting her. Kara coming to Angels Landing had changed him. It was the first time, other than working the 8:00 p.m. to 8:00 a.m. shift that he hadn't slept in his own bed. When he'd called his grandmother to let her know he was spending the night with Kara, her response had been, "It's about time." He knew Corrine liked Kara because she was always asking about her.

Jeff let go of Kara's hand and smoothed her mussed hair. "You're a young, beautiful, intelligent, educated woman. Why wouldn't men be knocking down your door to take you out?"

A wry smile parted Kara's lips as she stared at him. "It's not that I couldn't get a date."

"Then what was it?"

"My job had taken over my life."

Jeff wanted to tell Kara it had been the same with him. For twenty years his life centered around serving his country. He'd known men who had addictions: drugs, alcohol, gambling, and women. For him it had been the military. And he knew if his grandmother hadn't had a heart attack, he still would be on active duty.

"My hours were eight to four, but most times I didn't leave the office until six, sometimes seven," Kara continued after a pregnant pause. "Updating case records had become an uphill battle I had no chance of ever winning. Whenever a social worker retired they were never replaced, so when the supervisors divided up their case-loads that meant a few more cases that I had to deal with."

"How many cases were you required to carry?"

"The ideal ratio is thirty to one, but there were times when I carried as many as fifty."

"It's a wonder you didn't burn out."

"Now, when I look back, I realize I was close to it." Kara smothered a yawn with her free hand.

He smiled. "Let's go to sleep, sleepyhead."

Kara yawned again. "I'm scheduled to meet with an engineer and a historic preservation specialist tomorrow."

He extinguished the light and eased Kara down beside him, pulling her close until her hips were pressed against his groin. "Good night, baby."

"How's Oliver?" Kara whispered.

He didn't want to believe she was worried about her dog when it should've been her own safety. "He's sleeping. Your baby's going to be a good watchdog because he reacts to every sound."

"I know," she said softly. "He's like an early warning system letting me know whenever Mrs. Todd comes and goes. I think she's a little put off with him being underfoot."

"Your baby is spoiled."

Kara laughed. "That's because he's so adorable."

"So is his mama. Go to sleep, Kara."

"Yes, Daddy."

Jeff left at dawn, warning Kara to keep the

doors locked. He told her he would contact the security company the Cove used when they installed the cameras in the downtown business district.

Kara had taken care of Oliver's needs and then called a Haven Creek glazier, leaving a voice mail that she needed to replace broken windows at Angels Landing. The man had called her back an hour later, promising he would be there before noon.

She told Mrs. Todd about what had happened but not the rocks' message. "All of the doors to the house must remain locked at all times," she told the housekeeper.

"Miss Teddy and Mr. Taylor never locked the house until it was time to go to bed."

Kara gave the older woman a warm smile. "There will be a lot of workmen coming and going for months. Even though everything in the house is insured, I still need to take measures just in case something is stolen. I want to try and avoid having to have to deal with the insurance company."

Mrs. Todd sucked her teeth. "Ain't no one stealing from here."

She decided to take another route. "When was the last time you had someone working in the house?"

"I don't rememba."

"And because you don't remember that

means it's been a long time. It's not going to be one or two people, Mrs. Todd, but a lot of people coming and going."

"What you havin' done?"

Resting her hands on the housekeeper's shoulders, Kara steered her over to the table in the corner of the kitchen. "Sit down, I'll bring you your coffee while we talk."

"No!"

"Please, Mrs. Todd, allow me."

Mrs. Todd narrowed her eyes behind her glasses. "Okay. If you say so."

"I say so. Every morning you get up to make breakfast for me. Today's my turn."

"You can cook?"

"Why does everyone believe I can't cook?"

"Who said you cain't?"

"Jeffrey Hamilton."

Mrs. Todd angled her head. "Corrine raised a fine young man. The gals all over the island were after him at one time. That ended when he went into the service. He came back in his uniform looking all handsome, and it started up again. But he paid them no mind."

Kara didn't want to talk about Jeff, not when she woke to find his erection pulsing against her hips. His soft snores and the gentle rise and fall of his chest verified he was asleep when another part of his body

347

wasn't. She was still in bed when he got up, dressed, and leaned over to tell her to get up and lock the door behind him.

"I'm going to have people come in and strip all of the walls," she said, deftly switching the topic from Jeff to restoring the house.

"Are you going to put up more paper?"

Kara nodded. "Yes." She filled a cup with coffee, then added a generous splash of evaporated milk, handing the cup and saucer to the housekeeper. Mrs. Todd had admitted she'd grown up using canned rather than cows' milk because she was lactose intolerant.

Mrs. Todd took a sip. "It's jest the way I like it. What about the paper?"

"The paperhangers will probably have to repair the walls before they put up new wallpaper. Personally, I would leave the walls bare, but that wouldn't be in keeping with what this house looked like in 1862."

Kara busied herself filling a pot with water for grits, then opened the refrigerator and took out eggs, butter, and breakfast links. "Do you want biscuits, Mrs. Todd?"

"You make biscuits, baby?"

"I sure do."

"Who taught you to cook?"

"My mama, who learned from her mama."

Jeannette's mother was actually her aunt. Kara's maternal grandmother had died when Jeannette was two, and the aunt for whom she'd been named adopted her. Kara didn't remember either of her grandfathers. By the time she was ready to go to elementary school, both had passed away.

Mrs. Todd touched the coronet of hair she braided every morning. "You're nothing like these young girls nowadays who cain't even boil water. They always eatin' out or orderin' in."

"I order in and eat out, but I prefer eating home-cooked meals." Kara removed the top to a large crock shaped like a chicken and scooped out enough flour to make at least a dozen biscuits.

If she'd been in New York, her breakfast would've been a hastily eaten bowl of cereal with a cup of coffee. Lunch was usually on the run, and when she worked late, dinner hardly figured into the equation of having three meals a day. If she didn't heat up leftovers in the microwave, she would pick up something from the corner deli. One time she'd brought enough to take for lunch the following day, she woke to find it half-eaten; it was the last time she'd done that.

Her cell phone rang, and Kara took it out of the back pocket of her jeans, staring at the display. She tapped a button. "Hi, Daddy."

"Did I wake you, baby girl?"

Kara glanced at the clock on the microwave. It wasn't quite eight o'clock. "No. I've been up for hours."

"This is supposed to be your vacation. Don't you know how to relax?"

"I am relaxing, Daddy. I'm making breakfast for the first time in what seems like ages."

"Good for you. Your mama told me everything about the will."

Kara turned her back when she saw Mrs. Todd staring at her. "What do you think?"

"I think you're getting what you deserve, Kara. What Taylor didn't do for you in life, he made up for in death. And I'm glad he never stepped up to be the father he should've been because then I never would've had my baby girl. I don't know why me and your mama didn't have any more children, but we were blessed to have had you."

"And you're the best father in the world, Daddy," she whispered into the phone. "I want you and Mama to come to Angels Landing and spend some time with me."

"You know I have all the time in the world, but it's your mama who has a problem getting off from work."

"Please, Daddy, try and talk her into taking some more time off. I can even introduce you to a few ex-marines."

"Didn't I teach you that there's no such thing as an ex-marine. Once a marine, always a marine."

Kara laughed. "Sorry about that."

"I know she's taking off Good Friday and Easter Monday, so maybe we'll come and see you then."

"Thank you, thank you, thank you, Daddy. When do you plan to leave Little Rock?"

She'd thought her father would view her accepting her inheritance from Taylor as an act of betrayal, when Austin had been the one who'd married her mother and given her his name. Austin was her father in every way; the exception was sharing DNA.

"If we leave Thursday night, with the both of us driving, we should make it to Charleston early Friday morning."

"That'll work. After you rest up I'll take you around to show you the island. This year you and Mama are going to relax while I prepare Easter dinner."

"That'll work," Austin repeated.

"I'll see you guys at the end of next week . . . Daddy?"

"What is it, baby girl?"

"I love you."

There came a long pause before Austin said, "I love you, too, Kara."

She ended the call, staring at Mrs. Todd who'd watched her between furtive sips of coffee. "That was my father."

"Humph. Your father or your daddy?"

Kara went back to adding baking powder and salt to the flour, then sifted the dry ingredients into another bowl. "He's both," she replied, cutting pieces of cold butter into the mixture until it resembled fine meal. She added a small amount of milk until she'd achieved the right consistency.

Mrs. Todd set down the china cup Theodora had used for her special guests. She'd told Kara that had all changed once Teddy died and Taylor began using them every day until he too passed on. "It wasn't that Mr. Taylor didn't want to be your daddy."

Kara's hands stilled, and then she turned on the oven. "Why would you say that?"

Mrs. Todd stood up, walking over to join Kara at the cloth-covered oaken table. "It was Miss Teddy. She ruined every friendship he had with a woman. And when she found the letter your mother sent him 'bout carryin' his baby, she was like a crazy woman. She went on and on 'bout how could he be so irresponsible to make a baby out of wedlock. Miss Teddy didn't even know your mama, yet she claimed she was out to trick her boy into marrying her."

Picking up a baking sheet from a shelf under the table, Kara took a forkful of dough and rolled it between her floured hands, then placed it on the ungreased sheet. "If Taylor knew my mother was carrying his baby, why didn't he contact her?"

"Miss Teddy knew how to work her son. She nagged at him day in and day out until he finally gave into her. Out of all of her children, Taylor was the only one who couldn't stand up to her, and she knew it. Her daughters are jest like her. They have tongues like switches, and they raised they kids to be nasty, too. In the end Taylor wouldn't have nothin' to do with them."

And now they're angry with me because I'll have nothing to do with them, either, Kara thought. "Don't they know they can catch more flies with molasses than with vinegar?"

Mrs. Todd sucked her teeth again. "You cain't tell them nothin' because they are Pattons, and 'round here that means everything."

"What do they do besides being Pattons?"

"They are doctors, lawyers, and teachers. Supposedly respectable folk. But they sure can act like heathens when need be."

Kara finished rolling out a dozen biscuits. She wanted to tell Mrs. Todd that she'd witnessed the Pattons' behavior in living color. "I'm glad my name isn't Patton."

"It doesn't matter what your name is. You still a Patton."

She didn't want to tell Mrs. Todd that her so-called relatives had fired the first salvo by having rocks thrown at the windows painted with a message she would have to be a complete idiot not to understand. What would be their next move? Have someone shoot at her?

Kara would take Jeff's advice and keep the doors locked at all times. She would also stay close to the house until the security company set up cameras around the property.

"What do you want with your grits and biscuits, Mrs. Todd?" she asked.

"I seasoned some whitin' 'cause I was fixin' to have fish and grits this morning."

"Well, fish and grits it is. Would you mind if I make it in the oven instead of frying it on the stove?"

"Will it be crispy?" Mrs. Todd asked. "My Willie likes his fish real crispy."

"Yes, Mrs. Todd. It will be crispy." Kara was aware that Mrs. Todd was old school, frying everything from chicken to fish and spareribs. The ribs were delicious, cooking in hot oil two to three minutes when compared to more than an hour in the oven.

What Kara had found startling was that even with their diet of fried foods, the Todds were slender, and she attributed that to them being in constant motion. Mr. Todd spent all day walking around the property, pruning and weeding trees and shrubs or cleaning out the pond where a flock of ducks had taken up residence. The highlight of his day was when he sat on the riding mower.

Mrs. Todd sat on a stool, watching Kara as she sprayed the seasoned fillets with a cooking spray, dusted them in cornmeal, and then sprayed them again before placing them gently on a parchment-covered baking sheet. "Where are you going to stay when they start working inside the house?"

"I'm going to move into the other guesthouse."

"Let me know when you are ready to move in, and I'll air it out for you."

"Thank you."

She'd thanked Mrs. Todd when she wanted to tell the older woman that she didn't want or need a personal maid. She made her own bed, cleaned her bathroom, and did her own laundry, leaving the housekeeper to dust and vacuum. If she hadn't walked the beach or passed the time digging up dead roots and vines that had been Theodora's award-winning garden, Kara would've gone completely stir-crazy.

Her cell phone rang again, and Mrs. Todd moved off the stool to check on the biscuits and fish while Kara answered the call. It was Jeff, informing her to expect the security company technician within the hour. Her entire morning and afternoon would be filled with meetings with the engineer, glazier, and now the security company.

"I really appreciate your help. How can I repay you?"

"Go to the movies with me."

"When?" Kara asked.

"Tonight."

"What time are you picking me up?"

"Nine."

"I'll be ready."

Kara hung up, smiling. She had a date — the first one in more than two years.

CHAPTER FOURTEEN

Jeff's grin spoke volumes. Kara had chosen to wear black again, but this time it was a pair of stretch pants, high-heeled booties, and a long-sleeved T-shirt and a wide leather belt that showed off her narrow waist. She brushed her hair and secured it in a pony-tail, and the light cover of makeup accentu-ated her lush mouth and shimmering eyes. Dipping his head, he pressed a kiss to the gold stud in her ear.

"You look incredible."

She gave him a demure smile. "Thank you." She opened the door wider. "I just have to get my bag and keys."

He stood in the entryway, staring up at the plasterwork around the hanging fixture. If the walls could talk in the three-story, twenty-room mansion, they would probably tell secrets known by only the people who'd lived there. His grandmother knew more about the Pattons than he had. His only interaction had been with Harlan who'd bullied him relentlessly until by virtue of Jeff's height and weight it had stopped.

Jeff had decided to ignore the animosity between him and Harlan until the mayor of Angels Landing opened his mouth to defame Kara. The man's twisted mind had him assuming they were sleeping together when nothing was further from the truth at that time.

Kara had come to Cavanaugh Island a month ago, and during that time Jeff was aware that his feelings for her had changed dramatically. What had begun as a favor to his cousin was now an all-encompassing need to take care of her, though he suspected she didn't care for him the way he was beginning to care for her.

As Taylor Patton's heir she'd become the largest single landowner on Cavanaugh Island, and if the rumors were true, then she was also quite wealthy. If she did need him, it would only be for protection. He could do that as sheriff of the island, but his protective instincts were deeper than his civic duty. Jeff wanted to love her and take care of her — something he hadn't done for any woman other than his grandmother.

"Come back here!"

He turned just in time to see Oliver scurrying away from Kara. Moving quickly, he scooped up the puppy. "Where are you running to?"

"I opened the crate to give him fresh water, and he escaped."

Cradling the dog as if he were a football, Jeff carried him back to his crate. "Personally, I'd let you have the run of the house, but it's apparent your mama wants to keep you on house arrest."

"I heard that, Jeffrey Hamilton," Kara said behind him.

"I intended for you to hear that, Kara Newell. Do you let him out during the day?"

"Of course, I let him out. I only put him in the crate whenever I go out. Right now, he's teething and gnawing on the baseboards. He hasn't attacked the legs of the furniture, so hopefully they'll be spared."

Jeff placed the terrier in the crate and slid the latch shut. "I thought you bought him some chew toys."

"He doesn't want his chew toys. The only time he's quiet is when we sit out on the porch together. I think he's more feline than canine because he loves the sun. He looks for a patch of sunlight, then settles down to sleep for hours."

Reaching for Kara's hand, Jeff brought it to his mouth, kissing the back of it. "I hope you aren't thinking of replacing me with Oliver as your companion."

Smiling up at him through her lashes, Kara nodded. "He's a nice little companion. He barked so much today that it's a wonder he isn't hoarse. Every time the doorbell rang he went ballistic. But . . . there's no way he can replace you."

Jeff waited for Kara to lock up the house, then led her to where he'd parked his car. During the short drive to the Cove, she told him the windows had been replaced and the security technician had recommended wiring the house with different zones. The guesthouses and garages would also be secured. Cameras would be installed along the path leading up to the house and in trees around the perimeter of the property as far as the slave village. Everything would be monitored from a central location with access to the local police and fire departments. He would install control panels on all three floors, with no delay signals at the back and rear entrances.

"If anyone were to come in the back door after I armed the system, then the alarm would go off immediately."

"And the call would come in to the station house," Jeff said. "We'll answer the call and alert the Charleston PD in case the perp tries to get off the island using the causeway."

"I hope it doesn't come to that."

"I feel the same way."

Jeff parked in the lot behind the courthouse. He knew parking was limited at the movie theater, and on the weekends it was similar to trying to find a space at the mall during Christmas shopping season. "We'll walk from here," he told Kara as he opened the door to come around and assist her.

The downtown area was illuminated with streetlamps and tiny white lights throughout the town square. Water spilling from the fountain was a sure sign that spring had come to the island. The benches surrounding the fountains were filled with teenagers and other townspeople taking advantage of the warm weather.

He tucked her hand into the bend of his elbow. "You can tell when it's springtime on the island. Everyone is out at night, especially on the weekends."

Kara sniffed the air. "It smells like spring. I've been trying to clear away the overgrowth of weeds that had been Theodora's garden. I had Mr. Todd cut back most of the brush because I didn't want to have to deal with snakes."

"Are you afraid of snakes?"

"No. I actually have a healthy respect for them. If they don't bother me, then I won't bother them."

"We have at least six poisonous snakes here on the island. There are the three Cs: copperhead, cottonmouth, and eastern coral. The rattlers are eastern diamondback, timber, and Carolina pigmy. The pigmy is the most dangerous because most of the time you can't hear the rattles until it's too late."

"Now you're scaring me."

Jeff tightened his hold on her hand, nodding and smiling to several permanent boarders at the Cove Inn. "I don't want to frighten you. I just want you to be careful."

"How's David?"

"Other than a pounding headache, he says he'll survive. He claims he's going to call you and thank you for looking out for him."

"I'm sorry he broke up with his girlfriend. How long were they together?"

"They must have dated off and on for about five years."

Kara stopped, forcing Jeff to stop with her. "He dated her for five years and only now was he ready to propose marriage?"

"What's wrong with that?"

"What's right with it, Jeff? If a man can't commit to a woman after two years, then he should get out of her life and let someone else willing to commit step in. It's no wonder she cheated on him."

Jeff started walking again, she keeping pace. "Would you cheat on a man who didn't commit?"

"We're not talking about me."

"I'm talking about you."

"No, because I'd leave him before I cheated. I don't know what men are afraid of," Kara continued. "They find a good woman, but for some asinine reason they're always looking for someone better. Most times there isn't anyone better than what they have. Look at some of these entertainers who father children with either one or different women. And because they don't marry them, they don't think of themselves as adulterers. Well, in my book they are lower than a snake's belly."

"Damn, baby! Calm down."

"I won't calm down, Jeff. Did David tell you before last night that he was going to propose to Petra?"

"I don't think so."

"I'm not judging him, but he had to have known his girlfriend was getting restless; otherwise he wouldn't have suddenly decided to propose."

"I don't know."

"He's your cousin. Don't you guys talk?"

"We talk, but David has always been a very private person."

Kara stopped again, her free hand going to the middle of Jeff's chest. "I like David, and it bothered me to see him hurting like that."

"Do you ever stop being a social worker?"

"You're impossible," Kara spat out.

Jeff cradled her face. "I had a long talk with my cousin. He's not as fragile as he appears. He realizes he should've asked Petra to marry him a long time ago, but she always gave him mixed signals."

"Did you like her?"

A hint of a smile played at the corners of his mouth. "I like her but not for David. She's a party girl, while David is a homebody. You talk about David when it would be no different with us."

Vertical lines appeared between her eyes when she frowned. "What are you talking about?"

"We date each other for five years; then one day you tell me you're going back to New York. Would you expect me to remain faithful to you if I know what we have isn't going to last?"

"It's not the same, Jeff," Kara argued softly.

"Because you say it isn't, darling, but actually it is. Can you stand here right now and tell me you'll commit to staying longer than five years?"

"You know I can't do that."

"If that's the case, then we'll drop the subject and head over to the theater before the movie begins." She opened her mouth to come back at him, but Jeff placed his thumb over her parted lips, shushing her. "We'll discuss this later."

Kara smiled as if she'd won a small victory. "Fine. Later. What's playing?"

"*The Help.*"

Her eyebrows lifted a fraction. "I've read the book but missed seeing the film."

They made it to the theater with time to spare. Jeff paid for the tickets, ignoring the stares of moviegoers looking at Kara. He knew they were curious about her and even more curious about them as a couple. Plus, it was the first time any of them had seen him with a woman.

He looped his arm around her waist. "Would you like popcorn?"

"Only if you'll share it with me."

Kara watched Jeff as he stood in the concession line. She noticed the sidelong glances directed his way by several women, who whispered to one another, and she wondered how often he came to movies. He'd admitted that he had never dated a woman from the island, so there was no doubt tonight would spark talk about him being seen with Taylor Patton's daughter.

She saw him turn around and speak to a man with Deborah Monroe, assuming the tall man with salt-and-pepper hair was Dr. Monroe, Deborah's husband. Kara smiled when Deborah waved to her, mouthing hello. Kara nodded, returning her smile. It was Saturday night, date night, and couples were filing into the movie theater.

The Cove Theater claimed a single screen, unlike the cineplex theaters in New York City and its suburbs where moviegoers could choose from up to a dozen films. And for someone who'd spent the past fifteen years of her life in the big city, small-town life was beginning to appeal to her. She'd become accustomed to smelling fresh air and damp earth rather than exhaust fumes from cars and buses. Sitting on the porch had become a luxury when she was serenaded by the sound of crickets rather than the sirens from first responders and other emergency vehicles.

Moving to Angels Landing had given Kara a chance to restart her life. She was still a social worker at heart, but she wasn't forced to get up every day and go into an office. She no longer had to share an apartment with a roommate because she couldn't afford to live alone. A twenty-room antebellum mansion went beyond anything she could've ever imagined.

When she listed all of the reasons why she'd been so amenable about leaving a lifestyle she'd become accustomed to, Kara knew Jeff had a lot to do with it. He hadn't done more than kiss her, yet she'd come to look for his kisses. They'd shared a bed, and he hadn't tried to coerce her into making love.

She was a normal woman with normal urges, urges she'd forgotten existed until she'd sat across the table from Jeff in Jack's Fish House. Though Jeff was a friend, the feelings she was beginning to have for him weren't very friendly.

Kara's gaze lingered on his strong, distinctive profile. A myriad of emotions assailed her, and she refused to acknowledge that she could be falling in love with him. She closed her eyes and shook her head as if banishing the notion. She couldn't and wouldn't, not when she could not commit to living in Angels Landing beyond the five-year mandate.

Jeff beckoned her, and she took a large tub of popcorn from him as he picked up two cups of soda. Kara rarely drank soda, but soda and popcorn at the movies was like peanut butter and jelly. They just went together.

"I hope there're still some seats in the balcony."

They made their way into the theater where the screen was filled with images of trailers for upcoming movies. Kara followed Jeff as he climbed the stairs to the balcony. There were two seats but not together. Jeff leaned down and whispered to a young man who nodded and moved to another seat.

"Thanks, Wes."

"No biggie, Sheriff," the teenager mumbled.

Kara sat down, smiling at Jeff when he dropped down beside her, anchoring the drinks in the cup holders. "Did you get napkins?" she whispered. He'd added butter to the popcorn.

Rising slightly, he took a handkerchief from the pocket of his slacks. "You can use this."

Seconds later the lights dimmed and the filled theater settled down to view the featured film.

Jeff cast a sidelong glance at Kara as she pressed her head to the car's headrest. "Did they do the book justice?"

"Yes. I can't tell you how many times I read a book, then go and see the movie only to be disappointed. This time I wasn't."

He downshifted as he approached the road connecting the Cove with the Landing. It was scheduled to be paved at the end of the month, and that couldn't come soon enough for Jeff. He never complained publicly because there was a time when the Landing was virtually inaccessible except on foot. And there weren't too many people brave or reckless enough to attempt to drive or walk through the swampy area with poisonous vipers, quicksand, and alligators.

"My parents are coming here for Easter, and if you and Miss Corrine aren't planning anything, I'd like for you to join us," Kara continued when he didn't respond. "I told my father that I'd introduce him to several marines."

Jeff gave her a quick glance. "How long are they staying?"

"Just for the weekend. They plan to arrive on Friday and leave Monday."

"I'll make certain to join you." He'd given Kara's suggestion about a corps' week a lot of thought. He'd even called one of his buddies and ran the idea past him, who promised to contact the others in their group for their feedback.

"What about Miss Corrine?"

"I'm certain she'll also come with me. I usually give my deputies off on Christmas and Thanksgiving because they have families. Easter's the only family holiday I claim for myself. So if there's someplace your dad would like to see, let me know."

"I'll give Daddy your cell number, and the two of you can talk."

A deep chuckle filled the interior of the small car. "Are you saying you don't want anything to do with the corps?"

Kara's laughter joined his. "Just say I've heard enough corps stories to last several lifetimes. I don't know what it is about marines that make them —"

"Don't go there, baby," Jeff warned softly. "The corps is sacred."

"And that is sacrilegious," she countered with a laugh.

Jeff winked at her when she met his gaze. "We'll get along just fine as long as you don't dis the corps."

Fisting her hands at her waist, Kara gave

him a "no you didn't" look. "Are you saying you like the corps more than me?"

Jeff didn't want to believe, couldn't believe Kara had just repeated what Pamela had asked him when she'd issued her ultimatum. Six months into their engagement, they'd begun making plans for their wedding, and without warning his fiancée revealed she wasn't cut out to become a military wife. When she'd asked if he'd loved the corps more than her, she took his slight hesitation as an affirmative and gave him back his ring. What Pamela failed to realize was that the military was all he knew. It'd been ingrained in him like involuntary breathing.

Before he'd left the Cove to attend college, Jeff wasn't certain what he wanted to do with his life. He'd always excelled in math and science and had thought of becoming a doctor. It was when he was approached by a recruiter to enroll in the NROTC that he realized the military suited his temperament.

He'd come to love all things military, the corps becoming his wife, mistress, and child, his fellow officers brothers and sisters, and the men under his command his extended family. But that all changed when he got the phone call that his grandmother had been hospitalized due to a heart attack.

Twenty years of drills, parades, and two tours in a war zone were forgotten when he stood at his grandmother's bedside, holding her hand while promising to take care of her. And he had.

"No, Kara. I don't like the corps more than you. In fact, I like you much more than I'd planned to."

"Are you saying you didn't want to like me?"

"That's exactly what I'm saying. David asked me to check on you after the Pattons threatened you, but you and I know my checking on you has progressed beyond protection. One of the most difficult things I've ever had to do was *not* make love to you last night. For a few minutes I forgot that someone tried to frighten you into leaving. And I wanted to forget the images from my dreams . . . men being blown apart by explosive devices, some whose bodies and minds would never be whole again."

Kara rested her hand over Jeff's on the gearshift. "I don't want you to want me to chase away your demons, Jeff. I want you to want me for me because I know in my heart I want *you,* not the marine or the sheriff."

He drove along the allée of oaks, slowing and driving around to the rear of the house. Kara had left on lights on the first and second floors, giving the appearance that the house was occupied.

Jeff felt an indescribable emotion of rightness. It was the first time he'd become involved with a woman where he felt a gentle, soothing peace. The only other time he'd experienced a similar feeling was when he'd stepped off the ferry at the Sanctuary Cove landing as a civilian. His decision to resign his commission had become a no-brainer. Nothing, not even the corps, was more important to him than his grandmother. But unknowingly Kara had also become important to him, much more important than she could've imagined. There were times when he couldn't keep his hands off her, and he found any and every opportunity to kiss her when he'd wanted to do so much more.

The one thing that kept him from aggressively pursuing her was the disclosure that she hadn't planned to stay on the island. And Jeff had to ask himself whether he was willing to engage in a relationship with a woman with an expiration date. His grandmother had begun to nag him that he was getting older, not younger, and it was time he think about his future. Did he want their branch on the family tree to end with him? Was he really so selfish that he refused to share his life with a woman? He'd given her a lethal stare when she asked if perhaps he preferred men to women. Corrine knew he was heterosexual, but she admitted she was just repeating some of the gossip she'd heard from those in the Cove.

He parked the car, shut off the engine, and turned to look at Kara. "There will only be Jeffrey and Kara, not Captain Hamilton or Sheriff Hamilton."

Unbuckling her seat belt, Kara leaned into him. "And there will only be Kara, not the social worker who must analyze everyone and everything."

Laughing, Jeff held up his hand, pinkie extended. "Pinkie swear?"

Kara looped their pinkies together. "Pinkie swear," she repeated.

"Don't move. I'll come around and get you."

Reaching for the small automatic strapped to his ankle, Jeff pushed it into the small of his back as he got out of the car. He held Kara's hand in a firm grip as he helped her to stand. All of his senses were on full alert when he walked with her to the side entrance, waiting as she unlocked the door. Within seconds of walking into the house, they heard Oliver barking.

Kara glanced at Jeff over her shoulder.

"What did I tell you about my early warning system?" Kneeling, she opened the crate and Oliver launched himself at her, wiggling and whining in his excitement to be let out of confinement. She kissed the top of his head as she cradled him to her chest. "Hi, baby. Mama's glad to see you, too."

Jeff knew Oliver was a dog, but he tried to imagine Kara with a child. She and the dog had bonded instantly, and it had taken a very short time for her to spoil her pet. Would it be the same if she had children? But then he remembered her statement that she wasn't ready for marriage and children, and he wondered if she would ever be ready for it. Some women were destined not to become wives or mothers. Maybe Kara was one of them.

"I'm going to check around to make certain there're no more broken windows."

"As soon as I change Oliver's pad, I'll be up."

Jeff started at the third floor, opening and closing doors to closets and looking under the beds in the bedrooms. He repeated the action on the second floor, knowing the action would be unnecessary once the security company wired the house and property.

He'd just set the automatic on the bedside table in Kara's bedroom when she walked in. He extended his arms and wasn't disappointed when she walked into his embrace. He held her, heart to heart, man to woman, silently communicating feelings he couldn't put into words. The scrappy, intuitive woman in his arms had captured a part of himself he'd withheld from every woman in his past, including Pamela.

Jeff hadn't stopped to ask himself whether it was because he was different, that his focus had changed when he'd become a civilian for the first time in two decades. Whatever it was, he didn't want to spend time trying to analyze himself or why he felt so strongly about Kara. Burying his face in her hair, he pressed a kiss to her scalp, when she anchored her arms under his shoulders.

She lifted her head, and he stared at the serene expression that had spread across her delicate features. "I want to make love to you. Will you allow me to do that?" The question had come from some place Jeff was totally unfamiliar with. In the past he'd never asked. It was something that just happened.

Kara's eyelids fluttered as she blinked back unshed tears. "Yes, Jeff," she whispered. "Make love to me."

One minute she was standing, and seconds later she was on the bed. He removed his shoes and socks, then lay over her, his body pressing hers down to the mattress. Time stood still, and the earth stopped spinning on its axis as Jeff slowly, methodically undressed Kara, his mouth charting a course over her silken flesh from the scented column of her neck to her slender feet. Her clothes had concealed a curvy, womanly body that had shocked him with its lushness. Her firm breasts were full, perched high above a narrow rib cage and flat belly. Her hips were rounded, thighs firm, legs shapely.

Her eyes were wide, trusting as he sat back on his knees and removed his own clothing: pullover sweater, belt, slacks, and underwear. He paused long enough to remove a condom from the pocket of his slacks and placed it on the table. They shared a smile when she held out her arms, and he sank into her perfumed embrace. Jeff lay between her outstretched legs.

"Do you know how long I've wanted to do this?" he confessed in her ear.

"No. How long?" she whispered.

"Since the first night I came here, and you opened the door wearing next to nothing."

She laughed softly. "That's what you get for making unannounced night calls."

"I find myself losing control whenever I'm

around you."

"Since we're into true confessions, I have one to make."

"What is it?"

"Since meeting you I've had a few erotic dreams and —"

He stopped Kara's words when his mouth covered hers in a smoldering kiss that left him feeling light-headed. Jeff had thought he'd been the only one harboring erotic fantasies, but apparently he was wrong.

He realized he was falling in love with her. What he didn't want to think about was losing her like every other woman he'd lost in his life.

He didn't know his mother, but she had to love her unborn child to hold on long enough to give birth to him. Then there was Pamela — the only woman he'd confessed to loving and she'd left him. Jeff didn't want to think of his grandmother, who, at seventy-nine, had most of her life behind her. And now there was Kara.

Could he afford to walk into a situation where he was certain of the outcome? As much as he'd tried to stay away from the pull, it was too strong to resist because he discovered that he wanted her in and out of bed. And if she'd insisted they wait a year before making love, Jeff knew he would've waited. She'd come to mean that much to him. "Having you here with me is good," Kara admitted. A small gasp of surprise escaped her when Jeff fastened his mouth to her breast, suckling her like a starving infant, and her body responded, arching up to meet him.

Nothing was rushed. His kisses started at the base of her throat and trailed lower to her belly. His teeth grazed over her nipples, turning them into hard buds. But everything changed when he placed his hands against her inner thighs, spreading her legs, sending a rush of moisture between them. Then the sensual assault began.

Kara rose off the mattress as he searched for the tiny bud of flesh at the apex of her thighs, and once finding it, laved it with his tongue until he knew she was close to climax.

She gripped the sheets, swallowing the moans trapped in the back of her throat, gasping as if unable to take a breath.

Cupping her hips in both hands, Jeff plunged his tongue into Kara's quivering flesh over and over until he lost count of how many times he'd drank deeply. He felt her entire body trembling and heard her plea for him to stop, but he couldn't. He'd wanted to brand her as his possession like a permanent tattoo and make her forget all the other men who'd been in her life. And for a brief crazed moment, he wanted to be the last man in her bed and in her life.

He did heed her pleas to stop, but it was to open the packet, remove the condom, and roll it down his tumescence. Taking her hand, he stared at her and together they guided his erection inside her. She gasped, going still until he was fully sheathed inside her hot throbbing flesh.

Jeff made slow, deliberate love to Kara until he established a rhythm she followed as if they'd choreographed it in advance, their bodies keeping perfect tempo with each other. Even with the thin barrier of latex, he still could feel her heat as he quickened his thrusts. Soft moans filled the room, and she rose to meet his strong thrusts, their bodies in exquisite harmony with each other, hurtling him to a point of no return.

His scrotum tightened painfully, and the burning sensation at the base of his spine was an indication that he was going to ejaculate. Jeff tried concentrating on anything but the woman writhing underneath him. He closed his eyes, shutting out the sight of her thrashing head and the rush of color darkening her face and chest.

Burying his head between her neck and shoulder, he quickened his movements and then released the desire, lust, and passion that had been building since the first time he walked into the garden room to find Kara rising off the chair like an apparition in a dream.

He felt Kara's orgasm as her flesh squeezed his penis, released him, and then squeezed him again and again. It was his turn to plead with her to stop when her vaginal muscles held his semierect penis in a viselike grip.

"Oh, baby, baby, baby," he chanted over and over until her throbbing flesh stilled and he was able to pull out. Rolling off her body, Jeff lay on his back, arms above his head as he tried slowing down his runaway heartbeat. He let out an audible sigh when Kara climbed atop him.

"Are you all right," she whispered in his ear.

"I don't know yet."

Kara rested her cheek on his muscled chest. "Don't you dare pass out on me, Jeff."

He smiled. "I'm not going to pass out. I just need to catch my breath."

They lay together, he barely feeling the weight of the body molded to the length of his. Jeff wasn't certain when Kara had fallen asleep because he had also. When he did wake, it was hours later. Kara lay beside him, curled into the fetal position. He went to the bathroom to discard the condom.

He returned to the bed, got in next to the woman whose scent was stamped on his skin like a tattoo, and pulled a sheet and lightweight blanket over their bodies. He fell asleep again. His internal alarm clock woke him at six, and Jeff managed to get out of bed, dress, write a note explaining his absence, and leave the house through the rear door, the door locking behind him.

It wasn't the way he'd wanted to leave Kara, but he was scheduled to relieve Nelson Lambert at eight that morning. It was early Sunday morning, and the Cove had yet to stir when he maneuvered his car under the carport next to his grandmother's.

Jeff used the back staircase to his bedroom. He shaved, showered, and dressed, then went downstairs to the kitchen to prepare breakfast. His cooking skills weren't four star, but he was able to put together a more than passable breakfast.

He'd just finished flipping buckwheat pancakes, placing them on a plate next to a bowl of sliced strawberries and peaches, when his grandmother walked into the kitchen. She was dressed for church in a becoming shirtwaist dress and sensible pumps. The single strand of pearls around her neck matched the pair in her ears.

"Good morning, Gram."

Corrine smiled. "Good morning, Jeffrey. Slept out last night, did you?" She picked up her favorite coffeepot and filled it with water.

Jeff refused to look at her. "Why are you asking a question you already know the answer to?"

"I just needed to hear it for myself."

His hands stilled before he set the plate on the table. "Who told you?"

"Hannah Forsyth called last night, waking me out of a good sleep to tell me she saw you and Kara at the movies. And I figured when you didn't come home, you were with her."

Jeff shook his head. "Damn, Gram!"

"Jeffrey, you know I don't abide with cussin' in my house on Sunday."

"Sorry about that. What did she do? Put a GPS tracker on my car?"

"You haven't been away that long that you don't know how fast gossip spreads across the island. The next thing you know they'll have you and Kara married with a house full of kids."

"That's not going to happen, Gram."

"Why not?"

"Because she doesn't plan on living here past five years."

Corrine frowned. "That's nonsense. If she stays five, then why not ten or even thirty? That will doesn't mean anything. He could've said thirty years. And what would she have done? Live here for that length of time, then pick up and leave? I don't think so, Jeffrey. You know I've never been one to get into your personal business, but it's going to be up to you to change her mind. And you don't need five years to do that. My sister called and told me how David messed up his life stringing that girl along for so long. In my day no girl would wait around for a man to get up enough nerve to marry her. But you young folks hem and haw, and when the girl leaves you for another man, suddenly you realize what you've lost. My mama used to say, *'You don't miss your water 'til the well runs dry, and you don't miss your baby 'til she says good-bye.'* Don't be a fool, Jeffrey. If you want Kara to stay, then you better start now trying to change her mind."

"Kara's parents are coming for Easter, and she's inviting us to Angels Landing for dinner."

"Tell her we're coming and find out what

she'd like me to bring. And don't try and change the subject, Jeffrey. If you let this girl get away, then I'm going to disown you."

Jeff pulled out a chair at the table. "Please sit down, Gram, and eat before your pancakes get cold." Leaning down, he kissed her soft, curly hair. "Love you."

Corrine waved him away. "Don't try and sweet-talk me, Jeffrey. I mean what I say."

Sitting opposite his grandmother, Jeff blew her a kiss. He knew she was angry with him, but there wasn't much he could do to get Kara to change her mind short of proposing marriage. He'd done that once, and one thing he'd learned was not to make the same mistake twice.

He would enjoy the time given them, and when Kara packed up and left Angels Landing, Jeff knew he wouldn't have any regrets.

CHAPTER FIFTEEN

Kara felt as if she was on a roller-coaster. At first she'd complained about not having anything to do but read and weed a garden, and now she couldn't find enough hours in the day to complete her to-do list. However, keeping busy was the perfect excuse to keep from thinking about Jeff. Whenever she did think of him, it was always thoughts of their lovemaking. The image of his hands searching between her thighs, his mouth on her breasts, and his hardness moving in and out of her body invaded her dreams, and she'd wake gasping, struggling to breathe until the throbbing and pulsing subsided. She'd curse her traitorous body; then she would lay motionless until sleep claimed her again while praying the erotic dream wouldn't return. But it did return — not every night, but often enough to remind Kara of what she'd had for one blissful night and wanted again. She couldn't wait to see Jeff again, but had so much to do in preparation for the upcoming holiday.

Not only were her parents, Jeff, and Corrine coming for Easter dinner, but Dawn had called to say she was closing her dance studio for a week and had decided she needed a change of scenery. Dawn, who didn't like flying, had decided to take the train into Charleston.

Sitting in her car at the Amtrak station, Kara closed her eyes. She'd ordered all the food she needed from the supermarket in the Cove. Back in New York, she would have traveled to the grocery store herself. But Mrs. Todd told her that she hardly ever went to the supermarket. She'd call in her order and had the groceries, meat, and produce delivered. The market would bill Taylor, and he would mail them a check. Now that she handled all the expenses for the household, Kara found herself doing the same, in addition to writing checks for electric, gas, and other household incidentals. Even though there was no mortgage on the house, there were still property taxes. The insurance premiums on the vintage cars, the house, and its contents were astronomical.

The engineer had sent his report, stating the foundation was sound, and the historic preservationist had sent her a copy of the estimated costs of restoring the interiors and re-creating the exterior buildings and gardens. Morgan had recommended him because he'd been one of her instructors at SCAD before he retired to go into business for himself while hiring a few of his interns. Now she knew why Taylor had bequeathed her so much money. A large portion of the inheritance would go to restoring Angels Landing.

It had taken the security company three full days to wire the house and property. They'd placed tiny cameras in trees that were barely visible at first glance. Kara now felt safer, especially once she armed the system before retiring for bed.

Jeff came to see her whenever he was off duty but had only slept over once since the system was installed. She wasn't certain whether he didn't want to leave his grandmother home alone too often or if he wanted to keep gossip to a minimum.

Mrs. Todd had warned Kara that folks were talking about the sheriff spending the night at Angels Landing. What Kara didn't understand was how anyone knew he'd spent the night when he'd parked his car where it wasn't visible from the path leading up to the house. The nearest residence was more than two acres away, so unless someone had a powerful telescope trained on her property, it would be impossible for them to monitor anyone coming and going. She decided to wait a week, then contact the security company to review surveillance footage to ascertain who was watching her home.

Kara heard the sound of the train pulling into the station and got out of the car and walked to the platform to wait for Dawn. Her former roommate was the last one off the train. Kara waved to get her attention. "Hey, Miss Dee."

Dawn turned when she heard her name. "Miss Kay!" Shouldering a large tapestry bag, she rushed over and hugged Kara.

Kara returned the hug, then pulled back to look at her friend. Dawn's pixie hairstyle suited her. With her natural blonde hair, peaches and cream complexion, and tiny round face, she could be the perfect Peter Pan.

"Welcome to the Lowcountry."

Dawn pulled her sweatshirt away from her chest. "I can't believe this heat. We're still wearing winter coats in New York, and here you are in a T, shorts, and sandals."

Reaching for Dawn's bag, Kara slung it over her shoulder. "You probably want to shower and get into something lighter than sweats."

Dawn closed her sky-blue eyes. "You're singing my song." She gave Kara a long, lingering stare. "You look good, roomie."

"I feel good. Come on, let's go before we run into traffic. Of course, it's nothing like rush hour traffic in New York —"

"Please don't mention New York until it's time for me to go back."

Kara led the way to the parking lot where disembarking passengers were hugging friends and relatives and loading trunks of cars and taxis with luggage. She put Dawn's bag on the rear seat, slipped behind the wheel, and drove away from the train station.

Dawn slumped against the leather seat and closed her eyes. "I envy you, Kara."

"What for?"

"For being brave enough to change your life."

"I've only changed my lifestyle, Dawn."

"Life or lifestyle. Same difference. Look at me. I'm a professional dancer who suffers from occasional stage fright, so in order to make ends meet I open a dance studio and teach kids whose mothers believe they'll be the next Nureyev or Dame Margot Fonteyn. But my students could care less about first, second, or third position. I don't want to teach, Kara. I just want to dance, dance, and dance some more."

Kara and Dawn had talked at length about her inability to perform in front of a live audience. The talented dancer had tried hypnosis and antianxiety medication, but she wasn't able to overcome the disorder that kept her from doing what she'd been trained to do.

"What other alternatives do you have?" she asked. "Think of Nureyev or Baryshnikov. What did they do after they stopped dancing?"

"They never really stop dancing. Most times they become mentors or teach."

"What about choreographing, Dawn? I know if I were in your class, I wouldn't want to come in once or twice a week and learn steps and positions. That's boring as hell."

Dawn opened her eyes, sat up straight, and stared at Kara's profile. "What would you want to see?"

"*The Nutcracker, Sleeping Beauty,* and *Swan Lake* with an urban spin. Bernstein and Robbins took *Romeo and Juliet* and turned it into *West Side Story,* and the rest is history. Give your students something they can relate to: street dancing."

"You're a genius!" Dawn said punching

her shoulder.

"Ouch! You don't know your own strength."

"My bad, Kara. Can you imagine my kids putting on an updated version of *The Nutcracker*? The mouse king has to be a real badass."

Kara smiled. "There you go."

Dawn kept up a steady stream of conversation during the drive to Cavanaugh Island, falling silent only when Kara drove along the allée of oaks draped in Spanish moss. Her mouth formed a perfect O when the house came into view.

"You *are* freaking Scarlett O'Hara."

"Scarlett lived at Tara. This is Angels Landing."

Dawn stuck her head out the open window, staring up at the three-story structure. "I see why you decided not to come back. This place is awesome."

"It needs a lot of work," Kara explained when she parked her car near the garages.

"What are those?" Dawn asked, pointing to the two one-story structures several hundred feet from the main house.

"Guesthouses. The groundskeeper and his wife live in one. I plan to move into the other once the workmen begin their restoration. What's nice about the guesthouse is that it has two bedrooms, a full bath, utility kitchen and living/dining area." Kara opened the car door. "Let's go in and get you settled." She led Dawn to the second floor and opened the door to a bedroom in the west wing. "You'll have your own bathroom."

"Where's your room?" Dawn asked as she placed her bag on the bench at the foot of the queen-sized bed.

"I'm at the other end. Have you eaten?"

"I stopped and had something to eat before I got on the train. Once it pulled out of New York, I reclined my seat and went to sleep."

Kara stared at the petite woman who barely tipped the scales at one hundred pounds. "We'll go out for dinner."

"Fancy or casual?"

"It's casual." She decided she would take Dawn to Jack's Fish House. "By the way, my parents are coming in tomorrow for the weekend."

Dawn's face split into a smile. "I love your folks."

"I know they'll love seeing you again. I'm going to shower and change. Meet me in the kitchen."

"Where's the kitchen?"

Kara pointed to the nearest staircase.

"Take the stairs and turn left. It's the second room off the hallway."

She left Dawn, retracing her steps until she entered her bedroom. She wondered how Theodora would've reacted if she knew her son's daughter had become mistress of Angels Landing and that the house would be filled with people she probably would've deemed beneath her.

It wasn't the first time Kara had tried to imagine meeting her paternal grandmother. Would the woman reject her outright, or would she embrace her because they looked so much alike?

What she found strange was that anyone who mentioned Theodora's name didn't have anything nice to say about her, and Kara shuddered to think of how she would've turned out if her mother had married Taylor instead of Austin.

Walking into the bathroom and stripping off her clothes, she covered her hair with a shower cap. It was easier to think about Teddy than Jeff. She missed seeing him every day, sleeping with him, and making love with him. He'd become a drug, a very addictive drug she didn't want to shake.

Kara and Dawn walked into Jack's, and the room suddenly quieted before conversations began again. Most of the muted televisions were tuned to the Atlanta Braves baseball game while others were tuned to ESPN. As usual the restaurant was crowded with regulars and out-of-towners.

Dawn, wearing a pair of black cropped pants with a white man-tailored shirt and four-inch heels, leaned close to Kara. "Does this happen every time you come here?" she whispered.

"No. Folks are curious because you're a stranger."

Bright blue eyes grew wider. "Please don't tell me everyone knows one another."

Kara smiled. "They do."

"How do you deal with that?"

"I just deal. Tuesday, we need a table for two," she said to the waitress that had approached them.

"Please follow me."

They were shown to a table in a secluded corner. It was only when she sat down that Kara noticed Jeff sitting at a table with another man. He turned his head and their eyes met. Her pulse quickened when he said something to the man, stood up, and came over to her table. Those close enough to watch the interchange had stopped eating while craning their necks.

Rising to her feet, Kara smiled up at him.

"Hey," she said softly. He smiled, bringing her gaze to linger on the attractive cleft in his strong chin.

"Hey yourself. I didn't expect to see you here tonight."

"I brought my ex-roommate and house-guest for the next week. Jeff, this is Dawn Ramsey. Dawn, Jeffrey Hamilton."

Dawn, who was usually never at a loss for words, stared up at the tall man with a gun strapped to his waist. She recovered enough to offer him a limp wrist. "It's a pleasure to meet you."

Jeff's raven-black eyebrows lifted. "The pleasure is all mine." His gaze shifted back to Kara. "Call me when your folks come in."

She nodded. "I will."

"I'd join you, but Mayor White and I have rescheduled this meeting several times, and there are some things we need to discuss."

Kara nodded again. "That's okay."

"How's Oliver?"

"He's allowed out of his crate during the day, but I still cage him at night. Other than that, he's perfect."

"You tell him Daddy will be over to see him in a couple of days."

Kara smiled and stared numbly at the man who made her look forward to every moment spent with him. For the past week, she hoped to get just a glimpse of him even though he called her every night. She went to bed thinking of him and woke looking for him.

"What's going on between the two of you?" Dawn asked when Kara sat down again.

She blinked. "What are you talking about?"

Dawn leaned over the table. "Only a blind person wouldn't see the sparks between you and that delicious-looking lawman. You've never kept a secret from me, sister, so please don't start now."

Kara picked up the menu. "I'll tell you after we order."

Dawn studied her menu. "What are chitlins?"

"They are small intestines of the hog."

"Ewww," she said, wrinkling her nose.

"Don't 'ewww' until you taste them," Kara said. "I'll order a side dish so you can try them."

"What do you recommend?"

"Everything's good, but I'm partial to the red rice."

"I like Southern food, but there's too much to select from."

Kara had introduced her friend to Southern cuisine when she used to prepare elaborate Sunday dinners, but all that stopped when her caseload increased and she spent the weekends doing laundry and trying to catch up on her sleep.

"I'll order for the both of us; that way you'll be able to sample dishes you've never eaten."

As promised, Kara ordered for the both of them and then quietly told her about Jeff, leaving out the fact that they had slept together. "I went to Haven Creek yesterday, and within seconds of walking into a gourmet shop, I overheard someone whisper that I was the sheriff's woman."

Leaning back in her chair, Dawn shook her head in disbelief. "It's like that?"

"I'm afraid it is."

"We don't even know our neighbors like that."

"Tell me about it, Miss Dee," Kara drawled.

"Doesn't the gossip bother you?"

"Not really."

"It would bother me. That's why I moved from upstate to New York City. Where I lived everyone knew everyone else's business. If they didn't gossip about you, then they made up crap."

Dawn stopped talking when the waitress

set out a pitcher of sweet tea and a plate of hot, buttery biscuits on the table. "What saves me is that Angels Landing is somewhat isolated from the other houses in the town. I come to the Cove to do some banking, occasionally eat at Jack's, and visit the local bookstore. I prefer Haven Creek because it has a lot of craft shops and local farmers that sell fresh fruits and veggies."

"So you've really become a country girl," Dawn teased.

"I've always been a country girl. All I have to do is open my mouth and folks know I'm from the South. What I hadn't realized until I moved here is that I still have small-town sensibilities."

Dawn's pale eyebrows met in a frown. "Are you saying you never felt like a New Yorker?"

"No, I'm not saying that. Although I lived there for fifteen years, I still found myself feeling like an outsider. Aside from my accent, I could never get used to the fast pace of the city. It's different here because everyone is so laid-back. I don't know if you noticed, but there are no traffic lights or street signs. There's not that frantic rush to get somewhere. Life expectancy here is twelve years higher than it is for people who live in urban areas. Maybe it's because there's no industry polluting the air or that most of the food is locally grown."

"Does your change of heart have anything to do with your new boyfriend?"

"What are you trying to say?" Kara knew she sounded defensive, but it was too late to retract her words.

"You're in love with the man, Kara. Don't forget, I've seen you with different guys. Some you liked and some you didn't. Your face completely changed when Jeff came over here. And if the man can't see what's so obvious, then he's more obtuse than me when I play the airheaded blonde."

"I'll admit that I like him."

"That's BS, Kara. You more than like him."

"Will you please lower your voice," she said when diners at a nearby table turned to look at them. "Can we finish this conversation back at the house?"

"Sure. Here comes our order. Wow." Dawn gasped when dishes of catfish fritters, black-eyed peas, greens, red beans and rice, fried chicken, and chitlins were set out on the table. "There's no way we can eat all this food."

"What we don't eat we'll take home with us. You know I'd rather have dinner for breakfast."

"How do you not gain weight living down here?" Dawn asked as she spooned a portion of rice and beans onto her plate.

"I go for walks along the beach."

"I never saw the beach living upstate. The closest I got to water was a stream that ran along a farmer's land he used to irrigate his crops."

Kara picked up the dish with the chitlins. "Taste a little bit, and tell me whether or not you like them."

Dawn speared a small portion with her fork. She took her time chewing, then smiled. "They're delicious."

"Now, when you speak to your parents, you can tell them you ate chitlins."

"That's not all I'm going to eat. When I go back to New York, I know I'm going to have to work out extra hard to shed the weight I'll gain here."

Kara smiled. "There's worse things than being round and happy."

"No shi—" She put a hand over her mouth to cut off the expletive. "I forgot where I was. Back home no one pays attention to four-letter words."

That was one thing it'd taken Kara a long time to get used to. She wasn't a prude, but she wasn't used to hearing people curse as eloquently as New Yorkers. And unfortunately it was taxicab drivers who were usually on the receiving end of their vitriolic rants.

Kara and Dawn fell into the comfortable camaraderie that had been the hallmark of their longtime friendship. They talked about mutual friends, the men they'd dated, and those they never should've dated. Dawn disclosed she'd given her freeloading friends the boot and it felt good to have the apartment to herself once again.

"You have an admirer," Kara whispered when she noticed a well-dressed man seated at a table to their left staring at Dawn.

Dawn ran a hand over the nape of her neck. "Not interested."

"Weren't you just saying that you were looking for someone new?"

"Someone closer to home, Kara. I'm not cut out for long-distance relationships."

"What makes you think he's from here? I'm willing to bet half the people in this restaurant are tourists. Besides, he's a little too buttoned up to be a local."

Dabbing the corners of her mouth with a napkin, Dawn shifted on her chair and gave the gawking man a dazzling smile. Then she did something that shocked Kara. She stood up, approached him, and introduced herself. The interchange lasted a few minutes, the man handing Dawn his business card.

"Satisfied?" she crooned, grinning at Kara.

"I didn't tell you to roll up on him like that."

Dawn dropped the card into her drawstring bag. "You know me. I'll strike up a conversation with a flea. He's with a film company, and he's here researching locales for a movie. I told him I was on vacation and would call him after I return home. I didn't tell him home is New York."

"Where's his home base?"

"New York. He's with Tribeca Film Company."

The two women exchanged high-five handshakes. They finished eating, and their server bought containers and boxed up the leftovers. Kara settled the bill, leaving a generous tip, and she and Dawn headed back to Angels Landing.

She punched in the code to disarm the alarm system, waiting for the signal to turn from red to green, then opened the door leading into the rear of the house. "I'll show you the house and grounds tomorrow morning before my parents get here."

"How long are they staying?" Dawn asked, following Kara into the brick-walled kitchen.

"They're leaving Monday. After that I'll

take you around the island, and one night we'll hang out in Charleston. I still haven't taken the Gullah tour, so that's something we can do together."

Dawn watched Kara store the food in the refrigerator. "You don't have to babysit me, Kara. I came down here just to kick back and veg out. And I'm certain you're going to want to see your boyfriend."

"Jeff and I have plenty of time to see each other."

"Are you sure?"

"Very sure. We —"

"Do you have a dog?" Dawn asked.

"Yes. Come meet Oliver."

Dawn sat on the floor, laughing hysterically when the tiny Yorkie jumped on and off her lap. "He's adorable, Kara. Where did you get him?"

"Jeff gave him to me."

Picking up the puppy, the dancer held him to her chest as he tried licking her chin. "You have the house, a beautiful classic car, and a dog. Now, all you need is a husband and a couple of kids. And I'd better be at the top of your list when you pick a maid of honor."

Kara sat on the floor next to Dawn as Oliver jumped from one lap to the other. "*If* I ever get married, then of course you'll be my maid of honor, but I'm willing to bet you'll get married before I do."

"I don't have the temperament to be a wife and mother. The only constant thing in my life is dance. You're the grounded one, Kara. Even though you had a very challenging and stressful job, you always kept your cool." She rested her head on Kara's shoulder. "I know I invaded your privacy when I allowed my friends to crash at the apartment, but I just didn't know how to say no. It wasn't until after you left that I realized how much you meant to me as a roommate, friend, and sister from another mother," she said.

Kara patted Dawn's flaxen head. "Don't you dare get maudlin on me, Dawn Renee Ramsey. You know where I am, and anytime you want some place to crash, you're always welcome to come here. It'll probably take a couple of years to restore every brick and stick of furniture in this house, but there's still the extra bedroom in the guesthouse."

"We can be roomies again. That is . . ."

"That is what, Dawn?"

"That is if you don't marry Jeffrey Hamilton."

"Please give it a rest. I'm not going to marry Jeff." Kara stood up. "I have to clean Oliver's crate."

The notion of marrying was not an option for Kara. He didn't believe in love, and she would never consider marrying a man who didn't love her. Kara had carefully mapped out her five-year plan in order to comply with Taylor's mandate. She would move into the remaining guesthouse and oversee the restoration of the property.

Dawn also stood up. "I think I'm going to turn in. I got up before the chickens to take the 6:00 a.m. train down here." She hugged Kara. "Thanks for dinner. I'll see you in the morning."

"Good night."

She cleaned her puppy's crate, but instead of putting him in for the night, she took him with her to the front porch. A near-full moon silvered the countryside. Sitting on a cushioned rocker, Kara inhaled the scent she'd now come to associate with the Lowcountry.

Oliver turned around and around until he found a comfortable spot on her lap, tucking his muzzle against his side. Running her fingertips over his soft fur, Kara rocked back and forth in a measured rhythm until she found her eyelids closing. She wasn't certain how long she'd dozed off before the sound of an approaching car jerked her back to wakefulness. She sat up straight, smiling when the headlights flashed twice. Kara knew the driver.

Jeff unfolded his body out of the Miata and mounted the porch steps. Bending over, he kissed Kara, then sat down beside her. "I'm officially on vacation for the next ten days."

Kara placed her hand over his on the armrest. "Who's filling in for you?"

"The deputies are going to hold it down for me. They're both family men and could use the overtime pay."

She started rocking again. "What do you plan to do while on your vacation?"

Stretching out his legs, Jeff crossed them at the ankles. "My original plan had to be revised once I discovered my girlfriend has a houseguest."

"I didn't know that I was your girlfriend."

"And why not?"

"Because we never talked about us."

Jeff stared at her profile. "I didn't think we had to talk about it."

Kara closed her eyes for several seconds. "I think we do. Are we a couple?"

He smiled. "Of course we're a couple." He angled his head and brushed his mouth over hers, deepening the kiss until her lips parted. "What else do I have to do to prove to you that I want us to be together?"

She smiled. "I think you've made your point."

His eyebrows lifted a fraction. "And that is?"

"We're a couple."

Jeff pressed a kiss to her hair. "I'm glad we settled that. Now, back to your house-guest."

"I just found out yesterday that Dawn was coming down."

"It's all right, baby. I would never interfere with you being with your friends. Now if that friend had been a dude, I don't think I would be so magnanimous."

"Do I detect some jealousy, Jeff?"

"Hell yeah, you do."

"There's no need for that."

"And why is that?"

"The only man I'm involved with is you."

"You think I don't know that," Jeff countered. "If you were seeing someone else, I'd know it immediately."

"Like everyone knows about you coming to my house and spending the night?"

Moving off the rocker, Jeff sat down at her feet. "I've heard the gossip, too, but I don't care, Kara. I knew when I took you to the movies, folks would talk because they've never seen me out with a woman. We're both consenting adults, so whatever we do together is our business."

"How do they know you come here at night?"

Chuckling, he shrugged his shoulders. "It beats the hell out of me. I've checked my car inside and out for a tracking device, but I couldn't find anything."

"I told Mrs. Todd that maybe someone has a powerful telescope trained on the house."

"Perhaps you're right, but there's no law against someone owning a telescope."

"But is it legal to spy on people, Jeff?"

"It would be if they were Peeping Toms. But we've never given anyone a show. The drapes are always drawn." He paused. "It could be they recognize my car because it's the only Miata on the island."

Kara trailed her fingertips over his head. "I'm not bothered that people see us together."

"If it's not that, then what's bothering you?"

"I just have this eerie feeling that I'm being watched."

Rising to his knees, Jeff held on to Kara's shoulders. He leaned closer, brushing his mouth over hers. "I think you're being just a little paranoid. You've secured your property, so if you feel something's wrong, then call the company and have them review the surveillance tapes. I think you're still spooked from the rock-throwing incident."

"I don't think I'll ever forget it."

"Kara, baby. Do you trust me to keep you safe?"

"Jeff —"

"Just answer the question. Do you?"

She nodded, then said, "Yes."

"Then let me take care of you."

Kara closed her eyes and pressed her forehead to Jeff's. "How are you planning on doing that?"

It was the first time since meeting Kara that Jeff felt her vulnerability. Even the rock-throwing incident hadn't appeared to unnerve her, and he wondered what had happened, which she wasn't telling him, to shake her resolve. She'd been so adamant about not running away, yet people talking about their relationship had her rattled. It just didn't add up.

"When are the workmen scheduled to begin working on the restoration?"

"A week from now. Why?"

"I want you to move in with me and my grandmother instead of you staying in the guesthouse."

Kara shook her head, her ponytail swaying with the motion. "I can't do that."

410

"Why not?"

"Because it wouldn't be right."

Jeff angled his head. "It's not what you think, baby. I would never disrespect Gram by sleeping with a woman under her roof. You'll have your own room."

"I can't give you an answer now. Please let me think about it."

The fact that she hadn't said no made Jeff feel a modicum of hope that Kara would eventually accept his offer. She'd told him of her plan to move into the guesthouse for the duration of the restoration. And when he'd informed his grandmother of Kara's intent, it was Corrine who'd offered to open her home to Kara.

Initially, Jeff had believed his grandmother was playing matchmaker but quickly changed his mind when she mentioned overhearing several churchgoers talk about how the Pattons were trying to prove that Kara was a fraud. Corrine normally eschewed gossip, but in this case what she'd heard had been helpful.

He kissed her again. "Don't worry, sweetheart. We'll find a way to make love."

Kara laughed, the sound disturbing Oliver who stood up and shook himself. "Your car is too small for a quickie."

"Wow, I haven't done that since I was a

kid. I was thinking more along the lines of renting a bungalow on one of the other islands."

She smiled. "So you want to set up a love shack."

"I'll do whatever it takes to keep you safe."

"Safe and happy."

Jeff nodded. "Safe and very happy," he repeated. "How long are you going to sit out here?"

"Oliver's up, so I'm going in now."

"I'll wait here until you go in and activate the alarm."

He eased Kara up off the chair, kissing her again; he watched as she walked into the house and closed the door. He waited a full two minutes before returning to his car and driving back to the Cove.

Jeff hadn't wanted to believe that he'd managed to take vacation for the first time since becoming sheriff; he'd planned to surprise Kara and spend the time with her, but the unexpected arrival of her ex-roommate had ruined it, at least for him. But if Kara did accept his suggestion to come and live with him, then he would get to see her every day for the next fifty-nine months.

CHAPTER SIXTEEN

Jeannette walked into the formal dining room, stopping short. "The table looks spectacular."

Kara's head popped up. She'd just finished setting the table with the silver, crystal, and bone china that she and Dawn had spent hours polishing and cleaning.

"Thank you. Mama, please turn on the chandelier. Wow," she crooned when the prisms in the chandelier reflected off the faceted fully leaded stemware. "It does look nice." Looping her arm through her mother's, Kara led her back to the kitchen. Dawn sat at a small round table in a corner with Corrine while Jeff and Austin were perched on high stools talking about the corps.

Kara had gotten up early to season and stuff the turkey and score the ham she'd studded with cloves and topped with crushed pineapple. Her mother had joined her, and together they'd made potato salad, collard greens with smoked turkey, macaroni and cheese, and corn bread. She'd never perfected making gravy from pan drippings and enlisted her mother to make the giblet turkey gravy. Corrine had volunteered to bring dessert, and sweet potato pie, lemon coconut cake, and peach cobbler sat on a serving cart. And when she'd spoken to Corrine, Kara also invited her and Jeff to spend the night so everyone could be in one place, and much to her surprise the former schoolteacher had accepted because she wanted to spend more time with Jeannette.

The doorbell chimed, followed by Oliver's barking. Kara had locked him in the crate to keep him from being underfoot. He seemed to understand what she was saying when she told him she would let him out after dinner was over.

"Are you expecting anyone else?" Jeannette asked.

Kara shook her head. "No. Jeff, could you please get the door?"

"Sure, babe."

They shared a smile as he left the kitchen to answer the door. Her gaze shifted to her father who smiled and winked at her. Austin had put on a few pounds since she'd seen him at Christmas. Either he was eating too much of her mother's cooking or he was spending too much time sitting in front of the television in his newly converted man-cave. Jeff had taken him into Charleston the night before to meet some of his buddies, and it was close to dawn when they returned to the island.

Austin came over and kissed her cheek. "You picked a fine young man," he whispered in her ear.

Kara patted her father's shoulder. He'd affected a short beard since his retirement, and the neatly barbered white hair gave his nut-brown face character. He'd begun losing his hair in his midthirties and now shaved his head like so many other men. Austin wasn't tall but appeared much taller because of his ramrod-straight posture. "I like him, Daddy."

"And he likes you, too, baby girl."

"Kara, someone would like to see you," Jeff said when he returned to the kitchen.

"Excuse me, Daddy." She walked out of the kitchen, Jeff following her. "Who is it?" she asked him.

"I don't know. He wouldn't tell me."

"I guess I'll find out soon enough." Jeff had left the front door half open, and when Kara opened it wider, she saw a tall, slender man with cropped light brown hair standing on the porch. He wore jeans, running shoes, and a College of Charleston sweatshirt. "May I help you?"

"Are you Kara Newell?"

She felt the heat from Jeff's body as he moved closer. "Yes, I am."

The young man reached under his sweatshirt and handed her a sheet of paper. "I was told to give this to you." That said, he loped off the porch and got into an updated Volkswagen Beetle and drove away.

Kara opened the sheet of paper, scanning it before she handed it to Jeff. "I don't believe it," she whispered. "They waited for Easter Sunday to serve me with a summons to submit to a DNA test."

Jeff shook his head as if in disbelief. "The Pattons just won't leave it alone."

Her eyes met his. "That's because they refuse to believe Taylor is my biological father." She let out a groan of exasperation. "Please don't say anything to my parents about this."

Jeff folded the single sheet of paper and handed it to Kara. "Don't you think they should know?"

"No, Jeff. I'll handle this by myself. I'll go to the lab and give them a sample along with something that has Taylor's DNA."

"Do you have anything?" he questioned.

"Yes. Mrs. Todd packed away all of his clothes and personal items in a closet on the third floor. There's an engraved silver-backed comb and brush set that belonged to him. I'm certain the technician will be able to lift some strands of hair from the brush."

"I'll go with you to the lab. I'll also call someone I know at the Charleston PD lab to conduct their own test just in case your relatives decided to bribe someone to say it's not a match. Meanwhile, you should call David and let him know what they're up to."

Wrapping her arms around Jeff's waist, Kara leaned into him. "Thanks. I don't know what I'd do without you."

He ran a hand over her hair. "You would do just fine. I don't think you realize how strong you are."

Leaning back, she smiled. "It takes a great deal of energy trying to stay strong. Promise me you won't mention any of this to my folks."

"I promise."

Kara left the summons under a hand-painted bowl on the fireplace mantelpiece where she would retrieve it later. When she'd gotten up earlier that morning, it was to look forward to sharing a festive dinner with her family and friends, not being served with a summons from a bunch of spiteful relatives with whom she shared blood ties. Mrs. Todd, who at first had been reluctant to talk about her former employers, now felt comfortable enough to reveal that Theodora had raised her children to be as malicious as she was.

What the Pattons didn't know was that the more they pushed, the harder Kara would push back. If they wanted a fight, then they were going to get one. When she walked back into the kitchen, she saw four pairs of eyes looking at her.

"It was some college kid looking for work," Kara lied smoothly.

"On Easter Sunday?" Dawn asked.

"I guess he figured it was the best day to find folks at home," she replied. She affected a smile she didn't quite feel at that moment. "Daddy, could you and Jeff bring the turkey and ham into the dining room? Mama and I will bring the side dishes."

Dawn jumped up. "I'll help with something."

"So will I," Corrine volunteered.

Kara gave her a pointed look. "No, Miss Corrine. We've got everything covered here. You and Dawn please have a seat at the dining room table." Corrine mumbled something under her breath about not being an invalid as she left the kitchen. An hour later, Kara covered her wineglass with her hand when Jeff went to refill it. "No more."

Dawn extended her glass. "I'll take a little more, please."

"So will I," Jeannette said.

Kara had filled crystal decanters with red and white wine to accompany the meal, and after her second glass, she was beginning to feel the effects. Picking up her water goblet, she took a sip while peering at Jeff over the rim. She'd removed several leaves from the table that seated fourteen to accommodate six. Her parents were at either end, Jeff with his grandmother, and she and Dawn sitting opposite them. Thankfully she hadn't lost any of her cooking skills. The turkey was moist, the ham tender, and the side dishes savory.

"Not only do I miss my roomie," Dawn admitted, "but I also miss our Sunday dinners."

"I told Dawn I'd teach her to cook, but she said why should she learn when I did all of the cooking."

Corrine wagged a finger at Dawn. "How do you expect to get a husband if you can't cook?"

Dawn blushed a bright red color as she

lowered her gaze. "I've dated men who didn't care if I could cook or not."

"Did any of them ask you to marry them?" Corrine asked.

"No, ma'am."

"Gram," Jeff warned in a quiet voice.

"Stay out of this, Jeffrey. I'm trying to school the young woman so she can get a husband. You do want to get married don't you?"

Dawn gave Corrine a direct stare. "Yes, ma'am."

"You spend a couple of days and nights with me, and I'll teach you how to make rice, bake a chicken so tender that the meat will literally fall off the bone, and a few other side dishes. I know you say you're a dancer, but you're nothing but skin and bones. And no man wants a bone. Don't look at Kara because she knows how to cook."

"Yes, ma'am."

"Yes, ma'am, what?" Corrine asked.

"Yes, I'll spend a couple of nights with you."

Corrine smiled as if she'd just negotiated a peace treaty. "Jeannette, could you please pass me the collards?"

Kara stared across the table at Jeff, wondering if he was thinking what she was thinking. His grandmother suggesting Dawn spend several nights at her house would give her and Jeff time alone together. She had to have known Jeff would never stay over at Angels Landing with someone else in the house. He smiled at her, and she returned it, glorying in the shared moment, knowing in a few days they would reunite in the most intimate way possible.

The conversations around the table turned to sports with Jeff and Austin debating who would make it to the World Series. It segued to a discussion about a young actress who purportedly had slept with her leading man *and* a supporting actor and didn't know which one had fathered her baby.

"That is so grimy," Kara stated.

"It's worse than grimy," Dawn quipped. "It's downright stink. And why did she have to make that public?"

Austin dabbed his mouth with a linen napkin. "The real question is how much did she sell the story for? It has to be about money."

The topic segued again, this time to reality television. Everyone agreed that even though exhibiting bad behavior translated into big bucks, it also sent the wrong message to young impressionable people. Dinner stretched into more than two hours, and no one seemed ready to leave the table to retreat to the parlor where Kara had planned to serve dessert and coffee.

"Are you all right?" Kara asked Corrine when Jeff stood up and pulled back her chair.

"I'm fine. I just need to get up and walk off some of this food. Jeannette, will you please walk with me?"

"Of course." Jeannette looked at her husband. "Honey, you need to get up and walk, too. You keep saying you have to exercise."

"She's right, Daddy," Kara agreed. "You're getting a little round in the middle."

Austin patted his belly. "I wouldn't be round if your mama's cooking wasn't so good." Pushing back his chair, he rose to his feet. "We'll be back later to help you clean up."

"I'll help with the cleanup," Jeff volunteered. "By the time you get back it'll be time for dessert."

Kara, Dawn, and Jeff made short work of clearing the table and putting away leftovers. Kara turned on the radio on a countertop, tuning in to a station with R & B and old school jams. Dawn rinsed while Kara stacked pots in the dishwasher. They alternated hand washing and drying china, crystal, and silver; they sang along with some of the songs made popular in the '90s.

"The downside of setting a formal table is that the good stuff has to be hand washed," Dawn said as she held up a water goblet checking it for water spots.

Drying her hands on a dish towel, Kara nodded in agreement. "We only had to wash place settings for six. Can you imagine hosting a dinner with twenty or thirty people?"

Dawn pushed out her lips. "That's lunacy. I can barely put together a meal for myself, and you're talking about thirty people."

"That's when you hire a chef and have him bring everything. That way they're responsible for cleaning up."

Dawn's eyes sparkled like polished blue topaz. "That's what I'm talking about."

"I hope you didn't let my grandmother intimidate you," Jeff said when he reentered the kitchen with the tablecloth.

"Of course not. She's right. I should know how to cook, but whenever my mother tried to teach me, I always found something else to do," Dawn admitted. "Eating out isn't always the healthiest because some of my friends have really put on weight. Their funds are limited, so they're forced to eat fast food."

Jeff nodded. "You hang out with Corrine for a couple of days, and she'll teach you enough so that you can put together a palatable meal that will cost no more than a few dollars a day. Even though she grew up during the Depression, the folks here never went hungry. They grew their own vegetables, owned milk cows, and raised their own hogs and chickens."

"Do you cook, Jeff?"

He smiled. "Just say I cook enough not to starve to death or give someone food poisoning."

Dawn waved a hand. "Well, it doesn't matter because you have Kara to cook for you."

"She can cook for me anytime," Jeff said with a smile. "Everything was delicious."

Kara opened her mouth to tell Dawn that she'd never cooked for Jeff before preparing Easter dinner, then held her tongue. She still hadn't revealed that she and Jeff were sleeping together. She took the tablecloth from him, folding it. "I'll take this to the dry cleaner next week."

"Do you think anyone is going to want dessert?" he asked.

"I don't know. We'll play it by ear. I'm going to let Oliver out so he can get some exercise." Forty-five minutes later Corrine,

Jeannette and Austin returned from their walk, and Kara sat back with a satisfied grin on her face. She knew this Easter would remain with her always. Angels Landing was filled with the sound of laughter for the first time in years. After everyone had dessert and coffee in the parlor, Miss Corrine and Dawn sat out on the porch until midnight talking to each other. Her parents had bedded down in a third-floor suite, and Jeff had selected a room on the second floor that doubled as a study/bedroom with a connecting door to what had been Teddy's office. Once Dawn and Jeff's grandmother came in for the night, Miss Corrine retired to a first-floor room so she wouldn't have to climb the staircase.

The house was still quiet when Kara got up at seven to see after Oliver before making preparations for breakfast. Her parents had mentioned they wanted to be on the road before noon. She didn't find Oliver in his cage but found fresh food and clean water. When she did find Oliver, he was in bed, the puppy curled up against Jeff's back, asleep.

Kara was tempted to pummel Jeff with a pillow for doing what she'd told him she didn't want to do: have the dog sleep in the bed. She closed the door and went into the kitchen.

Mrs. Todd was already there. The woman and her husband had celebrated the holiday with his cousins in Haven Creek. "Good morning, Kara. I didn't expect you to be up this early."

"Good morning, Mrs. Todd. How was your Easter?" Kara didn't want her to know that she'd slept fitfully because she couldn't stop thinking about the summons requesting a sample of her DNA.

"It was nice, but Willie knows I only tolerate his family. After all these years I still can't get used to the folks in his family talking over one another. It's a wonder they hear what the other is saying. Enough about Willie's folks. How did your dinner turn out?"

"It was wonderful. Thanks to my mother and Miss Corrine's desserts."

Mrs. Todd smoothed down the front of her crisp gray uniform. "Miss Corrine's desserts are as good as those Mabel and Lester sell at the Muffin Corner."

"You may be right. I think I'm going to fix a buffet breakfast."

"I'll get the warming dishes," Mrs. Todd volunteered. "Where do you want me to set them up?"

Kara glanced around the kitchen. The

426

oversized table in the middle of the kitchen doubled as a dining and preparation table. "Put them on the table. We'll eat in the breakfast nook." The table in the corner of the kitchen was hewn from the same oak as the larger one and bore initials and dates going as far back as 1886. She'd had the portraits of Shipley and Oakes Patton taken down from the wall, put into slipcases, and stored in a third-floor closet. The canvases would have to be cleaned before they could be restored to their original vibrancy.

"After breakfast I have to take Willie to the VA hospital," Mrs. Todd announced. "He's been complaining about headaches and pain in his legs, so the doctors want to keep him for a few days to give him some tests. He still has shrapnel in his head from when he was in Vietnam. I'm going to stay at a hotel, so I can be available to him if he wants me."

Kara patted the older woman's back. "Do whatever you need to take care of your husband."

She'd just finished chopping ingredients for omelets when Dawn walked into the kitchen. Her short hair was pasted to her scalp from her shower. "Good morning, Miss Dee."

Dawn smiled. "Morning, Miss Kay. Yesterday was awesome. I'm glad I decided to come down, but I don't want you to get mad at me."

"Get angry with you for what?"

"I told Miss Corrine that I would go home with her today for cooking lessons. It's not that I really need to cook to land a husband, but I need it for myself. I grew up with a lot of sisters and brothers, and after that I always had roommates. This is the first time I've really lived alone, and it's made me realize I have to take care of myself, and that includes cooking for myself. So I hope you don't mind if we don't see each other for a few days."

"Dawn, please. You're here on vacation. You can do whatever you like. And I'm going to expect you to cook for me when you get back here."

"That's a bet. And I promise not to give you food poisoning."

One by one everyone filed into the kitchen as Mrs. Todd and Kara flipped pancakes, grilled waffles, and broiled bacon and breakfast links. Someone mentioned grits, and Jeannette put up a pot of water for the Low-country staple. Breakfast was more subdued than dinner had been as Kara's parents prepared for the drive back to Little Rock. She packed food for their trip, storing the containers in an insulated bag with ice packs.

Kara and Jeff stood on the porch, waving to them until their car disappeared from sight. Her father had announced he was returning to Cavanaugh Island for the Memorial Day holiday weekend for a corps reunion with Jeff and six other marines.

Jeff moved closer, resting a hand at the small of Kara's back. "I'm going to drive Gram and Dawn back to the Cove; then I'll be back later."

She gave him a sly sidelong glance. "We're going to have the house to ourselves. Dawn is staying with your grandmother, and Mr. and Mrs. Todd will be in Charleston to-night."

"What do you want to do?" Jeff asked, when his hand slipped lower to her hips.

"I don't know. I'll leave that up to you."

He patted her behind. "I'll think of something before I get back."

Once everyone left, Kara had the house to herself. She'd put away food, rinsed and stacked dishes and flatware in the dish-washer, and was sweeping up the brick floor when the doorbell rang. "I hear it, Oliver," she said when the terrier raced into the kitchen. "Let's go see who's at the door."

Kara peered through the sidelight to see

429

the figure of a woman. She opened the door, stunned to see one of the Pattons standing on the porch. "May I help you?"

The stylishly coiffed and dressed woman smiled. "May I come in, Kara?"

Kara peered down at Oliver who was barking furiously. She managed to close the door. "I still don't trust him not to bite. Please sit down." She waited for the woman in the tailored suit to sit, then sat down opposite her. "It's apparent you know who I am."

"I'm Eden Patton-Cox. Taylor was my uncle."

Crossing one denim-covered leg over the other, Kara met a pair of smoky-gray eyes. The diamond studs in Eden's ears and those in her wedding set must have set her husband back a pretty penny. Eden's smooth dark skin, chemically straightened black hair styled into a chignon at the nape of her neck, and subtly applied makeup made her a very attractive woman.

"How can I help you, Eden?"

"It should be how I can help *you*, Kara. My cousins don't know I'm here. I wanted to warn you to be careful because there are people who don't want you in Angels Landing."

Kara's expression was impassive even

though she couldn't stop her stomach muscles from contracting. "Who are these people you speak of?"

"I can't name names because I don't want to incriminate myself."

"You're an attorney." Eden nodded. "Are you telling me you've broken ranks with your family to come and warn me that my life may be in danger?"

"I'm just telling you to be prepared to fight to keep what you inherited from my uncle."

"Don't you mean my *father?*"

"That will be verified once the results of the DNA test are in."

"So you know about that?" Kara asked.

"I was present when the vote was taken." Eden stood up. "I must leave because I have to meet a client." She held out her hand. "Good-bye and good luck, Kara."

Kara rose and shook her cousin's hand. "Thank you, Eden. It's too bad this meeting couldn't have been for a different purpose."

Eden smiled. "I agree."

Leaning against a marble column, Kara watched the taillights of Eden's Cadillac CTS as she drove along the allée of oaks. First the summons and now a warning. She wondered if the Pattons would ever give up their quest to deny her her birthright. Kara knew it wouldn't stop until the DNA test proved conclusively that she was Taylor's daughter.

When Jeff returned, she was sitting in the rocker on the porch while Oliver lounged on a chair with cornflower-blue seat cushions. The puppy got up, whining for Jeff to pick him up. Jeff scooped him off the chair, setting him down on the porch.

Kara raised her chin for Jeff's kiss. She held his wrist. "I don't want Oliver sleeping in the bed with you."

"Jealous, sweetheart?"

"Of a dog, baby?"

"It's a warm body," Jeff teased.

"I guess I'm not warm enough for you," she said, pouting.

"That's where you're wrong, Kara." Reaching down, he pulled her smoothly to her feet. "You're hot. Hotter than a ghost chili."

Her arms went under his shoulders. "That's the hottest chili in existence."

"That's you, baby."

Wrapping his arms around Kara's waist, Jeff lifted her off her feet. "Open the door," he whispered in her ear. She complied, and Oliver darted inside. Using his foot, he kicked the door shut and managed to lock it while still holding on to Kara who'd locked her legs around his waist.

She tightened her hold on his neck. "Where are you going?"

"I'm going back to bed, and you're going to join me."

The smell of his cologne still clung to the linen in the bed where Jeff had spent the night. She watched, transfixed, as he undressed seemingly in slow motion. Making love in daylight was different from when they'd come together in a darkened room. Her blood warmed and raced through her veins with a desire that resulted in a gush of wetness bathing her core. She couldn't believe the perfection of his toned body when he stood over her, fully aroused.

If she'd wanted to look away, Kara couldn't when he reached into an overnight bag and removed a length of condoms. Her gaze did not waver when he removed one and rolled it down the length of his erection. Their dance of desire began when Jeff got into bed with her and pulled her T-shirt over her head, then unhooked her bra. His hands were steady when he unsnapped her jeans and eased them and her panties down her hips in one, smooth motion. Like a sleek, large cat, he moved over her.

Kara gasped as his blood-engorged arousal

brushed her inner thigh. Instinctively, her body arched toward him, she caressing the length of his spine, smiling when her finger-nails raised goose bumps along his skin.

"Love me," she breathed out. Jeff answered her entreaty when he eased his swollen flesh into her, both moaning in satisfaction as their bodies melded as one.

Closing her eyes, Kara's heart rate sky-rocketed along with the uneven rhythm of her breathing as Jeff's hardness slid in and out of her. She experienced extreme heat, then bone-chilling cold that made her teeth chatter.

Jeff had set a pace that quickened, slowed, then quickened again until she was mind-less with an ecstasy that became a mind-altering trip, shattering her into millions of tiny particles before lulling her back to a euphoric state. What had begun as a groan escalated until it became a low growl when Jeff pumped his hips until he collapsed on top of her.

They lay joined together, waiting until their hearts resumed a normal rate. Kara issued a small cry of protest when he pulled out. She curled into a fetal position, still savoring the aftermath of a lovemaking that made her want more and more. Jeff came back to the bed, pressing his chest against her back.

"Don't tell me you're going to sleep on me," he whispered against the moistness of her nape.

"I am. I need to rest so when I wake up we can do this again."

A laugh came from his throat. "You want more?"

"How many more condoms do you have?"

"Five."

It was her turn to laugh. "Then I'm going to want five more courses. You should've asked before you took up with me. I like five- and six-course meals. Next time I'll be the one doing the eating." He sucked in a breath. "Did I shock you, baby?"

"A little."

"It's all right. I'll go easy on you." Jeff cradled her hip. "Go to sleep, sweetheart. But let me warn you I've been known to overindulge."

"Consider me warned."

She lay in the protective cocoon of Jeff's strong arms as he pulled her closer. Within minutes Kara forgot everything, including Eden's warning and the summons for her to take the DNA test.

CHAPTER SEVENTEEN

Kara opened her mouth and closed her eyes as the police department technician swabbed her inner cheek. She knew the drill because she'd gone through the procedure twenty minutes ago. As promised, Jeff drove her to the private lab where she left samples from Taylor's brush and razor, while allowing the technician to swab her cheek and take several strands of hair. She'd thought it overkill but wanted to put the issue of her paternity to rest. Forever.

Even though the ME claimed to be backlogged, she'd promised Jeff she would make the Taylor-Newell test a priority.

"Don't you need a sample of my hair?" Kara asked the police techie. They'd taken hair samples at the private lab.

"No. Your cheek cells are enough."

She slipped off the examining table. Jeff's ten-day vacation had come and gone much too quickly, and they tried to spend every day in bed making love. The only time they had left was to go to the Cove and spend time with Corrine. Although on duty, Jeff had taken the time to drive her into Charleston for the tests. "I'm ready," she told him when he approached her.

Cupping her elbow, Jeff escorted her to the parking lot where he'd parked his official vehicle. Kara hadn't mentioned Eden's visit to him because she felt once the results of the DNA tests were revealed the Pattons would end their character assassination.

Dawn called her every Sunday with an update on what new recipe she'd attempted. Corrine had given Dawn her prized gumbo recipe, and her former roomie could not stop talking about it once she'd duplicated the dish. When Kara asked her about taking in strays, Dawn had laughed, declaring she'd gotten over that phase and she liked having a clean and quiet apartment all to herself. She'd also begun teaching street dancing, and her young students took to the new routines like ducks to water.

Today Kara wouldn't return to Angels Landing to spend her days and nights, but to Sanctuary Cove where she would stay with Jeff and Corrine. The restoration staff had moved and covered all the furniture as they removed ceiling fixtures and began the arduous task of stripping wallpaper. Mrs. Todd had assumed the responsibility for deactivating the alarm for the foreman when he arrived in the morning, and she reset it at the end of their workday.

It was Corrine who'd convinced Kara to move in when she mentioned she'd always wanted to learn hand quilting. Living with Corrine was a win-win for both of them. They could keep each other company, and Kara would have the advantage of seeing Jeff every day. She'd brought Oliver to the Cove the day before so he could become acquainted with his new surroundings. Even when coaxed, the terrier refused to leave his crate.

"I have to stop at the house to pick up my car," she told Jeff as he reached the causeway.

"I thought you were going to use my grandmother's car."

"I have all my summer clothes in the trunk." It was May and daytime temperatures were in the mid-80s. Dawn had packed up her clothes and personal items and shipped them to Angels Landing.

"Do you want me to wait for you?"

"You don't have to. I've taken up enough of your time today." Jeff gave her a quick glance, glaring at her from under the worn bill of his baseball cap. Kara couldn't understand why he continued to wear it. The cap was falling apart.

"Let me judge whether you're taking up my time."

"Touchy, touchy, Jeff?"

"I'm not touchy. I merely stated a fact."

She looked out the side window. "Forget it," Kara mumbled under her breath and bit down on her lower lip to keep from smiling. She liked teasing Jeff because he was always so serious.

"Are you spoiling for a fight?"

"No!"

"Now who's touchy?"

"If this is the way it's going to be when we live under the same roof, then I'll just move in the guesthouse like I'd planned to."

"I doubt whether we'll even get to see that much of each other. I've switched my hours from 8:00 p.m. to 8:00 a.m. When you and Gram are out and about, I'll be sleeping. And by the time you two are winding down for the night, I'll be going to work."

She may have promised Corrine she would move into her home, but the Hamiltons were also aware that she *did* have some place to live: the vacant guesthouse.

Having to deal with DNA testing and Eden Patton-Cox's warning was weighing heavily on Kara. It was obvious the people who didn't want her there were of Patton blood. Greed had turned them into ravenous beasts that would probably resort to more drastic measures to force her to leave the island.

She and Jeff slept together whenever he was able to come to Angels Landing and not once had he ever mentioned the word *love,* not even in the throes of passion. The endearments flowed freely: *baby, sweetheart, darling, babe,* but never *love.*

Kara had told herself it was futile to fall in love with Jeff, but she had. It was impossible to tell the heart what to do or how to feel.

She'd come to love the Lowcountry: the food, local shops, the unique language of the Gullah, the tradition of sitting on porches or residents gathering in groups under trees, vegetable stands and craftspeople selling their trademark baskets, seeing the brightly colored houses with their windows often trimmed in blue to keep out evil spirits. The blood of the Gullah ran in her veins, yet Kara still did not feel a sense of belonging, and she knew it had to do with Eden's warning.

They didn't want her, and she didn't want them. She'd promised Jeff that she wouldn't run, but Kara wondered how many more times she would be put to the test before they broke her spirit. Knowing Jeff loved her, truly loved her as much as she loved him, would help make her plight easier. Make her rethink her decision to leave after five years.

Kara was out of the Jeep as soon as it stopped. "I'll see you later."

Not waiting for his response, she reached into her bag for the key to Taylor's Mercedes-Benz. She didn't know why, but she couldn't think of the car as hers even though it was now registered in her name. It was Taylor's house, Taylor's land, Taylor's cars, and Taylor's money.

Taylor had left her all of his worldly possessions to make up for abandoning her mother when she needed him most, but it still wasn't enough. Those who resented and hated him resented and hated her, too. Kara had given David her word that she would fulfill the terms of the will, and she would. However, she would not stay on the island one day longer than required.

She put the key in the ignition, turned it, and the engine roared to life. Instead of heading east to the Cove, Kara drove west to the Haven. When Miss Corrine had asked what she wanted to quilt, her response had been a crib blanket. Blankets she would donate to needy families.

"Always the social worker, aren't you?" Jeff's words echoed in her head. She smiled. Yes, she would always be a social worker because that's who she was and always would be.

Kara sang along with the radio as she maneuvered the car along the narrow road. It'd taken her more than an hour to select the squares she wanted for her first quilting project. The soft pastel colors of blue, green, pink, and yellow in solids and prints would make a beautiful quilt for a baby.

A scream caught in her throat when large objects appeared in the middle of the road. In the split second it took for her to identify them as hogs it was too late to slow down. She swerved at the last possible moment, the car crashing head-on into a tree. The impact of metal slamming into the tree sounded like an explosion as shards of glass littered the dash, passenger seat, and Kara's lap.

There was a burning sensation along the right side of her neck, and when Kara pressed her fingers to the area, it came away wet. Blinking, she stared at her trembling fingers covered with blood. She looked down at the front of her blouse and it was dotted with red.

Luckily her cell phone sat on the console next to her. It took two attempts, but she was finally able to grab it and punch the speed-dial button on the screen. Jeff answered after the second ring. "What's up, baby?"

"Jeff." His name was a trembling whisper. "What's the matter?"

"I'm hurt." The blood was flowing faster. "Where are you?"

Kara couldn't remember what she'd said, but she did remember Jeff telling her he was on his way.

Kara lay on an examining table, staring at Dr. Asa Monroe. He leaned closer. "I gave you an anesthetic that will make you a little groggy."

She blinked slowly. "Why does it hurt so much?"

"You have a piece of glass embedded in your neck. I stopped the bleeding, and in a few minutes I'm going to take it out."

"Where's Jeff?" She was slurring her words.

He moved into her line of vision. "I'm here, baby." He took her left hand, gently squeezing her fingers.

Her eyelids fluttered wildly. "I don't think I'll ever eat swine again."

"Why not, sweetheart?"

"There . . . there were hogs in the . . . the road. I . . . I . . ." Her words trailed off as she drifted off to sleep.

Jeff exchanged a look with the doctor. "Judging from where I found her car, I know who those hogs belong to."

"People have to be responsible for their livestock," Asa said as he sat on a stool at the head of the table. Reaching up, he adjusted a bright light, then swabbed the swollen area with a disinfecting solution.

"How bad is it, Doc?"

Asa's gloved fingers touched Kara's neck. "It looks worse than it is. One millimeter lower and you would have lost her. The shard is close to her carotid artery."

Jeff watched intently as Asa opened a package with a sterilized scalpel. The doctor adjusted the light again and seconds later deftly removed the glass, dropping it in a metal bowl.

Kara's chest rose and fell as she slept through the entire procedure. Quickly and neatly, the incision was closed with four tiny sutures.

Asa covered the wound with gauze and a waterproof bandage. "She needs to keep it dry for several days. Bring her back before the end of the week so I can change the dressing."

"What about the sutures?"

"They'll dissolve on their own. I'm going to give you some painkillers for her. If she complains about the pain, then give her one every six hours."

Waiting until the doctor discarded his gloves, Jeff shook his hand. "Thanks, Doc. Please send me the bill."

CHAPTER EIGHTEEN

Corrine put on her half glasses and looked closely at the faint scar on Kara's neck. "Dr. Monroe did a real fine job. You have to look real close to see where he took out the glass."

It had been two weeks since the accident. The Mercedes was towed to a garage on the Cove where the insurance adjuster documented that the vintage car was totaled.

Jeff had hovered over Kara like a hen with a brood of chicks. He'd gone as far as to sleep with her for two nights until she threatened to lock the bedroom door, because whenever she moaned when turning her head or changing position, he'd ask if she was in pain. The result was he forced her to swallow a pill that made her lose track of time. For several days she didn't know where she was or whether it was day or night.

It didn't take long for news to spread across the island that she was convalescing at the Hamiltons' house. Mrs. Todd and Morgan had come to visit, bringing flowers, get-well cards, and sweet breads from the Muffin Corner.

Eddie Wilkes, editor in chief of the *Sanctuary Chronicle,* also stopped by for an interview. He was forthcoming when he said it was the first time in nearly seventy years that hogs were responsible for a road accident. There had been a time when feral pigs were destroying the farms on Haven Creek, but farmers had concocted elaborate traps and hunting parties to capture them. What had been estimated to be more than one hundred pigs decreased dramatically over a three-month period until the numbers dwindled to single digits.

Eddie also interviewed her as the new owner of Angels Landing. When the article appeared in the *Chronicle* with news that she had no intention of selling the house or the land surrounding it, and that it was currently being restored to become a museum, the Pattons fired another salvo at her. This time they were contesting Taylor's will, stating he wasn't of sound mind and body when he had it drawn up.

Kara touched the spot where Dr. Monroe

had made the small incision. "It's only slightly tender."

Corrine removed her glasses. "The Lord was watching over you that day because that glass could've struck you in the eye."

"You're right about that."

"You gave us quite a scare. Jeffrey in particular. You know that he's in love with you, don't you?"

"That's where you're wrong, Miss Corrine."

Corrine folded her arms across her chest. "When it comes to my grandson, I'm seldom wrong. Jeffrey is in love with you."

"Has he told you that he is?"

"He doesn't have to tell me, Kara. I see the way he looks at you. Even when he was engaged to that teacher, he never looked at her the way he looks at you."

Kara stared at the woman she'd begun to relate to as her own grandmother — tall and slender with soft, curly, silver hair; smooth skin that reminded her of dark brown velvet; and a sweet fragrance of gardenia. She and Jeff had talked about a lot of things, yet he'd neglected to mention that he'd been engaged. She managed to mask her surprise with a deceptive calmness.

"Why didn't he marry her?" she asked Corrine.

Corrine smoothed the crease in her cotton slacks. "It wasn't Jeffrey but Pamela who didn't want to marry him. She said she couldn't be a military wife."

"But didn't she know he was a career officer when she'd accepted his proposal?"

"She did."

"That is so wrong, Miss Corrine." A rush of relief replaced Kara's annoyance. Now she understood why Jeff had failed to mention his engagement. There was no doubt he was too embarrassed to tell her of his former fiancée's rejection.

Corrine smiled. "You're preaching to the choir, child." She stood up. "I'm going to put up water for tea. Would you like a cup?"

Kara pushed to her feet. "Please sit down. I'll make the tea."

"Okay. I'll set up the table in the sunroom."

Walking out of the parlor, Kara made her way to the kitchen. When she and Jeff had discussed David's inability to commit to his longtime girlfriend, he'd never mentioned that he'd been engaged. They'd talked about how men were reluctant to propose marriage, and not once had he taken himself out of that equation.

Kara didn't expect Jeff to profess his undying love for her after three months, but hearing the word would make it easier for her to consider changing her future plans to include possibly spending the rest of her life on Cavanaugh Island.

She'd come to appreciate the homey warmth of the Hamilton residence. Although the house was larger than those along Waccamaw Road, it was one-fourth the size of Angels Landing. Corrine had disclosed that her neighbors were quite curious when a contractor had begun knocking out walls to expand rooms, replacing old windows with those that would withstand the force of tropical storms and replacing the clapboard siding with maintenance-free vinyl that Jeff power washed twice a year. Not to be outdone, one by one the residents began updating and renovating their homes. The ongoing renaissance on Waccamaw Road had become a blueprint for many of the older homes in the Cove.

Filling a kettle with water, Kara placed it on a cook-top stove, then took down two cups and saucers from an overhead cabinet. She moved around the kitchen with the familiarity of someone who'd lived there for years instead of two weeks. Corrine had become her mentor when she instructed her in preparing traditional Lowcountry dishes. She'd taught her how to make and perfect old-fashioned brown gravy, crab cake sauce, and sweet potato pone.

Without warning Corrine would speak Gullah, and Kara would have to try and figure out what she'd said. One day when Corrine was going on and on about Jeff, she'd stopped and said, *"Ebry frog praise é own pond."* That she understood to mean that every frog praises his own pond.

She finished brewing the tea, pouring it into a hand-painted teapot. Tiny jars of locally made honey, a small pitcher of milk, the teapot, cups, and teaspoons were placed on a tray. Kara carried the tray into the sunroom.

Corrine sat in her favorite club chair, feet resting on a footstool. Oliver lay on the chair beside her. Her pet had quickly switched his allegiance from her to Corrine who'd permitted him the run of the house. No room was off-limits. Not even the kitchen. What she wouldn't permit him to do was beg for food. Kara also suspected the tiny dog slept in the bed with Corrine but loathed accusing her host of the infraction as she'd done Jeff.

She set the tray on the coffee table before filling a cup with the steaming fragrant blueberry tea. "Do you want honey?"

"Not today. But I could use a couple of

those shortbread cookies you made yester-day."

Kara smiled. "Okay."

She'd just entered the kitchen when the doorbell rang and Oliver began his frenetic barking that echoed through the house. When she returned to the sunroom with the plate of cookies, Corrine handed her an envelope.

"A messenger just delivered this."

Sitting, Kara opened the mailing envelope with the return address from the lab that had conducted the DNA test. Her heart was pounding, hands shaking, as she broke the seal on the flap and opened the envelope. Slumping back in the chair, she smiled. The results of the test were irrefutable. The medical examiner had signed the letter, then covered her signature with the department's official seal. She handed the single sheet of paper to Corrine.

"Only a fool would doubt you were Taylor's baby girl."

Kara nodded. "If I know, they have to know. Maybe now they'll drop their crusade to challenge Taylor's will."

"Please don't tell me they're going to try and prove Taylor was crazy. He may have been a little strange, but he wasn't crazy." Corrine handed Kara back the paper.

"Don't you worry yourself none 'bout those silly folks. I think we can go out and celebrate."

"Where do you want to go, Miss Corrine?"

"There's always Jack's, but Jeffrey told me that someone in the Creek opened a panini café last week. All of the bread is baked on the premises, and it's become very popular with the college students that come over from the mainland."

"It sounds good to me."

"Maybe we'll go after we finish our tea, so we can avoid the crowds."

Kara wanted to ask Corrine if they should invite Jeff to go along with them but quickly decided against it. Sleeping under the same roof had changed them and their relationship. She knew he'd been more shaken than he appeared about the car crash, but that didn't explain why he'd cleverly devised ways not to be around her.

The doorbell rang again, and Kara and Corrine exchanged a look. It wasn't often they had visitors, and to have two within the span of half an hour was indeed rare. Oliver, barking frantically, stood up, turning around and around to indicate he wanted to get down.

"Stay, Oliver," Kara said firmly. "Should I

get the door, Miss Corrine?"

"Please."

The doorbell rang again before she opened it. "Eden."

Eden flashed a plastic smile. "I need to speak to you. May I come in?"

Opening the door wider, Kara shook her head. "We can talk out here." She stepped out onto the porch and pointed to a cushioned chair. "Please have a seat." Waiting until she sat on the chair, Kara sat opposite her on a matching love seat. "What do you want to talk about?"

Eden leaned forward. "I want to be honest with you, Kara."

"Honest about what?"

"What you need to ask yourself," Eden continued as if Kara hadn't spoken, "is do you really belong here. If you did, then you never would consider turning our ancestral home into a museum. You have no connection with the land or the people who've lived here for centuries. Folks will never accept you, so why would you want to live someplace where you'll always be thought of as an outsider?"

"That's enough out of you, missy." Kara and Eden turned to find Corrine standing a few feet away. "Please leave my home."

Eden stood up. "I have no quarrel with

you, Miss Corrine."

"And I won't have one with you if you leave my home."

"I haven't had my say with Kara," Eden insisted.

Kara knew it was time to take charge of a situation that was quickly spiraling out of control. "You heard what she said, Eden. Get the hell out!"

Eden's eyes grew wide. "Who do you think you are to speak to me like that?"

"She is who she is," said a softly spoken deep voice. Jeff had walked out of the house without making a sound. He'd pulled on a pair of jeans but had left his chest and feet bare. He beckoned Eden. "Come. I'll see you to your car."

"You can't protect her forever, Jeff."

He shook his head. "I hope that's not a threat, Eden."

"Of course not." She nodded to Corrine, then Kara. "Good afternoon."

When Jeff returned, Kara shook her head. "She just won't give up."

"What are you talking about?" Jeff asked. He listened when Kara told him about Eden coming to Angels Landing. "Why didn't you tell me about this before?"

"There's no need to raise your voice, Jeffrey."

He glared at his grandmother. "Gram, this is between Kara and me."

"And this is my home, Jeffrey, and you know I don't tolerate folks raising their voices."

"Gram, you don't understand." He told his grandmother about the rock-throwing incident.

Corrine pressed a hand to her chest. "Oh, my word!"

"To answer your question, Jeff, I didn't tell you because Eden said she'd come to warn me that her family wasn't going to give up fighting for what they believe belongs to them."

"A dog that brings a bone will take a bone," Corrine mumbled under her breath.

Jeff approached Kara. "Gram is right. The Pattons sent Eden as a decoy. She wanted you to believe she was on your side, but she was really sent here to intimidate you."

She stared at the stubble on his lean jaw. "The DNA results say I'm Taylor's daughter."

He smiled. "I know. The ME called me the other day. She didn't want me to say anything until you got the official notification." He took a step and cradled her face. "Now you know why I wanted you to stay here."

"I thought it was to keep your grand-mother company," she whispered.

"That's only half of it."

"What's the other half?"

"I'll have to show you."

Corrine grunted loudly. "I'll leave you two alone to *talk*."

"I'm off this weekend. If you're not doing anything, then I'd like you to come with me to Myrtle Beach."

"Should I bring a swimsuit?"

"Of course. But panties are optional."

Turning on his heels, he walked out of the parlor leaving Kara staring at the space where he'd been. As exasperated as she could be with Jeff, Kara never doubted her love for him.

Kara opened her eyes, peering at the clock on the night-stand. Even after three months on the island, she still woke up without an alarm clock. Knowing she wasn't going back to sleep, she slipped out of bed and went into the bathroom across the hall. The house was as quiet as a tomb.

She completed her morning ablutions in twenty minutes; slipped into a halter top, shorts, and flip-flops; and went downstairs to sit on the front porch. Corrine had unofficially adopted her dog. Oliver slept at the foot of Corrine's bed and sat in her lap whenever she read or watched television. He also claimed a spot beside her on her favorite chair whenever she did her needle-work projects. Oliver was now Corrine's pet because she'd taken over the task of feeding him. Kara was tempted to rename him Traitor.

She'd discovered Waccamaw Road didn't begin to stir until six thirty when high school students piled into cars to drive into Charleston for classes. She returned the wave of a pretty coed who lived several houses away. The girl's older sister, a local college student, came twice a week to clean Corrine's house to earn extra money.

It was after seven when Kara stood up to go into the house. As soon as she opened the screen door, she heard breaking glass. Running into the house, she was met with smoke and the ringing of smoke alarms. The smoke burned her eyes and lungs as she raced frantically, maneuvering through the thick haze trying to find Corrine.

"Miss Corrine!" Gasping, she went in and out of rooms, looking for her. Holding a hand over her mouth to keep from choking, she found Jeff's grandmother on the kitchen floor. Oliver lay beside her, shaking uncontrollably.

Snatching a dish towel off the countertop, she wet it and placed it over her nose as she dialed 911. She gave the operator the address and told him to hurry because smoke had filled the entire house. Anchoring her hands under Corrine's shoulders, she managed to drag her out of the kitchen, through the living room, and onto the front porch. She returned to get Oliver, nearly panicking as he lay limply in her arms.

By the time she returned to the porch a small crowd had gathered. Kara had begun administering CPR when Jeff and Dr. Monroe arrived at the same time. Sitting on the floor, she pulled her knees to her chest, rested her head on her knees, breathing deeply to clear her lungs of the smoke. Then she cried. Tears blurred her vision as she watched the doctor give Corrine oxygen, waiting until she began to stir before he shifted his attention to Oliver.

I can't do this. It can't continue like this. The silent voice shouted what she couldn't form her mouth to say. Whoever wanted her gone had won.

Jeff hunkered down beside Kara. He was frightened. More frightened than he'd been when he and his men were pinned down by sniper fire. Cradling her in his arms, he rocked her back and forth.

"Baby," he whispered over and over, placing tiny kisses all over her face.

"How is she?" Kara asked hoarsely.

"Gram is going to be all right. Asa is calling the mainland for a chopper to have her airlifted to a mainland hospital."

Kara pulled back, her eyes wide with fear. "I thought you said she was going to be all right."

"She is. It's just a precaution because of her heart condition." He smoothed back her hair. "Oliver is also breathing on his own, but I'm going to take him to the vet just to make certain he's okay. Meanwhile, you're coming with me to the hospital so they can check your lungs."

"I'm okay, Jeff. I didn't inhale that much smoke."

"That wasn't smoke, Kara. It was pepper gas, the same gas used by the military." He kissed her mouth. "Don't get up. I'm going inside to open the windows. And when I come back, I'm taking you to Charleston."

Taking a handkerchief from his jeans, he covered his nose, entering the house and opening windows on the second and first floors. A light breeze coming in through the screens did little to dispel the acrid smell, and Jeff knew it would take hours before it dissipated completely. His foot hit an object on the kitchen floor. The moment his hand touched it Jeff experienced déjà vu. The message glued to the brick was different from the last but held the same meaning: "KN — Get out of town."

It was the second time someone had threatened Kara. And he planned for it to be the last. Whoever had tossed the pepper grenade cared little for who else was in the house with her. He'd lost every significant woman in his life, and he swore an oath that he would hold onto the last two until his final breath. He loved his grandmother and had fallen in love with Kara.

CHAPTER NINETEEN

Kara sat on a gurney in the ER's examining room, waiting for Jeff. She was examined, her chest x-rayed, and medically cleared to be discharged. Home for her wasn't Sanctuary Cove or Angels Landing. It was nowhere on Cavanaugh Island. Home was Little Rock. She was going to forfeit her birthright. He walked into the room, and she didn't know how, but she'd managed to hide her love for him behind a façade of indifference. The strain of possibly losing his grandmother was apparent by the lines bracketing his firm mouth.

"How is she?"

"They're going to keep her for a couple of days."

Kara couldn't stem the tears filling her eyes. "She's in this hospital because of me."

"Stop it, Kara! I'm not going to let you blame yourself for something you couldn't control."

"But I could control it, Jeff. If I'd packed up and left the first time someone threw a brick through the window, your grandmother wouldn't be lying in a hospital fighting for her life."

"Gram is not fighting for her life. She has a little trouble breathing, so they have her on oxygen."

"Don't, Jeff."

"Don't what?"

"Don't try to minimize what happened. What if I hadn't been there when that smoke bomb came through the window? What if I'd gone for a walk instead of sitting on the porch? Your grandmother would've died, Jeff, because I'm too stiff-necked to accept the truth. Eden is right. I'm an outsider, and the people on the island will never accept me. And the fact that I'm Taylor's daughter is of no consequence to anyone. At least not to the Pattons."

Jeff moved closer. "I told you I would protect you."

"I know. But the truth is you can't. No one can." Kara couldn't stop her chin from trembling. "I'm trouble, Jeff. I've been trouble since the moment I discovered I was Taylor's daughter. It's like there's a bull's-eye on my back that says hit her with a brick. What's next? A bottle filled with gasoline and a lighted rag? I may be some crazy's target, but how many others will become collateral damage if they were to come after me again? I'm going to call David and let him know that I'm giving up the house and the two thousand acres. After that, I'm calling my mother and father to tell them I'm coming home."

A shudder shook Jeff as he met her eyes. "You can't leave."

"Why not?"

A beat passed. "Because I love you."

Kara couldn't stop the sob that began in her throat. "And I love you, Jeff. I love you so much my heart hurts. But our love isn't enough to protect those we love."

Bending slightly, Jeff scooped her off the gurney. "I didn't visit hell, not once but twice, while losing my soul when I did unspeakable acts all in the name of war, to let you walk away from me, Kara Newell."

"You can't stop me from leaving."

"Yes, I can. I'll lock you up and keep you in jail until I find out who's trying to run you out of town."

"You can't."

He gave her a lethal stare. "Do you want to test me? I thought not," he said when she didn't answer. "I'm going to hire someone to watch Angels Landing around the clock. Wherever you go, they go. Think of yourself as the first lady with a secret service detail."

"That's not funny," she countered.

"No, it's not. Now, we're going home where I'll pick up a change of clothes. I'm going to drop you off at the station house where you'll stay until I return. Then we're going to Angels Landing to stay in your guesthouse for the night. You will come with me tomorrow to bring my grandmother home before your house arrest begins."

"You're really going to lock me up?"

"You can stay in our break room. It's where we bed down while on duty."

"Will I be allowed one phone call to my lawyer?" she teased.

"You can call anyone you want."

Kara laid her head on Jeff's shoulder. *Why now?* she asked herself. Why did he wait until she was ready to walk out of his life to admit that he loved her? He'd promised to protect her from a phantom who struck without warning, not caring who stood in their way.

"Can I see Miss Corrine before we leave?"

"She's resting."

"What about Oliver?"

"I called my clerk and told her to take him

to the vet. I'll stop by and check on him, too."

I can't believe I'm doing a bid. Kara tried to find a comfortable position as she lay on a cot with a too thin mattress in a room that looked directly into a cell. She may not have been behind bars, but she definitely was spending time in a police station. She and Jeff had returned to the Cove where she changed clothes and packed an overnight bag with enough clothes for two days.

Kenny peered at her through the half-open door. "Do you need anything, Kara?"

"No, thank you. I'm good here."

"I'll have you know the boss told me to change the linen."

"Thank you, Deputy Collins."

"Please call me Kenny."

"Okay, Kenny."

"You can turn on the TV if you want."

Kara just wanted to tell the deputy to go away and leave her alone so she could think. She'd called David, but his secretary told her he was out of the office and wouldn't return until the following day. She left a message for him to call her.

Everyone on the island was chatting about the incident at Corrine's house. There was talk that if and when they found the person, he or she would beg the police to get them before they meted out their own form of Cavanaugh Island justice.

Turning on her side, she closed her eyes and miraculously fell asleep.

Jeff walked into the Angels Landing town hall, heading for the mayor's office. He knocked on the open door, garnering Harlan's assistant's attention. "Good afternoon, Erin. Is Harlan in?" There was something about Erin that reminded him of Kara's friend Dawn.

"He is, but he's in a meeting with someone very important."

Bracing both hands on her desk, Jeff leaned closer. "Who is he?"

Her round blue eyes looked like marbles. "I can't tell you his name."

"Why not?"

"Because Harlan told me I was never to mention his name in or out of the office."

"Do you have his business card?"

She smiled. "Yes." Opening her desk drawer, Erin took out a card and slid it across her desk.

"Bingo." The man with Harlan was from the same company who'd sent Porter to soften up Kara. "Don't bother to announce me."

"Wait, Jeff. You don't have to go in to hear what they're saying." She handed him a tiny earpiece, then flipped a switch on a box in a drawer in her desk. "Sit over there and pretend you're waiting."

"Why are you doing this?" he asked.

"Because I hate the greedy bastard. If Harlan knew that I listen in on his meetings with these vultures, not only would he fire me, but he would also have me arrested."

Jeff winked at her. "I promise not to out you." He placed the listening device in his right ear, then sat on a wooden bench.

He recognized Harlan's voice immediately: "You can't come in here and threaten me."

"And why not, Mayor Patton? You told me the girl wouldn't stay. Not only is she staying, but she's turning the house into a museum."

"The house, Scott. The house isn't two thousand acres."

"Take your head out of your ass, Patton. If the house becomes a museum, what do you think is going to happen with the rest of the property? It will become a mini-Williamsburg. I want you to put more pressure on her."

"Eden tried talking to her."

"I'm not talking about lip service, Patton.

I'm talking about action. I had my people send her a message by throwing a brick through her window, but apparently it didn't work. I'm certain this morning's brick with the pepper grenade got her attention. There won't be any more bricks. The next time there will be a bullet with her name on it."

"You're nothing but a piece of shit if you think I'm going to be a party to murdering my cousin or hurting anyone else on this island. We protect our people, not take them out. And the other woman in that house just happened to be the sheriff's grandmother. What do you think is going to happen when he finds out you were behind the latest bully scheme?"

"I'm not concerned about *your* sheriff. Let's get back to Miss Newell. I thought she wasn't your cousin."

"Of course, she's my cousin. We asked for the DNA test and said we were going to contest the will to intimidate her."

"Well, apparently intimidation doesn't work with your *cousin* because she's still here. And that means we now are going to do things my way."

"You're not going to hurt her, Scott."

"You're right. What we're going to do is eliminate her. I know people who can make her disappear just like Jimmy Hoffa."

"Get the hell out of here before I call the sheriff."

"Call him. She's still gone."

Jeff had heard enough. He stood up, walked past Erin, and pushed open the door to Harlan's office. "What's this I hear that you were looking for me, Harlan?" Both men stared at him as if they'd seen a ghost. "Scott Pierce," he crooned. "May I call you, Scott?"

The slightly built, deeply tanned man in what appeared to be a three thousand dollar suit and imported footwear, perfectly barbered black hair, and equally black eyes glared at him. "I'm sorry, but I don't know you."

"And you really don't want to know me, Mr. Pierce. I just happen to be the sheriff of this beautiful island you're looking to turn into your own personal playground. And the woman you plan to make disappear is someone I love very much." He rested his right hand on the butt of his gun. "How are we going to do this? The easy way or the hard way?"

"You can't arrest me."

"And why not?"

"You can't prove anything. Patton and I were discussing business."

"Business that included you threatening my cousin," Harlan said. He opened a desk drawer and pushed a button.

Jeff watched the natural color drain from the man's face when he heard his words played back on the tape. "You can't tape me without my permission."

Harlan smiled. "That's where you're wrong. Legally I can tape every meeting in my office. Jeff, please get this garbage out of here."

Jeff took a pair of handcuffs off his gun belt, stood behind the dapper developer, and cuffed his wrists. "Scott Pierce, you're under arrest for conspiracy to commit murder. You have the right to remain silent. Anything you say or do can and will be held against you in a court of law. You have the right to speak to an attorney. If you cannot afford an attorney, one will be appointed for you. Do you understand these rights?" He turned to Harlan. "Please call Charleston PD and tell them to have a bus waiting at the causeway."

"It'll be my pleasure. I'm sorry I ever got involved with this pond scum, but I hope to make up for it when I get to testify against him in court." He offered Jeff his hand. "Thank you. And please let Kara know how sorry we are for the way we treated her. As

471

you know, we can be a lethal bunch when we feel threatened. To make up for our behavior, I'd like to arrange a get together so we can give her a proper welcome and apology."

Kara lay in bed with Jeff, her leg resting over his. The room was pitch-black. A thunderstorm had temporarily knocked out the power on the island. When she couldn't find any candles in the guesthouse, they'd decided to go to bed early.

"How long do you think we'll be in the dark?"

"It all depends."

"On what, Jeff?"

"If it's a blown transformer or if a line is down. The one thing I know is there will be zero crime on the island tonight."

She laughed. "Cavanaugh Island is dark enough without a blackout."

Jeff shifted on his side, pulling Kara to his chest. "Thankfully it doesn't happen too often. After the last one most folks bought generators."

"What time are we leaving tomorrow to pick up your grandmother?"

"Any time after ten. We'll pick her up, then go to Haven Creek to get Oliver; then we're going home."

"Miss Corrine and her baby both had overnight stays in the hospital."

Jeff chuckled. "You know the first one she asked about was Oliver. I told her he was at an animal hospital in the Creek, and the vet wanted to keep him overnight for observation."

"Do you think I'll ever get my dog back?" Kara asked with a smile.

"That's something you're going to have to take up with Gram."

A beat passed. "I still can't believe Harlan knew who was behind the threats against me."

"He didn't know until this morning, Kara. Your cousin felt he could intimidate you by forcing you to take the DNA test and by contesting Taylor's will, but he had no idea Scott was resorting to violence."

"Did you suspect Harlan was behind the brick throwing?"

"I wasn't certain whether he was behind it, but I suspected he knew something. Instinct told me the Pattons were involved in some way because of Eden's visits."

"What about Porter?"

"I gave the DA his name, and he says he's going to subpoena Mr. Caldwell as a witness for the prosecution."

Kara didn't want to believe it was over,

that she didn't have to leave the people she'd come to love. "Will I be called in to testify?"

"If the DA can convince Pierce to accept a plea, then you won't. It would be in his best interest to accept it because legally you could sue him and his company, and I don't think he'd want that."

"If he does take the plea, what will he get? A suspended sentence? Probation?"

"I don't know, baby. I'm not an attorney."

"But Eden is," Kara countered.

"What is it you want?"

"I want restitution. If Pierce accepts a plea, then I want Eden to sue the hell out of him and his company. I want them barred from doing business in South Carolina, and I want whatever money we get to go to charities dedicated to advocating for women and their children. And don't you dare say it, Jeff. Yes, I'm still a social worker. Now that I've decided to stay I'm going to apply for a part-time social work position with either the public schools or a municipal hospital."

"What other plans have you made, baby?"

"That's it," she said.

"What about us?"

She smiled. "What about us, Jeff?"

"How long do you think we're going to

474

shack up together without getting married?"

Kara tried turning over, but Jeff's arm wouldn't permit her to move. "You were the one who invited me to live with you and your grandmother."

"That was before you were in jeopardy and before Gram needed someone to keep her company. We've uncovered who was behind the threat to force you to leave, and Gram has bonded with Oliver, so there's no need for us to live together."

"Your grandmother can't take my dog!"

"You can fight with Corrine Hamilton if you want, but you'll wind up on the losing end." They both shared a laugh before Jeff cupped Kara's chin in his hands. "I love you, Kara, and I don't know how else to say it."

"Say what?"

"Marry me."

Kara felt her heart beating through her chest. Jeff had just uttered the two words that lay in her heart when she'd been too much of a coward to acknowledge that was what she'd wanted from the first time they'd slept together. She'd fallen in love with Jeff. He was someone who made her feel safe, someone she could envision growing old with. She knew living with him was fodder for gossip, and as sheriff his morality would be called into question when it was time for his reelection.

"I marry you and what happens after that?"

"That would depend on you, Kara. I want children, but if you don't, then I'll accept your decision. I want to spend the rest of my life here, but if you don't, then I'll follow you wherever you decide to go. And if I was still in the corps and you didn't want to become a military wife, I would resign my commission. I love you that much."

Tears of happiness pricked the backs of her eyelids. A man who'd told his cousin that he should've let his girlfriend love him more than he loved her had just flipped the script. Kara loved Jeff, and she suspected he loved her more. "Love is not about giving up what you want for the other person. It's about sharing what you have. I want to marry you and give you a baby, lots of babies before I get too old, and I want to spend the rest of my life on Cavanaugh Island. And when I die, I want to be buried in the cemetery with the Pattons who came before me. I'm home, Jeffrey Hamilton, because you've become my home."

Jeff moved over Kara, supporting his greater weight on his forearms. "You have just made me the happiest man in the entire world."

"Kiss me, babe. Kiss me and make love to me so I know this is real."

He nuzzled her neck. "I can kiss you, but I can't make love to you because I didn't bring protection with me."

Kara's fingertips trailed up and down Jeff's back. "I thought we'd get a jump on starting a family."

"I guess you don't want to have a long engagement."

"Of course not. I've always wanted to be a June bride, and that means we'll have to plan something quickly."

"Your father and my buddies are getting together over the Memorial Day weekend. We can use the occasion to get married and have a blowout of a reception on the beach."

"I love the idea of having a beachfront ceremony, but I'd like to hold the reception here at Angels Landing. A caterer can set up tents and tables, and we can invite the entire island to attend."

Jeff caressed the length of her leg and thigh. "Do you plan to invite the Pattons?"

"Of course. If they choose not to come, then it's okay. But if they do, then I'll know they're serious about extending the olive branch."

"You are a lot more forgiving than I would be."

"The animosity has to stop somewhere, darling. I was raised by two people who loved me and were never shy about letting me know. We're not perfect, but I didn't grow up fighting with my relatives. It wasn't about who had more than the other or a parent favoring one child over the other. I may look like Theodora, but I hope and pray I'll never be like her."

"You won't, baby."

Kara gasped softly when she felt Jeff's growing erection against her thigh. Her hand found him, caressing the hardening flesh until it pulsed against her palm. She opened her legs, sighing when Jeff eased inside her.

She'd asked him to love her and he did. It was the slowest, sweetest love she'd ever experienced. Minutes before she fell asleep Kara thanked Taylor for doing in death what he hadn't been able to do in life — reuniting his family.

CHAPTER TWENTY

Jeannette walked into the bedroom at the Hamilton residence and stopped when she saw her daughter in her wedding finery. "Oh, Kara, you look so beautiful. Does Jeff know how lucky he is?"

Kara nodded. "I think he knows, and I know how lucky I am to have fallen in love with him. Have you seen him, Mama?"

"I have. He looks so handsome in his dress uniform."

She and Jeff had discussed whether or not he would wear his dress uniform, and they'd decided he would for the ceremony, then change into a suit for the reception. She'd sent invitations to the Pattons, and much to her surprise they'd all accepted. As promised, Dawn was her maid of honor, and she'd come down the week before to select her dress from a local bridal boutique.

Kara had selected a stark white, strapless ballgown with a hand-sewn pearl-beaded bodice of matte satin and a tulle skirt. Dawn floated into the room in a cornflower-blue halter A-line gown that was an exact match for her eyes. Her headpiece was a coronet of fresh violets and tiny rose petals that made her look like a fairy-tale wood sprite.

"Oh, my!" she gasped. "You are truly a princess, Miss Kay."

Holding out the skirt to her gown, Kara inclined her head. The stylist at the Beauty Box had rolled her hair on narrow rods, turning her straight tresses into tiny ringlets that framed her face. In lieu of a veil, she'd opted for miniature roses and jeweled hairpins.

"Thank you. I'm so nervous my knees are shaking."

Dawn took her hand. "I saw the groom, and he looks good enough to eat. And his best man isn't too shabby, either. They were getting into the car to drive to the beach."

Kara had noticed that the man Jeff had selected to be his best man was also a retired marine captain who'd appeared totally enthralled with her ex-roommate. Never one to act as matchmaker, Kara hoped the two would become more than friends.

She picked up her all-white bouquet of

roses, gardenia, and lily of the valley. "I'm ready."

Jeannette pressed her cheek to her daughter's. "Your father is waiting downstairs in the limo with Corrine."

Kara lifted the skirt of her gown as she walked down the staircase in the house that was to become her permanent home. She and Jeff had decided to live in the house where he'd been raised, and they would use the guesthouse at Angels Landing as their private getaway whenever he was off duty. Corrine and Oliver had become inseparable, and Kara had come to regard him as Gram's dog.

The permanent residents of Cavanaugh Island had warmed to the idea that when restored, Angels Landing would be listed on the Lowcountry and Gullah tours because it would mean more tourists and additional revenue for the businesses on the island.

She and Jeff had delayed having a honeymoon until late fall. He'd wanted to wait until after the local elections were over because the Cove's incumbent mayor was being challenged by the first female mayoralty candidate in the island's history. Alice Parker, wife of US Representative Jason Parker, had announced that she wanted the town council to pass a law that would limit developers wishing to do business in Sanctuary Cove. Scott had posted bail, surrendered his passport, and was scheduled to return to court at the end of the summer, so Kara had the entire summer to concentrate on being a wife to a man she loved unconditionally.

They'd decided on a late-morning wedding before the temperatures made it prohibitive to remain on the beach for an appreciable amount of time. Austin stepped out of the limo to help his daughter into the vehicle. He repeated the action with his wife and Dawn before sliding in beside Corrine. Kara thought she saw tears in her father's eyes before he averted his head. He'd admitted he had gained too much weight to fit into his uniform and had purchased a tailored suit for the occasion.

Kara tightened her hold on her bouquet when she exited the limo and placed her hand on her father's arm when he led her along the path to the beach. She would never forget the expression on her groom's face when he saw her for the first time in her wedding finery. She saw the blood stripe on the leg of his dress blues and the Mameluke sword carried by all Marine Corps officers in the gloved hand of his best man.

"Daddy!" she whispered as her knees

buckled slightly.

Austin caught her elbow, holding her until she regained her balance. "It's all right, baby girl. Take your time. If Jeffrey waited this long to marry, he'll wait a few more minutes for you to pull yourself together."

A string quartet played softly as she struggled to regain her composure. She nodded, smiling. "I'm ready, Daddy."

She smiled at those sitting on chairs under a large tent that had been erected for the ceremony. She recognized Dr. and Mrs. Monroe and their children, some of the women who quilted with Corrine, and when she glanced to her left, she recognized the faces of those she'd encountered when she walked into the law office for the reading of a will that forever changed her life. She smiled at Morgan, who sat on the side of the groom's family and friends with David. Turning her head, she nodded to Willie and Iris Todd.

Her smile was as dazzling as the sun when her father placed her hand on the outstretched one of the man who would become her husband. She met Jeff's gaze under the shiny bill of his cap. She lowered her eyes demurely when he mouthed the word *beautiful*.

Malcolm Crawford, the pastor of the

Cove's interdenominational church, had been selected to officiate because it was where Jeff had been baptized and attended services as a child. It was the church where they planned to baptize and send their children.

They repeated their vows, and when Jeff slipped his grandmother's wedding ring on her finger, Kara knew it was for keeps. She was now Mrs. Jeffrey Malachi Hamilton. When the minister told Jeff he could now kiss his wife, she looped her arms around his neck and pressed her mouth to his.

"I love you, Gullah man," she whispered in his ear.

"Not as much as I love you my beautiful Gullah woman."

They were showered with rice, birdseed, and flower petals as they followed the procession to the beach to where they would pose for pictures before returning to Angels Landing for a reception that was rumored not to end until after sundown.

Kara had spared no expense when she hired three caterers to have enough food on hand for more than two thousand people. It would be the first time the entire island would come together en masse to celebrate a single event.

She kissed Corrine's gardenia-scented

cheek. "Now that I'm married to your grandson do you think I can now call you Gram instead of Miss Corrine?"

Corrine touched her cheek in a loving gesture. "Of course. I've always wanted a granddaughter. But I didn't think I would get one as perfect as you."

Kara hugged her grandmother as she exchanged a loving smile with her new husband. Eden approached her, arm extended. "You look beautiful, Kara. I know my uncle is smiling down on you today."

Returning the hug, Kara looked at her cousin. "We have to get together one of these days."

Virgie joined them. "Let her get used to sleeping with her gorgeous husband before talking about getting together."

Kara smiled at her cousins. "That's something I don't ever want to get used to." The three women exchanged high-five handshakes, then dissolved into laughter.

Those standing around watching exchanged knowing looks. It had been Theodora who'd torn her family apart and her granddaughter who would bring them together again. Good things were happening for the folks in Cavanaugh Island, and those who lived there were looking for better days ahead.

FROM THE DESK OF
ROCHELLE ALERS

Dear Reader,
I would like to thank everyone who told me they couldn't wait to return to Cavanaugh Island. And like the genie in the bottle I'm going to grant your wish.

You will get to revisit people and places on the idyllic island, while being introduced to others who will make you laugh, cry — and even a few you'd rather avoid. It is a place where newcomers are viewed with suspicion, family secrets are whispered about, and where old-timers are reluctant to let go of their past. Most inhabitants believe what happens in Sanctuary Cove, Angels Landing, or Haven Creek stays in Cavanaugh Island. Angels Landing — or "the Landing," as the locals refer to it — takes its name from the antebellum mansion and surrounding property that was and will again become a crown jewel on the National Register of Historic Places.

In *Angels Landing* you will meet newcomer Kara Newell, a transplanted New York social worker who inherits a neglected plantation and a house filled with long-forgotten treasures and family secrets spanning centuries. Kara finds herself totally unprepared to step into her role as landed gentry, and even more unprepared for the island's hunky sheriff. Her southern roots help her adjust to the slower way of Lowcountry life, but she finds herself in a quandary when developers concoct elaborate schemes to force Kara into selling what folks refer to as her birthright. Then there's hostility from newfound family members, as well as her growing feelings for Sheriff Jeffrey Hamilton.

Jeff has returned to Cavanaugh Island to look after his ailing grandmother and to assume the duties as sheriff. His transition from military to civilian life is smooth because, as "Corrine Hamilton's grandbaby boy," he's gained the respect of everyone through his fair, no-nonsense approach to upholding the law. However, his predictable lifestyle is shaken when he's asked to look after Kara when veiled threats are made against her life. When Jeff realizes his role as protector shifts from professional to personal, he is faced with the choice of whether to make Kara a part of his future or lose her like he has other women in his past.

So come on back and reunite with folks with whom you're familiar and new characters you'd want to see time and time again.

Read, enjoy, and do let me hear from you!!!
Rochelle Alers
ralersbooks@aol.com
www.rochellealers.org

The employees of Thorndike Press hope you have enjoyed this Large Print book. All our Thorndike, Wheeler, and Kennebec Large Print titles are designed for easy reading, and all our books are made to last. Other Thorndike Press Large Print books are available at your library, through selected bookstores, or directly from us.

For information about titles, please call:
  (800) 223-1244

or visit our Web site at:
  http://gale.cengage.com/thorndike

To share your comments, please write:
  Publisher
  Thorndike Press
  10 Water St., Suite 310
  Waterville, ME 04901